Mon

CW01457348

Edited by

H.K. Hillman

and

Roo B. Doo

The Twenty-fourth Underdog Anthology
from Leg Iron Books

Halloween 2024

J Forbes

Disclaimer

These stories are works of fiction. Characters, names, places and incidents are either the product of the authors' imaginations or are used in a fictitious context. Any resemblance to any persons, living or dead, or to any events or locales is entirely coincidental. If any of the events described have really happened to you then I'm afraid that's your own problem.

Copyright notice

LEG IRON BOOKS

https://legironbooks.co.uk/

Cover image © Jana Fewkes, 2024

ISBN: 9798345582916

Contents

Foreword

H. K. Hillman

Welcome to the Monster.

The twenty-fourth Underdog Anthology seems to have hit a tipping point. The first twenty-three attracted maybe fifteen or fewer submissions but this time, it really took off. Over forty submissions, all of excellent quality, of which thirty-nine (well, thirty-eight, I can't really count mine) stories made it into this tome of horror.

I still think, sometimes, about that first anthology and how I wondered whether I was being overly optimistic by calling it 'volume one'. I had no idea if there would ever be a 'volume two' and here we are at volume twenty-four. It started as a hobby...

It's running very late this time because for all these years, Leg Iron Books set the closing date on the basis that we'd get enough submissions to deal with in a week or two. Next year we'll have to set opening and closing dates earlier. It seems we've at last been noticed.

Until now, we were delighted if we attracted one new author to each anthology. This volume contains some of our regular contributors surrounded by an entire host of new contributors. All with their own take on the spookiness of the season. Some gentle, some not so gentle. All of them show incredible imagination in their work.

There are some stories involving monsters, but really, the title more reflects the astonishing size of this volume. It's truly a monster of a book.

The cover image was made for us by an artist before she read any of the stories – but it does encompass several of the stories about haunted houses.

You are bound to find stories to entertain you in here so I'll stop writing and let you read on.

This time, I have such sights to show you.

The Bone Train

Jane Nightshade

Einar Miller lost his job for stealing a severed arm from the local hospital's biowaste depository. That was a year ago, but the memory of his forced departure from his long-time position as a radiology technician still stung. Hospital administrators were known for turning a blind eye to petty thievery now and then, but stealing an arm was beyond the pale.

"What on earth possessed you to take something like that?" demanded his boss, Mr. Price. Thick and dull by Einar's estimation, he looked at Einar with barely concealed disgust.

"Nothing on *earth*," Einar mumbled under his breath. He regarded Mr. Price as a plodding plebeian. Price could never see the greatness of the Presence who'd dominated Einar's life for... *what?*... going on five years now?

"I meant, nothing you would find understandable."

"What's that? Of course, I don't understand a crazy action like this. What you've done is sick—mentally sick. You need psychiatric help!"

"It was only a piece of waste. A gangrenous arm from a junkie who'd shoved his infected needle into the same diseased hole one too many times. He didn't need it anymore—no one did. Who got hurt by my actions, really?"

"Removing biowaste endangers our entire community. I've no choice but to let you go. If this got out into the news..."

Einar grew quiet; there was no point in defending himself. Later, he cleaned out his desk and his locker under the watchful eye of the hospital's security manager, and that was the end, more or less, of any real participation in the rhythms of normal everyday life. He got by on a pension—he'd just passed his twenty-year anniversary at the hospital when he got canned—and did occasional freelance work for a radiologist in private practice downtown.

Not that he minded having all that extra time on his hands. Retirement meant that he could devote most of his time to fulfilling the wishes of the Presence, the main objective of which was to build an elaborate miniature Town in his basement, crafted of human bones (he had come to think of it in capitalized form, such was its importance). A Town that had everything a town could have, except for a church. Never a church.

It was Halloween, the season when the Presence spoke to him most often. As in years past, it reminded him to get ample candy and decorations at the supermarket for the upcoming holiday.

The pumpkins, sadly, were mostly gone from the bins in the produce section. Not much of a selection awaited those who, like Einar, dawdled until the last possible minute. There were still some decent-sized white ones, but he considered a white Halloween pumpkin to be almost a sacrilege. He fished through the bin until he found a single orange one (proper color at last!) that satisfied him. The orange one was much smaller than he would have liked, but beggars couldn't be choosers. He sighed and put it in his cart.

"I should have come last week," he thought ruefully. But he'd been busy with his model city all week. The Presence had instructed him to build a train station, very clearly outlined in a sudden vision. And Einar had worked all week until far into the night to clean, carve and sand his creation. He used Materials that were left over from last Halloween's—uh—*supply run*—but now they were mostly depleted. He had to collect new ones. The Presence had helped him understand that it was an essential part of the collection process to decorate his house in an eye-catching way for Halloween.

He wheeled his cart past the candy aisle. He didn't bother looking for the special Halloween assortments of mini-chocolate bars or small packages of Skittles. Instead, he bought a bunch of regular-sized candy bars from the shelves up near the register. The Presence had told him years ago to buy the big candy bars to give out for trick-or-treating, not the little ones. Expensive, but what else did he have to spend his money on? And if things worked out this Halloween evening, he could justify the extra expenses as an investment. Yes, *an investment.*

He bought thirty-five full-sized candy bars: divided among Snickers, Milky Ways, Hershey's, and Three Musketeers, all at around eighty-nine cents apiece—a little bit more for the Hershey's.

"You are going to be the most popular person in the neighborhood tonight," said the check-out girl, chuckling. "There's a

10

special place in heaven for people who give out full-sized candy bars."

"*Heaven*—oh dear—I hope *not*," answered Einar, without thinking. The girl goggle-eyed him and he caught himself.

"I mean, I hate being fussed over and treated special. Always have. I'm a modest sort of guy, I guess."

She smiled a lovely smile, with big white teeth, rectangular and even; piano key teeth. "Well, you have a great Halloween this evening, sir."

"I'll bet she has excellent bones," he thought wistfully, as he exited the store. "Judging from those teeth."

Einar set his less-than-optimal pumpkin on the front porch when he got home. Once inside, he found a large bowl for the candy bars. He also groped around in the hall closet to find his Halloween decorations. There they were, in the back, waiting to come out.

There was the dancing witch that hung on the door. Then, the big, puffy blow-up black spider. Fake spiderwebs and cardboard cut-outs for the big front window, and there was Mr. Boney, a motion-activated skeleton, which he usually posed on a children's lawn chair on the front porch. When trick-or-treaters approached the door, Mr. Boney would sing:

Boney Bone Collector's my name
Can you give me a hand?
I've got a bone-crush on you, sweetie pie
Wanna see me shake, rattle and roll?

The younger children would, in rare cases, take fright; the older ones would laugh delightedly.

"Good ol' Boney," he thought, as he posed the skeleton on the chair. "He's served me so well for years."

The Presence had told him to rescue Boney from the bargain bin at the local discount store one Halloween past, and he'd been grateful for the advice ever since.

When Einar finished decorating the front of his house, adding a bright orange string of lights as a last touch, the Presence finally spoke to him again.

Build a train next, to go with the station.

And a vision of the train popped into Einar's mind in exquisite detail: a bulky, steaming Victorian locomotive hauling five cars, including a passenger car, a boxcar, a coal car, a cattle car, and a hopper car. He savored the challenge and waited quietly for dark and the start of trick or treating in his neighborhood. Waiting for the new Materials to come to his door.

The first buzz of his doorbell sounded, and Einar heard the door witch and Boney Bone Collector go off, to the squeaks of startled children. He went to the front door and opened it to three munchkins ranging in age from about five to seven, each dressed like giant green peas.

"We are three peas in a pod," one sweet-voiced child inside a large, green felt ball explained, as the children's mother beamed on approvingly.

"Very clever," said Einar, handing each green ball a candy bar. "Did you make these costumes?" he asked the mother.

"Sure did," she trilled. "Look at those full-size chocolate bars! Don't see that every day! Thank you, and Happy Halloween."

Einar closed the door as the little party scampered off in search of other houses and other treats. It was the opening salvo of a busy night, with numerous trips to the door while bearing his bowl of candy bars; numerous children's costumes to (falsely) admire; and numerous incidents of Boney and the dancing witch sounding off when activated by their motion sensors.

Each time he opened the door to a childish knock, he expected the Presence to issue instructions, but nothing came. It was a quarter to nine now, and he knew the kids would stop coming after the clock passed the next hour. His bowl of candy bars was almost empty.

At five till nine, there was a lone rap on the door, and Einar hurried to it. The motion sensor that activated Boney and the witch didn't work this time—he thought that was odd. But perhaps Boney and the witch needed battery changes after a busy night.

His latest visitor was a teenager: a lone boy of around fourteen, who was on the tall, husky side for his age. Large-boned, Einar thought a bit greedily. The teenager was wearing a Darth Vader cape and partial helmet.

The Presence spoke very clearly in his mind.

"Materials," it said. "No parents, no friends. No one will notice where he went tonight." Einar understood in an instant. This boy would provide the Materials for his beautiful, bountiful train.

The teen boy held out a pillowcase. "Trick or treat," he chirped.

Einar gave him the rest of the candy bars left in his bowl. "I think you're the last to come tonight, my boy."

"Gee, thanks, Mister. Four full-size candy bars—the other kids at school won't believe it!"

The teen boy turned to go. "Wait!" said Einar. "If you like that candy, you'll probably like my special candy even more."

"Sure. Where is it?" The teen boy's pale, freckled face flashed a guileless smile.

"Inside. It's up high in a closet and I'm afraid I just don't trust myself to climb a stepladder anymore. But you look like you could scamper up a stepladder in double-time."

The young teen boy hesitated. "My mother wouldn't like it. I'm not supposed to go inside with strangers."

"Even for a whole box of gourmet Belgian chocolates? Your Mom would probably love it."

The boy shifted on his feet. He was clearly leaning toward coming in.

"I'm a good guy, I swear," said Einar. "I worked at the hospital for twenty years, helping sick people get better. My name is Mr. Miller."

"I guess it wouldn't hurt to come in for just a minute ..."

"Excellent, my boy," said Einar, opening the door wider and moving aside to let the child enter his house. The teenager walked in, looking all around Einar's living room, as if reassuring himself that it was all normal and above-board. He seemed to relax at the sight of Einar's spare, spotless decor.

Einar noticed the boy was carrying a small toy weapon on the belt of his costume.

"My lightsaber," he said, following Einar's eyes. "The large ones were sold out, so I had to settle for the little kid's model, which I'm way too big for." He made a face of disgust.

"No one would notice it's a little kids' toy," Einar said soothingly. "The hall closet is right this way."

He led the boy to the closet, where a stepladder was already leaning against the wall next to it.

"There's a stack of boxes on the top shelf. It's the first box you reach," said Einar, unfolding the stepladder and positioning it in front of the closet. "The slim one, wrapped in gold foil paper."

As the boy moved to retrieve the candy box, Einar remembered the first year he had collected... Materials... besides that of the hospital's biowaste disposal.

That was a thirteen-year-old, also a boy, who said his name was Patrick. Patrick was out alone that night also, and was big for his age. He wore a Batman costume, which Einar later burned in his fireplace.

The Presence had walked him through every step. He had purchased the lye and the huge cast iron vat as instructed before Patrick showed up at his door. The vat was difficult to find, but he located a good used one from a craft soap maker on eBay, and prepared a place in the basement for it. Next, he built a brick fire pit into the floor of the basement and connected a makeshift smokestack out of aluminum tubing, to be used boiling the lye.

He gave Patrick some fudge poisoned with chemicals stolen from the hospital. And then he'd waited for the lye, the vat, the water and the fire to do their work. It was absurdly easy, once it was all in place.

Not so easy were the carving and creating afterward from the clean bleached bones, but he'd managed in the end to produce a brilliant piece, a white-pillared courthouse with a clock tower. The miniature clock, cannibalized from an old wristwatch, actually worked—something that Einar regarded with immense pride.

"That's it," said Einar aloud, turning back to the present. "That's the candy."

The teen boy was holding the gold foil box and looking expectantly at Einar.

"You've got it, my clever boy! Step down now and let's open it up to see the delightful things that are inside." The candy was actually stale, but no one could tell that from the unopened package. Einar had stolen it from a hospital volunteer's cart more than a year's past, before he got canned from his job. He had purloined gifts meant for patients frequently when he worked at the hospital.

Einar led the young teenager into his dining room and bade him to sit at the small table. He told the boy to open the box and choose a treat to eat—or several, if that's what the child wanted. Einar had injected all of them with poison.

"I just can't choose," fretted the teen boy. "They all look so good!"

"Go ahead," urged Einar. He looked at the clock on the wall above the table. "Heavens! It's getting late and your Mom will be worrying about you. Maybe you'd better choose quick and go!"

The boy cocked an eyebrow. "*Heavens*? I should hope not!"

Einar was confused at this statement; it sounded like something he would say, or rather what the Presence would say through him. He looked into the boy's eyes, really noticing them for the first time. They were a greenish-hazel and there was something about them that startled him. Something hard. He felt suddenly that it wouldn't be as easy as he thought to collect his Materials for the train he was planning to make.

"Choose something," Einar urged again, pushing the gold box closer to the boy. He tried not to sound desperate. He hoped to hear some instructions or advice in his mind from the Presence, but there was nothing.

"I think I will," said the boy. "But later." He stood up and pushed the gold box of candy gently away. "I think I want to stretch my legs first. How about showing me the rest of your house?"

What an odd request, thought Einar. *This kid is a handful. He's nothing like Patrick or the other people the Presence sent to me. What do I do? What do I do?* He prayed fervently to the Presence for help, but his prayers remained unanswered.

Aloud he said: "There's not much to my little house. Just a kitchen, a couple of small bedrooms, a tiny bathroom, and what you've already seen. Very boring."

"What about the basement?" asked the boy. He looked and sounded innocent enough, but Einar could have sworn he heard more than a hint of malice in the teen boy's voice.

"*Wha...what about it?*" Einar gulped, shocked to the core. "It's just an odd dusty place, full of white elephants and laundry supplies. You'd be bored to tears."

"I think I'd like to see it anyway."

Einar tried to think. His mind was racing. His eyes caught a heavy stone vase on the dining room sideboard, and he thought wildly that he should grab it and conk the troublesome boy on the head with it. It would be messier than the poisoned candy, but sometimes a body needed to improvise. But then he stopped himself. The kid was big and strong. And Einar was old, thin, and not much taller than the boy. There could be a struggle that Einar wouldn't win.

He was flying solo now. The Presence had deserted him. He tried to think why that was so, but the solution would not come. For a moment, he even considered forgetting about the train and letting the kid go. Why obey the Presence when it had deserted him and left him in this unpleasantly sticky situation? But then he recalled, with a deep shudder, the one time he had disobeyed the Presence and the terrible price he'd paid for it. The only time he had ever glimpsed the hellish black face and smelled the sulfurous body, and felt the white-hot blood-red claws upon his neck...

No, the Presence was absent for reasons opaque to Einar, and it was not Einar's place to question why. He had his last marching orders and must carry them out to the letter, unless he received other instructions to replace them.

I know what to do. I'll lead the kid down to the basement and finish him off there. Einar's basement was full of tools hanging on the walls—including several hammers, a saw, and an axe. *I'll surprise him from behind with a blow from one of the hammers. Or maybe the axe.*

"All right," Einar said finally to the boy. "I'll show you the basement. Don't blame me if you find it dull and a waste of time, though. Come this way, young man."

He led the boy to the door that connected the kitchen down to the basement. He flipped on the lights at the top of the basement stairs and began descending them slowly. Einar realized as he did so that he felt uncomfortable with his back to the boy, for some inarticulable reason.

I really don't like this boy at all. It occurred to him that he had not asked the kid's name. He was almost afraid to ask now, at this point. It was possible the teen boy had a name that would reveal something threatening about him, a nature of malice...*I am a fool,* he thought. *Letting a fourteen-year-old spook me like this. I am not worthy of the Presence. I must see this task through and prove myself worthy again of it.*

At the foot of the stairs, the first thing the boy saw and remarked upon was the vat, perched expectantly on a stack of wood that Einar had stuffed into the fire pit. He'd already filled it with water and leaned a large bag of lye against it.

16

"That looks like the pots that witches make spells in!" cried the boy, pointing at the vat. "It's cool!"

"I make homemade soap in it," said Einar, thinking quickly. He felt some of his old confidence return. This strange boy wasn't going to break him or humiliate him in front of the Presence. In fact, shortly, this vexatious boy's bones would be stewing in the very vat he so admired.

"It's a hobby. You make it with lye and animal or vegetable fat. I sell the soap at the farmers' market."

"How interesting." The boy scanned the room and Einar could tell he was sizing up the hammers and other lethal things on the wall. Then his eyes alit on the alcove where the Town rested on a large table. The alcove was darkened, and Einar could only make out a few shapes; he wondered if the boy could make anything out of what he saw.

"What's over there?" asked the boy.

Einar gulped. "It's...it's another one of my hobbies. Just some old models and things."

The boy moved across the basement and into the alcove. He pulled the light string that was hanging overhead and flooded the alcove with harsh illumination.

"Wow!" he exclaimed. "It's a whole mini town! Where did you get this stuff?"

Einar couldn't help but brag a little. It wasn't at all apparent what the town was made of at a casual view. Most pieces were painted or carved in such detail that the original nature of the source was undetectable.

"I made it. Carved every bit, except for a few things like the clock in the tower. Over there are my carving tools." He pointed to a leather case perched in a corner of the table.

"Cool! Can I look at the tools?"

Einar hesitated. He didn't want anyone's grubby hands pawing his precious carving implements. On the other hand, the tools could provide a needed distraction...

"Sure, you can, my boy," he said with false enthusiasm. He handed the case over. "And here's a little practice block of wood you can try them out with. But please be careful—these are expensive, professional carving tools. Not a kid's set of toys." The "block" was actually a small piece of bone that Einar had carved into a cube and stained to look like wood, but he figured the teen boy wouldn't notice. "Go ahead, start carving! Whatever you wish."

The boy sat down in Einar's chair and began fiddling with the block of bone and the set of carving tools.

"Why don't you take off your costume's headgear? It must be hot!"

The boy nodded, and then removed his Darth Vader helmet and set it on the floor next to Einar's chair. In short order, he was engrossed in his work, and Einar was silently congratulating himself on his own cleverness at getting the boy to shed his head protection.

"I'm afraid I have to excuse myself for a short moment," he said. "Continue with your practicing—you're doing very well."

The boy did not bother looking up from his carving. "Okay, Mr. Miller."

Einar smiled to himself and walked slowly over to the other side of the basement, where the hardware tools were—the axe, the saw, the various hammers. After some deliberation, he chose the hammer with the most lethal looking head—it had double-sided pounding surfaces like a mallet, heavy and large. Then he crept back toward the alcove, hammer clutched in his right hand, hidden behind his back.

He hoped to catch the boy from behind by surprise. He envisioned the first smashing blow on the boy's bent, absorbed-in-his-work head, blood and perhaps bits of skull flying everywhere in the alcove. The thought of it gave him great satisfaction. He had actually felt sorry for Patrick and the others, but not this troublesome brat.

Einar crept closer behind the boy and brought his right arm and hammer out from behind his back. He began to raise the hammer when suddenly, the boy looked up from his carving experiment and turned around to face Einar.

Einar stopped his hammer in mid-air, shocked at the boy's reaction. He was further disconcerted when the teenager sprang from the chair and faced Einar with a hard, menacing look.

"What were you planning to do with that hammer?" came the question, drenched in cold fury.

Einar's face flushed and sweat began forming profusely under his arms. He felt rooted in place and the hammer seemed heavier and heavier, until he could hardly hold on to it. It fell from his rigid fingers to the basement floor with a loud thud.

"I...I was just going to clean it," Einar responded lamely. *Where is the Presence? Where is it?* his mind screamed hysterically.

"Funny thing is, I thought you were going to kill me with it," the boy said, in a chilly mechanical tone. "And then cook me in your big old witches' pot over there."

"Wh...why would I do that?" Einar stammered.

"I dunno...maybe you were planning to use my bones to carve a few more pieces for your town? I noticed you have a train station...but no train?"

Einar was in full panic mode now. *How could that brat have known about the Town... the vat...and the train?* He was trembling and felt faint. Then he noticed an amber glint in the teen boy's eyes and it looked familiar...but where had he seen it before?

Then he remembered: It was in his own eyes, when he once looked at himself in the mirror as the Presence was speaking to him in his mind.

Slowly, he backed away from the boy in a wretched, terrible fear, but it was too late.

The boy had pulled up his "lightsaber" from his belt, and Einar saw that it wasn't really a toy after all. It was a slender, wicked-looking knife with a blade that was covered in shiny, glow-in-the-dark paint. He advanced on Einar with it, amber eyes radiating and a mocking grin distorting his face.

"You see, Mr. Miller, I too have a Presence that talks to me in my mind. And *my* Presence wants me to finish building your Town. You will make quite a nice train, I think, despite the age of your bones. Thank you for laying the fire and filling the pot for me so nicely."

The Fizz Man

Stephen Johnson

"It's ten o'clock!"

Logan grunted, pushing the recliner seat rest down with a loud crunch. Laughing from the couch, I pointed towards the door, "Your turn this time, bro!"

His irritated eyes cast a short glance back to me. Without a word, I caught his full meaning in only a twitch of his eye. With a hint of frustration, he opened the door. The chorus rang out, "Trick or treat!"

Sighing, Logan grabbed the half empty plastic pumpkin and dumped the remains into the paper bags the three kids shoved his way. Shaking his head, he slammed the door and switched off the porch light signaling he was done for the evening.

"Kids didn't even have costumes on! No way I get any candy back in the day going out like that!"

With a flick of the wrist, he locked the door and headed upstairs, "Good night, little brother. Any more of them and it's your problem. Gotta work in the morning. Some of us have a job!"

I waved a dismissive hand back, "Oh, I'll be working real hard. Don't you worry."

He flashed a sarcastic smile and disappeared upstairs. I closed the calculus book and threw the unsolved integral homework on the coffee table.

This college calculus class is a lot worse than work.

I settled back in the couch to flip on the first horror movie that came up when a soft knock interrupted the opening scene of The Conjuring.

"Are you kidding? The light is off!"

I turned my attention back to the show, intent on ignoring the rude kids on the other side of the door when the knock came again. This time with a loud thumping. Jumping up I ran to the door, "Please don't wake up Logan. I will never hear the end of it."

The banging increased to a crashing hand as I swung open the door. Fuming, I looked out, "What is your ..."

At the bottom of the steps stood a man. I could just make out an outline. The hulking figure looked crouched under a tattered dark robe. I flipped on the light and was repulsed at the sight nearly tripping as I stepped back over the threshold of the door.

"Who are you? What do you want?"

A garbled deep voice stammered from beneath the dirty cloak, "Trick or treat!"

The man stepped closer, emerging from the shadows. The sight was horrific, but it still paled next to the putrid smell. He stepped forward and stopped about four feet from the porch before settling onto the ground. The strange man sat cross-legged, his arms and hands covered by the long robe hanging rudely over his shoulders. With a sudden jerk, he flicked open the robe exposing his grisly face and sinister smile. His clothes were drenched and smelled as if he had not bathed in quite a while. Ratted white hair hung down in knotted strands over his forehead, his eyes visible through the wet bangs. He ignored me and simply continued his gaze into the night, all the while bearing the uncomfortable grin.

"That's enough, all right. Just get out of here or I am going to call the police."

I glanced back over my shoulder, hoping Logan would heat the commotion and come down.

This guy is really creeping me out.

The man started humming. Not loud but with a gravelly voice. After a short time, he added lyrics to the same tune.

"In your closet, under your bed
Beware of the Fizz Man in your head
He waits till midnight to seek his prey
Never to wake to see the day"

I jerked back as the odd man began his chant. He continued the same verse a few more times. Inching closer back into the house, I reached for the door. He continued his song, increasing toward a high-pitched scream.

Underneath the filthy robe, the old man wore only a dirty grey T-shirt, and jeans filled with holes. His face was covered completely by a shaggy uneven reddish beard, and he looked down at a small tin cup that sat in his lap. He turned from looking out into the random dark night and fixed his eyes on me. He lifted his head and met my eyes with a nasty smile full of rotten and missing teeth. Slowly, he lifted the small, dented tin cup towards me. His face looked ancient, but his eyes seemed to glow with life as he changed his tune now singing in a much deeper and clearer voice,

"Into the cup a sacrifice be made
The Fizz Man demands this to be paid."

A thick brown mucous ran down the side of his grin dripping off his arm onto the floor as his eyes never left me. Repulsed I began to back away when the old man jumped towards me quickly. I fell back startled as he stood over me holding the tin cup out like an offering, muttering incoherently, "He demands a sacrifice! The Fizz Man is coming for you."

Logan bounded down the stairs as the old man lay flat in the entrance way. He never stopped his eerie chant.

"Get out of here!"

Logan picked the man up and tossed him outside the door. Peeking through the side window, he watched as the man fled off into the night, still cackling his odd poem about the Fizz Man.

"What was that all about?"

Logan turned to face me as I sat up against the bottom stairwell. My heart punched at my chest, sweat covered my tussled hair. I wiped my forehead and felt my hands shaking. I murmured back, "I... I am ... not sure. Just some crazy guy."

I staggered to the edge of the couch. The television erupted with screams from the movie.

"Why don't you turn off that mess."

Logan flipped the movie off and threw the remote into the recliner. He kneeled down next to me, "You sure you are alright? Want me to call the police?"

I attempted a laugh, but it came out more as an exasperated cry, "No, I am fine. Just need to go to bed. Enough of this Halloween night."

That old man really shook me.

My face flushed with anger but also more with embarrassment. Logan snickered and walked back upstairs to bed.

"Sweet dreams!"

"Just leave me alone," I said intending to be forceful but the words actually coming out in a cracked and scared voice.

Logan shook his head and hopped back upstairs as he made spooky voices and waved his hands. Blood returned to my face, and I could feel my pulse relax. I took a deep breath and suddenly felt a wave of exhaustion come over me. Anxious to put the night behind me, I plodded back to the couch ready to crash for the night. Nervously, I glanced around the room and looked toward the large window next to the door. I pulled out the couch bed and shut the drapes fully.

"Hope I can fall asleep. Hopefully no more trick or treaters tonight."

The sound of the old man rang in my ears with his strange poem.

"In your closet, under your bed
Beware of the Fizz Man in your head
He waits till midnight to seek his prey
Never to wake to see the day"

A boom of thunder rattled the room, and a flash of lightning illuminated the sky. I shielded my eyes as the lightning produced a strobe effect across the window. The light produced a clear view of a man standing outside staring into the window. I jumped back and instinctively yelped in shock as the strange man stood frozen staring directly back at me. The crashing of steps coincided with Logan running downstairs clearly concerned.

"What is wrong? What are you yelling about?"

I mumbled and pointed toward the window. My hand shook as I pushed closer to the head of the bed, pointing frantically toward the open curtains.

"Th... there is ... someone outside!"

Irritated, Logan bolted over to the window cupping his hands to peer through the glass.

"Be careful. There is someone out ..."

He turned, eyes narrowed, and lips pursed, "What is wrong with you tonight?"

He grabbed the curtains and forcefully shoved them closed. Shaking his head, he grabbed me by the shoulders.

"You really need to chill, man. I am so tired. I don't feel like dealing with this tonight. Just go to sleep!"

He started back upstairs rubbing at his tired eyes and yelled back, "Turn off the lights. I am going to sleep!"

My body trembled as I pleaded with my brother. "I swear there was someone there. I saw ...."

I stopped mid-sentence deciding not to describe what the man looked like. If Logan thought I was a little crazy now, then he would have me locked up if I explained what I witnessed through the window a few moments ago.

"Just go to bed. I don't feel like your games tonight. I have to leave early tomorrow."

The room went silent, and I sat on the couch bed staring at the ceiling, afraid to close my eyes. About ten minutes later, a familiar snoring echoed throughout the house from upstairs. I tried to rest but my mind drifted back to the old man in the lobby and the song he kept singing over and over.

"In your closet, under your bed
Beware of the Fizz Man in your head
He waits till midnight to seek his prey
Never to wake to see the day"

The vision of the old man was replaced in my head by the monster I witnessed outside the window. The grotesque head punctuated with pieces of teeth protruding from all over its scalp and face. A thick scar lined with odd, placed teeth rolled down the creature's face as its eyes rolled uncontrolled around the sockets. It carried the same sinister smile as the man in the lobby. Looking down, my hand would not stop shaking.

Was that the Fizz Man?

I took a deep breath and slowed my breathing.

I must be going nuts. That old man is really in your head.

I tried closing my eyes. The vision of the monstrosity smiling towards me with the tune of the old man played in my head. I fought the vision for what seemed an hour before the tune was drowned out with weariness. Finally, my aching and tired body dispatched the memory and sleep found me. Dreams filled a fitful sleep as I tossed in the sweat filled bed. The old man's tune rang loudly in my head as I tried desperately to escape his demented song of the Fizz Man.

A piercing stab to the side of my cheek awoke me from the devilish tune. I opened my eyes to something much worse than my nightmare filled dreams. Hovering above me, the Fizz Man's cruel snarl stared down at me. The putrid smell of death whiffed across my cheek as he sat inches from my face. His heavy breath beat down on my trembling face. His head warped and bulged in time with the unrelenting tune in the background. Bloody jagged teeth protruded covering not only its face but also its hands and neck. The old man in the cloak laughed loudly standing behind the monster.

As the Fizz Man gripped the side of my head and reached into my mouth, the old man held out the tin cup laughing hysterically. Joyfully he watched and sang softly the tune from the porch, delighting in the creature finding its prey.

I sat helpless in the bed looking from the Fizz Man to the old man as I felt the pull of a tooth. Watching in horror, the creature added its new trophy to the rest that occupied its sadistic head. I grimaced in pain as tears filled my eyes and I felt the warm breath of the old man close in my ear whispering as darkness overtook me,

"Into the cup a sacrifice be made.
The Fizz Man demands this be paid.
A single precious tooth is your only plight.
For his special Halloween treat on this night."

On Carney Hill

Ian Caswell

Thursday, 3ʳᵈ October. Carney Hill, near Holywood, Co. Down.

"For God's sake Mick, could you not have got that damned bead off her. Deirdre could have choked on it. And where did it come from anyway? I nearly had to prise it out of her hand when she went to sleep."

Mick, already in bed, looked up from his book as his wife tapped the bead down on the shelf over the sink in their ensuite. "We were out looking at Deirdre's little patch of garden while the men brought the new furniture into the lounge. She was deadheading those little yellow coneflowers that you got her, even telling me all about how this would make the plant produce more flowers, then she saw something sparkle in the grass under the border. You know her; glittery things and all that, we had to investigate."

Edith smiled, "She loves that little patch. Giving her responsibility for it is teaching her a lot. So, knowing you, you made a big game out of the bead. Carefully extracting ancient relics from the ground. Go on, admit it, you're the one that has her thinking she is a great hunter of archaeological treasures, aren't you? It's no wonder she wouldn't give it up. She'll be looking for an Indiana Jones hat next."

Edith moved to the bed and kissed her husband's forehead before climbing in beside him, then cuddled up with his arm around her. "The house is stunning Mick, and everything came together so well. You hear so many stories of bad builders these days. I was worried that we were making a big mistake, but even the landscapers seem to have gone above and beyond. I never for a moment thought that those old, blackened foundation stones that the builders dug up when they were digging the foundations would be good for anything, but they cleaned up well, and the little terrace the landscapers made with them is beautiful."

She teased him then, knowing his lack of belief, "Maybe a little prayer once in a while didn't go amiss after all?"

He pulled her in, tickling her stomach, "Get real girl, hard work, and long hours by the pair of us got this place built, not superstition. If I could pray for anything, it would be to keep your parents from visiting for another week. We will be hard pushed to get everything unpacked and tidied up before lunch on Sunday. We should have got them to do two weeks in a row. Still, all this will pay off when we get to do the big family Christmas."

Mick's hand then traced a semicircle above their heads, as if he were drawing the scene, "Can you imagine next spring when it is a little warmer? We can have breakfast in the sun out on that balcony while watching those big cruise ships go up and down the lough."

For a moment Edith looked lost in the vision of that view, then, more down to earth, "I'm just glad we were able to keep the house in Belfast while all this work was going on. I don't think I could have been like those people you see on the TV property programs; you know, living through the winter in some leaky old caravan or something."

Mick turned to face Edith with mirth, "It's the start of a new life, my girl. Now if only all my clients were as friendly as you!"

Edith put on a mock frown for him, "Now now. Don't get ideas above your station. If you were this friendly with everyone you drew up plans for, you have no idea of the trouble you would be in! Besides, aren't most of your clients male?"

She laughed as he made a joke of acknowledging this, then moved even closer and kissed him, then kissed him again more passionately.

Sunday, 6th October. Carney Hill.

Chatter fed softly through the open plan living area to where Mick stood behind a large, granite topped kitchen island, his left hand laden with cutlery. As he glanced behind to the eye level oven to check the roast, Edith's mother walked over, wine glass in hand.

"Mick, the house is beautiful; and so big! I mean, these spaces, wow! You must be very proud." She held her arms wide and almost pirouetted a full circle to emphasise the point. "I suppose every architect has a secret dream to design their own home?"

"Thanks Roselyn. Yes, it's great to see it all come to fruition, and finally move in. The house seems to have taken over our lives for so long now. It's good to get out of the city too, although I didn't realise how pervasive the noise would be from the road at the bottom of the hill. It is constant during the rush hour."

28

"Oh Mick," she replied. "I know it took a lot of work to get here, but just look at the result. The old 1960's bungalow that was here just doesn't compare! As for the noise, there is none when you are inside, and even when we looked around the garden earlier there was barely a whisper from the road. The view across the lough to the Antrim coast is to die for! Carrickfergus Castle looks nearly close enough to touch. I could easily forgive a little traffic noise for a view like that.

I know too that you both worried about the effect of the move on Deirdre, but she seems to be settling in well. She was so excited to show everything to Jim and I, and she says she has a new friend, someone called Katie?"

"Really? That's news to me. I mean, we've all walked up to the top of the lane and back a few times, but other than a brief hello to a few of our new neighbours, I didn't think Deirdre had had a chance to make friends yet. Did she tell you anything about her."

"She said Katie talked; in her words, 'funny'. Perhaps Deirdre means the girl has a foreign accent, although the name doesn't sound foreign? Anyway, by the time you come round to us next Sunday, I'm sure the girl will be like a new member of the family."

Mick glanced over towards the double height picture window at the front of the house, where Edith sat chatting with Deirdre and her father, Jim. Deirdre was on her grandfather's knee, her left hand, palm open while she was pointing into it with her right. She appeared to be in the middle of some long, childish explanation. Jim was nodding his agreement but rarely getting a chance to break into the monologue.

Mick smiled at his father in law's predicament, "Perhaps we should rescue Jim? He seems to be getting the full history of the finding of that bead."

"Oh, don't worry Mick. It's his own doing. He thinks the bead may be very old, so he has been taking photos of it to show to his friend George. Jim thinks he can help stimulate Deirdre's new-found interest in history if he can get an estimate of just how old the bead is. I think Jim spent so long getting involved in other people's lives when he was working that he just can't stop. If he thinks he can be an influence in someone's life, he will do it. He would probably have made a good psychiatrist rather than just a GP.

George is our neighbour, by the way. His garden backs onto ours, so he and Jim share a beer or two over the hedge when they are supposed to be gardening. He is a retired history professor from Queen's University."

"George sounds like an interesting neighbour to have. By contrast, I've talked to the couple in the house below us a few times during the building work. The husband is called Samuel; not Sam or any shortened version you will note. He's an accountant in the Civil Service, with all the personality that job implies. In conversation, he always seemed more interested in the amount of dust our building work would create, and in consequence, how much extra time he would have to spend washing his prized BMW. I can't ever see me wanting to share a beer with him! His wife seems as bad. Without any prompts, she was instantly boasting about their 'marvellous' holiday trips, and how their son had landed such an important job with the Foreign Office in London, straight out of Oxford."

"Poor Mick, they sound awful. Perhaps it's just first impressions and they will come around in time."

Mick smiled, "Neighbours aren't the worst problem in the world to have I suppose. But I bet you wouldn't want to swap George for them, Roselyn?"

That brought a momentary grimace to Roselyn's face. "Come on then Mick, give me that cutlery and I'll set the table for you while you get the roast out to rest for a bit and sort out the veg."

Sunday, 13ᵗʰ October. At Edith's parents, Malone Road, Belfast.

Roselyn smiled broadly while opening her front door as Mick and Edith crunched their way across the gravel driveway to her door. Deirdre, as usual, ran ahead; her arms outstretched for the traditional swinging hug that she always received in the welcoming arms of her grandparents, the one passing her to the other to swing her across the porch and into the house. Jim then stayed in the porch to welcome Mick and his daughter, kissing her cheek, while Roselyn almost ran into the house to keep up with the child.

"Sorry we're late Dad. If I could get just this man of mine to go to chapel with us, we could all come up here directly rather than me having to go all the way home to get him." She gave Mick a sideways but not very serious glance, "And if he was ready when I did get home rather than sitting in his slippers watching football, then we wouldn't be spoiling Mum's good cooking."

Mick shrugged, "What can I tell you Jim? I'm a football loving heathen. It looked like a good match though."

"Don't worry about it, Mick. We aren't quite ready yet anyway, so come on in and sit down. I got a few cans of Guinness Zero since I knew that you would be driving. By the way, that match is well worth watching. I saw the highlights last night, so I'll not spoil it for you with the final score."

Inside, the detached 1950's house was spacious, but much older in style than the new house at Carney Hill. Its kitchen, though big enough to have a small table in it, was separate from the dining and living rooms. Deirdre was there, 'helping' her grandmother. In the living room, where Jim left his guests momentarily while he went to get them drinks, the low-level sofa sat below formal land and seascapes in gilt frames. It was comfortable but old fashioned other than two things. A huge flat screen TV in the corner, and a small Sonos speaker, linked to a music system that was playing quiet classical music throughout the house. The room's decor simply looked like it had failed to make the transition to the current millennium.

Edith was sitting on the sofa, while Mick wandered over to the patio doors to look out on the well-tended back garden. As she looked around her old home, Edith suddenly felt the loss of her own childhood years.

"It's funny Mick. This old house always felt so comfortable, as if it was part of me and I of it. But something has changed since in the week or so since we moved to the new house. Suddenly it looks different to me; sort of old fashioned and distant."

She rose from the sofa and sidled up behind her husband, wrapping her arms around him from behind as she reached him, "Do you remember sneaking in here for a kiss when you would leave me home at night?"

Mick turned in her arms, his eyes shining as he encircled her with his own, "As I remember it girl, the kissing was only for starters. It's as well that your dad didn't walk in on us!"

"He might do now Mick when he comes back with my wine! I guess we've just found our place, haven't we?" She broke away from him, still embarrassed that her father might catch them in an embrace. "Do you think Deirdre will find our house old fashioned when she grows up?"

"Hmm, after our visit to the Cultra Folk Museum yesterday, I'm beginning to wonder if she'll want to live in a traditional cottage rather than a modern house. The more basic the houses were up there, the more she seemed to like them. And the one she said was like the one that Katie lived in, was about the most basic of the lot! No glass, just wooden shutters, a dirt floor. I mean, where does she get these ideas from?"

"Oh, come on Mick. The Halloween displays just looked better in the darker, more basic houses. She loved that. And you've seen her at home, playing with her toys and talking to this Katie creation of hers at the same time. She's just an imaginary friend. Deirdre even said she has had dreams about staying over at Katie's house. It's probably just something she picked up from a book."

At that moment, a bump on the door signalled Jim's arrival as he backed into the room with a glass in either hand. "Sorry but I couldn't help overhearing the end of that conversation about Katie. Deirdre has talked of little else while she has been in the kitchen. Our granddaughter is blessed with a very vivid imagination it seems, and that's not a bad thing. She is probably just feeling a little uprooted and lonely after the move. Believe me, when I was in practice, many worried parents came to me about their children's imaginary friends. It is much more common that you would think. As soon as she settles in and gets to know some of the local kids, she'll be fine."

Edith looked worried, "I know Dad, but this Katie thing is just so all pervasive at the moment. I don't think Deirdre wants other friends. She even says that the bead she found was Katie's, and she has it on a thread around her neck now, and even wears it to her new school."

Jim smiled softly at his daughter, taking her free hand in his, "Oh love. I didn't want to bring this up in front of Mick, but do you remember when you were young, your best friend's family moved to England. You spent almost the whole summer that year playing on your own, except that you weren't actually on your own, you too had an imaginary friend. What was it you called her?"

Edith blushed, "God, Dad. I haven't thought about that in years. Jennie, I called her Jennie, but I can't even remember much about her now, only that she felt the same way I did and gave me someone to talk to."

"Then let me give you the same advice that I used to give to all those other worried parents. Humour Deirdre in this. If she wants to talk about Katie, or if Deirdre passes on questions from Katie, then direct your answers back to Katie. In effect, Deirdre becomes the teacher to her 'friend', and the lesson will be learned much more easily as a result."

In the background, Mick had been listening intently, his brow furrowed, "I can almost see the logic in what you are saying Jim, but it seems counterintuitive to pay acknowledgement to something that is so obviously unreal."

Jim just smiled knowingly, "The human mind is a complex thing Mick, especially when it is developing. It requires subtlety. In this as in many other aspects of life, have faith, all will be well."

Mick, still thinking, nodded his thanks, then looked back towards his wife, "At least I know now where Deirdre gets her imagination."

At that break in the conversation, Jim suddenly realised how long it had taken him to deliver the drinks, "Come on you two. I was supposed to have you seated in the dining room by now and be back helping to serve. By the way, I can't get hold of George to get an evaluation of the bead. He and his wife, Sandra, often spend weekends with their family. They have a daughter who keeps up the family tradition; she lectures at Edinburgh University. Their son works in Dublin, film graphics or something. If they are away for long, they usually let us know, so that we can keep an eye on the house, put the bins our and all the usual routine things. If I can get hold of him, I'll let you know. Perhaps half term comes a little earlier for the schools on the other side of the pond."

Soon enough they were sitting down to this week's roast. Edith's father said grace as all but Mick bowed their heads.

Sunday, 20th October. Carney Hill.

The clear and bright weather had gone, and more traditional autumnal weather had returned to Ireland over the preceding few days. Once crisp autumn leaves had blown into soggy piles in the corner of the garden at Carney Hill. Jim and Mick stood watching as a heavy squall from the north was whipping up huge waves on Belfast lough, and the wind was beating torrents of rain against the large window at the front of the house.

"That's quite a storm."

"Mmmm. Edith and I had cleared all the leaves from the garden, but it's as bad as ever again. Did you have any trouble on the drive down?"

"We weren't rushing Mick. There were a few small branches and leaves on the road, but there wasn't much traffic on a day like this. Getting to and from the car is the worst and wettest part. It was worth the drive, just to be able to stand here and watch the waves in comfort. I wouldn't fancy being out on Belfast Lough in a boat today, but it's kind of invigorating watching all the action from here, don't you think?"

"It's better than what's on the telly if nothing else, though that's not saying much. You're right, there is something very comforting about standing here watching the storm. There was lightning last night. That was truly spectacular."

"I can imagine."

"You know, since we went to the Folk Museum last week I've been wondering about the contrast between this house and the ones in the museum. How did people survive in those draughty old houses, with just an open fire for heat? It must have been a dreadful existence."

"Ah, now there is a question even a retired doctor can answer. You know of course that life expectancy has been rising for many generations now? Around 1900, the average was only about 45 for men, but that includes child mortality. If you were poor and did manage to live to the ripe old age of 50, the chances are that you would have lived a life of hard labour, and as a result suffered from diseases like arthritis. Poor sanitation, bad diet, and a host of other factors would also affect your life chances. I take it that you weren't a history student then?"

Mick shrugged, "I like my facts to be precise. All that nuanced stuff about 'meanings', just seemed like chasing your own tail to me. Besides which, isn't that what all the ex-terrorists over here used to justify their actions?"

"Yes, I suppose it is Mick, but not everything in life is so black and white. It's like the amount of salt and pepper you add to season your food. Everyone is different."

"Perhaps you're right. That might explain why I'm such a rubbish cook. By the way, I presume that your own daughter knows your likes and dislikes well enough. Edith has cooked duck this week, just to add a little variety to the roasts. Your whole family has such culinary skills compared to my own. It's as well that we built a gym in the basement, or I would soon be too big to even fit through our own front door!"

"Yes. It comes from Roselyn's mother, Mick. She worked in the catering trade. An exclusive club on Royal Avenue for the cream of the city's businessmen. Apparently even during the troubles, it was always busy. I know what you mean though. That woman was a bad influence on my waistline. We used to go to their house every Sunday for years, sort of like our reciprocal arrangement now. That is, we did once Roselyn became brave enough to introduce her unruly young student doctor! Her mother's knowledge of fine wines was astonishing, especially back then. And her baking, that, as they say nowadays, was to die for. Roselyn has many of her recipes written down, and I know that Edith uses them too."

"When I first met Edith, I was in awe of your daughter's cookery skills. My own mother used to say that she could hardly boil an egg when she got married. It wasn't that bad of course, but we ate a lot from tins and simple things like fries and Bolognese. A few tried and tested recipes if you know what I mean. There was nothing like this." Then after another second Mick added, "Not that I'm complaining of course."

Jim looked at his son in law pensively, "I would have liked to have met your parents. They must have been good people."

Mick looked down sadly, "Thanks Jim, they were. Too good to be taken like that as part of some political nonsense over a line on a map. Too good to be taken just because some idiot couldn't make a phone call in time to make sure that the shop was evacuated before their pointless bomb went off. I'm no saint, I resented everything to do with this province after that. My parents always avoided all the rubbish that is talked about causes and creeds; they didn't deserve to be sucked into it like that.

You know, I was still at school when it happened and with all the anger and resentment it put into me, I had planned to emigrate as far away from this damned place as I could. Australia, New Zealand, somewhere like that. Living with my Grandparents was strange after my parents. Then I met Edith, and everything changed. She was a real breath of fresh air for me. Someone I never thought I would find here during those dark days. You know that I tried to persuade her to emigrate with me, but she wouldn't. She saw hope here where I saw only madness."

Jim was aware of the growing emotion in his son in law's voice as he had been speaking. He had known the story of Mick's parents, but never realised just how raw the feelings from those times still were. When he spoke, he spoke softly, "She discussed it with us Mick. I hope you aren't too disappointed about not getting to Australia. I'm afraid we told her to stand up to you if she really didn't want to emigrate. She was worried about losing you if she did, but yes, if you want someone to blame for having to live with this Irish weather, I'm the one."

"God, Jim. I'm sorry, I shouldn't have said all that. You must think me a fool? I've worked for years to live up to my parents, and to get the qualifications and experience to escape this place, yet here I am. Still in Northern Ireland, and yet with all the things that I ever could have dreamed of. With this house now finished, I have had more time over the last few weeks to sit and think my life over than I have had in years. It's unsettling for someone like me."

"Don't worry about it, son, you're doing OK. Just cling for dear life to your family and the things you love. I've found over the years that every one of us is doing the exact same thing; just trying to live life by making it all up as we go along."

Mick nodded slowly but couldn't look his father-in-law in the eye, even though his thoughts were lighter now, "You're a wise man Jim. I guess I'll have to learn to stop trying to be a hard man. I shouldn't have been so self-absorbed. You know I'd do anything for my girls don't you?"

"That much is obvious. Shall we change to a more flippant subject?"

Mick smiled, happy that his father-in-law was steering them away from delicate subjects, and glad to get to something more light-hearted, "That would work for me Jim."

"OK, thanks for sending those photos earlier in the week. George, when I eventually got hold of him, seemed much more interested in the stonework you found than in the bead for some reason."

"No problem. Did he say why he wanted to know about those stones"?

"He said that this hill has a history, and that there had been some historical investigations here in the past, but that nothing had been found. He wanted to talk to you both, so we have invited the two of them to come for lunch next Sunday. You don't mind, do you? He did ask if either you or the builder had taken any shots of those stones in situ. I got the impression that he wanted to try to estimate the size and shape of the original dwelling. I had been tasked with taking a few close ups of the stones too, but not in this weather. George thought he might be able to see how the stones had been dressed."

"They are a bit rough, and certainly not heavy enough to be part of a castle or anything important, but that sounds intriguing. The building's footprint looked more like that of a traditional cottage than anything else. I do have pictures uploaded to my cloud storage. There are more there than a project like this would normally justify, but the desire to document all this was irresistible. I'll have a look later and share them with you."

The two men walked over towards the dining area as they spoke, only to have bowls of steaming vegetables thrust at them for delivery to the table. When everyone was settled and eating, Edith re-started the conversation as she cut Deirdre's meat up into more manageable pieces.

"Mum was telling me about how George thinks there may be something of historical interest here. Imagine that Mick, our Deidre's archaeology may be very important after all." Edith kissed her daughter's hair as if to prove the point.

"Hmmm, a brand new house with a history. I wonder what it can be. I suppose it will make for a good yarn to tell any guests."

To which Jim replied, "Roselyn and I are both keen to hear what George has to say too. He was making something of a melodrama of it over the phone, but he wouldn't explain further until he sees us."

"And on that point, Mum and I have made an executive decision. Since George is so interested in those stones, he should really see them for himself. There is bound to be a limit to what photographs can show, so next Sunday's lunch will be here again. We've swapped weeks, and you, Dad, are going to ensure that George and his wife Sandra receive the invite. They will be due a little hospitality for generating such a stir."

"Are you sure you don't mind having them round when you have never met them? They hadn't moved in next door to us when you were at home."

"They sound lovely, Dad. Anyway, our mind is made up, isn't that right Mum? Besides, my only problem with this is waiting a whole seven days to find out what George has to say."

Sunday, 27th October. Carney Hill.

Even Edith had skipped chapel to ensure that everything was as perfect as possible for the lunch to come. With a little help from Mick and Deirdre as sous chefs, she had roasted a pork shoulder, the crackling of which was always a firm favourite.

All four guests arrived a few minutes after noon, a full hour earlier than was normal for these lunches, to give time for introductions and discussion. This was George's idea. He had suggested that they might want to talk through his findings away from the dinner table, and from Deirdre. He had given no reason for the request.

None the less, on arrival, after introductions had been made and flowers presented to the hosts, both he and Sandra made a real fuss of the little girl. While at first Deirdre had almost hidden behind her mother at the sight of the two unknown faces, she was easily encouraged out when Sandra handed her a present of chocolates, and her very own small posy of flowers. Deirdre was still a little shy when George then knelt to be at her level as he asked to shake her hand, but with a little encouragement, and her index finger pressed firmly into her cheek, Deirdre listened as Edith told her that George had come to examine her bead. She shook hands, then almost reluctantly removed the thread it was on from around her neck and placed it in George's outstretched hand.

He made a show of examining it carefully, producing a magnifying loupe, and turning the bead over and over to see every part. George then gave the loupe and bead to Deirdre, showed her how to focus on the bead, pointed out the miniscule scratches on it, and that its shape was not perfect, 'slightly lumpy' as he phrased this for his young audience. He then told Deirdre she could keep the loupe because he has others, which pleased her immensely.

"The bead is old Deirdre, but I cannot say with any precision exactly how old it is. Its shape tells me that it was hand-made and the scratches on it show that it is likely to have been in the ground for many years. Your grandfather told me that the area where you found it was rotovated before being re-planted with grass. It's a miracle that it the bead is still in one piece. Someone probably lost it there many years ago."

At this Deirdre looked serious, nodded slowly, then shyly mumbled, "It was a part of Katie's treasure."

"Ah, Katie. Your Grandad told me about her too." He smiled at Deirdre before scanning the faces of the other adults, "And how old do you think Katie is?"

"She's very old. Even older than Daddy."

At that, everyone laughed although Deirdre didn't seem to understand why.

"Perhaps you could show me where you found it?" said George. "It is very cold out there though, so you will need a coat."

Deirdre didn't need a prompt and ran off to get her coat. Before she returned, George stood, then turned to talk to Edith, "There are a few things about the history of this place that probably aren't suitable for young ears. We all discussed this in the car on the way down, so Roselyn will ask Deirdre to give Sandra and her a tour of the house so that the rest of us can talk for a bit. What happened here is interesting if a little gory."

After a short tour to the garden to see the find site and the stones that had been reused in their terrace, Roselyn duly requested that Deirdre show Sandra the house, so off they went. The others were silent for a moment until the house tour was out of earshot.

Then, while Jim went off to the car to collect something, George began, "I'm sorry to keep you both in the dark for so long. Mick, I'm told that history is not your forte, so a little background information first. Does the year 1641 mean anything at all to you?"

Mick shook his head while Edith nodded. Both looked puzzled.

"In England, the events which precipitated the civil war started that year. There were moves within the English parliament accusing the King, Charles the first, of a Catholic conspiracy to destroy Protestantism. I'm sure that you can see how this may have split society on this side of the Irish Sea, especially with Protestants, mainly from Scotland having been planted into confiscated Catholic lands since Elizabethan times. As you will know, the scale of the plantations was greater here in the province of Ulster than in other parts of Ireland, because this was the most troublesome part of the island for the English.

Anyway, On the fourth of January 1642, the King entered Parliament, trying to impeach his enemies, but they may have been warned of this move because they were not there. The King left London to be with more secure supporters in the north only five days later. In his absence Parliament raised a force against him. Of course, Charles did the same, asking his followers to raise an army on his behalf.

Personally, I find it difficult to believe that the raising of these armies was limited only to England. Why, if the strength of the two opposing sides was to be tested would such requests not have circulated throughout the whole kingdom? I also find it difficult to believe that the King would not have been canvassing for whatever support he could find a long time before this big showdown.

Which brings us to Ireland. In October 1641, so before the start of the real hostilities in England, Sir Felim O'Neill, who was part of the old Catholic gentry in Ireland, attacked a government fort just outside Moy. He claimed to have a document signed by the King authorising this attack. This, of course was denied. After the massacre of about 100 Scots settlers, who were driven into the freezing waters of the river Bann near Portadown, the conflict quickly deteriorated into sectarian violence throughout Ireland, and because of the pending conflict in England, there were no reinforcements for government forces here to deal with it, and those local forces were sectarian in their own right.

By May in 1642, the Catholic church had pronounced this rebellion to be a just cause, and the old Catholic Gentry had set up their own proxy government, yet forces loyal to the English government still held Dublin and many other important areas. The whole conflict went on for roughly ten years until Cromwell came to Ireland after the English Civil War, and we all know the esteem in which he is held here in Ireland! Are you with me so far?"

Mick, interested, but a little confused, replied, "Yes, but are you telling us that there is a link between this area, which must only have been empty countryside at that time, and Cromwell?"

"You are getting ahead of me Mick. Actually, there are still the remains of lime kilns from that time further up the hill here, and there was a small community who lived on this hill who would have worked them. Being an architect, you will know that lime is pretty nasty stuff, very caustic. Working lime kilns was not a good job so it fell to the lowest strata of society, which at that time was the native Irish."

"OK, so what happened?"

By this time Jim had returned from the car, carrying a hardbacked book. George reached out to take it, "This is an old book written by a local history society based near here. It has a first-hand account of what happened, and there are more, similar accounts online at Trinity College, Dublin's website. I've marked the page so that you can read it later when you have more time. I'm afraid that even the name of the road here, hints at these events. The name Carney Hill has evolved over the years. Its original name was Carnage Hill."

Both Edith and Mick were stunned to silence. It took a few seconds before Mick could even form a response, "Carnage Hill? So, from what you have already told us, there must have been an attack on the people living on this hill back then? Is that why you were interested in the old foundations we found during our build? How many people died here?"

"I'm sorry. This is the bad news for you both. Contemporary reports say that 73 people were murdered on this hill on the night of 26th January 1642. Most seem to have been from an extended family group called O'Gilmore. Revenge bred revenge following the start of this conflict in Ireland. These people, and many others, were simply caught up in a conflict they had no part of. There was, for example, a similar massacre on the other side of Belfast Lough, at Island Magee."

Although his brow furrowed, only one word escaped Mick's lips, "Christ!" Internally though, he was in turmoil, thinking, *Even at the site we bought to build our home, I can't escape this stuff.*

George continued, unaware of the impact of the facts he was giving, "There have been digs here in the past, but they were always further up the hill towards the old kilns. Rumour said that the bodies had been buried up there, although nothing was ever found, not even any signs of a settlement. It may be that because of the dust from the lime that their homes were constructed here, further from the kilns. No excavations were ever done in this area because it was already built over."

Edith made a grab for Mick's hand, squeezing it tight, "It's alright George. All that was a very long time ago. What we have built here is obviously a much happier place that it was back then. Anyway, we don't know if this is the exact spot of the massacre. There may have been other buildings here over the ages." Then, turning to Mick, she whispered to ask if he was OK.

He nodded, squeezing her hand in return, smiled back at her, and tried to crack a joke, "Isn't it good to see how far we've come in the last four hundred years or so?" He was recovering himself quickly, shaking off his memories, and rejoining the conversation.

The smells and tastes of their hearty lunch did much to revive him, although his thoughts of the massacres in his life remained in the background of his mind. Sandra and George proved to be full of knowledge and humour. Sandra had also been a lecturer and told stories of the best and worst of her students, which even raised a laugh from Mick. George was full of tales of the Lough behind them, shipwrecks and smugglers, WW2 conveys and raids by John Paul Jones during the American war for independence. Both the adults and Deirdre were enthralled.

Only later, as Edith was putting Deirdre to bed, did he get a chance to read the account below from the book that George had lent him.

26th January 1642

(Exerpt from evidence given to a Government Commission led by Ambrose Bedell to enquire into the events known as The Ballydavey Massacre. The enquiry took its evidence some 11 years later, and the depositions are now held at Trinity College, Dublin. More details relating to the numerous massacres and other events from the rebellion that started in 1641 can be found at: https://1641.tcd.ie/)

"After '.. that party of Scotch men did abyde with them and supt with the said Irish and were very merry till about midnight, the party fell upon ye said Irish and stript them and a little aforeday fell a-killing of ye sd. Irish.' At the end of this treachery, 73 Irish had been killed.

Katherine O'Gilmore, who subsequently moved to Ballynahinch, escaped by hiding in a ditch. She told the Commission, which appears to have involved the High Court of Justice sitting at Carrickfergus: '8 days before Candlemas next, after ye Rebellion, shee then living in ye townland of Ballydavy, in ye Barrony of Castlereagh, altogether with tenn familyes more, of all which 11 familyes there were (of men, women, and children) killed to her own knowledge, seaventy and three by a great company of people (being) to her estimacon in number about 200, who were brought thither by one Andrew Hamilton of the fforte, James Johnson the elder, and James Johnson the younger, both of Ballydavy, John Crafford of Craford's Burne; and further she saith that James Johnson the elder killed one Henry O'Gilmore, brother to the examinat, at her own sight, and likewise she saw the sd. James with his sword slashing at one Edmond Neeson, who was killed but shee knoweth not whether he made an end of him or not, for on the recept of the first blow, the sd. Neeson rann to the lower end of the house, among the rest of his neighbours, the cause of her knowledge is that a short space before, the said Andrew Hamilton had putt her out of the door of the house in consideracon of her tartan, after which shee lay her down in a ditch which was right before the door where she was unespied of any as she supposeth, the night being very darke, rayny and windie.

The Examt. Further saith, she saw one Abraham Adam kill James O'Gilmore, her owne husband, and Daniell Crone O'Gilmore, and Thurlagh O'Gilmore; shee further saith, that at her going forth of the house, a sister of hers tooke houlde of her for to go out with her, and the sd. Abraham Adam strock of her sd. sister's arme from the elbowe, with a broade swoord, the sister's name was Owna O'Gilmore.' Owen O'Gilmore escaped by hiding himself in a limekiln on Ballydavey Hill. He told the Commission: 'Andrew Hamilton, now of Crawfordsburn in Bangor parish came to them who was to bring order for that work, and came and shott off his pistoll before Bryan Boy's doore, whereupon ye sd. Scots party fell upon killinge ye sd. Irish, and so killed of men, women and children, three score and odd, and ye names of ye persons yt this examt. remembers yt were at ye place yt night were ye sd. Andrew Hamilton, John Crawford, James Johnson senior, and James Johnson junior, Captain Will Hamilton, Robert Morris, John Watt and Gabriell Adam, and did see ye sd. Watt and Morris kill seven of ye sd. persons. Also this examt. saith, yt he, escapeinge this danger by hydeing himself in ye kilne, did so soone as he could escape thence towards one Hen. M'Williams M'Gilmore's house to secure himself, and as this examt. came nere the sd. house, he heard the Scotchmen aboute the sd. house, and so durst not go thither, but perceived yt ye sd. persons were the two James Johnsons, aforesd., and the said Watt and, others not known to this examt.; but this examt. heard ye sd. James Johnson junior, say to ye sd. Gilmore,

Open the door, but ye sd. Gilmore denyed, and then ye sd. Johnson said, You know me, to wch. Gilmore said, yes he did, but for all ye must not open ye door; then ye sd. Johnson desired ye sd. Gilmore to light some straw, ye wch. Gilmore did, whereby ye sd. Johnson put in his pistoll and shott and kild ye sd. Gilmore, whereupon they broke open ye doore, and went in and kild one of ye children of ye sd. Gilmore and did wound ye sd. Gilmore's wiffe and one child more, and left them for dead, but ye sd. wiffe recovered and tould this examt. the foresd relation.'

Thomas O'Gilmore survived the massacre but only for four days. Owen reported what happened: 'Ye constable one Robert Jackson of Hollywood, did bring with him one Thomas O'Gilmore, uncle to this examt.; whom ye sd. Jackson brought to ye sd. place with his hands bound behynd his back with match, ye sd. Jackson brought ye sd. prisoner to Bangnell to ye .... And ye sd. Capt. would not receave him at all; so so sd. constable took ye sd. prisoner back, and this exampt., thinking yt they would cary him to Bangnell accordingly did follow them; but as ye constable (and another man) went up ye mountaine betwixt ye sd. Kirkdonnell and Hollywood, this exampt. did see ye sd. Jackson, constable, kill ye sd. prisoner, Thomas O'Gilmore with a sword, and this exampt. did goe to him after yt ye sd. constable was gone away and perceaved severall wounds yt ye sd. Tho: had, both cutts and stabbs.' We also have information about the planning of the event, which was clearly premeditated. James Gourdon of Clandeboye was pressed to join in the attack: 'His mother told him that there were some of the town, two or three tymes looking for him, to speake with him, and that she heard it was to goe out with them to kill the Irish that lived neere and about the towne; therefore she advised him to put himselfe out of the way and not to have any hand in the busines; whereupon he tooke his bed clothees and went and stayed and lodged in his mault kilne, a pretty distance from the sayd towne of Bangor. And he furthermore sayth that within a night or two after most of the towne of Bangor and the parish together made a compact with those of Ballydavy about Holliwood to fall out in two partyes in the night upon the neighbouring Irish to kill and plunder them.

And they went forth in the night and killed of men, women and children (poor labouring people and their familyes) a great number. His cause of knowledge is, for that the next morning after the sayd murder was comitted he saw those of the towne of Bangor that had beene acters in it come in with bloody brakans (a kind of tartan or plaid) and other goods, cattle and household stuffe; his further cause of knowledge is that there was a collection made through the whole towne of Bangor for burying those were killed, wherefore this witness played a part but cannot now remember how much."

When Edith rejoined him on their couch, he passed her the book. She immediately noticed the girl's name.

"My God, Mick. This girl was called Kathleen. You don't think all this has anything to do with our Deirdre's Katie, do you?"

"Oh, come on Eadie, you can't really believe that can you? Kathleen was here nearly four centuries ago. And she survived and moved on."

Edith, still reading the book's account was becoming increasingly horrified by it, even as she kept up the conversation with Mick, "Yet Deirdre chose her name. What are the chances?"

Mick turned to her rolling his eyes, saying nothing. Edith although concentrating on the book, eventually looked up, "Yeah, OK. Our daughter being haunted by a four hundred year old woman seems a bit of a stretch. But look at this stuff, this massacre that happened here. Don't you believe that people's souls can leave a trace?"

Mick just resumed his wide-eyed puzzlement, but this time with a smile on his face.

Edith gave up on that argument, reached behind her, grabbed a cushion and swiped her husband, "Don't make fun of me Mick. Something awful happened here; or at the very least within a few hundred yards of this house. Just because you cannot see logic in something doesn't make it untrue. So tell me, knowing what we know now, how would you explain Deirdre's bead and the name she gave to its owner? And while we're at it, you have been a bit distant recently, thinking more about your past than you have done in years. You would tell me if I can help, wouldn't you?"

Mick reached over and cuddled her in against his shoulder, "I'm sorry love, I don't deserve you. I just seem to have had a lot of time for reflection since this little project of ours finished. It's not only the past that I've been thinking of either, it's our future too. I promise to make more time for the two of you. You know, holidays, weekends, all that kind of thing. I'm not going to be an absentee father for Deirdre growing up, and just as soon as we can find a good local babysitter, how do you fancy a night out for just the two of us?"

Edith cuddled closer, "The night out would be lovely Mick. There are some very good restaurants in Holywood, I'm told. But you don't get away so easily. You didn't give me an explanation about Deirdre."

"Damn," Mick squeezed her, "I thought I'd got away with that one. I can't explain a coincidence, no matter how much meaning you read into it."

"You're an awful man Mick, but somehow, I still love you. It's Halloween on Thursday. They say that the veil between us and the spirits is thinner at this time of year. Maybe you are getting spiritual in your old age but just don't know it yet!"

Thursday, 31st October. Carney Hill.

It was school half term, and both Edith and Mick had taken time off too. Mick however had left the house early that morning to see a client with an urgent problem. He had promised to return early so they could all go as a family to the National Trust estate at Mount Stewart for their Halloween celebrations. Knowing his forgetfulness for all things not related to architecture, Edith had texted him so that he remembered to pick up some trick or treat sweets on his way home.

In the meantime, both she and Deirdre shared a leisurely breakfast with the TV on. Then, when Edith could stand no more children's programs, she suggested they go out to the garden to plant some of the Winter Cyclamen they had bought the previous weekend. With Deirdre doing the planting it was a slow but thorough task. By the time Mick returned a few hours later, they still had half a dozen plants to put in the ground.

Finding the house empty, Mick left a pile of Halloween themed sweet packets on one of the kitchen worktops, along with a good bottle of red wine in a conspicuous place where Edith would notice it. The rest of the food he had bought to try his hand at the red Thai curry that Edith had been teaching him, he put into the fridge, then went in search of his family. Looking back into the kitchen area as he went out, the pile of sweets looked a bit excessive, but in his defence, he had no idea how many costumed kids would call at their house that evening.

Deirdre's constant stream of chatter and conversation made them easy to find, and on sight of her father, she ran to welcome him, planting trowel still in hand. Edith too rose to from the kneeling pad she had been using, dusting her hands as she got up. After Deirdre's welcome, Mick stepped forward to hug his wife.

"Hello love, you see, it didn't take so long to sort out after all, and I even remembered the sweets. Plus, I got a little something for the two of us to share later on as well."

"Mmm, I hope by that, you mean something made with fermented grapes?"

Mick performed an exaggerated bow, "Your wish is my command, my lady." Then as an aside, "In the meantime, shouldn't the two of you be getting cleaned up so that we can go out?"

Edith acknowledged this and made to move off, placing her hand behind Deirdre's back to bring her along too, but their daughter stood firm. Deirdre eyed her father fixedly, then moved off towards the hedge at the side of their garden. The two adults looked at each other, puzzled, then Edith called out, "Deirdre, where are you going?"

"I have to get something for Daddy."

Both adults were now really confused but started to follow their daughter. She was moving towards an old, gnarled Hawthorne at the side of their property that made up part of a hedge with a drainage ditch on the far side, which separated their garden from the fields beyond. As Deirdre stooped to duck under the thorny lower branches, Edith broke into a run, calling to Deirdre to be careful. Deirdre made no reply and was now at the tree's roots.

She still had the trowel and started digging a short distance from the trunk. Edith, now on her knees crouched down to see what was happening, but even with autumn's fallen leaves, everything there was in shadow. Edith could barely see her daughter let alone see what she was doing. Mick was on the grass on his stomach, yet could see little more.

"It's OK Mummy, I have to get this for Daddy."

She could not be moved, no matter how much Mick and Edith tried to persuade her to come out. Eventually, Deirdre rummaged in her pocket for a tissue, which she then set on the ground beside her before reaching into the small hole she had excavated and lifted a few things onto the tissue. She then dug again and repeated the process. Eventually, Deirdre seemed satisfied with her work and squirmed out from under the tree again, straight into the relieved arms of her mother. Deirdre was filthy yet seemed unaware that she had done anything odd. From her mother's arms, Deirdre then turned to Mick, her father, holding out the crumpled tissue and its grubby contents.

"Katie says you need to have her treasure before she goes."

Mick took the package in silence and solemnly opened it. A few glimpses of something bright glinted from clay bound scraps of earth, among which sat one larger dull lump. In amazement, he rubbed one of the scraps between his fingers, revealing a bead similar to Deirdre's one, and then yet another until there were eight of them in total. Then he moved to the larger piece. It was heavy for its size, and as he cleaned it, a small cross made of lead emerged, crudely fashioned. On one side something that looked like a human shape had been scratched on the surface of the cross; a crucifix.

Mick looked at his daughter in wonder as she said, "The string broke when she ran, so she left her treasure here. It's yours now."

There was a silence between them for a few moments, from which Edith managed to recover first. She swallowed, feeling like even a breath would be sacrilege, then said, "Well Mick?"

Mick looked around him trying to detect the presence that he had failed to see. The sky was still as it had always been, as similarly were the waves of the Lough. Even the spot where Deirdre had found the first bead was just grass and earth. He looked at Edith winking at her before looking lovingly into the innocent eyes of his daughter. "Thank you Deirdre." Then, looking over towards the Hawthorne again, "Thank you Katie."

The Monster in the Dungeon

L.N. Hunter

So, here I am, stuck in a dungeon, surrounded by monsters.

Yeah, I know, what's a dungeon doing in Crake's Landing, the most boring town in the universe? Nothing exciting ever happens here.

At least until now.

I find it hard to believe, myself, but here I am in a genuine, old-fashioned, grimy-walled dungeon. I'm not alone: I've got a zombie and a ghost for company. We've been trapped in here by a vampire.

All I need is a werewolf to complete the set.

I'm not entirely sure how we got here…

Courtesy of the parental units – who else? – my name's Amanda Amelia Moon, but everyone just calls me Mel. Everybody apart from my mother, that is. I'm always and only Amanda to her. But the bit of my name that really matters is Moon.

The most exclusive group at school is the *Maidens of the Moon*: me, Becky and Kevin (don't ask, it's complicated). Becky's the bright one – yes, she does wear glasses – and Kevin is the artist, but I'm *numero uno*. It's my name and it's my group. I'm not a brainiac, I'm definitely not cheerleader material, I'm too well-balanced to go the emo route, and I really don't see singing and prancing around on stage as my thing. So, I set up my own club: my rules, my people.

Despite the name of our little association, we're all thoroughly grounded in reality. We don't dress like goths or hippies, we don't pretend to cast spells, and we definitely don't prance around in the nude during full moons. We love the idea of the supernatural; who doesn't? It's all entertaining twaddle – I'm a fan of Twilight and Sookie Stackhouse, Kevin's a real Walking Dead-head (don't get him started on where the TV series diverged from the comic books!), and Becky's favourite characters are Eve and Kristof from the Otherworld series, not to mention Patrick Swayze, but I think that's because he's a hunk, not because he's a ghost.

Everybody knows there're no such things as vampires, zombies and ghosts.

Kevin found some pictures of a Ouija board and created a gorgeous copy for an art project. You can imagine how well the board went down with the teachers at our overly-conservative school, in spite of the effort Kevin put into it. The obvious craftsmanship of the polished oak. The delicately inlaid teak lettering. He even spent days creating varnish from some old recipe, and weeks of applying layer after layer, to make the surface shine.

Letters were sent home, and parental visits were endured. Were we being corrupted (though, by whom was never specified), or were our parents too lax? Were we going to flip one day, and burn the school down, or douse it in pigs' blood? Come on, people, it's just a plank of wood with some pretty letters on it! It's a good thing that only head-spinning is considered a sign of possession, and not eye-rolling, because Kevin, Becky and I did an awful lot of that.

Anyway, it blew over eventually, and the Ouija board was all but forgotten.

A few months later, I suggested we dig out the board; it was Halloween, after all. We gathered in my room with a sneaky bottle of vodka that Becky had liberated from her older brother. I closed the curtains to cut down the sunlight and hide the pink wallpaper (thanks again, parentals), then lit some black candles to create the proper atmosphere.

We were having a giggle, passing around Halloween make-up and my silver hand mirror, the one with the handle in the shape of a gothic cross. Becky had used up pretty much all the white make-up, going for the ghostly look, and Kevin was painting his arms a decaying grey with the occasional suppurating sore.

We weren't getting much from the Ouija board, though: so far, the planchette had spelled out D-G-N-V-M-P-Yes-B-E-G-H-S-T-K-L-Yes-Z-M-K. Kevin said it seemed to be using text-speak, and we must have contacted a very modern spirit. I suspect our laughter had more to do with the booze than with Kevin's statement.

I spilled half a glass on the Ouija board, totally an accident, somehow making a smiley face pattern. Before I could wipe it off, the vodka reacted with the varnish, emitting a foul smell and a bubbling hiss. As I stared, the smile seemed to get wider, and then…

I'm not sure what happened next, but I must have passed out. I came to with my cheek pressed against cold, damp stone. This wasn't my bedroom. In the light of sputtering, greasy torches, I took in slimy walls and rusty chains, and Becky and Kevin slumped on the floor.

A heavy wooden door indicated the only exit.

It was locked, of course.

I peered through the huge keyhole and saw some keys hanging up on the wall, so far away. There was an oddly-shaped crate in the outer room too. I felt my heart stutter when I realised what it was.

"It's a coffin!" I shouted.

"What's a coffin?" Becky seemed confused, as if she wasn't seeing the same as me.

Kevin's gaze skipped around the room, not settling on anything, like he was stoned.

I struggled to make sense of our surroundings. *Who has a coffin in a dungeon?* a small voice in my mind asked. Another voice answered and, all of a sudden, the first part of the Ouija board message made total sense: D-G-N was dungeon and V-M-P must be vampire. We're definitely in a dungeon, and vampires really do exist. Somehow, one had discovered that we were on the verge of uncovering his secret, so he kidnapped us. Crake's Landing had a vampire, and that must be his coffin!

The others refused to believe me, ignoring the evidence right in front of them. Maybe Becky isn't as clever as we all thought, when she's under pressure.

Or maybe it was the effect of the vodka and the fumes from the varnish. I still don't understand why the others were so much more affected by it than me, but at least one of us still had a clear head.

"We have to get out of here and warn the town," I whispered.

"Warn the – what? I don't know what's going on, but we definitely need to get away. What's wrong with the door? What happened to your room? And what's wrong with Kevin?"

Kevin had pulled his shoes and socks off, and was counting his toes.

Becky and I beat on the door until our hands were scratched and bruised. The dungeon contained a rough wooden chair and table. The hand mirror from my bedroom sat on the table; how did that get here? No time to think about that. We poked at the keyhole with the handle of the mirror to no avail: lock picking really isn't as simple as it looks in the movies. We searched every inch of the walls, even tried scraping at the mortar with the mirror handle, but all we managed to do was break the mirror.

We lay back against the wall, making no sound apart from exhausted panting, as we each sank into our thoughts. I was thinking about the Ouija board and, with a snap, the next bit of the message became clear.

"Hey guys, B-E-G-S-T-K-L means Becky, ghost, kill! B-E for Becky, G-S-T ghost, and K-L is kill – obvious. When Becky's a ghost, she can pass through the door and open it from the other side."

"What? Wait a minute, Mel! That's a bit drastic, don't you think? The letters could spell anything: begin, strike, lock – we ought to start hitting the lock with, erm," Becky petered out. "With something."

"Look, you're not going to die – well, you are, but you won't be really dead, you'll come back as a ghost. That's got to be better than becoming a vampire's buffet."

It seemed so completely logical to me, but I didn't have time to convince the others. I grabbed a bit of the broken glass from the mirror, and plunged it into Becky's chest. She really wasn't getting with the game and tried to fight me off, but I knew that the only way to save the town was to kill Becky. Kevin watched with huge eyes as I pushed harder, cutting my own hand too.

Becky's body went limp and, after a few moments, I detected a faint wispy shape easing out of her. It was her ghost, just like the Ouija board had told me. It looked at its body and seemed to sigh.

I pointed at the door, and Becky drifted out of the dungeon towards the key. I held my breath as she reached for it.

And then her hand passed right through it.

I smacked my forehead, splashing blood in my eye, and wincing from the sudden pain in my injured hand. Something I hadn't realised was that, while she could get out of the dungeon because she's incorporeal, she couldn't pick up the key, let alone turn it in the lock.

Becky re-entered the room and shrugged. Still, she would be able to make some noise and attract the vampire down here, where we could overpower it and escape. Somehow...

I looked at brain-dead Kevin and, in a flash, the rest of the message came into focus: Z-M-K – Zombie Kevin. Of course! Zombies are strong and, because they're not alive, the vampire wouldn't be able to exert his Jedi mind powers on them. And he wouldn't want to drink dried-up, rotten zombie blood.

I sliced the broken glass across Kevin's throat – not too deep, I didn't want his head to fall off – and he gurgled, then became very still.

After what felt like hours, he twitched and slowly sat up. I guessed I'd have to watch out for him attempting to eat my brains, but that'd be a worry for later.

"Right, Becky, you go out again, and make some noise to draw the vampire down here. Kevin can grab him when he comes in."

I threw the chair against the door, breaking it into pieces but barely marking the door. I grabbed one of the legs to use as a weapon. Kevin moaned in the corner, but he was doing his best, bless him.

The plan worked. The door opened, and there he was. Long white fangs, blazing red eyes, black cape – the whole shebang. I held up the mirror handle cross in an attempt to slow him down.

"What's all the crashing? What are you lot up to?" There was something familiar about his voice. Then he shouted "What the –?" He called behind him, "Martha, call an ambulance!"

The vampire morphed and, for a moment, looked like Dad. Was my dad the vampire, or was this some mind trick to fool me into submitting to his will?

I took no chances, and pushed him into Kevin's arms. He was a bit slow to grab the vampire, but somehow they ended up getting entangled. I stabbed the broken chair leg into the vampire's chest. The blood-sucker struggled for a few moments before expiring with a gasp. I expected him to collapse into a pile of dust, but the body just lay there, on top of Kevin.

Strangely, it took on Dad's appearance again. Maybe there was some residual magic that made him retain this shape – despite all my reading, I didn't know much about real monsters.

We'd done it. We'd opened the dungeon and even killed the vampire. Crake's Landing was safe again!

I pulled Kevin out from the vampire's embrace and on to his feet, and dragged him towards the door. It was heavy work, and Becky was no help – ghosts really are useless. Before we could make our escape, something else materialized to block the exit.

"What's all this commotion, Amanda? And what's that about an ambulance?" A pause. "What have you done to your father?" The voice had started quietly, but ended on a choked-off shriek that pierced my mind.

I saw a flash of pink. And damaged walls. And Mom at the door. And Kevin in my arms. And Becky and Dad slumped on the floor. And blood dripping from the furniture and seeping into the carpet. And the Ouija board, with a bubbled pattern in the varnish that looked like the laughing face of a demon. The demon winked at me. The flash faded, and I was back in the dungeon again.

The werewolf that had once been my mother lifted her fur-covered head and howled. Demonic laughter still echoing in my ears, I grabbed the broken mirror, hoping the handle really was silver, and launched my attack.

Bag of Tricks

Jim Mountfield

He hadn't known it was Halloween. These days he lost track of the date for long stretches. Only when it was printed on plane tickets, for errands Toshi has assigned him, did the date loom clearly in his mind. Otherwise, while he numbed himself with alcohol, opium and Prozac, the numbers on the calendar retreated into the murk that, for him, veiled much of the world now.

But tonight, he'd realised it was October 31st, 2023. He was riding on Bangkok's Skytrain when, at one of the elevated stations, there boarded a group of young Thai people dressed for a Halloween party. Several wore Western costumes – a white-sheeted ghost, a pointy-hatted witch, a zombie who, he thought as he observed from a few seats along, probably looked no more decrepit than he did. But a couple were inspired by local folklore, for instance, a girl with a corpse-white face and blood-smeared lips, clad in a traditional red dress and cradling a cloth-swathed bundle that represented a baby.

While the Skytrain resumed its motion and the lights of another portion of Bangkok glided past its windows, the associations struck him like hammer-blows. Halloween. The Thais had started celebrating it, at least in the parts of their country more subject to Western influences. Youngsters were out and about in scary costumes, and back in Scotland – he couldn't help checking the time on his phone – it'd be getting dark soon and kids would be donning costumes too, mobilizing to go trick-or-treating, or 'guising' as many Scots still called it. When *he'd* done that one Halloween night, long ago… 30 years ago…

It'd started then – his life going wrong. That evening when he'd learnt that nobody, no matter how benevolent they appeared, was to be trusted.

He shambled into the room Toshi had rented for him in Sukhumvit. Getting from his Skytrain stop to here had consumed the last of his strength and he barely managed to lock the door behind him before his knees buckled and he slid down it to the floor. The plastic pharmacy bag he was carrying ended up in a heap beside him, handles still entwined around his fingers. As well as Lomotil tablets, the bag contained a bottle of SangSom he'd bought in a 7-11. He fished the bottle out, broke its seal and tried swigging from it. His hand shook so much that more of the sweet Thai rum splattered down his chest than entered his mouth.

He'd collapsed before he could switch on the lights and aircon. The room was dark and suffocatingly warm. Hidden in one of its hot, black corners, already well-wrapped in cling-film, were the pellets of hashish that he had to swallow and carry inside him during his next run for Toshi. The constipation-inducing Lomotils were meant to slow the movements of his bowels, so he wouldn't expel his cargo too soon – not until he was in the privacy and safety of a hotel room at his destination.

But something was wrong. The batch he'd been entrusted with was smaller this time. Why? Was Toshi setting him up? Maybe their routes were being monitored and Toshi intended him to be arrested – a sacrifice offered to the uniforms in the hope they'd ease off and watch those routes less intently in future. Or was there someone with a bigger load taking the same flight? Did Toshi plan to snitch on him to create a diversion?

The smuggling was wrecking him physically and mentally. His guts crawled hideously from what was stashed inside them. His mind boiled with fear and paranoia each time he made his way through an airport... But this would finish him. Toshi, the person he'd regarded as his best, his only friend in the world, betraying him.

Just as at Halloween in Scotland long ago, another person he thought he could trust betrayed him.

Not bothering to pick himself off the floor, he slurped back the rest of SangSom. He felt small and defenceless, as if he'd shrunk in size and spirit and regressed to being the little boy he'd been on that awful Halloween night. Finally, his face wet with sweat, rum and tears of despair, he decided he'd had enough.

He remembered the pharmacy bag beside him. It would suffice.

Louisa declared, "Headcount!"

She managed to gather the diminutive ghosts and ghouls together and count them. All present and correct. Seven. Her lad Dominic in his scarecrow costume, complaining that the stalks of straw sticking from the ends of his sleeves and from under his hat were scratching his skin. Mr. Muir's two girls, Kirsty and Katie, dressed as witches, one in a glittery dark-blue gown and hat, the other in glittery dark-purple ones. And the four Drummond children...

Irritation flared inside her. Barry and Ginny Drummond had been the ones most enthusiastic about this expedition. Why, they'd practically *suggested* it. But tonight, it transpired, neither was available to accompany the kids. The outing had become a childminding session, with her and Mr. Muir as the childminders... Worse, Mr. Muir was such a distant, dreamy type she found herself doing 90 percent of the childminding.

The Drummonds were the last ones counted. "Four... five... six... seven!" The seventh, a boy called Martin, wore a mask with a jutting nose and jaw she'd assumed represented Mr. Punch from the old seaside Punch-and-Judy shows. But now she noticed strange red spirals painted on the mask's cheeks. "Who are you supposed to be?" she asked him.

Behind the mask, a voice snorted, "Billy."

"Who's Billy?"

"The puppet frae the *Saw* movies. Ye *saw* any o' them?" Martin chuckled, pleased with his joke.

"I haven't had the pleasure..."

"Best yin's *Saw V*. Especially the bit where the guy gets injected with acid an' melts frae the inside oot."

Another Drummond boy, wearing a not-very-frightening werewolf head that made him resemble a fluffy, bipedal puppy, turned to his brother and said, "No, eedjit. That wisnae *Saw V*. That wis *Saw VI*."

They moved on. Louisa fell behind while she Googled the *Saw* films on her smartphone. She skimmed through a web-article entitled *All Saw Films, Ranked by Goriness* and her eyes widened... Then something odd happened. The night had a wintry chill but, suddenly, warm air wafted by her. She might have been next to the door of a heated room that'd just opened. Yet there were no doors or rooms near her. She was on the pavement that encircled most of the cul-de-sac, and strips of front lawn separated that pavement from the houses. The thing closest to her was the last of the kids, hurrying to keep up with the posse while Mr. Muir escorted them through the fuzzy yellow glow of the streetlights. Instinctively, she counted again: ...five... six... yes, seven.

Around her, the inexplicable warmth had disappeared. The night was properly cold...

A voice whined, "Mummy, I *hate* this straw."

She spun and found Dominic behind her. He was holding his scarecrow-hat and shaking it up and down, trying to dislodge the straws that were pasted to the inside of its rim. "It's *itchy*."

She took the hat, stripped the straw from it and planted it back on his head. His face was painted white, though two pairs of black crisscrossing lines, meant to resemble stitches, covered his eyes. But without the hat he didn't look very scarecrow-like – more like a Pierrot in scruffy clothes. Taking his arm, she led him after the others. She felt troubled. Half-a-minute ago, she'd counted seven children ahead of her when Dominic *hadn't* been.

The group divided because they'd reached two adjoining houses with Halloween decorations. On Facebook, the neighbourhood committee had advised householders happy to receive trick-or-treaters and guisers on October 31st to put lanterns, fake spider-webs, crepe-paper ghosts and bats outside their front doors as signs of welcome. Undecorated houses were to be left alone. While three kids went along a path to one door, and three – *four?* – approached the other door, Mr. Muir dithered behind, as if unsure which faction to join. Louisa caught up with him, counting again. Three plus *three*. Correct.

"I'll take the left, you take the right?"

"Aye..." Mr. Muir looked from side to side. "I'm sure there were seven weans a moment ago. Now I see six..."

"Here's number seven." She bundled Dominic onto the path of the left-side house. Before following him, she leaned close to Mr. Muir and whispered, "Barry and Ginny Drummond let their children watch *torture* films."

Mr. Muir showed a glimmer of interest. "Really? Which ones?"

"The *Saw* ones."

His expression became nostalgic. "I mind watchin' the video nasties as a lad. *The Driller Killer, Cannibal Holocaust, Zombie Flesh Eaters*... That bit in *Zombie Flesh Eaters* when the lassie gets dragged through a hole in a door and a big wooden skelf goes intae her eye..." He noticed Louisa's unenthusiastic expression. "It wis... very cinematic."

"I'm sure."

They'd decided that, because some houses belonged to older folk who remembered how Halloween had been in Scotland before it got Americanised, the children wouldn't just chant, "Trick or treat!" and expect to receive sweeties. No, they had to be traditional Scottish guisers and perform – delivering a joke, a story, a song – so that they earned the confectionary.

Thus, when the door opened in front of Louisa's four charges, Dominic told a joke: "Why is it easy to know when ghosts tell lies? Because you can see right through them!" The Drummond boy with the werewolf head told a joke too, a risqué one involving a toilet that made Louisa squirm with embarrassment but made the sixty-something couple living in the house roar with laughter. And Kirsty and Katie Muir, who'd managed to end up in the faction not supervised by their father, sang one verse of a song. It was seasonally inappropriate, but the only song-verse they claimed to know – the opening one of *Jingle Bells*.

When they'd finished, there was an expectant silence. Then the sixty-something man inquired, "Does the other yin do something too?"

Louisa looked along the row of children: Dominic, the Drummond boy, the Muir girls… She glimpsed a bobbing round whiteness beyond the cones of the girls' hats. What was it? A balloon? A bag? Someone with a bag on their head – another Drummond child dressed as something from a horror film? But when she looked again, the whiteness was gone. She had four charges, not five.

The man was discombobulated too. "Sorry, ma mistake." He removed his glasses and rubbed them on his sleeve. "It's ma age. Seein' things."

Louisa collected their payment, which was a slab of tablet – a teeth-eroding Scottish delicacy made from condensed milk, butter and sugar – and brought it to Mr. Muir, who added it to the goodies bag. The parents had agreed he'd keep custody of the booty until the evening's end, when it'd be shared among the seven children.

Seven… She was spooked now. While they visited more houses around the cul-de-sac, then emerged onto the street that served as the estate's main artery, she counted, re-counted and re-re-counted. Seven? Definitely seven.

They looked along the street in the direction of the town and saw another group trick-or-treating their way towards them. Louisa suggested they visit some doors in the other direction and they headed towards the top of the street, where the estate ended. The darkness of the nocturnal countryside was discernible past the final houses' lights, which made her glance at Dominic protectively. The fact the countryside was on their doorstep had been a major reason for buying a house here. But its proximity also bothered her slightly. In the wilds beyond the estate, there were trees children could fall out of, ponds they could fall into, cows they could be trampled under, farm machinery they could be mangled by…

While she mused about this, she became aware of a pale thing at the edge of her vision, like a giant white bubble floating alongside her at the height of a child's head. Sharply, she swivelled sideways. The yellow radiance from the streetlights fell on an empty area of street. She swivelled again, to face the way they'd come, but found nothing there, either. Finally, she swivelled towards Mr. Muir and the kids and counted. Still seven.

She joined Mr. Muir and asked, "You don't suppose we've picked up an extra child from somewhere?"

He sounded bemused. "Cannae see how. Unless Barry an' Ginny have popped oot another yin but didnae tell us."

The end of the street gave way to a narrow, unlit country road that, prior to the estate's construction, had extended all the way to the town with fields, trees, drystone dykes and sheep on either side. A lantern – a shrunken, wizened turnip lantern rather than a plump, orange pumpkin one – burned on a windowsill of the last house before the road. They rang the doorbell, a middle-aged woman emerged and the guising began. First, the Drummond boy repeated his unsavoury joke about a toilet…

Then several things happened, almost at the same time. A big golden retriever bounded out of the doorway, past the woman's legs and towards the children. Though they'd been lined up to perform one by one, the children immediately abandoned the line and crowded chaotically around the dog, making delighted "Oooh!" and "Aaah!" noises. For a moment the dog seemed to enjoy their attention. But then something upset him and he barked furiously. The children squawked and retreated, making the scene yet more chaotic. And…

A white-headed figure tore past Louisa. It left the street, entered the country road and vanished into the darkness.

Without thinking, she chased the figure. She'd run only a few yards when, it seemed, the lights of the estate faded behind her and the night enveloped her. She tugged out her smartphone and turned on its torch, so she could follow the road without crashing into the tree-trunks, bushes and drystone dykes that flanked it. She saw no sign of the fleeing child. Who was it? She'd glimpsed a white head... Alarmed, she recalled Dominic's white-painted face. Was it him, running without his scarecrow's hat? But surely he wouldn't have reacted so badly to a barking dog...?

The road both dipped and curved and a few panels of light, muffled by curtains, leavened the darkness ahead. She found herself among some houses whose doors almost opened onto the roadsides. Their window-lights, plus an outside light burning above the furthest house's door, let her see they were stone cottages – built originally for farmworkers, perhaps, though now they'd be desirable country properties worth as much as the houses on the estate. There were four of them, not enough to even make this place qualify as a hamlet.

On the last cottage's doorstep, in the hazy light descending from the external bulb, she observed a small figure with a white, round head.

Her phone chimed. She looked down in time to see a WhatsApp message arrive in the recently-created 'Halloween 2023' group-chat. Mr. Muir asked: *Where are you?* When she looked up again, the figure was gone from the doorstep.

Louisa approached the final cottage whilst typing a reply: *Kid ran away. Trying to find him/her.* She got to the cottage's door, sent the reply, then peered into the darkness beyond the door-light. She saw nothing, even when she probed with the torch-beam. Then, turning towards the door, she pressed a button on its stone jamb and heard a bell jingle distantly.

Another WhatsApp message: *But all are here.* As she read that, a photo materialized in the group-chat. It showed seven children, including Dominic, crouching around the happy-again golden retriever and making thumbs-up signs...

"Yes?"

The photo had so distracted her, and the door had opened so silently, that briefly she was frightened. But then she saw the voice belonged to an old man. Well, oldish – 60 or 65. He was thin and slightly stooped, making him the same height she was. His receding grey hair revealed a broad crescent of wrinkled forehead and he wore a knitted, burgundy-coloured cardigan. He looked as unthreatening as was humanly possible. Feeling foolish, Laura explained.

"I'm looking for a child."

"A child?" Oddly, the man had flinched.

"We were trick-or-treating, guising as they say around here, and... Well, we stupidly lost one of our kids." She remembered Mr. Muir's photo – they hadn't actually lost anyone. But she pressed on. "I saw him on this doorstep a minute ago." Him? Yes, Louisa was sure now the child was male. "I wondered if he'd gone inside. If you'd taken him in."

The man's eyes expanded and his forehead creased even more. His mouth opened and closed a few times as if he was attempting to speak but his throat had suddenly become too dry to allow it. He finally managed four words. "Took in a child?"

"Yes, a lost one."

The man's face became wildly contorted. When his mouth opened again, it released a stuttering croak.

"I'm sorry, I didn't mean to suggest you were a..."

She realised the man wasn't apoplectic with rage but stricken with fear. She also realised he wasn't looking at her but at something to her side and below the level of her face. Then his hands clutched at his chest, his croak gave way to an agonised wheeze and he fell against the doorpost.

Louisa wasn't wholly surprised to find the small figure on her right, standing a few inches back from her. As she turned and her gaze alighted on it, its head tilted upwards and showed its face. A bag enclosed it. A blue cross covered its left eye, a squiggling black line descended its nose, a row of small, cramped, green teeth ran across its mouth. Otherwise, the bag was white – and plastic. What made it hideous was the bag's tightness around the head. The eyes bulged against it. A lower part of it, with the green teeth, sank into a gaping mouth and was contoured by the ridges of the real lips and teeth underneath.

Her fright this time was many times greater. She shrieked, sprang back and lost hold of her phone, which clattered onto the doorstep. Then she crashed against the afflicted man and both of them stumbled through the doorway into the cottage. The man managed to grab her with a hand and stopped himself falling. The apparition remained at the threshold. She lunged forward, slammed the door on it and snibbed the lock.

She couldn't spend any more time being scared – the man needed attention. He was unable to stand by himself and one hand was still at his chest, claw-like, twisted amid the wool of his cardigan. She dreaded to think what'd happened to the heart underneath. They were in a hall with, along its side, an open doorway that had light filtering out of it. So she dragged the helpless, voiceless man towards the doorway.

"You have to sit down. Then I'll call an ambulance."

The room's only sources of light were a study-lamp and a laptop screen on a desk by its far wall. She lowered him onto an armchair and left him there, gasping in pain and incoherence.

Because she couldn't countenance going outside to retrieve her dropped phone, she ran to the desk and hunted for the man's phone. Surely he had one – but she couldn't find it. She noticed the laptop. The screen's background picture was of the Glenfinnan Viaduct in the Scottish Highlands, famously traversed by the Hogwarts Express in the *Harry Potter* films. Two chains of yellow folders and different-coloured icons hung down the picture's left side. Could she call the emergency services from this? Were they contactable on some app or platform? WhatsApp, Facebook, Twitter…?

Not knowing what to do, increasingly panicked, she sent the cursor skittering down the folders and icons, then along some additional ones in the bottom taskbar. There, it crossed a minimised jpeg image, which fleetingly popped open in a little window. Something about it caught her eye. She shifted the cursor back onto the jpeg and made it fill the screen.

She recoiled, almost gagging.

Earlier, when she'd thought about the dangers of the countryside, some horrible images had flashed through her head – Dominic's body sprawled brokenly under a tree, afloat face-down in a pond, trampled by livestock, chewed up by agricultural machinery. The picture on the screen was bloodless, but what was happening to the child in it was much, *much* worse than anything she'd imagined.

She returned to the armchair. Pain still racked the man but he'd regained some control. He knew what she'd discovered and he could speak again. "Please understand," he rasped, "I get urges... Seein' those images satisfies the urges... Stops me doin' what I did before..."

Her voice was ice-cold. "Before?"

"Yin Halloween night, a wee boy guisin'... got separated from his friends... appeared at ma door... lost, askin' for help... I took him in... That night wis the only time I did it... Afterwards, I moved here, away frae the toon, away frae temptation... An' the images kept the urges in check..."

The pain worsened again and he convulsed. But he continued, sobbing, "The laddie wis very young... He never said anything tae anyone... I thought he'd blocked oot the memory... But tonight he came back... As a child again, after all them years... after *30* years..."

His pain reached a peak. He lurched up and wailed, "How's that *possible?*"

Then, spent, he slumped against the armchair. The only words he managed after that were a wretched plea: "*Help me.*" Otherwise, she just heard his breath, slobbering in and out of him.

But he attempted one last, desperate movement, which was to grope across a low table beside the armchair, his quaking hand trying to get to a smartphone – *that* was where it'd been. Briskly, Louisa went and shunted the phone beyond his reach.

She waited for the tortured breathing to cease. She'd leave then, picking up her phone on her way. The dead man and his laptop could be someone else's find.

Meanwhile, a small figure – head shrouded in white plastic, face frozen in a scream – stood in the room's doorway. It nodded at her approvingly.

On November 2nd, the day the Westerner was supposed to vacate his room but didn't, the landlord forced open the door. He had to force it because the Westerner was lying against its other side. An empty SangSom bottle and some packets of medicine were scattered on the floor around him.

Staring down at the huddled body, the landlord marvelled at how small, even child-like it looked now. But he was far more shocked by the white plastic bag from the pharmacy and how its humdrum details

– the blue medical cross in a corner, the symbol of a snake entwined around a staff in the middle, the green Thai lettering spelling out the shop's name at the bottom – were grotesquely superimposed over the asphyxiated man's features: a goggling eye, the nose, the screaming mouth.

Indeed, he was so shocked that something snapped inside him and he fled from the room. His wife was mopping the floor halfway along the corridor. As he ran towards her, and before she spotted the genuine panic in his face, she couldn't help commenting.

"What's the matter with you? Seen a ghost?"

The Last Night of October

Nicola Lombardi

Translated by J. Weintraub

It was horrible, and at the same time sublime, to admire the infernal paradise staged by autumn outside of the dingy, dirtied glass. Martino, seated immobile in front of the window, was staring from within the endless silence lingering in his room. And he was thinking. After all, there was nothing left for him to do, and thinking offered him a mixture of anguish and exhilaration.

The dry leaves, whipped up by the wind, soared like drunken grey bats colliding against each other as they followed the sudden, breezy swirling of the air. The sky, toward the west, was the wonderful color of cinders, cinders beneath which a bed of bloody and trembling embers were dying. With a gradual shifting of his eyes toward the east, the inevitable, creeping advance of the night, already about to swallow the world, could instead be viewed. The lights going on in the houses were tiny rectangles, steeped in a poignant serenity, brilliant hearths of redemption, peace, warmth ...

Martino had only the candle with its sickly flame, wavering and sputtering, shaken by fiery convulsions. For the rest, the house had fallen into shadow, as always. The shadow that saturated the walls, that breathed, that gripped the heart. The shadow of his mother, lost in some other room. The shadow of his wheelchair from which Martino would never again arise.

Outside, in the meantime, the first ghosts began to streak past in the distance, as if emerging from a daydream. And there were also skeletons, witches, the cadaverous walking dead with their outstretched arms and uncertain steps. They appeared and disappeared in small groups, through alleyways and yards, and from time to time they stopped to ring at a door, looking forward to getting a treat.

Martino would have given anything, at least in the past, to be with them, to be one of them. To collect caramels or chocolates or candied fruits, and then return home to taste the euphoria following those abundant Halloween raids. But he had never put on a disguise nor worn the makeup of a monster. Nor, after all, had he ever been invited or sought out... His mother would not have allowed it, anyway.

His mother ...

She came into the room just at the very instant he was thinking about her. Martino remained motionless as he listened to the creaking of the door behind him, opening so slowly and then closing with that slack clicking he would have recognized anywhere. The light steps, shuffling a little, crossed through the stale, dusty half-light to approach him by the window.

The woman did not say a word. Only a hand on her son's shoulder, and she stood, stunned, as she viewed the agony of the day glowing beyond her own face reflected in the glass. What terrible eyes she had ...

Martino had always thought that they were the unkindest eyes in the world. But with the passing of the years, he came to understand that they were only pained eyes, distant. Hers was the look of a stranger, the wrong person. She was as sick in her head as he was in his body. And their life together had always been a sleepy siphoning of anxiety, solitude, and, especially, silence. His mother ... She had never accepted help from anyone. It would have been an insult. The two of them were enough for each other. In a head muffled by despair, there had never been room for anything else but herself and a poor son unable to keep close always, always protected, always a prisoner. All out of love, naturally. Poor mama ...

A volley of shrill, childish giggling arose from somewhere, sailing in with the warm wind. The flame of the candle twisted, bending beneath the burden of the thoughts now permeating Martino's room. It was the last night of October. And also the first of a new life, for him. All in all, it had been easier than expected. He was afraid his mother would not have gone along with him. Instead, among tears, sighs, and prayers muttered to invoke the forgiveness of whatever god lay hidden among the creases of her troubled mind, she had done everything he had asked of her.

"You'll see, mama," he had told her. "You will give me the greatest satisfaction in the world. And all those out there, all those who hate us, they won't be laughing at us anymore."

And so the day had, little by little, like a page covered with red scribbling near a fire, crumpled into itself. Slowly, hour after hour, the shadows had crept, trembling, into the interior of the house to observe the work of the mother and her son, both hopelessly lost among the webs of a mournful silence.

"Thank you, mama," thought Martino. This was a strange kind of vengeance, in the face of all the friends he had never had, against a life that never had made much sense, if it ever had any at all. Maybe the shadows reveling disdainfully in his mother's brain had also infected him over time. It would not have been very surprising. And, besides, it didn't matter to him at all. He felt it had been the right choice.

The little monsters arrived cackling in small, scant groups. But just as they came up to Martino's house, they instinctively lowered their voices, peering at the front door with their eyes circled in black or sunken behind heavy, papier-mâché masks. Martino knew that they would have wanted to ring the doorbell, but they were struggling with their fear. Fear of his mother. They had always called her, without giving it a thought, "that crazy woman." Yet he had stopped being troubled by that. He probably would have acted in the same way if he had been one of them.

But he had never been one of them, nor would he ever become one. Nor was there any way to turn back. Now he was there, and for always, on the side of the night. He watched those little kids with a contempt allayed by just a hint of compassion.

His mother withdrew into the shadow, dead quiet, a moment before the little monsters raised their eyes toward that window. Martino sensed her bringing her hands to her face, striving to stifle her sobbing.

"Don't worry, mama," he would have liked to tell her. "I'm fine now. I've never been happier than this." But, by then, he could no longer say a word.

His mother's feet, falling back, bumped against the thick, heavy ladle lying on the floor, almost covered with the red and greyish pulp spilling over and spackling the dust. A sticky, metallic noise rebounded from one wall to the next, like the clanging of a rusted cowbell. The hacksaw, too, lost in the darkness, was probably not far away.

"Don't worry, mama. I wanted you to do it. And I'm grateful that you did."

And when the little kids saw him, finally, they began to scream.

The flame, inside Martino's emptied head, suddenly swayed lightly back and forth, as if the children's cries from the street had touched it. Through the hollow eye sockets, the light still wavered just a little, emitting a pair of faint, restless beams cast out to probe the night. Martino felt himself shaking with the thrill of exaltation.

His mother was now laughing and crying. Soon, people would certainly be coming, and they would be taking them both away. It didn't matter. Regardless, Martino would still be in that house, for always, inescapably. He had forced his entry, by then, into the minds of those little kids running away as the most terrible of dreams, nightmares that could not be forgotten. His image, seated by that window, his skull opened up and the lit candle plunged inside his head hollowed out like a pumpkin, with its insane glow glimmering there where his eyes should have been, would never ever be erased from their souls.

His mother had been perfect. In her entire life, she never would he have had the chance to carry out a more glorious, memorable, and merciful act. Whatever happened to her then would not have meant anything.

A few dead leaves, like severed and withered hands, slapped against the glass, almost as if intending to drive away the madness settled in that room, maliciously poised at the window. And Marino knew he already belonged to the night, to that night, an eternally damned specter, living forever, brilliant and terrible.

Three, four, five doors swung open along the street, and people with alarmed and confused faces responded to the children's cries. Everyone looked toward "the house of the crazies," as it was known, and they began to approach, running, ready to invite the horror in, to poison their dreams for the rest of their lives.

The Ghost of Cornelius Bush

Mark Ellott

"Did you hear that?"

Joshua Hill stirred, looked at the clock showing 03:00 and turned to Sadie. "Hear what?"

"That."

"Nope." He groaned. *Here we go again.* It had been the same every night since they moved in. "There aren't any ghosts, Sadie. Just go back to sleep and forget about it."

"So, I'm imagining it?"

"I didn't say that."

"No, but you implied it. I'm not going mad. I heard it. *There, there it is again.* How can you not hear it?"

Josh sighed. "I can't hear anything."

Sadie poked him with her elbow, and he turned in the bed to face her, blinking the sleep from his eyes. "'kin' Hell, Sadie, I need to get a decent night's sleep."

"There," she said. "That low moaning."

Josh shook his head. "I can't hear anything. It must be your imagination."

"It is *not* my imagination, Josh!"

The house was old. Parts of it were medieval, apparently. Although a listed building, requiring eye-wateringly expensive repairs and renovations, all using period methods and materials, the purchase price made it perfect for Sadie and Josh. Located on the outskirts of Malton, it once stood alone in the open countryside. It had appeared perfect. They paid the deposit, arranged the finance and set about planning the renovations. Finding craftsmen who were able to carry out the work to the standards set by the authorities for a listed building proved costly and took time, but, again, things moved along smoothly with Josh supervising the project and it was always going to be a long-term project, so time wasn't an issue for the couple.

It was when they moved in that the problems started.

The nightly moaning. At least that's what Sadie described it as. "A low moan," she said. "It starts low and then goes on and on. As if someone is in pain."

Josh could hear nothing and at first dismissed it as the wind blowing through a gap somewhere and promised to look around and find the cause. Despite spending a few days trying to locate the source, every night it would commence.

"It's human," she said. "I'm sure of it."

Josh on the other hand was sceptical and made no bones about it. Talk of ghosts and ghouls irritated him. Such things didn't exist.

Sadie woke with a start. She lay down with her face in the mud. Disoriented, she looked about her. She was wet and cold. She heard shouting.

"Cornelius, get up!"

Cornelius?

She lifted her head and looked at a young man staring back at her. Dressed in a doublet and hose, his brown hair was cropped short and he sported a neatly trimmed moustache and goatee beard. A white ruff adorned his neck and he held out a hand covered in a fine leather glove.

He looks Elizabethan.

"Cornelius," he said. "Come on, the soldiers aren't far away now. They will hang us if we are caught."

She lifted herself to her knees and looked down. Like the young man, she was wearing hose with breeches and a leather doublet. Men's clothing, not a woman's. She was a man. She frowned as she struggled to make sense of it all. She wiped her face to get the mud off and felt the roughness of a beard. She looked at the young man. "Who are you?"

"Cornelius, you've taken a bump to the head, it's me, Thomas. Now, come on, we must make haste, or we will hang. We have no time to waste with questions."

Clambering to her feet, she followed Thomas as he seemed to know where he was going.

"What happened?"

Thomas turned to look at her without breaking his stride. "You must have hit your head hard, Cornelius," he said. "We have failed. The queen has sent her men north to put down the rebellion. Now we are all hunted men. Condemned to the scaffold if we do not get out of the country. Neville and Percy have fled to Scotland, leaving the rest of us to get away as we can. Sussex is marching north with his militia now."

Sadie shook her head. Vague memories of distant history classes swirled in her mind. "The northern earls plot? Northumberland and Westmoreland have tried to oust the queen?"

Durham. Yes, Durham cathedral. That was it, they raided the cathedral and held a catholic mass. The fools.

"Yes, now come on. I have a plan. Your sister's house has a priest hole. We can hide there until Sussex's troops have grown tired of looking. Then we will have to seek our fortunes abroad. We will take a ship from Whitby and make for France."

Sadie jerked awake. She blinked at the light flooding though the curtain. Josh was still asleep. She reached across to the bedside clock. 06:03. She sighed.

"What?" Josh said, opening his eyes.

"Oh, I was dreaming."

Josh grunted and turned over. Sadie threw back the duvet, pulled on a robe and went downstairs to the kitchen table and switched on her tablet. By the time Josh came down, she had been browsing for over an hour.

"What are you doing?"

"Research."

"Uh, huh." He opened the fridge and took out the milk as he prepared his morning coffee. "And what are you researching?"

"A pair of Elizabethan conspirators. More precisely, their involvement in the northern plot."

Josh poured his coffee and raised his eyebrows. "Uh, huh."

"That was what I was dreaming about," she said. "In 1569, there was a Catholic uprising against Elizabeth I."

"So?" He sat and sipped his coffee.

"So, I was inside one of them. We were running away."

"It was a dream," he said. "Just that. Dreams are weird."

She shook her head. "It was so real. And," she turned the tablet so that he could see the screen. "This was the guy. Cornelius Bush. The other one, Thomas, referred to him as Cornelius. He was running somewhere. The plot had failed."

"Maybe you read it somewhere before. The mind plays tricks."

She scowled and turned the tablet back. *I am wasting my time.*

Josh went about his day once breakfast was over, the bathroom needed work ready for the new suite that was booked to arrive in a couple of days. She was aware of him moving about as he disconnected the bath, accompanied by groans and grunts.

Sadie looked at the screen and as she looked, she felt as if she was being drawn into another world.

The room was cast in shadows. The faces of the men sitting around the table sipping mead and talking in low voices were lit only by the candles sputtering in their holders. Across the room, Sadie could see Thomas, his eyes animated in the candlelight, with a brightness of their own as he talked about the plan. The excitement of the zealot.

"We will ride with Northumberland into Durham on November the 14th," he was saying. "There we will celebrate mass in the cathedral. It is time to restore our ancient customs and liberties and the old faith."

There were murmurs of assent around the room. She realised that she was nodding along.

"Isn't that so, Cornelius?" French was looking directly at her.

"Yes, Thomas," she said.

She looked around the room. It was different but the same. The modern accoutrements of the kitchen were gone and the window looked smaller. Outside, the night was clear and she could see the pricks of light as the stars poked though the ink of the firmament. She had moved in time, not place. It was this house. The centre of a plot against the queen and she was a part of it. Her heart stirred as she looked about the room at her co-conspirators.

Later after the others had left, she was alone with Thomas French and Cornelius' sister Iona. Iona's husband, Titus was outside, seeing to the horses. He came back in a few minutes later.

"Well, we are all set, Thomas?"

"The 14th, then?" Thomas smiled. They raised their glasses and toasted the plan.

Sadie jerked awake again. Josh had come back downstairs. "I could do with some help up there," he said.

"Sorry, I dozed off."

"Well if you spend half the night down here looking up old stories, what do you expect?"

They spent the rest of the day clearing out junk. Sadie's mind was too occupied with the job in hand to think about her strange dreams or what happened to Cornelius Bush. Until that night.

She was hungry. She hadn't eaten for days. The small cot was squeezed into a space below the rafters, so she was high up in the house. When was it she had come in here? She couldn't recall, but she did have visions of it being night. They had fled from the militia and eventually arrived at the house. Thomas had insisted that she come in here, but he hadn't come in himself, which she thought odd at the time. She recalled the clunking of the latch as she was enclosed in the narrow space. She had climbed the narrow staircase, barely wide enough for one person to fit through. She smiled as she thought to herself that the old king would never have managed it. But then, no one came. She went downstairs to the entrance, but it wouldn't open. And still no one came.

They will come soon, she thought. *They must. Unless they have been captured. What then?*

She wasn't sure how much time passed, but the bread and cheese that had been left out didn't last long.

She heard voices. She went to the window. It was the garden she recognized, but this room was new to her. Outside on the grass she could see a body and several soldiers standing round, their faces concealed from this height by their helmets. The captain dismounted.

"Well, have you searched the house?"

"Yes, sir," one of the soldiers said.

"And?"

"No one here. Apart from this one." He kicked the body so that it was now on its back. Sadie gasped. *Titas! Where were the others?*

"Have you checked for priest holes?" the captain was saying.

"Yes, sir, but there is nothing. At least, nothing that we could find. The birds have flown if you ask me."

"I didn't," the captain said, wheeling his horse around. "Come on, no point waiting here. They will have been making for Whitby, like as not."

"We are likely too late," the soldier grumbled as they fell into line behind the captain.

She watched as they marched out, leaving the body of Titas Bird to rot.

"What the hell are you doing?" Josh leaned out of the window and called down to Sadie who was standing on the front lawn looking back up at the building, clad only in her nightdress and dressing gown. The dew made her feet cold, but she didn't notice. "It's not even six, for crying out loud. What is up with you?"

"Come on down and look," she said, waving frantically at him. "Come on!"

Josh swore and closed the window. He came out of the door a few minutes later and walked across the lawn, still buttoning his shirt.

"What?" he said. "This had better be good."

"Look up there."

"Where?" his gaze followed her pointed finger.

"How many windows do you see?"

Josh frowned. "That's odd."

She smiled. "Isn't it? We never really looked before."

"So... There's another room?"

"A priest hole. These old buildings are known for them."

They went back inside, and Josh started to go upstairs.

"No," she said. "The basement."

76

Josh shrugged and followed her down into the basement. "There's nothing here. The entrance must be upstairs."

"Sadie shook her head. "No, it's here." She put her hand against the wall. "Behind this wall. There's another wall."

"How do you know all this?"

"I dreamed it."

He rolled his eyes. "Oh, you dreamed it. What are we supposed to do? Knock down what is a load bearing wall because you had a dream?"

"This isn't a load bearing wall. That's behind this one."

Josh went outside and came back with a sledgehammer. He looked at her as if expecting they would regret it, before swinging the sledgehammer and breaking out the bricks. They came away easily, partly because the mortar was old and crumbling, but partly because the wall wasn't tied and had been built hastily. As it fell away in a cloud of dust, it revealed a panelled wall behind.

"Well," said Josh, "I wasn't expecting that."

"The load bearing wall is behind it," Sadie said. "This is why the soldiers didn't find anything."

"What soldiers or shouldn't I ask?"

"The soldiers looking for the conspirators following the failed rebellion I told you about."

She walked up to the wall and ran her hand along to the edge of one of the panels feeling her way until she found what she was looking for. Sliding her fingers into the small opening, she felt the latch. She tugged at it and there was a clunk as one of the panels moved outwards, revealing an opening behind. Fusty old air came out with a cloud of dust causing them to cough and gag as she pulled it back.

The gap was just wide enough for one person to stand. The steps leading up were so narrow that their shoulders rubbed the walls either side. They followed the light coming down from the space above. Once at the top of the stairs, they found a tiny room about six or seven feet wide below the rafters. Tucked into the furthest side was a cot just big enough for a man to lie down. On the cot were the skeletal remains of Cornelius Bush.

Josh gasped, but Sadie remained silent. She had found what she had been looking for.

"I need to go back down and call someone," Josh said.

Sadie stayed as she heard him scurry back down the steps. "Hello, Cornelius Bush," she said.

Cornelius Bush watched. *Finally.*

In the shadows a figure appeared. At first, he was barely a subtle change in the darkness in the corner of Cornelius' vision.

"I know who you are," he said without turning.

"I have been waiting," Death said.

"I know, but I couldn't go. Not until now."

"I understand. But now that you have been found, they will bury you properly and you can move on. These poor people are tired of you moaning through the night. It gets on their nerves, you know."

Cornelius sighed. "But why?"

Death leaned on his scythe. It glinted in the weak light from the window. He had been polishing it and the blade was nice and sharp. His raven ruffled its wings with impatience on his shoulder, urging him to get on with it. "You would like to know?"

The raven squawked and Death lifted a bony finger to its head, smoothing its feathers to calm it down.

Cornelius turned to face him. "Of course. I've been here for these past centuries, rotting into dust. I'd like to know why. If we had been caught and executed, I could understand, but this... This makes no sense."

Death sighed. "Humanity is not always driven by noble motives. Sometimes it is as base as they come. Yes, I will show you. Come with me. You might not like what you see, though."

Thomas French finished putting the last brick into place. His shirt was damp with sweat, and he wiped his brow as Iona came into the basement. In her hand, she held a knife dripping with blood.

"It's done?" he asked.

"It's done," she said. She looked at Thomas. "It's different now. I am a murderess. I have slain my husband. We will be hunted for this for the rest of our lives, and we will burn for eternity. I hope it was all worth it."

Cornelius turned to Death. "I saw Titus on the grass. I assumed the soldiers had killed him. But Iona?"

Death shrugged. "I told you that motives are often base. Usually, it comes down to sex. It was in this case.

Cornelius exhaled. "Then it was my fault."

Death shook his head. "Your father forbade the match. You were merely carrying out his wishes. You weren't to know that they would kill for it."

"They got away with it. They killed Titus and walled me up, so they could elope? May they rot in Hell forever."

Death smiled. Not that anyone would have noticed. It was more a rictus grin, but it sufficed as a smile. "Oh, I'm not sure that they got away with it."

The sea grew as dark as the thunderous cumulonimbus above. The small ship bucked with each wave, its timbers creaking under the crash of each wave, the water rushing over the decks as it plunged into the next trough. The decks groaned with the strain and a sharp crack accompanied the foremast as it sheared, falling with rigging onto the deck as the next wall of water struck with such force, the ship seemed suspended in time.

Thomas French wasn't fast enough, the ropes tangled around his feet, and he was swept overboard, dragged away by the debris of the foremast and spars, never to be seen again. Iona drowned a few moments later as another wave swept across the stricken ship, breaking its back and spewing the remaining crew, passengers and cargo into the icy, watery clutches of the North Sea.

Death watched. *Justice*, he thought, *tends to find its own way*.

In the small churchyard, a new grave lay under the shade of the ancient cedar tree. Sadie stood and looked at it. The new stone they had commissioned was fitting, she thought. Now that the news media attention had subsided, she took a few moments to pay her respects and to lay flowers. After five hundred years there was no one else who would care. After five hundred years, Cornelius deserved some peace.

"Goodbye, Cornelius," she said.

"Well, at least we are getting a good night's sleep at last," Josh said, placing an arm around her and turning her away.

"Yes," she said before turning to look back at the grave. *And so will you.*

A Tall, Dark Stranger

Bill Diamond

When Britt left work, it was ominous, and threatening rain. Great for a somber Halloween ambiance. Bad for her already depressed mood.

Pulling on her rain parka and gloves, she walked toward the coffee shop. Once again, she asked herself, "How did I get here?"

Here was Harlan. A small farm town in western Iowa and culturally as far from her East Coast roots as she could imagine. Downtown was nearly deserted. The Halloween decorations did little to lift her spirits.

She was on a temporary assignment for the federal government. Britt did field audits for infrastructure projects to discourage and detect fraud. It didn't make her popular with the locals. As her first job, she didn't expect a glamour assignment, but didn't expect Harlan either. She felt isolated and lonely.

There was little to do. For her, Harlan was corn, flat and monotonous. The big activities were football, hunting and drinking. None appealed to her. Most weekends, she drove to Omaha or Des Moines. Her two month stint was ending. She was eager to leave.

At the Daily Grind, Britt ordered tea with honey. Chloe served her and said, "You look down. You should visit the Harvest Carnival at the Fairgrounds. It might cheer you up. And, the Haunted Halloween Cornfield is always great."

At home, the idea might intrigue her. But, she'd usually do something like that with friends. No friends here. "It's a little cold. I'll probably just get a bite to eat and go back to the motel."

When she left, Britt couldn't face another meal at the same restaurants. In the evening gloom, she saw the bright Ferris wheel lights a few blocks away and decided a change might shake off her funk.

A fine drizzle started. The traveling carnival had the typical game booths and rides. Despite the twinkling lights and upbeat music, it had a scruffy feel. The weather kept the midweek crowd down to a handful of stragglers. She bought slices of pizza and wandered the grounds.

Britt was about to leave when she spotted a faded sign in front of a worn tent. Ornate lettering proclaimed "Madame Gorgo - Psychic Palm Readings. $10". Normally she'd pass by. But, this might give her something to tell her folks on their next talk. Britt called out, "Hello".

A deep voice answered, "Enter".

The candlelit interior was murky. She'd expected an exotic-looking gypsy. Rather, a grandmotherly woman in a normal, long dress sat at a round table. A shawl covered her head, but more for warmth than as part of a costume. "Please sit, child."

After paying, Britt offered her hand. In flickering light, Madame Gorgo peered closely and kneaded the palm with a strong thumb. Looking into Britt's eyes, the mystic said, "You're a skeptic."

Britt blushed at the blunt statement.

"No matter. Take what I see as you will." Madame poked at the hand and started a sing-song chant. "You love family. You're ambitious in your career and get stressed at setbacks."

Britt considered these as easy and generic findings. The next pronouncements were similar. "You're unattached."

Obviously, no ring.

"You will have struggles in your life." Who doesn't? The reading proceeded in that vein for several minutes.

Things changed when the mystic said, "There is a violent trauma in your past."

Britt stiffened. The memory of the sexual assault flared.

Gorgo stroked her forearm soothingly, "But, you are strong."

The psychic leaned in again. Her face wrinkled and took on a troubled expression. "I see signs you'll soon meet a tall, dark stranger."

Britt giggled nervously at the abrupt switch to the cliché for pending romance. She dismissed any credence she'd given to this amusement. There were few 'eligible' men in Harlan. And, she wasn't interested at the moment. Her skepticism about the reading was validated. Thanking Gorgo, Britt rose to leave.

The seer gripped her wrist and said urgently, "Be alert and careful."

Britt nodded.

Restless, she took Chloe's advice and sought the Haunted Cornfield for scary relief. It was beyond the Fairgrounds at the stark break between town and sprawling fields. The attraction was run by the high school as a fundraiser. An inattentive teenager manned the ticket booth.

"Are you open?"

Barely looking up from his phone, he mumbled, "Yah. Almost no one's here tonight. You'll have the place to yourself."

She paid.

The drizzle was now accompanied by a swirling mist that complemented the spooky music. Set away from the carnival, the field was Stygian after the lights of the midway.

Tall corn formed a dark maze. Inside, Britt followed a narrow path from set to set. Amid rusted farm tractors and assorted farm implements, costumed students played famous Halloween villains. Freddy with his razor glove. Jason wielded a machete. Leatherface revved a chainsaw. The jump scares were effective. Britt yelped when they pounced from the dark. She scurried away as they chased her. The actors faded back to startle the next 'victims'.

In addition to the live performers, motion-activated skeletons and shimmery ghosts populated the stalks. She skittered through a pitch black crypt to deathly groans. At a funeral parlor setting, there was mournful music as a corpse sprung from a casket.

In the unseen distance, she heard shrieks followed by the girlish giggles of startled youths. The Haunted Cornfield was more elaborate than expected. The diversion relaxed her.

Ahead, Britt spied a figure in a black, Grim Reaper cowl carrying a tool. 'Time to meet Death', she thought. When they reached each other, the tall figure grabbed her arm.

Surprised, Britt barked at his masked face, "Heh! You're not supposed to touch."

He struck her temple with a strong blow and she collapsed to the mud. Dazed, Britt was dragged away from the maze by her hair and collar into real danger. Alone and vulnerable. Terror jabbed her.

She'd been traumatized by her earlier assault. Had become frightened and timid. As part of the recovery, she'd learned self-defense. Now, she tried to call on her training to combat fear. They broke from the corn stalks into a harvested field. Sliding through the mud on her back, Britt scanned the darkness. No houses or people. The loud soundtrack and rain would mask yells. She pretended to be unconscious and fumbled for the bag looped around her shoulder.

Her attacker dropped her and his tall bulk loomed. Waving long garden scissors, he hissed, "Scream or fight and I'll cut you."

It wouldn't happen again! Anger and adrenalin kicked in. As he bent down, Britt sprayed the mace she always carried. With an animal howl, he fell to the mud, dropped the scissors and clutched his burning eyes.

Britt shouted, "City girls are prepared, asshole!"

His mask partially protected him. Enraged, he rose and charged blindly. The rain was now teeming. She kicked at his knee and he went down again.

Britt scrambled away slipping on the furrows. She moved back toward the maze.

He recovered the scissors and waved the blades wildly. Limping after her surprisingly fast, he yelled," You're dead!"

In semi-shock and gasping, she reached the stalks. Lurching forward, she reached a scene with a ghostly scarecrow. Britt heard her attacker closing behind her. Unsure which way to safety, she crouched and hid near the stuffed figure. In her panicked head, her breathing sounded thunderous.

Seconds later, the Reaper reached the clearing. He sputtered in rage and spun seeking his quarry.

Britt tried to shrink and draw further into the dark of the corn.

"There you are!" he spat triumphantly. Her clothes were mud spattered, but he'd seen the splotches of light grey of her rain jacket.

Britt tried to rise, but was hindered by the leafy stalks.

The attacker charged. His cape snagged on a stiff cornstalk and he lost balance on the slick ground. To stop his fall, he lunged to hug the scarecrow.

His weight carried him down on top of it. He gave a guttural screech of agony.

Britt sidled back preparing to run again.

Her assailant squirmed, but didn't get up.

Peering close, she saw the prongs of the scarecrow's pitchfork had pierced his abdomen. He wasn't dead, but was on the way. The Reaper lifted a hand and reached out with an expression of pain and pleading.

Britt thought about going for help. She rejected it. She was an innocent victim But, this was probably his hometown. His friends.

She wouldn't go through the outsider scrutiny and victim-shaming again.

"Screw it." She rose and stepped away. The rain would erase any evidence of her presence. The circumstances and mystery surrounding his death would possibly start a local horror legend.

In an agitated fog, Britt took the long way to her car through empty fields and backstreets. Halfway there, some rationality returned. She paused for a breath. Looking skyward, Britt let the rain wash away the muck and mania.

"Damn!", she said to the October night. "The fortune-teller was right about a dark stranger. And, about my strength."

JUICE

Lee Bidgood

The woman wandered around the car park. It was nine at night and the place was deserted. Daytime was better. There were often men in their cars then, waiting as their wife shopped. Men hated shopping. Or more precisely, looking at things they had no intention to buy.

But the shops had closed an hour ago. It was an irritating paradox. More cars meant more marks. It also meant more potential witnesses. The best hope in a deserted car park was a man taking a time-out from home. From a domestic argument, perhaps. Or a break from loneliness.

She wandered up the malodorous stairwell from the second floor to the third. It was supposed to be summer. She still felt cold. The woman pulled her jacket tighter and pushed through the double doors. Her hopes rose when she saw a man walking to his car. He carried a holdall. There was a gym nearby. However, the man got into a sports car and left without delay. He would have been a waste of time, anyway. His strutting gait suggested he was impressed by himself. And her strategy relied on the opposite. Men who were lacking something. Men who would ask her to get in.

The woman kicked at a discarded plastic bag. It caught on her shoe, and she flapped the bag around. It was a puppet. Then a green cloud. A moment of distraction from the boredom of her job. For a job it was. It beat the tedious captivity of an office.

She walked around the few empty cars, then sighed and headed for the fourth floor. No one was there. She was about to turn around when she saw a shadow. Stepping closer, she saw him. Yes. A man was sitting in a dark saloon car. She waited a moment. He didn't drive off. Nor did he appear to notice the woman. She ruffled her long hair. Unzipped her jacket. Then she walked around the car and knocked on the passenger window.

The man did not respond. His head was bowed. For a second, the woman worried he was dead. She tried again and he turned to her.

"Hi," she said through the glass.

The man leant sideways and opened the door.

"Hi," she repeated. "Sorry to bother you."

The man looked her up and down. She was used to this, of course. She was twenty-five years old and knew she was attractive. But there was no leer on the man's face. He looked at her impassively and shrugged.

"Yeah," she said, "I just wondered if you had a phone charger?"

He looked at his own phone on the dashboard. "No, I don't, I-"

"But you have a USB slot, yes? I can see it. There."

The woman pointed at the slot beneath the car's infotainment screen.

"No," he said, "that's where I plug my phone in to play music. It's not a charger."

She sighed. Some nights were hard work. The man was in his mid-forties, at most. Technology should not be an alien concept to him.

"That slot charges your phone as you use it," she said.

"Oh." The man stared at his phone again. "I didn't know that."

"Yeah, so..." She pulled the door wider, slow enough to not concern him, and leaned forwards. Her jacket swung open. This was on purpose. Her low V-neck jumper hinted at the flesh beneath it. However, it hid enough to retain her dignity. She was no hooker.

"If I plug my phone in there, and you switch your car on for a bit..."

The woman waited. This was the part where they should want to help; to relish the chance to feel close to her body. Her phone would reach ten per cent and off she would go. Job done. If the guy's wife returned, then, well, the man was being chivalrous. Modern life was dangerous for a girl without a phone. No clothes had been shed; no money handed over. Only her perfume would linger.

"I'll be gone in a minute," the man said.

The woman looked around nervously. So he *was* waiting for somebody, then. Maybe his wife was in the gym. It was essential, she thought, that I get into the car. Otherwise, I'm just an attractive girl leaning into one. That would be misconstrued.

She moved the door so that it rested against her back. "That's cool," she said, "it'll only take a minute. My phone has fast-charge."

She took out her iPhone. The empty one. Not the other phone, still in her pocket with a full battery. This empty one was special. It only needed to be plugged into the infotainment system for a moment. He would turn the ignition key. Provide power to the system. And the phone would download the memory of the device which preceded it. Specifically, the man's passwords and bank details. Then she would take them home, plug in the phone and help herself.

Juice jacking. That's what it was called. But in her world, it was another shift at the office.

"So…" she smiled. "Can I…?"

The man stared at her. Not with suspicion, or attraction, or menace. His face was blank. He merely shrugged again.

The woman felt a pang of concern. She padded the small can of pepper spray in her pocket. There was no going back, though. She had to get in. Her debts demanded it.

"OK," she said, sitting in the passenger seat. She closed the door and held out her phone. The juice-jacking USB lead dangled from it like a hangman's rope. It was best to let the mark plug it in. It was less suspicious. Made them feel in control.

The man did not take the lead's jack. "There's no point," he said. "I'm not here for long."

"A ten per cent charge is all I need."

"Yes, but all the same."

The woman waited for him to continue. He remained silent. They stared at each other vacantly, as if strangers on the tube. Sighing, she held the phone against her breasts: *Look here. Look at them.* The man did not. He broke eye contact and stared at the steering wheel.

"I'll do it then, shall I?" she said as sweetly as she could.

The woman eased the lead into the car's USB port. Then she gave it a final thrust. The connection should be tight. Otherwise, data might be lost.

She put the phone in her lap. The man did not use it as an excuse to glance at her thighs. They usually did. Married men could not resist. Only one had ever tried to touch her. And he had got the pepper spray. Yet she doubted this man was married. He smelled of cheap aftershave, like most of them, but he didn't stink of desperation. He just sat there, staring at the Ford logo on his steering wheel.

The woman turned around in her seat. The car park was still empty. Yet this could be a police sting. People were more aware of juice jacking now. She had seen a few articles on the internet news. But if the police were here, they were hiding well. There were no shapes in the shadows. It was only herself and this man.

"So… could you switch the engine on, yeah?"

"It's like I said. You won't reap a benefit."

Which the woman thought ironic. She would reap the benefit only too well. But he didn't know that. Or maybe he did. Had he read the news, too? An impulse made her want to get out. No need to be hasty. Her phone was plugged in now. She would get the data, get away from here and leave the man alone.

"It'll be quick," she said. "Look - I'll hold my screen up to you as it's charging. You'll see it increase."

Another play from her book. People were less wary of things they could see. She had even placed a large battery-percentage widget on her home screen. He wouldn't need his reading glasses.

"What's your name?" he asked.

"What?" The woman moved her hand towards the door handle. They shouldn't ask that. It should never get personal. "I'm… I'm…" Her mind went blank.

"My name is Ian," he said. "Ian Foster."

"Hi Ian." The woman tried to sound breezy. "I'm Madison." It was the first name her brain could muster. She tried to remember where she'd heard it. An American TV show, perhaps.

"That's an unusual name," he said.

"Is it?" The woman glanced at the door handle again. "Well, anyway, I really need to charge my phone and call my boyfriend. I'm stranded, y'see. Someone nicked my bag in a shop."

Another strategy. Make them think that someone was waiting. That someone would miss them. Which was a lie in her case. Everyone had left her. People, generally, don't like to be stolen from. Or lied to. Or cheated on. With money or sex or pilfered cigarettes. It annoyed them. The woman wanted to protest to the man: I just can't help it. It's innate. I do it to them before they do it to me. Because everybody's like that, right? We're all out for what we can get. And if I had a car, then I'm sure someone would come along and steal my data, too.

Right?

The man studied her. Their eyes met again, but with meaning this time, with understanding. As if he could hear her unspoken protest. His hand lingered on the car's ignition. At last. Just get it over with. The woman hoped this was worth the wait and he had a fat bank account.

"Do you feel empty, Madison?" he asked. "Like there's nothing there?"

The woman frowned. She found herself nodding.

"That everything you thought important is actually... shite?" he added.

"Yeah. I do, as it goes."

Madison née Charlotte looked away. The car park was empty. There was no one waiting. She would return to an empty flat and congratulate herself on a job well done. But nobody would celebrate with her. Every can in the six-pack was hers. She could steal all of them.

Charlotte glanced at the man's left hand. No wedding ring.

"Look, Ian," she said, "have you fallen out with your partner? Or lost a job, maybe? Had the bailiffs round? I have. It's fucking humiliating. The neighbours lined the hallway."

Ian shook his head.

"An addiction, maybe? Gambling? Drinking?" She didn't mention drugs. He didn't look the type. "But you can get help, y'know? There are... groups you can attend."

And Charlotte asked herself: why am I saying this? I don't care about this man. I'm only here to steal his stuff. She looked down at her phone. It should be filled with the man's digital life by now. Instead, she was discussing being and nothingness.

She tapped the dashboard. "Look, Ian - I'm sorry that you feel like crap. But you'll sort it. Life's a forgiving mistress. It gives you a second chance."

And Charlotte thought: if it gave one to me, I'd probably run off with it. She felt guilty, suddenly. Empty and shite. She had read once that the criminal wants to get caught. They want someone to stop them. Well, that may be, but Charlotte didn't. She had a large credit card bill which wasn't going to clear itself.

Yet she had a bad feeling about this one. She reached forwards to pull her connection from the car.

Ian gripped her wrist. "I know what you're doing," he said.

Charlotte winced. "Let go, please. You're hurting me."

"I read about it recently. What do they call it?"

"Juice jacking," said Charlotte reflexively. She was panicking now. Her arm trembled. The pepper spray was in her pocket. But she only had one free hand. Which to reach for: the spray or the door handle?

"Do you hate yourself, Madison?" he asked.

Charlotte replied that, yes, she did. But give me a second chance, Ian, and I promise I'll change. There are groups. They sent me to one recently. Didn't do much good but I could try again. And you could change too, Ian. Don't give up on yourself. You're the most interesting person I've tried to rob.

"Really."

Ian released Charlotte's wrist. He locked the car and started the engine. Charlotte tried her door uselessly. She spun on her seat and looked around. Please come and help me. The car park was empty. Then she saw it. The hosepipe. The passenger window behind Ian was wound down slightly. Just enough to fit the pipe through. She tried to bat Ian's hand away, to turn the ignition off, but she gave up. He was too strong.

"Turn the car off, you fucking nutter!" she screamed.

Ian shook his head.

Charlotte tried again: "Whatever it is, Ian, you can sort it. Listen, we can sort it together. What do you want? A blowjob? A shag? I'm not attached so it wouldn't be cheating. And you wouldn't have to pay me so it wouldn't be illegal. Just... anything, Ian. Whatever you want. Just switch the fucking car off. Ian! Please!"

Charlotte took a deep breath. She felt light-headed.

"I'm sorry!" she continued. "It's just that I need to pay for stuff. I have debts. Ask Barclaycard. And I just can't cope with people, Ian. I hate being shut in. I could never work in an office or anything like that. Not a shop. Or a hospital, or... I dunno... a trampoline centre. But I'll try again, I promise. I'll stop treating everyone else like... like..."

Charlotte stopped talking. She was getting a headache.

"The problem with stealing, Madison, is that it makes you greedy."

"Charlotte!" she yelled. "My name is Charlotte Jones!"

Ian said nothing. He revved the engine.

Charlotte closed her eyes. She felt dizzy now. Dizzy and sick. The car park walls spun in her mind, and she tried to find her pepper spray until she fell asleep.

Afterwards, Ian's wife was shocked to learn he'd been having an affair. He had died with his mistress. A suicide pact. He had even given this Charlotte Jones woman all their details. Their shared passwords. Their joint account. He'd also tossed his wedding ring.

Such a betrayal. What a thing to live with. No wonder Ian Foster had been depressed.

The Pumpkin Carver

Gary Thomson

"Emma, I'm telling you, he'll help you get rid of your head mess, easy."

The chaos in my life. You mean the sudden loss of my mom to lymphatic cancer? Or my nagging resentment toward a cow of a stepmother, whose careless driving turned me into a shuffling misfit who can't walk without pain? Who stumped herself between me and my dad, probably forever? That mess?

"After all, look what he did for me and my situation," Sophie emphasizes.

My friend's 'situation' was her getting tangled with a half-wit dopehead boyfriend who used her as a ready punching bag when all she wanted was a standup guy who'd treat her with respect and decency. When Razi was shot in the park near his housing complex, the cops put it down to a drug deal gone bad.

"The Carver worked that one out. It's him I owe a new life to."

New life for sure.

If Soph could find herself enjoying school again, and get on with her mom like they were two best friends, then maybe the Pumpkin Carver could help me. Besides, I owed it to my mom, her wandering forlorn in her spirit realm, head full of questions, no doubt.

Momma's ghost first appeared at her funeral reception at our house. She strides through the living room wall and sidles close by my father where he stands greeting friends and associates come to offer their condolences.

She walks past these people, nodding her head in recognition or welcome. Her face draws tight in unspeakable sadness and confusion. She tries to draw my father close to her, but she holds onto nothingness. He shudders as she moves through him. Scheming Stepmom-to-be is milling with some of the wellwishers, looking downcast, glancing often toward my dad. Already sorting possibilities to replace my mother, and shift me to the sidelines.

Mom glides toward the kitchen door, where, if alive, she would have gathered mounded platters of sandwiches and nibbles for the visitors' comfort. She disappears through the kitchen wall.

"When can we see him?" I ask Sophie one day.

We were exiting Ayaaz's convenience store with lottery tickets for her couch-potato father, and maybe it was the sight of the first Hallowe'en pumpkins for sale at Randall's market stand, all plump and golden, that prompted my request.

Sophie jams the lottery tickets into her jeans pocket. "We'll go now. Most like he'll be in his workshop. I won't stay, hafta return these tickets to Ol' Grouch."

He was really Mr. Enright, elderly, stooped, with a shock of white hair that hung over his ears. He recognizes Sophie straightaway, and leads us both into his workshop. His voice is soft and reassuring, like that of a trusted granddad.

Sophie has a quick word with him apart, then leaves us.

His bench shelves are filled with pumpkins of varying attraction, plump and petite, smooth and nubbly, firm, robust and shiny. From the whimsy of his finished pieces I can understand the schoolkids' fascination, where he helped with Hallowe'en decorations and costumes.

"We always like his trolls," Sophie enthused. "Tangled hair over peering eyes, and hats askew." And his carved likenesses of parents or siblings – the whiny and clueless and hurtful ones. He gives the younger kids a place where they can have one over for inexplicable cruelties or sudden banishment.

Like the payback I crave for Horrid Stepmother's intrusion.

Mr Enright is fast and precise in his preliminary instruction: lop off top, scoop and discard innards. Black ink Sharpie to outline shaggy eyebrows over an aqualine nose. Watching the dark lines make sense I recall my childhood carving joy with dad, laughing and shuddering together as a malevolent face emerges from the nubbly casing. A sudden longing for his unhindered affection heats my skin.

Carver works a chin angled in aggression. Sketches in two narrow eyes – in defiance or growing resentment? Already the emerging face reminds me of a schoolyard bully at school.

96

"Sophie mentioned your anguish and concern at home. I must remind you, this is a serious exercise. There can be hurtful consequences."

His pen swishes over the pumpkin's surface, marking teeth that slant in barely restrained wickedness. I shudder in memory of Careless Stepmom driving me to the orthodontist for my retainers appointment. Texting her bridge partner in the rain and chaotic traffic. Abrupt smash of metal, searing pain in my leg. Darkness. Surgery and lengthy therapy. She expressed sympathy, but her eyes were empty.

He levels the bottom of the pumpkin's interior. Then places a candle in the slot. "The final step is to study the face you have carved, contemplate it until you can not only feel, but hold, its essence. The charm you recite will enable your power over the subject."

"How will I know it will work?" My voice feels raspy.

"The candle will light up."

As I ready to leave he hands me a printed note. "Your ancient charm," he says. "From Irish peasants, to protect against the banshee. Recite it when you are ready."

Returning home I stop under a broad oak to read it: I want you never / I need you never / leave my life now / and come back never. Simple enough, for superstitious farm folks afraid of bog spirits. But will it work for me?

After my practice sessions at home I can see the likeness of Devil Woman's features emerge over the side of the pumpkin, her arched eyebrows, discontented eyes, thin downturned mouth never open in song or banter.

I recite Carver's charm while walking to school and under the duvet before sleep. Soon it throbs unbidden in my head. Right there beside thoughts of pop's situation. Does he still mourn for mom, or has he let her go? When this trespasser is gone, can we continue as before, just we two, happy and together forever?

I phone Sophie, tell her of my progress. "What did I say? It'll work out, you'll see."

Then, over one intense evening I work the gleaming knife over the pumpkin's flesh. Taper the downturned mouth, slice out Witchwoman's hooded eyes, add slash marks over the forehead.

I cut a small slot to hold the candle. Will it really light up, as Carver promised? Take her out of my life? Or will the whole affair come to naught, leaving me angry for wasted time? For now I feel lightheaded and trembly.

Momma's ghost comes by next evening, out of a chill sky lightning-scarred with threatening rain. She approaches dad in the dining room as he is clearing the dinner dishes, comes to him through the heavy walnut table. Her face is pale and crinkled, half smiling. Of welcome or solace? Her dark eyes look expectant, at ease.

This time she cradles pop's elbow and makes to draw him toward her, nurse comforting patient. Her hand moves through his arm and midriff. He shivers in response, turns to the window, says, "Ugly weather approaching. Might need the fireplace tonight." The ghost tilts her head in calculated expectation. She looks toward Intruder with a triumphant expression. Then she glides through the buffet with its china plates and sparkling wine glasses, and through the wall into the gathering storm.

I think of momma's changed expression from her first appearance. I see there a sign of gratitude for my work, a relief that she is not forgotten. I want to tell my dad, She too is waiting, wanting you near her.

I leave the dinner table and force myself through some inane television program with excited family members chugging through a hazard course of giant beach balls and swinging plastic logs.

Dad and his Scold are standing by the front door, wrangling over his offer to drive her to her evening bridge game. "I don't mind the wet," he says. "You can come home with Diane Morrissey, or I'll come and fetch you." He holds stubbornly to the car keys as they go out the front door, huddled against the lashing rain.

I hear the car back out the driveway. Retreat to my bedroom, flop on the bed. Listen to the broken rhythms of nearby thunderclaps and pellets of rain smacking against the window. Hum the familiar words: I want you never / I need you never...

I will show pop my carved pumpkin on his return home. Just the two of us. We will laugh and regain our connection like we knew those Hallowe'ens when I was a little girl.

A lightning flash illuminates the yard beyond the window. A jagged limb crashes onto the lawn; acrid pall of charred wood seeps into my room. A chill ices my heart. A black rain-slick road looms across the windowpane. Carver's earlier warning throbs in my head. Hope turns to rising dread.

I lurch away from the bed. Pull back the cover from our pumpkin.

There, against the pale interior, the candle flickers in reddish-gold flame.

The Guy Who Saved Halloween

Daniel Royer

How it Started

She was found by a bird-watching troop early in the morning. Mutilated. Tortured. Dead. Her corpse lay prone under a Sycamore tree. And next to the body, a note just like the others.

The date was October Eleventh. It was the tenth murder since the beginning of the month. Ten killings. Ten notes. Ten letters to the press and police. He called himself *"Guardián de los Meurtos."* The victims varied in terms of age and sex. The oldest was eighty-seven, and the youngest was six. Five males. Five females. No discernible connection between them.

The local police were on the case. They scoured the evidence. They searched for clues.

DNA... none.

Fingerprints... none.

Leads... none.

Suspects... none.

The chances of catching the culprit any time soon... Slim.

The police were stumped. A curfew was put in place by the mayor. Be at home by sundown or be arrested. Locks were installed. Locks were changed. Locks were upgraded. Locksmiths were making big bread.

But not everyone in town was making bread.

Los Quatro

They met at Rosey's Bar. There were four of them. They were *Los Quatro*. All hailing from the oil derricks of Texas, they moved to town, cashing in that black gold for city green. They were...

Big Al. He coordinated the haunted carnival.

Old Earl. He owned the pumpkin patch.

El Ropo. He managed the candy shop.

Stoggs. He ran the Halloween pop-up.

These were *Los Quatro*. They accounted for the Halloween trade in town.

They met at Rosey's to discuss their decline in profits. Business had been good at the beginning of the month, tapered downwards, and by the Eleventh of October, had stopped completely. And it was all because of *Guardián de los Meurtos*. A curfew had been instated. Folks were terrified. Folks were staying home. Folks weren't buying Halloween fare. And absolutely no one was going to let their kids trick-or-treat in three weeks. October was on the verge of being canceled.

This could not continue. If it had been any other month of the year, it would have been fine. But this was October! Halloween was the livelihood of *Los Quatro*. If sales remained dormant they would be broke. If *Guardián de los Meurtos* remained at large they would be toast. The people were frightened. The cops were scratching their heads. *Los Quatro* was in a bind. Watching their bank accounts dwindle was not the Texas way. Something needed to be done.

A proposal was put forward by Big Al… A bounty. We pool our resources. We throw our money in a briefcase. We put out a reward for *Guardián de los Meurtos*. Like they used to back in the Wild West Days. Call it Lone Star Vengeance. Call it Texas Justice.

The police were useless. Let the citizens take a crack at it. *Guardián de los Meurtos*: dead or alive. And whoever gets him gets the briefcase.

The other three agreed. They settled on a number. One million bucks. They shook hands. Contracts weren't necessary. They were Texans. Calls were made to accountants. Calls were made to financial advisers. Calls were made to loan sharks.

By the next day, the million bucks had been collected. The dough was in a briefcase—a bread box. *Los Quatro* sent an ad to the local paper. Fliers were hung around town. Newsletters were hurled to doorsteps.

The bounty was in place.

The Bounty Hunter

The bounty hunter approached the old lady's house. His name was Bogart and he held a cat. The cat was going bonkers in his arms—an orange terror by the name of Custer. Claws tore into flesh. Bogart screamed, let go. The cat hit the pavement. Bogart dove, missed, made a blind grab. The cat sank its teeth. Bogart screamed again. He put Custer in a choke-hold, continued to the door.

Knock knock.

The old lady answered. "You found Custer!"

102

"Yes, ma'am," said Bogart. He extended the cat. It made one final swipe. Claws shredded his forearm. Bogart suppressed a scream, winced only. Displays of emotions were unprofessional for bounty hunters.

The old lady accepted the cat gingerly. He purred in her arms. *Good Custer,* she said stroking him. She frowned suddenly.

"His mane is all mussed up and his tail is crooked," she whined. "What'd you do to him?" She held the cat's paw, peered closer. "... Also, some of his claws are broken..."

Bogart was pretty sure those claws were in his arm. "I didn't do nothing, ma'am. I found old Custer here under a bridge eating batteries."

The old lady huffed. She put down the cat. It trotted into the house. The old lady withdrew a handbag, pulled out a bill. Bogart's heart raced.

It had taken him nearly a week to find that missing cat. He had pounded the pavement, knocked on doors, and scoured every back alley and alcove in town. He had been threatened, blackmailed, and harassed by teenagers. Plus, there was a ruthless killer out prowling— *"Guardián de los Meurtos,"* he called himself. The media was in a frenzy. The folks were scared. The streets were not safe. But the streets is where Bogart belonged. He was a bounty hunter after all. Bogart knew that this was all standard stuff to the profession he had chosen. But now came his favorite part of the job: payment.

The old lady handed him the bread. Bogart counted, paused.

"There's only ten here. Your ad said twenty for the mouser."

"My ad didn't say nothing about Custer's fur being all matted or his tail cattywampus. You're lucky you're getting any dough at all!"

"But—but..." stammered Bogart. He stumbled for words. Sometimes clients needed a rundown of the trials and tribulations of the bounty hunter. The life of a bounty hunter was fraught with complications, to be sure. Some clients required a summary. This was all standard procedure. Bogart took a stab at it. "I got threatened over that cat. I got cursed at. You should have seen the way some teenagers talked to me! Plus, my life was in danger. There's a murderer on the loose, you know. I spent a week looking for that mouser! I'm gonna need more bread than this."

"A week!" scoffed the old lady. "Last time Custer got out, it took Mancini less than an hour to find him! Plus he gave him a bath beforehand."

Bogart sighed. Mancini...

Mancini was the *other* bounty hunter in town. Mancini was big-time. He had a van. He had equipment. He had a whole crew working for him. Mancini got the good bounties: fugitives, missing heiresses, even a prince lost in the jungle. Mancini always got his man. He even had connections to the mayor's office. The cat-finding business was beneath him these days.

Bogart held the cash. Ten dollars. He needed more. Mancini or not, his work still warranted more jack than this! There were times when a bounty-hunter was forced to abandon his dignity. Bogart knew that this was one of those times. He got on his knees, cupped his hands: "Please...?" he whimpered.

"No!" said the old lady, her arms crossed. "And let me tell you why... You are the worst bounty hunter ever! I've dealt with a lot of you guys over the years, so I know. That's right, Custer escapes a lot. The only reason I'm forking over *anything* is because it's clear you haven't had a meal in a while. That's right! I feel sorry for your keister. Now get off my porch! Next time, I'm calling Mancini!"

"Do that!" shouted Bogart, all professionalism gone. "Don't ever call me or hire me again! I don't need no charity and I don't want no help!"

The door slammed. He stuffed the bread in his pocket. It was a disappointment to be sure, but it was still ten bucks. Ten bucks was enough for a slug or two at Rosey's. If he stiffed on the tip, maybe even three slugs.

Bogart shuffled to his auto. Brittle October leaves crunched under his feet. The car was an old Goat he had salvaged at the junkyard. It lacked mirrors, a speedometer, and a parking brake. Bogart got in. He inserted the key, turned it. Nothing. He pounded the gas pedal, turned again. Nothing. Dead battery.

Bogart walked back to the porch.

Knock knock.

The door flung open. "What?"

"You got any jumper cables? The jalopy needs a kick."

Felina

Bogart headed to Rosey's. The Goat thrust and jerked en route. It stalled at stoplights. It was smoke and steam the whole way. The auto died in front of Rosey's. It died in front of a big van. It was a locksmith truck. Bogart double-parked. Good enough. Bogart ditched the auto. He approached Rosey's. A workman kneeled at the bar's entrance. Bogart saw that he was changing the lock. With that maniac running around chopping off peoples' heads, Bogart had heard that folks were getting their locks changed in a heap. The locksmith trade was booming. Bogart stepped around the workman. He entered Rosey's.

It was noon, and the bar was sparsely populated. Mariachi music trickled from the jukebox. Bogart surveyed the saloon. Two truckers at the bar, plus a traveling salesman. An old couple at one of the tables, and a *vaquero* at another. And also… Felina.

Felina swayed next to the juke. She twirled. She swooned. She whirled. Eyes closed, Felina danced by herself as she always did. Her dress fluttered. It flitted. The men gazed. Bogart gazed.

Bogart took a seat at the bar, still looking. He placed the ten on the counter.

"A slug," he said to Rosey.

A glass plopped on the bar-top, a finger's worth inside. Bogart sipped, gazed some more.

The song finished. Felina took the stool next to Bogart's. She eyed the ten, still on the counter.

Bogart turned to Rosey. "This enough for another slug?" he asked, eyeing the ten.

Rosey nodded, poured, plopped a second glass. Felina sipped.

"You're flush today," she said.

Bogart smiled. "A big case."

Her eyes widened. "Really?"

Bogart summarized his week. He added some embellishments. This was pretty standard in the bounty-hunting biz. The old lady became an heiress. The missing cat became a tiger. The teenagers became a street gang. Also, the ten bucks became a thousand.

Felina's eyes danced. She stroked his arm. She squeezed his bicep. Her leg brushed Bogart's. "It's about time you fried that bacon," she said, her hands running through his hair. "I have to say, I've had my eye on Mancini for a while. He watches me whirl sometimes. He's been asking for a spin. He's a big-time bounty hunter, you know. I only date the big-timers. I must admit, I've always thought you were small potatoes. A second banana. A featherweight. But now, I think you're finally trading blows with the big boys. With this tiger business, it looks like you're finally giving Mancini a run for his money. Keep it up, and you just might get a spin with me..."

The saloon door burst open. "A round of drinks for me and my crew!" All eyes turned. It was Mancini. Mancini and his boys. Bogart turned away. The boys took a table in the back. Mancini strutted up to the bar, smug as a prom king.

He snagged the stool on the other side of Felina. He draped his arm over her. Felina purred. Mancini slapped a C-note on the bar-top. "Double slugs for me and the boys, Rosey, and keep 'em coming!" He winked at Felina. "Oh, and give this slinky thing a double as well. Some of that fancy stuff with the umbrella."

With her right hand still on Bogart's bicep, she placed her left on Mancini's. She eyed the C-note, stroking both men. "Bread like that's gotta have a story. What's yours, stud...?"

"Well I'll tell you, honey, it was a big case. Pretty complicated. Lots of twists and turns. You see, the mayor's wife went missing, and he flashed me the big bucks to find her. As you know, he comes to me first when there's a big case..." Bogart listened to Mancini tell his story, rife with the standard bounty-hunter embellishments. Mancini spoke of double-crossings and mistaken identities and red-herrings. He talked of forensics and gun powder residue and DNA evidence. Mancini knew all about criminal investigations. Mancini knew all about technology. He knew all about that science stuff. That's why he was top-dog in the bounty hunter game. That's why he had a crew. That's why he knocked double slugs. That's why he never paid Rosey in dish-washing-duty, as Bogart often did.

By the time Mancini concluded his tale, Felina was stroking his thigh. "What a lucky gal I am, to be slugging with two big-time bounty-hunter bucks. You see, Bogart here just wrapped a big case too..."

Mancini looked at Bogart for the first time. Bogart met his eyes. "A big case, huh? Let's hear about it, Bogart..."

"I don't kiss and tell."

"So humble," said Mancini.

Felina spoke. "Well if this stud won't tell the tale, then I will..." Felina told Mancini about the missing tiger and the heiress and the gang members and the thousand bucks.

Mancini pondered this. "This reminds me of a flier I saw last week. If I remember right, some old lady was looking for her missing cat... But that must be a different case... Right, Bogart?"

"Must be," muttered Bogart.

Felina turned swiftly to Bogart. "Well *is* it?" Bogart's face reddened. Felina knew. Bogart said nothing, sipped at his glass.

Mancini continued: "When me and the boys came across the ad, I told them not to waste their time with this chicken scratch. You see, we don't mess around with the peewee stuff. Missing cats and stolen lunch boxes... We only deal with the tough cases."

Felina turned back to Bogart. She frowned. "I don't understand. Why was this old lady offering a thousand bucks for a stinky old mouser?"

"The flier didn't mention nothing about no thousand bucks," said Mancini. "It *did* say something about a twenty-spot though. But if I know Bogart, he had to have botched this case somehow, so I'm guessing the old bird gave him half that..."

Mancini and Felina looked at Bogart's ten-spot, still flat on the counter. Bogart looked ahead, kept sipping. Felina removed her hand from Bogart's bicep. She was done with him. Her attention was now solely on Mancini. She stroked his thigh with extra fervor.

"So what's the next big case, stud?"

Mancini slapped a flier smack on the counter.

WANTED
DEAD OR ALIVE
GUARDIAN DE LOS MEURTOS
REWARD
ONE MILLION DOLLARS

Felina whistled. "That's quite a case, stud. You're talking some big bread. That nasty killer needs to be stopped, that's for sure. They say that no one's safe. They say that we need to get our locks changed. They say that Halloween is in jeopardy. Those are some pretty big stakes..." Bogart studied the flier. Felina noticed. She softened. "Tell you what... Whoever bags the killer, gets a spin with me!" Bogart perked up. "But until then," continued Felina, smiling, "let's have a few more slugs. Who's buying?"

"*I'm* buying," said Mancini. "I'll tell you what, Bogart. I'll get you another slug as well."

"I can buy my own," said Bogart. He looked down. The ten-spot was gone. Bogart looked around. One of the truckers at the bar held a ten-dollar bill. That was Bogart's bread. Bogart approached him. "Excuse me, sir. That's my slice."

"No, it isn't," said the trucker.

Bogart returned to his stool, his eyes downcast. He looked to Mancini. "Can you buy me a slug?"

The saloon door swung open. The locksmith entered. "Listen up," he said. "Someone's heap is blocking my van. It's getting towed."

Research

Mancini gave Bogart a ride to the tow yard. He lent him the bread to get it out. Bogart sat in his car. He was thinking about *Guardián de los Meurtos* and that sweet reward. Bogart needed to study up on this guy. That meant he had some research to do. Bogart headed over to the library. Parked in front, was the same locksmith van.

Bogart stepped inside the library. He gathered recent newspapers. He started with the October Second edition, the morning after the first murder, and worked his way up to the present day, the Twelfth. *Guardián de los Meurtos* had claimed eleven victims since the First of October. Some were men. Some were women. Some were home-invaded. Some were snatched off the street. All had been slain with a knife. And every one of them had been tortured prior to the murder, their corpse posed publicly after the evil deed had been done. Hand-written letters had been mailed to the local press following each incident. The newspapers provided copies of the letters.

I WILL NEVER QUIT!
MORE WILL DIE!
SOMEBODY STOP ME!

The letters seemed to indicate that the murders would continue for the length of the month, up to and including Halloween Night. The twelfth victim was expected to be murdered later that evening, its corpse, presumably, would be found the following morning.

The evidence left at the crime scenes had been scant. The police had reported no clues. They claimed that this was the work of a "serial killer." Bogart was unfamiliar with the term. He hopped on a computer. He clicked in a search engine. Apparently, a serial killer was someone who had killed three or more people on separate occasions. Bogart continued his research. According to the experts, there were twenty-five to fifty serial killers operating in America at any given time. Over eighty percent of them were both white and male, the median age being twenty-seven years old.

Bogart learned that a common characteristic among these rogues was a lack of empathy. This meant that serial killers had difficulty caring about other people's feelings. Bogart found out that the motives for these murders often involved some sort of psychological gratification, such as sexual fulfillment, anger-release, thrill-seeking, financial-gain, and even the pursuit of attention. Incidentally, it was not uncommon for serial killers to return to their crime scenes to "relive" the moments. The experts also claimed that serial killers never "stopped." They could be dormant for a particular stretch of time, but their murder-sprees would continue until they were either jailed or killed. Apparently, after that first taste of blood, the dopamine-kick was just too strong.

Bogart kept clicking. He learned the names of the game. There was Harvey Glatman, Ted Bundy, and Jeffrey Dahmer. There was Charles Manson, Samuel Little, and H.H. Holmes. But serial killers didn't just use their Christian names—sometimes they came up with fun nicknames. There was the Black Dahlia Avenger, Zodiac, and Son of Sam. There was BTK, the Co-ed Killer, and the Boston Strangler. These ruthless killers plied their trades in contrasting modes of instrumentation, including guns, knives, tire-irons, claw-hammers, and ligatures. They punched, kicked, bludgeoned, pistol-whipped, strangled, and tortured. Their methods may have varied, but the outcomes were always the same: a lot of people died.

Bogart kept reading. There was a serial killer in the 1980's that he found particularly intriguing, a young homeless Satanist by the name of Richard Ramirez. His nickname was the Night Stalker, and his confirmed kill-count was upwards of fourteen. For more than a year, the Night Stalker terrorized the Greater Los Angeles area, including the suburbs of Glendale, Monterey Park, and Whittier. After sixteen months of horror, the Night Stalker was caught, eventually being convicted of thirteen murders. Ramirez, reportedly, never expressed any remorse for his crimes, and even hailed Satan as his personal savior while rotting in a jail cell. Bogart exhaled. Talk about a lack of empathy! This was one tough cookie.

Bogart's research continued. As good as the Night Stalker was, the most notorious serial killer of all time was a dude named "Jack the Ripper." He committed his murders in the Whitechapel district of London, England, way back in the late nineteenth century. The guy was a pioneer in the art of serial-killing, as he set most of the trends still used by mass-murderers today. He hunted at night. He stalked. He tortured and he mutilated. He removed organs. His preferred victims were prostitutes. Once the Ripper's fun was through, he often dumped the bodies in public spaces for maximum shock-appeal, all before vanishing in the London fog. The dude would even mail cryptic notes to the police, including a letter claiming to be FROM HELL. The Ripper murdered at least five women, often referred to as the "canonical five," but the victim-count was suspected to be higher. Jack the Ripper was never caught, and his identity still remained a mystery after nearly a century and a half. Bogart learned that self-appointed "Ripperologists," scoured the Web dissecting clues, still trying to unmask the rogue's true identity. Upon further reading, Bogart realized that the Internet was flooded with shaggy-dog detectives, attempting to crack a variety of unsolved crimes from the past.

Bogart was impressed—and a little worried. It seemed that these serial killers were a slippery bunch. If Bogart wanted to out-think these psychopaths before Mancini and the cops, he needed to step up his game. He thought of Mancini. His rival had a van, equipment, and a whole crew working for him. So did the police. Bogart had no crew and no equipment. He didn't even have a van. Bogart pondered. A van and a crew seemed a little out of reach. Perhaps he could get some equipment? All the great detectives and bounty hunters used gadgets. Bogart would get some gadgets himself. The trouble was, he didn't have any bread to buy some.

Gadgets

Bogart stepped inside the pawn shop. He had stopped off at his apartment on the way over. All of his possessions, he had thrown into a rucksack. Clothing, silverware, blankets, and food. Bogart plopped the bag on the counter.

"How much can I get for this?" he asked.

The proprietor opened the bag, sifted through it. "I can give you twenty scoots," he said.

Bogart's eyes danced. Twenty bucks could get him four slugs—maybe even five if he didn't tip. Bogart shook his head. He was not out for slugs—he was out for gadgets—detective gizmos.

"No dice," he told the proprietor. "I want merchandise." He racked his brain. What kind of equipment did a detective use? What kind of gadgets did Mancini have? Bogart continued: "I want a magnifying glass, a flashlight, binoculars, a tape recorder, and a police scanner."

The pawn shop guy whistled. "Sounds to me like you're out to get *Guardián de los Meurtos*."

"I also need a gun."

"No-can-do, buddy. Selling guns without a permit is against the law. I don't do that stuff."

"Cut the comedy," said Bogart. "Just give me the goods. I've got a killer to catch."

The Investigation

Bogart visited the most recent crime scene. The hour was late. The scene was in a wooded park by a residential district. Old Victorian homes lined the park's perimeter. Bogart entered the wood. Yellow tape surrounded the zone. Bogart ducked under, advanced. He pulled out his flashlight and magnifying glass, inspected for clues. He found nothing. Bogart peered through his binoculars. He saw nothing. Bogart turned on his tape recorder and police-scanner. He heard nothing. He pointed his gun. There was no one to shoot.

What now? Most detectives would have found a piece of evidence at this point. Investigators often called this a "clue." Bogart needed to find one. Something. He had to keep trying. Bogart looked harder. Brittle yellow leaves lined the scene. He kicked at them. Under the leaves he found clumps of hair.

"Gross," said Bogart. Hair was definitely not a clue. Hair was not going to help him find his man.

Bogart was discouraged. He was about to give up when he heard a scraping sound. The noise came from a house adjacent to the park. Bogart looked through his binoculars. A man was stooped on the front porch of an old Victorian. He knelt by the door knob. Bogart watched. He saw the side of the man's profile. Bogart studied. A flash of recognition. It was the locksmith he had been seeing all over town.

Bogart sighed. The guy was probably on another call—the locksmith trade was booming as of late.

Bogart suddenly thought of the time. Why, it was late at night! Locksmiths didn't work these hours! And this was clearly not the man's house. So what was he doing on that front porch? Why was he kneeling by the knob? Bogart knew that this was what detectives referred to as "suspicious." The man on the porch was a "person of interest."

Bogart watched through the binoculars. The locksmith seemed to be jimmying the door. Was this *Guardián de los Meurtos?* Was he about to slay his twelfth victim? Bogart racked his brain. He remembered his research. The locksmith was a white male, as most serial killers tended to be, and he looked to be about the median age. He was also in close proximity to a recent crime scene. Bogart knew that serials often visited their former sites. But what about motivation? All serial killers had them. It was then that Bogart realized that financial-gain was a common incentive. With the locksmith market exploding, the dude was clearly profiting from the slayings.

The evidence fit. Bogart knew that this was *Guardián de los Meurtos.* Bogart had his man. He fingered the gun in his pocket. He would bring him in alive, or he would drag him in dead. The bounty paid off either way. The million bucks was his! Bogart kept watching. He heard a click. The lock had now been pried. The man opened the door. He withdrew a knife. Bogart needed to stop this. He charged, gun cocked and loaded.

Bogart reached the porch in seconds. He burst through the doorway, gun out. He swiveled left, he swiveled right, the gun shaking in his hand. Bogart stomped through a hallway, turned. An old woman sat at a dining table. On the table was a cake with a candle. Standing next to the old lady was the locksmith. He was poised over the cake, the knife in his hand.

"Freeze, buster!" shouted Bogart, the gun pointing right at his man.

"What's the meaning of this?" said the locksmith.

"I—what? I said 'freeze!'"

"How dare you come into Nanna's house! How dare you interrupt her surprise birthday party!"

Bogart stuttered. "Birthday…? But, aren't you *Guardián de los Meurtos?*"

"No. I'm a locksmith. And I was about to cut Nanna's cake. She's one hundred years old."

The old lady squinted through her glasses. She adjusted her hearing aids. "Who is this man?"

The locksmith huffed. "Just a bounty hunter, Nanna. A fool. A dunce. Forget about him. Now how about that cake?"

DNA?

Bogart found himself on a stool at Rosey's. He watched Felina whirl by the juke. Bogart knew he had been so close to giving her a spin. The locksmith had seemed like such a good suspect. That million bucks had almost been his. But Bogart would regroup tomorrow. For now he would wet his beak.

"How 'bout a slug?" he asked Rosey.

"Where's the cash?"

"Can I just wash your dishes?"

Rosey said, "Sure." She slid a slug over to Bogart. He drank.

Mancini and his crew burst through the front door. They whooped. They hollered. They ordered a round of doubles. The boys took a table. Mancini took the stool next to Bogart.

Mancini spoke: "Me and the boys have been at it all day. I'm talking about investigating. I'm talking about detecting. I'm talking about *bounty-hunting*. And son, we just hit pay-dirt... The boys and I found a clue."

"A clue?" asked Bogart.

"We found something at the park near the Victorians."

Bogart's interest was perked. He had just been over there. "What did you find?"

Mancini smiled. "A hair."

Bogart remembered the hair clumps at the scene. "How's *that* gonna help you?"

"You serious? Hair is everything. It's DNA. Deoxyribonucleic acid. I'm talking about science. I'm talking molecules..."

The song on the juke finished. Felina approached. She snagged the stool by Mancini. She rubbed his leg.

"Why you boys talking about molecules?" she asked. "I thought you'd be out there trying to catch that nasty old *Guardián de los Meurtos*."

Mancini spoke: "Molecules *is* bounty-hunting, babe. Molecules is clues. I was just telling Bogart that the boys and I found a clue this evening. A hair. You see, we're gonna take that hair out to our lab. Then we're gonna use polymerase chain reaction to make a bunch of DNA segments. When that's done, we'll analyze the results for variations in specific regions. Then we're gonna test the results against known and unknown samples, including the victim's, to see if the hair belongs to our man..." Bogart had no idea what Mancini was talking about. This was white noise.

Mancini turned to Bogart. "DNA is the name of the game my friend. That's how most killers are caught these days. Don't tell me you're out there still using a magnifying glass and a tape recorder. That stuff's obsolete. It went out of style with trench coats and fedoras! Science is where it's at. Without it, you don't got your man."

Mancini knocked down his slug, asked Rosey for another. He continued. "I've been doing some research at the library. I've been studying up on my serial killers. Ever hear of a cat named Richard Ramirez? They used to call him the Night Stalker. Anyway, he was convicted of thirteen counts of murder... But here's the switch... Twenty-five years later, they found out there was a *fourteenth* killing. A murder that happened before all the others, probably his *first*. And do you know how they discovered this? That's right... DNA. So... that little hair we found is gonna catch us a killer. And after that, a sweet reward. I'm talking about saving Halloween. I'm talking about a spin with Felina. I'm talking about a million bucks. And let me tell you something else. The boys and I are going to take that million bucks, and we're going to book a flight to England. And no, we're not going to visit the king. We'll be investigating the Jack the Ripper murders. We'll be visiting the crime scenes. We'll be collecting evidence. We'll be looking for clues. And we'll be taking those clues back to our lab, and we're going to uncover that scoundrel's identity."

Felina began to purr. She nuzzled against Mancini. She rubbed his leg harder. "So when are you going to take this hair to the lab?"

"Not until tomorrow morning," said Mancini. "We met a sweet old lady near the crime scene. She turned one hundred today. She invited us to her birthday party tonight. Everyone's gonna be there.

114

It's gonna be a rager. You wanna be my date?" He puckered up for a kiss. Felina brushed him away.

"Not until you catch *Guardián de los Meurtos*. You'll get a second kiss when you catch the Ripper." She began to rub his bicep.

Bogart's head spun. What was all this talk about molecules and laboratories? Mancini sure knew his stuff. That's why he got the good bounty-hunting gigs.

Bogart watched Mancini and Felina nuzzle. They touched. They giggled. They cooed. Bogart had had enough. He knocked down his slug. He got up from his stool. Mancini and Felina didn't even notice. Bogart headed for the door. He knew that Rosey would be hot that he left before the dishes were done. Bogart didn't care. He had bigger problems.

New Gadgets

Bogart drove aimlessly. He pounded the steering wheel. He had found that hair first! Any decent bounty-hunter would have known that a hair was a clue! But not Bogart! He had flunked out of science class. That million bucks would have been his! And now, Mancini was going to bag *Guardián de los Meurtos*. He had said that he would be taking the hair to the lab first thing in the morning. By noon, he would have a million scoots and the hand of Felina. Mancini was on the cusp of saving Halloween!

Bogart was no detective. Bogart was no bounty-hunter. The magnifying glass, the tape recorder, and the gun were all toy props while the grownups did the real investigating.

Bogart pulled up to the pawn shop. It was past midnight. He entered.

"I'm about to close," said the proprietor, the same as before. "I've got some business to conduct tonight."

"I got business too," said Bogart. He dumped the detective gizmos on the counter.

The proprietor eyed the goods. "I can give you ten scoots for that."

"I don't want scoot, I want merch."

"What you after?"

"I'll take a bottle, a hose, and a gas can with a splash. I'm running on empty."

The proprietor nodded. He reached under the counter, withdrew a tangle of garden hose. He shuffled to a back room. He came back with a bottle of Jimmy Goodtimes and a jerrycan. "That stuff's leaded," he said.

"The booze or the gas?" asked Bogart.

"Does it matter?"

Out of the Way

Bogart drove, sipping the Goodtimes. He parked on a hill. He let the engine run. The city sparkled below. Somewhere in that dark cruel city a serial killer was prowling—but Bogart would never catch him. Somewhere in that dark cruel city a beautiful lady was whirling—but Bogart would never spin her.

Bogart drank. Watched. Drank some more. He finished the bottle. Peed in it. Chucked it out the window. Bogart sighed. The time was now.

He walked outside and stretched. The brisk October air stung. Bogart shivered. He popped the trunk. The garden hose waited. Bogart grabbed it. He inserted the hose in his tail pipe. The hose fell out. Bogart peeled off a sock. He shoved the sock and the hose back in. He ran the other end of the hose through a crack in the window. Bogart stood outside, waiting for the gas to fill. He leaned against the car, head up, gazing at the stars. He had loved to do this as a boy. The world had seemed so full of hope back then. And now…?

Bogart leaned. Gazed. The car moved out beneath him. Bogart's butt hit the asphalt. The auto was rolling down the hill! Bogart remembered his car didn't have a parking brake.

Bogart ran after the car. He screamed. The car rolled faster. It was a little out of reach. It was *way* out of reach. The car barreled forward. Bogart screamed again.

Bogart saw a pedestrian at the bottom of the hill. The car was heading right for him! Bogart shouted. *Out of the way, out of the way!* The man didn't hear.

Bogart tripped, smacked the pavement, and that's when everything went black.

Manslaughter

Bogart awoke in a hospital bed. His head ached. He tried to stretch, but couldn't. He realized his wrist was cuffed to the bed. A policeman stood before him.

"You've been out for over an hour." Bogart looked at his cuffed wrist. "Yeah," said the policeman, "the pedestrian is dead. Roadkill. He probably never knew what hit him."

"Who was it?" asked Bogart.

"A pawnshop owner, apparently," said the cop. "We think he was walking home from work. You're about to be charged with manslaughter."

And that's when Bogart passed out again.

Return of Los Quatro

Bogart awoke once more in the hospital bed. His wrist was not cuffed. He looked around. There were balloons. Flowers. Teddy bears. Get-well cards.

At the foot of the bed stood four men—big men, mustached and suited up, cowboy hats crowning each of their heads. One of the men held a briefcase.

"You've been out for a couple of hours," he said.

"Are you the police?" asked Bogart.

"We're *Los Quatro*."

"I don't understand."

Big Al: "Never mind us, Mister Bogart, we're not important. We're just some business men from way out Texas. But, listen to me when I tell you, that the man you killed tonight... the pawnshop guy? Well, apparently his DNA matches a hair sample that some other bounty hunter collected at a crime scene. There's a bunch of other science stuff that I don't understand, but as it turns out, this pawnshop clown was *Guardián de los Meurtos*. The cops are sure of it. They found a manifesto in his apartment, plus his handwriting matched."

Old Earl: "The cops think he was on his way to slash an old woman. It was her birthday yesterday. One hundred years old! Do you believe that? Anyway, she was throwing a party. A real rager... Mister Bogart, we were *at* that birthday party. If not for you, *Guardián de los* Moron would have killed us too."

El Ropo: "As you know, our bounty was for 'Dead or Alive,' and this man was very much dead. If I don't say so myself, Mr. Bogart, you killed the crap out of him." *Los Quatro* chuckled. Bogart chuckled. *El Ropo* turned serious. "Now I must tell you that some other bounty hunter by the name of Mancini thinks the reward money should belong to him because his science stuff revealed the killer's identity. He thinks he's some hotshot investigator because he's got a lab and a Bunsen burner. But you and I both know that that's not how *real* detectives solve crimes. The real ones use magnifying glasses and tape recorders. The real ones use binoculars and police-scanners. And sometimes, the *really* good ones use rolling cars. We told that Mancini guy to get lost. We told him to step aside so the real bounty hunters can do their jobs."

Stoggs: "You ever been to Texas, Mister Bogart?" Bogart shook his head. "Well, we have a different way of doing things where we come from. Back in the old days, the Wild West Days, if the law took too long to catch a bandit, why the citizens just put a bounty on him. And it worked! Billy the Kid, Jesse James, Butch and Sundance...? Those misanthropes weren't arrested. They were shot in the head. They got what we call 'Texas Justice.'"

Big Al: "You ever hear of Richard Ramirez? The Night Stalker? Well, he wasn't caught by science, nor was he caught by the police... He was caught by ordinary citizens trying to protect their neighborhood. Now *that's* Texas Justice. Billy the Kid, the Night Stalker, this *Guardián de los* Maniac...? Do you know what those thugs have in common? That's right, a lack of empathy?"

Old Earl: "That means they don't care about our feelings. Well, if they don't care about my feelings, then I sure as heck ain't gonna care about theirs. Back in our Texas days, the local sheriff snatched one of them serial killers. He read him his 'rights,' he offered him a lawyer, and he interrogated him for more than an hour. All legal. And he got nothing. So we said, *Sheriff, why don't you let* Los Quatro *take a crack at him?* Well, we entered that room with a phone book and a roll of quarters, and in two minutes, that sucker confessed to everything, including taking his sister's babysitting money back when he was five... The point is, what the law calls 'justice...' well, it just don't work on some folks."

El Ropo: "We like your style, Bogart. This *Guardián de los* Malarkey character wasn't about to snap, and he wasn't about to stop. So you said, *Hey! Why don't I just run him over with my car?* Now that's some real lean and quick justice—Texas style!"

Stoggs: "You serve that Lone Star vengeance like a cowboy, Bogart. A man! And *that's* who we give our bounty-money to—*men!* Not science nerds who think pie is a math equation. Mister Bogart, you are a real bounty hunter. A real Texan, even if you don't know it yet. Thank you for saving Halloween. And more importantly, thank you for saving our profits." He handed Bogart the briefcase.

Bogart opened the breadbox. He had never seen so much dough. This was a whole loaf! A million scoots would get him about a billion slugs—not to mention the hand of Felina.

"Tell us, Mister Bogart, what are you going to do with all that cash?"

"I'm going to dance with a beautiful woman."

"Like a true Texan. Let me tell you a story about a night I had in El Paso..."

Hero

Bogart sat at the bar, the breadbox on the counter in front of him.

"Rosey, I'm sorry about the dishes last night. Now get me a double-slug and keep them coming! Forever." Rosey shrugged, did as she was told.

Felina took the stool next to Bogart. She rubbed his leg. She stroked his bicep. Bogart spoke once more to Rosey: "And get this *chula* a double too. One of those fancy ones with the fruit."

Felina purred. She nuzzled his neck. "Spin me tonight, stud."

Bogart smiled. A million bucks was sure going to change things. For starters, no more searching for missing cats, that was for sure! From now on, Bogart would only take the tough cases. From now on, Bogart would be the one the mayor called during times of trouble. From now on, his thigh would be the *only* thigh sweet Felina would be rubbing.

Bogart pondered. And maybe he would fly out to England and investigate the Ripper case. But no microscopes or petri dishes for him. DNA was out. Old-school detecting was back in. Maybe Bogart would roll his car down a hill over there and see what mysteries he could solve.

Mancini entered the bar, head down. He took the stool next to Felina. Felina ignored him. Mancini existed to her no longer.

Mancini spoke: "The boys left me. The mayor dismissed me. The van got repossessed. Buy me a slug, Bogart?"

Bogart ordered Mancini a double.

The phone behind the bar rang. Rosey answered. She handed it to Bogart. "It's for you."

Bogart spoke: "Hello?"

"I'm calling for Bogart," said the voice on the other end, a female. Felina leaned against the earpiece so she could hear. Bogart felt her heat.

"Speaking," said Bogart.

"This is Miss Velasquez, personal secretary for the mayor..." Felina stuck her tongue in his ear, cooed. This was hot!

"What can I do for you, Miss Velasquez?" asked Bogart.

"Something terrible has happened to the mayor, and he believes you are the only one he can count on... You see, Jasper has been missing since last night, and the mayor would like to retain your services to find him..."

Bogart found a pen. Picked up a cocktail napkin. He knew that a good bounty-hunter took notes.

"I'll need a description of Jasper," he said. "What's his height?"

"Eighteen inches."

"Weight?"

"Ten pounds."

"Hair color?"

"Spotted."

"Age?"

"Three."

"Last known location?"

"Litter box."

Bogart shook his head. He didn't understand. "Um, is Jasper the mayor's child?"

"No, it's his cat. A calico. Means the world to him. He's offering twenty scoots. He knows you won't let him down."

Felina recoiled. She removed her tongue from his ear.

Bogart spoke into the phone. "But—but, doesn't the mayor have any missing relatives?"

"Actually, yes," said Ms. Velasquez. "The mayor's daughter was kidnapped this morning. We found some DNA in her room. We heard your friend Mancini is a scientist. We heard he has a lab. Can you hand the phone to him please?"

Bogart tossed the phone to Mancini. Mancini snagged it. He spoke into the receiver. "Sure, I can do that for the mayor. A thousand bucks sounds okay to me." Felina stuck her tongue in Mancini's ear.

Bogart looked away. He sighed. He sipped at his drink. Well, maybe he wasn't going to get the girl or the good cases, but at least he had a million bucks. He could buy a better car. Get a new apartment. He could buy double-slugs for the rest of his life. No more paying Rosey with dish-duty.

Bogart looked towards the briefcase. It was gone. Bogart looked around. One of the truckers at the bar held a case. It was stuffed with dough. The breadbox belonged to Bogart. He approached the trucker. "Excuse me, sir. That's my loaf."

"No, it isn't," said the trucker.

Bogart shuffled back to his stool, head down.

He turned to Rosey. "Can I do your dishes?"

The Pop-Up

Daniel Royer

The pop-up shop almost didn't happen. Indeed, it would not have happened without a guy named Rockmash. It began when Rockmash grabbed his phone that morning. The date was September First.

Rockmash yelled into the receiver. He screamed at his secretary to bring him the files. He slammed the phone when he was finished. Rockmash wasn't angry. He just liked to yell—make threats—slam phones—speed in his car. That's how Rockmash liked to live. That's how Rockmash conducted business.

Rockmash was fifty-six years old. He was the founder and head partner of Rockmash & Associates, a law firm specializing in estate planning. It wasn't a particularly exciting business, but certainly a profitable one. Because of this, Rockmash and his wife Stella were able to live in a mansion. Because of this, Rockmash drove a Jaguar. The car had a turbo engine. The car had flames on the sides. Rockmash liked to drive it fast. The Jag was parked outside in a space specifically assigned to Rockmash. Rockmash liked his parking space. Rockmash liked his Jaguar. Sometimes Rockmash stared at it outside his office window just to watch it glisten.

The secretary knocked on the door. She placed the files on the desk. Rockmash yelled at her. She left. Rockmash studied the paperwork. One of the documents needed a signature. He grabbed the phone. He called Dave. Dave was one of the associates. Rockmash shouted at Dave and told him to sign the form. Dave came in and signed it. Rockmash threatened to fire him. Dave left. Rockmash grabbed the telephone. He had court in the afternoon. Rockmash screamed at the judge to confirm the time. The judge confirmed. Rockmash slammed the phone. The door opened. Skippy the lunch boy stepped in. Skippy placed a tuna sandwich on Rockmash's desk. It was exactly what Rockmash had ordered. Rockmash told Skippy that he got his order wrong. Skippy left.

There was a knock on the door.

"What!?" screamed Rockmash. He grabbed a stapler. Squeezed. Poised himself to hurl it. Sometimes Rockmash liked to throw things. Jackson stepped in the office. Jackson was one of the associates.

"Oh," said Rockmash softly. He put down the stapler. "... Hey there, Jackson."

"Hey boss. Here's the documents for court tomorrow."

"Thank you," said Rockmash, accepting the files.

"I'll email the client. You wanna be CC'd on this?"

"Yes please," said Rockmash.

"On it, boss." Jackson turned to leave.

"Have a good day, Jackson." Jackson stepped out, closed the door behind him. Rockmash threw the stapler at the wall. He massaged his temples. Breathed out.

Jackson...

Jackson's wife and kids had died last month. Rockmash couldn't be mean to Jackson. The HR guy had told him this. Rockmash couldn't throw things. Rockmash couldn't make threats. He had to be sensitive. He had to listen. He had to be *nice*. This was not how Rockmash liked to conduct business.

Rockmash sighed. Death. Rockmash had to admit it was an unfamiliar topic. His wife was alive. So were his kids. So were all his friends. Not only were his parents, but so were all four of his grandparents.

The HR guy had suggested that Rockmash attend the funeral. Rockmash attended. It was his first one. The funeral was at Rose Garden Cemetery. That's where Jackson's family was to be buried. The casket hung suspended above a large hole. Jackson gazed deadpan. Not a tear fell. *What gives?* thought Rockmash. *Weren't people supposed to be crying at funerals?* The HR guy informed him that sometimes people express sadness in different ways. And sometimes, they find themselves in something called "denial." Denial was when someone pretended that everything was okay when it wasn't—it was not recommended. The HR guy told Rockmash to be supportive of Jackson, even if he found his sadness to be awkward. As the casket was lowered, Rockmash patted his back. *There there.* Rockmash played nice at the funeral... and had been playing nice ever since!

Because of this, Rockmash was having trouble running his law firm as efficiently as he would have preferred. After the deaths, Rockmash had offered Jackson some bereavement time. A week. A month. A *few* months. Whatever Jackson needed. Whatever Jackson wanted. But Jackson declined. Rockmash offered him family medical leave. Personal time. A sabbatical. All paid. These too, Jackson declined. Apparently, the associate found work to be therapeutic. Tough break. Rockmash didn't know what to do. The man refused to take a break. Business was suffering. The accountants said that it wasn't, but Rockmash knew better.

Rockmash's intercom buzzed. "Your wife's on line one," said the secretary.

Rockmash threatened to demote the secretary to the mail room. He pressed line one. "What is it, Stella?"

"I need you to pick up some stuff on your way home," she said. Rockmash cursed. Made some threats. Called her a filthy name. "Quit your grumbling," said his wife. "I need you to buy some Halloween candy."

Rockmash looked at the calendar. Why, it was only September First! The Halloween season was still a month away! He told Stella this. She said that candy was cheaper this time of year. Starting next month, they jack up the prices. She continued: "And make sure you get it at Wiley's."

Rockmash hung his head. Old Man Wiley. Rockmash couldn't stand him. The old guy ran a convenience store. He carried just about everything. But Wiley was inconsistent. Wiley was unreliable. Wiley was eighty-two years old! Wiley marked his wares with price labels, but then charged you a completely different amount at the register. The guy made you *barter!* In *America*, for goodness sakes! Rockmash and Wiley argued whenever he shopped there. They screamed at each other. They made threats. Stella knew this. But Stella didn't care.

"Fine," said Rockmash, rubbing his temples. "I'll go to Wiley's."

"Get the sour stuff," said Stella. "And some of that licorice. Also, I need you to pick up some pantyhose. My old ones are worn down… Don't forget."

"I won't."

"Last time you forgot."

"No I didn't."

"You forgot," she repeated. "My stockings have holes in them." Stella hung up.

Rockmash closed his eyes. He swallowed some pills. Halloween candy. Rockmash hated the Halloween season. The candy. The decorations. The costumes. His kids running around scaring him. The whole month made him jumpy. Rockmash wished he could skip the season just once. He wished he could somehow fall asleep and not wake up until November.

Rockmash's phone rang. He picked up. "What!?" It was a client. Rockmash threatened to drop his case. He slammed the phone.

A knock on his door. "WHAT DO YOU WANT!!!" Jackson stepped in. "Oh hey there, buddy. How's your day going?"

The work day had ended. Rockmash stood before his Jaguar. The car sparkled in the sunlight. Rockmash admired it. He frowned when he saw that a bird had defecated on the windshield. Rockmash cleaned it up. He got in the car. He turned it over. He flipped on the radio. Heavy metal music blasted out of the speakers. Rockmash cranked up the volume. This was how Rockmash listened to music. He peeled out of the parking lot. This was how Rockmash left work. He sped down the street. This was how Rockmash drove.

It had been a tough day. Jackson was making him crazy! Rockmash had been nice to him for a whole month! How much longer could he keep this up? Jackson was clearly sad that his family had died. The HR guy had told Rockmash that Jackson was "grieving." Apparently there were multiple stages. Denial was one of them. Depression was another. Rockmash had been told that depression was similar to being sad, but usually for longer. After depression, there were other stages of grieving. The HR guy had said that a grieving period could take a few months. Sometimes even longer! Was Rockmash really expected to be nice for *that* long? And don't forget it was September First—the Halloween season was approaching. Somehow Rockmash would have to endure Jackson *and* Halloween.

Rockmash sighed. Again, he wished that he could skip the next few months. At the very least, he just wished that Jackson would take a break. Take some time off to walk the beach. To camp in the woods. To explore some childhood dreams that never got fulfilled. Wasn't that stuff supposed to be good for the soul? Rockmash was certain he had read that somewhere. But alas, this was clearly not to be. Jackson was sticking it out at work. And Rockmash would have to play the part of caring boss.

When Rockmash got stressed, he liked to drive the Jaguar extra fast. He liked to roll stop signs. He liked to run hard yellows, and even soft reds. Sometimes he liked to race. Sometimes he liked to put on a show. This was how Rockmash kept calm. As his Chinese clients would say, this was how Rockmash found his *'chi.'*

And so when the Corvette pulled up next to him at the stoplight, Rockmash didn't hesitate to rev the engine. The Vette revved back. Rockmash studied the vehicle. The windows were tinted. He couldn't see the driver. Not knowing what else to do, Rockmash revved the Jag some more. And that's when the Corvette began to bounce. But it didn't just bounce—it hopped. It jumped! It was clear to Rockmash that hydraulic pumps had been installed on the rival vehicle. He had read about this in trade journals. Hydraulic pumps were all the rage with car enthusiasts and drag-racers. Hydraulic pumps were expensive. Rockmash knew that with sufficient pumps, a car could jump several feet in the air. And that's exactly what the Corvette was doing!

Higher and higher went the Vette. The sled was clearing some sick air. Rockmash had to admit that it was quite a show. Pedestrians clapped. Drivers tooted their horns. A blonde blew kisses. Rockmash hung his head. He didn't have hydraulics. He continued revving his engine. But nobody clapped. Nobody tooted. Nobody blew kisses. Nobody liked his show. Rockmash needed to do something quick.

With the light still red, Rockmash crept into the intersection. He idled in the center. Cross-traffic halted. Pedestrians froze. The Vette stopped jumping. The whole intersection paused. *What was the Jaguar about to do?*

Rockmash smiled. The show was about to begin. He placed his left foot on the brake, then punched the gas with his right. The tires screamed. The smoke poured. The audience cheered. This was a burnout. The wheels spun while the Jag sat stationary. Rockmash continued the show. The intersection became a sea of smoke. Rockmash coughed. His eyes burned. He gripped the wheel. Rockmash went hard over to the left. He released the brake. The Jag peeled out. It leaped forward. It burned donuts in the intersection. Pedestrians clapped. Drivers tooted. Blondes blew kisses. A bouquet of flowers struck the windshield. Around and around went the Jag. This was a good show. A moment later, the Corvette joined him. Their shows merged. Together they scorched donuts. They busted figure-eights. They power-slid. More cheers. More kisses. More flowers.

Rockmash was amped. He was charged. He knew that he must take this show on the road. He straightened the wheel and stomped the gas. The Jag blasted out of the intersection. Tires screeched. Smoke bellowed. People yelled. They called this "burning rubber." They called this "making dust." Rockmash sped forward. The Jag roared. Rockmash watched the needle climb. He checked the mirror. Was the Vette behind him? Would this show continue? Indeed it would, as Rockmash watched the Corvette pull alongside him. Rockmash sped up. The Vette did the same. The shows sped forward.

They weaved through traffic. They slalomed. They ran hard yellows. They ran soft reds. Their needles climbed. Who *was* this man? Rockmash wondered. Where was he going, and where had he been? What kind of stress was he facing at work? Was there a Jackson in his life? Did he loathe Halloween? Did his wife force him to shop for seasonal candy a month early? Did she humiliate him with pantyhose runs? Was he headed for Wiley's too? Rockmash could not say. All he *could* say was that this man's show would not beat *his* show.

Rockmash goosed the pedal. The needle climbed more. An intersection neared. A yellow light turned red. Cross-traffic commenced. This was a hard red. Rockmash punched the gas. The Corvette did the same. They blitzed the intersection. Vehicles screeched. Pedestrians dove. Horns blared. The Jag and the Vette stormed through. They ran the gauntlet. They threaded the needle. They bombed through without a scratch. A pileup mounted in their mirrors. And still they accelerated. And still their shows went on.

More reds. More shouts. More smoke. Wiley's appeared in the distance.

Rockmash floored it.

Teddy was by the magazine racks when it happened. He was fifteen and liked to thumb through the superhero comics at Wiley's after school. That was where he had met Charlotte. She was also fifteen, and enjoyed flipping through the makeup mags. Teddy had been sweet on Charlotte for quite some time. Tragically, the girl had "friend-zoned" him. To be friend-zone was to be without hugs—to be without kisses—to be without hand-holding. To be friend-zoned was to talk. Charlotte talked to Teddy about makeup. Teddy talked to Charlotte about superheroes. This was the extent of their relationship. They talked.

Teddy was talking to Charlotte about superheroes when two cars crashed through the big front window at Wiley's. Teddy pushed Charlotte out of the way. Teddy was a real life superhero.

When the cops and the reporters interviewed him later, Teddy told them that his ankle was twisted a little. But that was okay because the doc said he would be good as new soon. When they asked him if he would be traumatized, he said "not really." You see, later that night after all that superhero business, Charlotte had given him a kiss. Teddy was no longer friend-zoned. In fact, Teddy had a girlfriend now. So, if Teddy thought about it, the incident had really worked in his favor.

Old Man Wiley was behind the register when it happened. He had been haggling with a customer over the cost of a frozen dinner. Wiley had marked the frozen dinner a particular price, but charged the man a different total at the register. You see, Old Man Wiley liked bartering. Old Man Wiley liked confrontations. And even as he shouted at the patron, he wondered to himself why he hadn't retired already. He was eighty-two years old, for goodness sakes! But the reason Wiley had not yet retired was actually quite simple: He didn't have enough money. Many of his contemporaries had IRAs and 401(k)s. They had pensions plans and social security payments. They had savings accounts. Some folks called these "nest-eggs." A nest-egg, Wiley did not have. There were times when he had seriously considered taking a match to his store so he could collect some insurance dough. And once that bread was in his pocket, Wiley would pack up and become the newest resident of Hawaii!

Old Man Wiley was thinking about Hawaii when two cars plowed through his window and the magazine section. A pair of teenagers dove out of the way. The other shoppers scattered.

When the cops and the reporters interview him later, Wiley told them that none of his customers were really injured. One of the teenagers had twisted his ankle, but apparently the doctor had told him that it would be okay. When they asked Wiley if he was sad that his store had been destroyed, he said "not really." You see, Old Man Wiley would be getting a hefty payday from the insurance company. Old Man Wiley would close the store, pack up, and (guess what?) move to Hawaii. So, if Wiley thought about it, the incident had really worked in his favor as well.

Stella Rockmash was at home waiting for her husband when it happened. She had been mending the holes in her stockings. Stella knew that there was a pretty good chance that Rockmash would forget the pantyhose.

She was stitching up the last hole when the phone rang. Apparently, Rockmash had been involved in some sort of car accident. When the cops and the reporters interviewed her later, Stella told them that her husband was in a coma. But that was okay, because the doctors said that he should snap out of it in a couple months. When they asked if she was worried about her husband being in a coma, she said "not really." You see, Rockmash wasn't too hot for Halloween, and had always expressed a desire to skip it. And besides, Rockmash probably would have forgotten the pantyhose anyway. So, if Stella really thought about it, the incident didn't have a whole lot of impact in her life.

Little Bubba was late to the commotion. Little Bubba was nine years old. Momma had given him five dollars to buy some milk. She told him to go to Wiley's. So Little Bubba hopped on his bike and headed that way. Tragically, Little Bubba hated milk. But Momma was the boss, so what was Little Bubba going to do?

Little Bubba pulled up to Wiley's. There was smoke and fire trucks. Little Bubba saw two cars inside the store. The cars were all smashed up. Little Bubba knew that cars didn't belong in a store. Little Bubba knew that something was wrong. A fireman confirmed this when he said that Wiley's was closed and Little Bubba wasn't allowed inside. Then the man put his fire hat on Little Bubba. He let

Little Bubba sit in the truck. Little Bubba was a fireman now! When the cops and the reporters interviewed him later, Little Bubba said he saw fire and a couple of smashed up cars. When they asked if he was scared, he said "not really." You see, Little Bubba wasn't afraid of fire—what scared him more than anything was milk! So, if Little Bubba really thought about it, the incident had really worked in his favor.

Later that evening, the police chief gave a press conference. A car accident had taken place in Wiley's Convenience Store. One man was in a coma, and the other was dead. When the reporters asked the chief if he was sad that the man was dead, he said "not really." You see, the dead man had several unpaid traffic violations, and was rumored to participate in underground dog-fighting. His neighbors said he was scum. His coworkers said he was trash. Even the man's grandmother said that he almost never visited. So, if the chief thought about it, the incident had really worked in everyone's favor.

The cops and reporters interviewed many people that day. The final witness was a man named Jackson. He had been at the register buying a frozen dinner at the time of the incident. Apparently, he was a recent widower. Jackson told the press that his employer Rockmash & Associates would be pausing business to honor their founder who was in a coma. All associates had been furloughed. When the press asked if he was bummed to be unemployed, Jackson said "not really." You see, Old Man Wiley was packing it up, and the landlord was looking for a new tenant. That new tenant would be Jackson. A two month lease had been signed earlier in the evening. Would the location remain a convenience store? asked the reporters. It would not, informed Jackson. It would be a pop-up Halloween shop.

And that is how the pop-up came to be.

The date was September First.

A week after his family had died, Jackson was summoned by the HR guy at work. *Step into my office, Jackson.* A comfy couch and a box of tissues awaited. A conversation ensued. The HR guy informed Jackson that he was "grieving." He told Jackson that there were five stages of grief. One of them was "denial" and another was "depression." The final stage was called "acceptance." Apparently, healing was not possible without it. The HR guy reminded Jackson that he had been offered some bereavement time. It was recommended that Jackson accept it. He suggested that Jackson take some time off to walk the beach. To camp in the woods. To explore some childhood dreams that never got fulfilled. That stuff was supposed to be good for the soul. Jackson declined. He preferred to ignore the pain—to focus on work. The HR guy said that this was "denial."

But then came the incident.

His boss and some other guy had wrecked their cars. Jackson was there to see it. Rockmash was in a coma and the other man was in a casket. A meeting was called at the law firm. The board of trustees gathered. They conferred. *What happens next?* The board voted to put a hold on business. They chose to honor their fallen leader. The office would be shuttered and the staff would be furloughed. Rockmash & Associates would reopen when its founder regained consciousness. The doctors said it could take a few months. The associates would wait.

And so Jackson had found himself with a severance check and an empty house. He considered the HR guy's advice. *Walk the beach. Camp the woods. Indulge a dream.* Jackson didn't care for beaches, and he wasn't too keen on camping. He thought about the third option: Childhood Dreams. Jackson noted the calendar. Summer waned and Fall approached. Halloween was near. Jackson had loved Halloween as a kid. The costumes. The decorations. The atmosphere. Halloween wasn't merely a day, but rather, a season. Not an October went by when Young Jackson didn't...

A) Explore a horror maze.
B) Tour a spooky graveyard.
C) Egg a neighbor's house.
D) Visit a Halloween pop-up shop.

One of the delights of Jackson's childhood was to probe the aisles of those funky little pop-ups that appeared every Fall. Where did they come from? How did they start? And where did they go when the season had passed?

There had been a pop-up that materialized every October, though always in a different location. Young Jackson visited that shop almost every day after school. Most times little Jackson didn't buy anything. How could he? He was just a kid. Young Jackson didn't care. He walked the halls. He perused the shelves. He explored the alcoves. Young Jackson just liked to be around the spectacle. To see it, feel it, breathe it in. As every child knew, Halloween had a certain smell.

Towards the end of the month, his mother allowed him to choose a costume. It was widely known that prices got cheaper as the Big Day neared. Retailers got desperate to sell their wares. *Everything must go!* After a month of careful deliberation, a costume was chosen and purchased. On October Thirty-First the costume made its debut. It was enjoyed. It was feared. It was loved by all. And the next morning it would go in the "Halloween Box." It would disappear as quickly as the pop-up from where it came. By the end of the week, that pop-up was a vacant building. It was a memory. It was a dream. Where did it go? Jackson wondered. All he knew was that it would faithfully, assuredly, and quite magically *re*appear the following season. Young Jackson would count the days.

Kids go through a variety of stages in childhood. *What do you want to be when you grow up, kid?* I wanna be soldier. A baseball player. The President of the United States. These phases come, and these phases go. Young Jackson had a phase himself—it lasted eighteen years. *What do you want to be when you grow up, Jackson?* I wanna own a Halloween store.

But then came college. *Choose a major, Jackson.* Halloween-Store-Ownership was not an option. Jackson learned the concept of careers. He learned the value of money. A Halloween pop-up was not a practical avenue in this pursuit. The dream was gone. Somehow Jackson found himself in Law School. He graduated. Then came Rockmash. Rockmash had a law firm. Rockmash was hiring. Rockmash paid well. Jackson worked for Rockmash. He had worked for him for twenty-one years. Jackson was now forty-six years old. In that time Jackson had married. Jackson had purchased a home. Jackson had raised children. Two boys and a girl.

The dream may have been gone, but not the nostalgia. Jackson passed his love of Halloween to his wife. They passed it on to their children. Not an October went by when the Jackson Family didn't...

A) Explore a horror maze.

B) Tour a spooky graveyard.

C) Egg a neighbor's house.

D) Visit a Halloween pop-up shop.

Jackson took the kids to the local pop-up most days after school. The kids touched. They giggled. They delighted. The dream began to itch again. Start a new career? Begin a pop-up? No, Jackson decided. He had a mortgage to pay. A family to support. Perhaps when he retired? Yes. When Jackson had a little nest-egg and a lot of time. Maybe his kids could help. They could run it together. The Jackson Family Pop-Up.

But now that family was gone. Buried at Rose Garden Cemetery. The family may have been gone, but was the dream? Definitely not, Jackson decided. An hour after the incident—after Wiley had announced his retirement and the building was available to rent—the dream, once again, bubbled to the service. Jackson signed the papers. A two month lease. September First through November First. The building now belonged to Jackson. A Halloween pop-up shop would grace the location. It would open October First.

But how does one start a pop-up? What is the process? Where does one begin? Jackson had a month to figure it out. He hopped onto the computer. He researched.

Jackson quickly learned that with the proliferation of online shopping, brick-and-mortar consumership was on a colossal decline. Ironically, this fact actually worked in his favor. Though true that consumers were ditching traditional in-person shopping, this didn't seem to affect the holiday pop-up business model. In terms of Halloween shopping, consumers still enjoyed the wonder and discovery of a physical location. And with so many vacant properties available, seasonal business owners like Jackson had an abundance of retail space from which to choose. Landlords were practically begging holidays pop-up owners to lease their properties.

Jackson continued his research. He learned that seventy-three percent of Americans celebrated Halloween, spending an average of one hundred dollars every year. In total, Americans were expected to spend close to thirteen billion dollars this Halloween season, with thirty-five percent of that number being spent at a Halloween pop-up store. Apparently, the three biggest pop-up chains were Spirit Halloween, Halloween City, and Halloween Express. The big boys. These were Jackson's competitors. He did the math. These retail chains were expected to make close to five billion dollars in gross this season. Even if Jackson could cut a sliver of that pie for himself, his profits could be massive.

Jackson kept himself busy that September. He obtained both a temporary business license and a seller's permit. He developed relationships with retailers and wholesalers. By the middle of the month, the shipments began to trickle into his store. Costumes. Decorations. Accessories. Candy. Jackson learned that Americans spent an annual total of four billion dollars on candy, four billion dollars on decorations, and four billion dollars on costumes, with over seven hundred million dollars of that costume-money being spent on their pets. Jackson filled the store. He decorated it real spooky. Tombstones. Fog machines. Fake blood puddles. Eerie music. Jackson went all out.

Next came the hiring process. Jackson posted a want-ad. A teenager on crutches came in the store. The kid's name was Teddy. Jackson recognized him. He had seen him at Wiley's on the day of the incident. Apparently Teddy had twisted his ankle saving a beautiful woman. This was a real life superhero. Jackson interviewed him. He thought that Teddy was a good kid. *You're hired, Teddy.* Teddy asked him if he would consider hiring his girlfriend. The girlfriend's name was Charlotte. It was the beautiful woman he had saved. Jackson said, *you bet.* Teddy also asked if Jackson would consider hiring his buddy. The buddy's name was Doug. Jackson agreed to hire the buddy. Jackson's staffing was complete.

On September Thirtieth, Jackson held a staff meeting with his employees: Teddy, Charlotte, and Doug. All fifteen year-olds, all good kids. Jackson told them that they would open for business the next day, October First. *But what's the name of the store, Mr. Jackson?* Jackson said, *step outside.* The staff walked out to the parking lot. A curtain was draped over the storefront. Jackson pulled a string. The curtain came down. The kids' eyes widened. JACKSON FAMILY HALLOWEEN. *But where's your family, Mr. Jackson?* Jackson paused. He smiled and patted his employees' heads—two boys and a girl.

Jackson adjourned the meeting. He dismissed the kids. He told them to do their homework and say their prayers. He encouraged them to get a good night of sleep. *See you tomorrow, Mr. Jackson.* Jackson surveyed his store. Everything was in place. Jackson was ready. He breathed deep, held it in. *What do you want to be when you grow up, Jackson?* I wanna own a Halloween store.

The dream that began over forty years ago was about to come true.

🐦

Little Bubba's momma gave him five dollars. *Bring home some milk, Little Bubba.* Little Bubba hopped on his bike. He pedaled over to Wiley's Convenience Store. The store had gotten smashed up over a month ago. Little Bubba and his family had gone that entire period without milk—it was one of the best times of Little Bubba's life!

Little Bubba reached the parking lot. He stopped short. Gone was the sign that said WILEY'S. In its place, a new sign: JACKSON FAMILY HALLOWEEN. Little Bubba gasped. He knew what this was… It was one of those Halloween pop-up stores! Little Bubba loved Halloween pop-ups. He leaned his bike against a fire hydrant and went inside.

There were decorations and cobwebs and spooky music! The shelves were loaded with costumes and accessories and lots and lots of candy! Little Bubba stormed the aisles. He perused the shelves. He handled the merchandise.

Costumes, candy, lights, smoke, noise machines… This was so much better than milk!

🐦

October started strong. Customers swarmed the pop-up. They flooded the aisles. They cleared the shelves. Jackson struggled to keep the store stocked. And as the month progressed, it only got busier. Halloween pop-up ownership was fairly profitable. Admittedly, it did not pay as well as his law practice, but it was still quite lucrative.

Jackson also realized that the only reason shoppers visited his pop-up and not another was purely due to proximity. His pop-up just happened to be closer to his customers than that of his competitors. In reality, his shop offered nothing that his rivals didn't already carry: costumes, decorations, candy. There was nothing to distinguish his pop-up from another. But that was okay with Jackson. His little shop brought in a steady customer base.

Jackson noticed that there were certain customers that visited the pop-up every day, the most noteworthy of which was a nine year-old boy named Little Bubba. The kid never bought anything—he just wandered the aisles with a curious smile. Jackson decided that he would let Little Bubba pick a special costume on Halloween.

Oddly, Jackson had also taken note of a menopausal woman consistently asking if he sold pantyhose. Of course, Jackson informed the matron that this was a Halloween pop-up, and he did not keep pantyhose in stock. But without fail, the lady would show up the very next day with the same request. Jackson decided that he would order a pair of pantyhose, and sell them to the old bird on Halloween.

In addition to the joys of cash and customers, Jackson also realized that he loved to spend time with his three employees: Teddy, Charlotte, and Doug. These were wonderful kids! They reminded him of—*stop right there, Jackson.* Anyway, with Teddy, Charlotte, and Doug, it was nothing but *Hello Mister Jackson, Yes Mister Jackson,* and *If you please Mister Jackson.* They were so polite! Whoever said that teenagers were rotten?

Teddy and Charlotte were in a relationship. They hugged and held hands. They kissed one another when they thought that Jackson wasn't looking. And Jackson noticed that they never made Doug feel like a "third-wheel." Teddy and Charlotte may have been a couple, but when Doug was around they were a trio of friends. It seemed to Jackson that Doug was a bit shy. Jackson knew that whenever Doug got over his shyness, he would be a terrific boyfriend to some girl out there.

Early on, Jackson had observed that Teddy read superhero comics, and Charlotte read makeup magazines. But deeper in the month, Jackson saw that they were both reading horror novels. Jackson inquired about this... *We do seasonal reading, Mister J.* Jackson got an idea. Costumes and decorations weren't the only seasonal Halloween products. What about books? Were other pop-ups selling them? Jackson had never seen a horror book section in one of them. This could be an untapped niche of the Halloween market.

Unfortunately, Jackson didn't know much about books... But he knew where to find out.

It was the first time he had stepped into a library since college. Jackson had arranged a meeting with the librarian. She was a brunette with creamy skin and an easy smile. Jackson noticed that her ring-finger was bare. Jackson looked away. The librarian told him about Edgar Allan Poe and Stephen King. She told him about H.P. Lovecraft and Ray Bradbury. *But who were Mary Shelley and Bram Stoker?* The librarian informed him. She told Jackson that there needed to be a section for the youngsters: R.L. Stine would be a good start.

Jackson thanked the librarian for the help. She smiled. He got on the phone and put in some orders. Within a week there was an entire aisle devoted to literature: Gothic Horror, Horror Fiction, Science Fiction, Juvenile Fiction, True Crime, Occult, and Folklore. Within a few days, the shelves had been cleared. Jackson put in another order. And then another. It turned out, his rivals weren't selling that stuff. Spirit Halloween and the big boys had missed the boat. By the end of the month Jackson began making lawyer-money!

Raking in the dough was nice, but that's not what this season was about. It was about taking a timeout. To rest. To heal. To explore a childhood dream, just as the HR guy had suggested. But didn't the HR guy say some other stuff? What else? He had said that there were multiple stages of grief, the final one being acceptance. Without acceptance, there could be no healing. Had Jackson really accepted the deaths of—? Jackson realized he couldn't even finish that sentence. It hurt too much. Had Jackson really accepted anything at all? In truth, he hadn't been out to the cemetery since the day they were buried. It was just too painful.

Take it easy Jackson, he told himself. The HR guy had said the grief process could take a long time. You'll visit that cemetery when you're good and ready. Let's just see what the rest of the month brings...

Halfway through October, the doc took Teddy off the crutches. *Go nuts, kid!* The new freedom of movement made his time at the pop-up so much better. Teddy really liked working at Jackson Family

Halloween. It was great working with his buddy Doug. And it was definitely great working with his sweetheart Charlotte, especially after she had dropped the friend-zone. Teddy also liked working for Mr. J. But the thing was, Mr. J was clearly sad about something. And why was the pop-up called "Jackson Family Halloween" when it was only Mr. Jackson? Teddy could draw only one conclusion.

And so he was nice to Mr. Jackson. Like, *really* nice! And so were Charlotte and Doug! In truth, they were all good kids, but even good kids like to misbehave from time to time. Teddy had to admit that he enjoyed throwing eggs, dropping F-Bombs, and even smoking the occasional cigarette. But with Mr. J around, Teddy felt like he and his friends couldn't do *any* of these things.

And so they were nice...

It was Halloween, and Little Bubba pulled up to the pop-up. He leaned his bike against the hydrant like he had every single day that month. He entered.

Little Bubba looked around. Everything in the store was on sale. As every kid knew, the prices all went down on the last day of the season. Little Bubba had five dollars in his pocket. Momma had given it to him to buy milk. But Little Bubba didn't want to buy milk. Little Bubba wanted to buy a costume. All month long, he had had his heart set on this scary monster outfit. Little Bubba liked monsters. He liked monster movies, and recently, since the addition of the reading aisle, he realized that he liked monster books. But tragically, even with the price marked down, Little Bubba saw that five dollars still wasn't enough to buy the monster costume.

Under normal circumstances, Little Bubba would steal the monster costume. He was nine years old, for goodness sakes! He had to be allowed *some* mischief. But the thing was, there was something clearly wrong with Mr. Jackson. Little Bubba couldn't put his finger on it, but Mr. Jackson looked the way Momma did after Daddy died.

And so Little Bubba would not steal the costume today. Instead, he did what he always did, and sat Indian-style in the reading aisle with a monster book in his hands. He had learned early on, that an author named R.L. Stine was pretty good. Pretty spooky. Little Bubba picked a book with a scary monster on the cover.

Some time had passed, and a tap came on his shoulder. Mr. Jackson stood above him.

"We'll be closing up soon, son," said Mr. Jackson. "It's getting dark now. Why don't you pick out a costume and go home?"

Little Bubba stood. He held out his five dollars. "This is all I have, Mister Jackson."

"I'll tell you what," said Mr. Jackson. "If you do something for me, I'll let you have one for free..."

Little Bubba's eyes brightened. "What's that?"

"On your way home, you use that five bucks to get your momma some milk. She's been asking for it all month."

"Yes sir," said Little Bubba.

"Good. Now let's pick you out a costume."

"But I've already got a costume picked out."

"Of course you do," said Mr. Jackson. "Which one?"

"That one," said Little Bubba, pointing at the monster costume.

"Good choice," said Mr. Jackson.

An old woman walked up to Mr. Jackson.

"Excuse me, young man," she said. "I'm looking for some pantyhose."

"Aisle Ten," answered Mr. Jackson.

"Oh," said the lady, surprised. She shuffled off to the aisle.

Mr. Jackson took the monster costume off the rack. Before handing it to Little Bubba, he placed a monster book in one of the pockets. "Run along home, Little Bubba. Happy Halloween... And don't forget the milk."

Little Bubba skipped out the store. He hopped on his bicycle. He stuffed the costume in his bike basket. The colors of the sky were soft. A breeze blew. Dusk approached. Little Bubba pedaled out of the parking lot. Leaves crunched under his tires. In an hour he would be out trick-r-treating with the best costume ever! Tonight, surely, would be the best night ever.

As Little Bubba rode up the street, he turned, looking once more at the pop-up, the sun setting behind it. JACKSON FAMILY HALLOWEEN. Would it be there tomorrow? Little Bubba sensed not. These shops were mysterious like that.

As Little Bubba pedaled, he remembered his promise to Mr. Jackson: milk for Momma. Little Bubba hated milk. But he would do as he was told because Mr. Jackson was clearly a sad man. Little

Bubba would be nice. He would get milk. Maybe chocolate milk? After all, nobody could be *that* nice.

It was dusk, and most of the merchandise had been cleared. Solo costumes hung from racks. Dog-eared books leaned on shelves. Candy bits were scattered on the floor. The cash register was stuffed. It had been a slam bang crazy busy day, and Jackson was tired.

The shop would close permanently this evening. The lease would expire in the morning. Jackson would hire some movers to haul his remaining wares to a storage unit. Would another pop-up sprout next October? Who could say? But unquestionably, it had been a successful month—successful in almost every possible way. Jackson had made money. Jackson had had fun. Jackson had realized a childhood dream. The experience was about as fulfilling as Jackson had always hoped it would be. He was certain that some healing had gone on this season. Perhaps not some of the other stuff that the HR guy had talked about, but that was okay.

Jackson thought about how he would spend his evening after closing the shop. The options were kind of limited. Halloween had been his favorite night as a child—a night of seemingly endless possibilities. Heck, Halloween had been one of his favorite nights as a husband and parent. Jackson reflected. In all his life, not an October went by when he didn't...

A) Explore a horror maze.
B) Tour a spooky graveyard.
C) Egg a neighbor's house.
D) Visit a Halloween pop-up shop.

Jackson smiled. At least he could check off one item from the list. As for the others, he would skip this year. That other stuff just wasn't as fun without family or friends. But that was just fine. Jackson would go home and pass out candy to trick-r-treaters. Contentment could still be found in that ritual. Leave joy to the youngsters.

Jackson eyed his employees. Teddy, Charlotte, and Doug. They were fifteen years old. It was kind of an awkward age, Jackson remembered. Fifteen was too old to trick-r-treat, but far too young to enjoy some of the more grownup aspects of the holiday. But it was

Halloween after all. The night was for everybody. There was plenty of mischief for enthusiasts of all ages.

Jackson addressed the trio: "Why don't you guys head home? I'll close up."

"You sure, Mister J?" asked Teddy.

"Scram," said Jackson, smiling. "Have fun tonight, okay?" He stopped himself short of saying, *Stay safe.*

"Happy Halloween, Mister Jackson!"

The trio walked out, laughing. Jackson sent a wish upstairs. *I hope they have a magical night, full of joy and wonder and mystery,* he prayed. *And also safety,* he added.

Jackson began to clean, then stopped himself. *I'll pay the movers to clean up this mess,* he told himself. *I just want to go home.*

Jackson surveyed the remains of his pop-up—his glorious experiment. He stepped outside, locking the door behind him.

"Wanna hang with us, Mister J?"

Jackson looked up. Teddy, Charlotte, and Doug were huddled by the hydrant, waiting for him. "I—what?" stuttered Jackson.

Charlotte spoke: "Could join us tonight, Mister Jackson?"

Doug stepped forward. "Please..."

Jackson blinked. His chest swelled. His throat lodged. Finally, a whisper: "Yes."

And so the trio became a quartet.

They toured a maze. They crashed a carnival. They told spook stories. They pulled pranks. And even though they were way too old, they trick-r-treated anyway! Some of the houses even gave them candy! And the ones that didn't got egged! They laughed. They screamed. They ran from the cops. At one point Teddy brought out a pack of cigarettes from his satchel. They smoked. They coughed. They dropped F-Bombs. It was one of the greatest nights of Jackson's life.

The four of them pounded the pavement. They scrambled through town. They found themselves standing at the entrance of Rose Garden Cemetery.

"Wanna tour a spooky graveyard, Mister J?" asked Teddy.

Jackson stopped short. He eyed the cemetery walls. *My family,* he thought. *My family is buried there… My wife and children are dead.*

Charlotte touched his arm. "We know, Mister Jackson. We know."

Doug spoke. "We'll go in with you."

Teddy withdrew a rose from his satchel. "It's going to be okay, Mister J. Everything's going to be okay."

Jackson inhaled. Breathed out slowly. He nodded. His three friends guided him forward.

They entered.

It was the morning after Halloween. Little Bubba rode his bike over to the pop-up. Last night had been a blast. His monster costume had been a big hit on the block. When it was all over, Momma had packed up the costume in the Halloween box. The Halloween box was in the garage. Momma said they would take it out next year. Also, Momma had given him five dollars to buy milk.

Little Bubba reached the parking lot. He braked hard. A big truck was parked in front of the pop-up. Men were loading boxes into the back. A big sign hung on the front of the building: FOR LEASE.

Little Bubba didn't know what that meant—only that there would be no more pop-up. He fingered the five-dollar bill in his pocket. He sighed. Maybe there would be another pop-up next year.

For now, he would buy some milk.

Stella Rockmash hovered over an ironing board, pressing the wrinkles on her new pair of pantyhose. She had purchased them the day before at that odd little Halloween shop that used to be Wiley's. Stella had needed a new pair of stockings for quite a while, and she was going to take really good care of these. Normally, her husband Rockmash bought her pantyhose, but he had been in a coma for two months now.

The phone rang. Stella put the iron down. She grabbed the receiver.

"Hello."

"We have good news, Missus Rockmash," said the voice on the other end. It was the trauma coordinator at the hospital. "Your husband is waking up from his coma."

Stella suddenly smelled burning. Something was on fire. She looked down. The iron was burning her pantyhose.

The date was December First. Little Bubba rode his bike down the street. He was heading to the building that used to be a Halloween pop-up. It had been a whole month since he had last visited. Little Bubba had been real busy that November. There was school of course, and baseball, and scouting, but also Thanksgiving. Plus Momma was always sending him out on errands.

A crisp five-dollar bill lined his pocket. Momma had asked him to buy more milk. But first Little Bubba wanted to check out what had become of the Halloween pop-up.

Little Bubba reached the parking lot. A new sign hung from the building: JINGLE SALES—GRAND OPENING.

Little Bubba scratched his head. Why, it was a new pop-up, but for Christmas! Little Bubba loved Christmas! The decorations, the songs, the presents… And also… Christmas cookies! But no Christmas cookie would be complete without, yes, a glass of milk! Little Bubba fingered the five-dollar bill in his pocket.

Maybe milk wasn't so bad after all.

Rockmash was back at the office. The law firm had reopened on November Second, the day after he woke up from his coma. Apparently Rockmash had been out for two months. In fact, he had completely skipped Halloween! Now, it was back to business.

It had been a great day. Rockmash had cussed out a judge, and had blackmailed a few clients. Rockmash swallowed some pills. He looked out his office window. Snowflakes drifted outside. A fresh sheet of snow lined his brand new Jaguar. Rockmash had purchased it the afternoon he woke up from his coma. The last Jaguar had been totaled. Rockmash made sure that the new Jag was accessorized with hydraulic pumps.

A knock came at his door. "What?" screamed Rockmash.

Jackson stepped in. Rockmash cursed him out. He made threats. He called him filthy names.

All of this was okay because the HR guy had given Rockmash permission. You see, it was like Jackson was a new man again. Whatever Jackson had done during his time off had clearly worked. Had he walked the beach? Camped in the woods? Explored a childhood fantasy? Rockmash didn't know. But the HR guy had said that Jackson was now finished "grieving." Apparently, he had gone through all the steps, the last one being something called "acceptance." In fact, Jackson had been spotted hanging out at the library on several occasions, a location in which he had previously never been seen. It was rumored that the librarian was a brunette with creamy skin.

All of this meant that Rockmash could once again run his law firm the way he saw fit. It was business as usual.

Rockmash ordered Jackson to sign some forms. He gave him instructions. He gave him dates. All of this was accomplished with F-Bombs and lots of shouting.

When the meeting concluded, Jackson stepped towards the door.

"Hey Jackson," said Rockmash. Jackson turned. "Welcome back... you scumbag."

Jackson smiled. "Thanks boss." Jackson stepped out.

Rockmash's intercom buzzed. "Your wife's on line one," said the secretary.

Rockmash swore at the secretary. He made threats. He pressed line one. "What is it Stella?"

"I need you to stop off at the store after work," she said.

"What is it this time?"

"Christmas cookies... Also, I need some pantyhose."

Ghosted

Greg Patrick

"Anything could move out there in the darkness, I think. A hook-handed man. A ghostly hitchhiker forever repeating the same journey. An old woman summoned from the repose of her mirror by the chants of children. Everyone knows these stories—that is, everyone tells them, even if they don't know them—but no one ever believes them."-Carmen Maria Machado.

To nervous children daring each other to stray into its forbidding shadow, the decaying mansion stood a gaunt, glowering ruin by moonlight. It was a pellucid specter, haunting the imagination and dreams of generations of neighborhood children. It was an eldritch structure, the product of a mad architect that seemed to construct a frankenhouse of Victorian and gothic styles, of gables, spires, and columns. That urban legend in stone dared the children with an annual rite of passage, to climb the creaking steps to touch the gargoyle knocker with trembling hand and smite the ornate door. Then they prayed nothing would stir in the shadows and answer. It remained a grisly relic that children hastened by in the twilight, shivering as they crossed its misshapen shadow, cast long by the crimson dusk.

"Blood manor" stood aloof from their daily lives in solitary darkness, mummified by swathes of cobwebs like ghostly tapestries.

On moonless nights it appeared more mausoleum than manor. It was rare to find a "ghost house" that lived up to its name, yet that "urban legend" in crumbling mortar, had a dark past that seemed to whisper its disembodied confession with the wind that hissed through its broken gables. Not all of it was mere lore, a certain young man had found. While cleaning up the old attic Patrick, a local high school student had found yellowed newspapers headlined "murder house" detailing the horrors investigators found inside. The prime suspect was never found.

Another man convicted as his accomplice was sentenced to the chair, tearfully denying his guilt. He swore he did not remember anything.

Later Patrick researched for a class assignment. Delving in the town's historic archives, he was chilled to uncover more of the history of "red manor." Patrick pored over grim headlines on yellowed pages and old faded images of crews taking cartloads of bones from the garden. A man was pictured being taken away smiling madly, while an elderly woman stood defiantly at the threshold holding a tommy gun and meat cleaver. That standoff would end with her falling in a hail of bullets, still scarring the walls, a bloody end to a deranged murderess. The article left little to the imagination, detailing the horrors investigators found inside. The manor was known eternally for its infamous tenant, but it had traded hands many times. Even the most unwitting tenant seemingly found themselves infected by the evil that seemed to ooze venomously from the walls.

Rumor and urban legend swirled around the manor like a reveling or danse macabre of dark ghosts haunting imaginations and dreams. It bore a charmed afterlife, enduring a number of plots to demolish it and whatever secrets remained buried under its grim foundations. That ominous shadow was cast long in the crimson dusk and passers-by shivered in its shadow as they hastened by that foreboding presence in the falling night. It was all something older generations never spoke of to the younger. "Life goes on" their elders repeated stoically.

To that end, Patrick hurried to don his costume for his eagerly anticipated Halloween date night. It was a Jon Snow costume he had been working on for weeks. Unbeknownst to him as he adjusted his costume in the mirror, that night his path would cross with the mansion once more and he would again ascend those steps to challenge whatever haunted the grim bastion of nightmares.

Patrick had taken the long way back from school that chill Autumn day to avoid the mansion, yet it seemed all roads led back to its ominous shadow. He found himself inexplicably facing the manor as if standing before an old enemy forcing a confrontation with a reluctant adversary...*as if it wouldn't let him go*...Patrick shook his head as he observed the graffitied walls along his path. The enigmatic vandal behind the display had proven elusive, despite the generous award for his capture. The vandal had graffitied his trademark cryptic symbol always painted in sanguine red. On his way to the meeting spot to a much-anticipated date, Patrick paused suddenly as his eye caught an enticing shimmer spotlighted by a lamppost. A mysterious cache of candy beckoned invitingly in front of the uninhabited murder house. His date's favorite kind of candy he observed. And it was untouched strangely.... or predictably so. The house was infamous.

"Take one," the sign offered with a winking jack o lantern lit on the table.

An ominous foreboding gave Patrick pause. Then something else drew his gaze. He cursed. The vandal had struck again. The new graffiti had been painted red in the blood of a ritually killed puppy.

"Sick devil whoever he is," Patrick growled.

A graffitied jack o lantern face smiled back red at him gloatingly, its seemingly following him. The paint seemed fresh. Patrick wondered if he was being watched by the vandal from the shadows. Suddenly he thought he heard the hiss of a spray can. Then he spied a stranger watching. He followed the dark shadowy figure furtively before shouting and giving chase. The vandal eluded him. The stranger seemed to dissolve into the wall known eternally for its evil tenant. And in the nights leading to Halloween, he was haunted by recurring nightmares with the mansion at the center of it like a dark lord enthroned in shadow beckoning for him.

As Patrick blinked in the bright dawn, he looked in bemused wonder at the grisly spectacle before him. As if a mad carnival rolled into town, the leaf-strewn street of the quaint picturesque village seemed to transform overnight in ghoulish metamorphosis into a riotous necropolis with skulls grinning and witches leering at every corner and lamppost. Like nocturnal or crepuscular scavengers emerging from their dens to feed, costumed children raced from their homes and gathered in the dusk to infest the streets with costumes representing the denizens of Halloween lore. Between the phantasmagoria of lavishly skull and witch-festooned houses lit welcomingly to bands of trick or treaters, was a dark gap where the long abandoned Victorian mansion, a gaunt shadow of its former stately grandeur, slowly rotted. It was shunned of course, hurried past to another lit house. Meanwhile Patrick stood in solitary vigil.

"Sweet for the sweet" he had rehearsed pocketing the gold-wrapped candy he found before the "red mansion". Looking across the dreamscape of lanterns and the interplay of light and shadow he envisioned her, Clare, the night of their first dance. It was at a themed masquerade ball. He felt painfully awkward yet rallied enough courage to ask her for the first dance of the night. Patrick sighed at how radiant she looked in her golden gown and cascade of red hair. A vision of beauty behind green eyes.

He remembered the softness of the fabric of her gown as he held her tenderly. Song lyrics became incantation. Steps were lost in the sensation of flight. Candles became constellations in the turns and sweeps of her gown and hair. They had danced every song together, losing all track of time till the lights went on and he escorted her outside and they laughed under the stars. He awoke to the present and he checked the time on his phone again. He desolately imagined her laughing at him with her popular friends. He lingered there by their appointed meeting spot by a lonely street lamppost. In his lonely vigil, he listened to the incessant creaking of decorative skeletons swaying from the bare branches of an old sycamore. The streets became eerily quiet otherwise.

"Where is everybody?" Patrick wondered.

He paced restlessly as the minutes then hours crawled by like a procession of insects crawling over his skin. His heavy sigh steamed in the chill air. He stood awkwardly. He distracted himself with trivia, morbidly reflecting on the metamorphosis of Halloween from an ancient feast ritual to a wild party night. Suddenly he was jarred from his musings by a goblin-masked figure. It was just some impish brat with his marauding gang of trick or treaters. He jeered, pointing. They howled with a chorus of laughter.

"Look at that guy just standing there all night! Ha-ha!" Their mocking cackling echoed back at him in passing as they ran past euphoric with the thrill of their hunt for candy. Dead withered leaves fell as if hailing him in mockery. Their cackling trailed away and the streets became eerily quiet.

Where did they all go? Had he really been there that long?

Patrick paced restlessly. The lamplight sputtered then went out, leaving him in darkness. Tempted to stress eat, he unwrapped the candy he found in front of the mansion. Then something strange caught his eye. It was handwriting in red on the pale underside of the golden wrappers. With startling recognition Patrick realized it was in Clare's handwriting. He recognized it from notes they passed in class. It had a simple desperate message:

"Help me. Please!"

Suddenly the phone lit up. He jumped. It was her finally.

What's this? A video?

150

Patrick raced the dying bars on his phone, texting frantically…He downloaded a video. He was horrified at footage of her trussed up in some warehouse-like chamber, struggling against sinister figures.

There were other messages…A photo of her chained in a dark room.

A prank? No. The fear in her eyes was real. She wasn't acting. That was real terror in her eyes.

"Where are you?" he texted.

"You know…" came the reply.

Then a picture of the mansion and a sinister figure standing in front of it.

"Think you can rescue her?"

A laughing face and devil emoji appeared.

For the girl of his dreams, Patrick would face nightmares. He ran for the mansion. In his memory the decaying mansion had always stood a gaunt ruin by moonlight yet by some eerie metamorphosis, some eldritch trickery woven by a master illusionist's art, of moonlight and shadows, the manor's facade rejuvenated to an opulent stately mansion by some eerie resurrection. Shadow and moonbeams caressed its newly restored walls as "the red mansion" loomed before him in lordly malevolence. Patrick had seen the symbol graffitied on random walls in the days leading to Halloween. Now he stood looking at it painted gigantically on the gate that was left ajar, swaying and creaking in the wind.

Patrick heard what sounded like ritual drums in the dark depths under the floorboards. He drew two butcher knives embedded in the jack o lanterns, their carved smiles leered crimson in reply. Patrick clutched the blades between his fingers like metallic claws ready to slash at anything skulking and lunging from the shadows. Patrick found himself in the midst of a sumptuous Edwardian era drawing room.

He found shelves brimming with occult books. He almost retched as he realized some were bound in stitched human skin. Old newspaper front pages reporting on the news of the mansion murders were framed proudly on the walls as if boasting. Deciding on a bold approach rather than stealth, Patrick strode through the labyrinthine catacombal tunnel. Patrick pulled a dark medieval chest plate from the wall and donned it. He wrenched a torch from the wall to guide his way, as well as a sword from the dark gauntlet of one of the suits of armor lining the halls.

"Winter is coming bitch," he growled.

Patrick recognized the music that had played when he had summoned up his courage to ask the girl of his dreams to a dance. It was being eerily played on an antique gramophone as he infiltrated the shadowed halls. He had been expecting a dilapidated abandoned house littered with years of broken beer bottles and thoroughly vandalized. Instead, it was sumptuously furnished with antiques. "Help!" was written on the wall in red letters. Patrick found a heart graffitied on the wall and touched it. A portal opened into a dark passageway descending into the sinister depths. He felt inhaled by darkness as he ventured further through the serpentine passageway. It seemed as if the mansion had been built over an elaborate subterranean cavern. The fluttering torchlight illuminated strange carvings on the wall like ancient petroglyphs. Patrick strayed further as his way slithered through a series of chambers.

Smuggler tunnels from prohibition, he guessed...*or something more sinister?*

Patrick recoiled at the grisly sight of the corpses of girls in brightly colored gowns like exotic tropical butterflies pinned as specimens to the wall. It was like some mad huntsman's trophy hall. He scanned their faces searchingly as the torchlight fell on their pale bloodless features. He was dreading seeing a familiar face among them, yet Clare was not there. Then he heard it, the eerie maddening sound of hearts beating in quickening palpitations...pulse quickening to rapid tempo.

Patrick recognized the symbols painted in red on the wall as the ones graffitied on the walls of the vaulted chamber. Among them were the red handprints by desperate captives trying to claw their way out of that hideous torture chamber. He suddenly gasped as he saw Clare. Her arms were splayed against a gargoylian statue like a gothic idol on a candle-lit altar. Her transfixed eyes saw through him. She was unresponsive. Patrick severed her bonds as he heard chanting in a strange tongue drawing nearer.

"I'm getting you out of here. Lean on me," Patrick urged.

Clare was frail and disoriented from enduring some horrific ordeal. Suddenly the gowned corpses pinned to the walls opened their eyes, seemingly revived and screamed as if in grisly alarm.

Confronting him was a blind-folded crone. The wizened figure pointed an overgrown curved fingernail like a talon and emitted a cringing wordless screech that echoed through the hallway in choir. Shapes moved then with a simian gait, closing in. He could make out lurching misshapen forms and grotesque hybridized features as if some mad scientist had bred some cave-dwelling creature to guard his chambers. Patrick ignited the torch and suddenly gasped as the deformed servants of these underground halls massing in the vulnerable interval of darkness were revealed. They were reaching for him with taloned hands.

Patrick brandished the torch to hold their pursuers at bay. They hissed and recoiled. The serpentine corridor echoed with their screeching echo locative cries, seeking them in the darkness. The torchlight cast the corpse-like pallor of their faces in hellish crimson. Their soulless eyes gleamed red in reply to the flame like smoldering embers. Patrick cast down the torch to cover their escape. Flames rose enveloping one in midstride. The others shrank back with a chorus of hideous cries. Patrick and Clare raced the flames and ran the gauntlet of cave-dwelling creatures lunging from the shadows. Patrick slashed machete-like through a mass of cobwebs shrouding the walls like ghostly banners of a netherworld. Patrick and Clare emerged from the grisly abattoir as the floor collapsed behind them and they burst into the night, inhaling the night air greedily.

Patrick was haggard and disheveled. He halted at the gothic threshold as he and Clare stood against a background of flame. The mansion burned behind them like an enormous bonfire. A horrific scream filled the air as if a living thing burned in agony. A solitary figure confronted them. The stranger had just turned from graffitiing his trademark symbol on the wall across the street. The vandal traced a red Cheshire cat smile and eyes on his blank soulless featureless darkness yawning under a black hood. The grin appeared like a reopened wound bleeding out.

"*Ah. now I see you,*" the vandal smiled.

His hissing voice was like a serpent's coils slithering over dry dead grass or flies buzzing around carrion.

"*I trust the hosts of the manor have not been remiss in their hospitality and you feel quite fortunate to be alive. Alas, I assure you that sense of relief is premature and your doom is quite imminent indeed. An avid follower of my art it would appear. Well tonight my dear friend, you will be witness to my final masterpiece. In fact, you will be quite instrumental in it...far from a mere spectator,"* the vandal said.

The trickster locked eyes with Clare's.

"Now, my acolyte," he commanded.

Suddenly Patrick felt Clare grasp his hair from behind and place a knife at his throat.

"The offering is ready master," Clare whispered in a ventriloquized transfixed voice.

"What are you doing?" Patrick cried out in alarm.

"You know nothing Jon Snow," the vandal mocked.

"She was never the intended victim. She was always merely the bait to lure you in. Yes, you were led astray by love. And to what end you wonder?

You see the ingredients were listed very specifically. One heart betrayed in love. That is where you come in. And don't bother to struggle in your last moments. You are quite outnumbered," the vandal smirked.

Silhouetted against the fire-reddened moon the trickster raised his arms as if in the act of conjuring and a horde of figures lurched from the darkness as if restless shadows were granted form and hideous face. Ranks of masked figures massed at his back in a chanting horde. They spread out, encircling them, like a besieging army. They clutched scythes, carving knives, and sickles. The blades shimmered crimson by the firelight as the mansion erupted in an inferno of flame. The vandal raised his dark-gloved hand to signal a halt. His possessed thralls were chattering like nocturnal insects. As if ritually- masked worshippers, the trick or treaters gathered with bags of offerings. They gleefully forced a candied apple into Patrick's mouth.

"So many hungry mouths to feed and such ravenous ones. There there my brood. I promise you a true feast of Samhain. But hark. Whatever is that sound?" the vandal asked.

Meanwhile in the chasmous depths under the mansion, a myriad of living things stirred as flames devoured the manor. A vast colony of bats infesting the subterranean darkness were roused by the fire. The darkness was lit in harsh crimson light and their eyes shimmered in the firelight. First instinctively alarmed, then their senses tortured as they burned and choked by the smoke pouring into their lair. The first Patrick heard of them was a shrill chattering, merging in a tidal-like roar. Suddenly Patrick shielded Clare from a showering of sparks and burning smoking debris as the horde of bats erupted explosively into the night like a torrent of underworld flame. Uttering shrill cries of agony, the bats rose in a great undulant wave towards the beckoning orb of the moon.

The rush of night wind extinguished some yet many were aflame, their membraned wings burning and constellating the night. They hovered in a maelstromic phantasmagoric mass of crimson and black, obscuring the crimson orb of fire-reddened moon and casting onlookers in an interval of darkness. The vandal laughed in maniacal rapture as several fell dead in mid-flight as they burned alive, trailing flame as if hailing him in nightmarish tribute. He basked in the crimson resplendence cast by the blaze.

"Trick or treat. Trick or treat. Give us something good to eat," a disembodied choir haunted the air.

"They all serve me now. At a word I can have them dismember you, yet I need you intact for now…Yes, they are entirely under my power…Perhaps a demonstration?" the vandal smiled.

The vandal pointed at two masked figures in the mob. They bowed and broke ranks.

Cheered on by the others they staggered straight into the flames to jubilant cries.

"Not to flaunt my power…but enough of false modesty…" the vandal boasted.

"This is a dream. This has to be a dream!" Patrick gasped.

"You can keep telling yourself that mortal…It was a quiet Halloween night much like this one when the eccentric master of Red Hall manor held a séance. He dabbled in the occult… a bored amateur merely, yet his coven delved far too deeply into the ancient ground's secrets. As they were playing at necromancy in the underground chambers of his manor they awoke something that night from its ancient slumber, then sealed it back with ritual sacrifice vainly believing they could harness and wield its power. They flattered themselves. That dark spirit gorged on their souls and infected them with its evil and insatiable hunger for victims. It lay dormant, all those years till I awoke it again and the portal to hell was reopened in all its fiery glory and power! Behold. Make way for your queen!"

"Hail! Hail!" they chanted.

They passed through the masked ranks. The torchlight shone sanguine red on their grotesque features.

"O grim lord Samhain accept this sacrifice, we humbly beseech thee," they uttered in invocation.

"*Test the blade for sharpness,*" the trickster bade.

A masked trick or treater offered his arm. Clare opened an incision as he laughed.

"*Sharp indeed. Let the ritual commence unhindered. Bring forth the sacrifice my acolyte!*"

She had donned a ritual mask of flayed skin like a grisly executioner's mask.

"*Priestess, bring me his heart!*" the vandal commanded.

"Sacrifice! Sacrifice!" they chanted as they writhed in wild atavistic rapture, cavorting against a foreground of flame as if dancing before a towering bonfire. He handed her a golden rune-inscribed sacrificial dagger.

"*I assure you that your mortal weapons are quite useless against me.*" He spread his arms exposing his torso.

"*See for yourself. Allow me to be sporting. You may retrieve your blade,*" the vandal offered.

Patrick stabbed and stabbed desperately to the vandal's mocking laughter.

"*Hahaha. Tickles. You, see? I am entirely invulnerable to your weapons. You imagined this was a duel. Do not flatter yourself. You are merely an offering. Now my thralls. Take him,*" the vandal commanded.

Patrick was grabbed and carried in a chanting torch-lit procession to a crude altar. A goat mask was forced on his face. He saw his own terrified eyes mirrored in the varnished blade. They forced a candied apple into Patrick's mouth.

"*So many hungry mouths to feed this feast of Samhain…and such ravenous ones. Fret not young master. You will be avenged. Your lady will perish screaming once she holds your sliced out heart dripping in her palm,*" the vandal gloated.

"*Hasten the hour grows late. Do not tarry,*" the vandal urged.

"You can stop this, Clare. Wake up!" Patrick urged.

Patrick looked pleadingly at her face, yet she was entirely mesmerized and unmoved. He cringed and closed his eyes bracing for the agony of the curved blade slashing through his flesh. It never came. Her hand faltered as the dagger hovered over his beating heart, as the first tolling of the steeple bell for midnight echoed sonorously over the rooftops.

It shook her from whatever trance held them all. The vandal screeched like a carrion bird deprived of carnage to scavenge by an advancing lion's roar. The mob shuddered convulsively as an impact ripple swept through them. Like a restless menagerie of dark spirits breaking loose at feeding time and consuming their captor they dropped their weapons and collided with him in wild disarray.

"I will not be thwarted by some lowly mortal! I will sacrifice you myself without these thralls!"

Gripping a reaper's scythe, the vandal launched at him with startling feline-like agility, evading Patrick's knife slashes. Finding an opening Patrick thrust the knife to the hilt with grim finality. The trickster's cry betrayed pain and his waning power. Its red smile shuddered like a speared eel as it faded. Like something cold-blooded and mortally wounded it still sought to kill his slayer in his thrashing death throes.

"I will carve you like a jack o lantern!" the vandal hissed.

Patrick then thrust a torch, setting his cloak on fire. Now enveloped in flame, the demonic figure charged at Patrick like a red ghost. Then as the last bell tolled midnight skeletal clawed hands reached for Patrick. The vandal drew back a hand to swing the scythe and decapitate his nemesis only to disintegrate in midstride. The scythe chimed on the pavement.

Meanwhile the trickster's "servants" exhaled dark vaporous mist that took human form before dissolving amorphously. The exorcised trick or treaters milled around, aimless and disoriented. Approaching sirens were heard. Patrick placed a coat over Clare's shoulders.

"Let me take you home," Patrick said softly.

He escorted Clare into the bright dawn.

Lorelei

Jason Battle

The spooky house at the end of the lane is mine.

I live behind the dirty windows, the peeling paint and the overgrown landscaping, with shrubbery whose twisted branches threaten to strike out to grasp anyone brave or foolish enough to venture to the crumbling front porch.

It's not that I'm an evil hag, drooling in anticipation for a juicy schoolchild to be shamed into ringing my doorbell by an undefeatable double dog dare of their peers, I just don't give a fig. I've become settled in my ways, and those are the ways of a forty-one-year-old bachelor with a dead end, mind-numbingly boring IT job, no prospects of female companionship, and an ever-expanding waistline, accentuated by a burgeoning addiction to the convenience of frozen pizza and easy access to hazy IPAs.

I'm actually quite a friendly guy. Not jovial, mind you, I'm not bloody Santa Claus. But I volunteer once a week down at the local animal shelter and buy a box or two of Thin Mints from the girl scouts, when they're hawking their wares outside the grocery. In fact, just earlier, after sleepwalking through another day at the office, I took out my garden shears and pruned the shrubbery that had grown wild enough to obstruct the steps to my front door because today is Halloween.

Several groups of kiddies in their store-bought costumes had rung my doorbell, gleefully making their standard request for candy before running back to their parents. But these few throngs of Pokémon clad adolescents were not nearly enough to warrant the purchase of five bags of peanut butter cups, certainly not at seven dollars apiece.

I was midway through my third pint, silently cursing the Hershey Company for their obvious corporate inflation exploitation and seasonal price gouging, when my doorbell chimed its generic two-toned ringtone.

As I passed through the kitchen, through the rear sliding door I noticed the sky had darkened and the digital clock on my microwave read quarter to seven, leaving just fifteen minutes until the township's trick-or-treating hours ceased and the leftover candy would become my responsibility. Grabbing a fresh bag of peanut butter cups, I ripped it open, spilling half of the contents on my foyer's floor. After a muttered expletive, I opened the door expecting the normal inquiry: 'Trick or Treat!'. What I got was something completely different.

Tears and snot oozed down the face of an elementary school aged girl, no higher than my waist, who stood on my front stoop. A plastic grinning pumpkin, overflowing with sugary loot, and a rubber mask hung loosely in her small, delicate hands. Her costume was that of a skeleton, white bones depicted on a black field, trousers and a shirt.

She looked up at me with a trembling chin, furrowed eyebrows and wide, pleading puppy dog eyes, "Can you help me?"

My initial impulse was the throw a couple peanut butter cups at the girl, turn off my lights and finish my pint, assuming the situation had resolved itself but, instead, I heard myself say, "What's wrong?"

She must have expected the same thing because, her face lit up and a glimmer of hope flashed in her eyes, "My brother and his friend played a mean trick on me. We were tricking or treating together, and I went up to a house to ring their doorbell and got candy but when I turned around, they were gone. I looked all over for them but couldn't find him anywhere. Now I'm lost and I don't know how to get home."

"That's horrible." I actually meant it, the girl looked like such a sweet, innocent thing. But just to make sure, I leaned out of the doorway a bit to peer up and down the street, straining to see a teenage rogue hiding behind my bushes or tailing his sister from afar.

"Yes, he's so mean," her voice changed midsentence, it deepened and was full of malice. "He's probably at his friend's house playing Fortnite by now."

"Tell you what," a proper plan began to form in my head. It began with me making a call and reuniting the girl with her mother. Then, I would watch the inevitable punishment laid out to the wicked brother. And who knows? Perhaps said mother is single, svelte and lissome, and generous with her gratitude. "Why don't you come in and I'll give your mother a call? She could come and pick you up."

She looked at me with a probing glance, "I don't know my mommy's number. I know we were supposed to remember it from school, but I forgot it." Then her face lit up, "but I remember our address, it is one-two-one-five Sugar Maple Street, Rolling Hills, Illinois, USA. I live there with my mommy and brother."

Slow recognition that my fantasy of the indebted single mom filtered through my fading IPA haze, and I asked her to repeat the address to me. When she did, there was a flicker of recognition as I realized that her house was no more than two blocks away, five minutes at most, an insignificant investment for such a potentially lucrative payoff.

"I can walk you there," I hurriedly grabbed an old pair of tennis shoes and shoved my feet into them without bothering with the laces.

Before leaving my house, I flipped off the patio lights and my entryway was instantly flooded in shadow. My key scraped against my front door's deadlock as my eyes adjusted to the darkness and I struggled to locate the keyhole.

"Thank you so much mister...", her voice trailed off, waiting for me to fill in the space.

"Dan, you can just call me Dan, no mister needed," I tested my front door, ensuring it was secure and walked down my front path with the girl in tow, the chilled air instantly made me regret not bringing a windbreaker. "What's your name?"

"Lorelei. My mommy says it comes from a place called Germany, where some woman lived long ago on an island in a big river," Lorelei scurried to catch up to me, so unused to accompanying one with such short strides that I had outpaced her once I hit the sidewalk. "My mommy is going to be so happy that you brought me home, maybe she'll give you cookies. My mommy makes the best cookies."

The possibility of her mother's cookies, or other, more carnal sweets, lightened my step and I had to restrain myself from breaking into a jog.

We passed beneath the sole streetlight on the way, and it was only then I noticed how the sky had darkened. Many of the houses on the block had extinguished their porchlights, signaling the end of their Halloween commitment and left the street to the will of the shadows. On either side of us, the tall, narrow houses' eaves stabbed into the indigo sky, daggers cutting through dusk. Even the insects had relented in their incessant whirring and the ever-present hum of traffic from the main road nearby seemed swallowed by the murky atmosphere.

I hesitated, doubt bored into my being from somewhere within, and a pinch within my gut held me in place. There was no one else about in the neighborhood, an oddity even at this time of night. Usually, one could count on cars driving through the area or people sitting on their front porch, indulging in idle gossip, and I was near to suggesting that we turn around when Lorelei, with her innocent, cute eyes and regal cheekbones, stopped beneath the fluorescent glow.

"We don't live here," Lorelei shivered, perhaps from the cold, perhaps from the nagging doubt that crept into my being.

"Just catching my bearings," I lied and then continued walking. I took a few strides with the girl beside me and then felt something warm and clammy wriggle its way into my hand. It was Lorelei's hand and as I looked down at her, the silver glow of the moon gleamed in her shining turquoise eyes.

"You have blue eyes," I stammered, instantaneously unsure of the appropriateness of the statement.

"Yes, my mommy says she gave them to me, she has hair like me too," we came to an intersection and crossed to the other side. We followed a side street which I knew from my frequent walks was Sugar Maple, the street where Lorelei's house was. "She told me when she was back home, people used to come and take pictures of her.

"Like a model?" I began to feel stressed, a model would probably be out of my league, no matter how grateful she may be.

"Sort of," Lorelei's hand tightened, her grip was firm. "She does other things too. She sings and she knitted my costume. Well, not the mask, but the shirt and pants."

"That's impressive. It looks like it came from a store," I couldn't recall the details of the skeleton outfit she wore, but distinctly remembering it recognizable as what it was intended. "Skeletons, they are spooky, right?"

"Not really," Lorelei's sigh was that of a deflated teenager's ennui. Her expression lightened as she remembered something, "in one of my readers, one about mythology, I learned about something called a Siren, do you know that one?"

The buxom, leather clad episodes of Xena: Warrior Princess being the extent of my knowledge of the subject, I shook my head at her question. She sensed my ignorance and carried on.

"Well, supposedly the Siren lived by a river and was so pretty that men would go crazy when they saw her. When she sang, her voice would paralyze them," Lorelei tugged at my hand, urging me on as we continued our way to her house. We were getting close. We passed a mailbox which read the number: 1211, and I knew her house must be but two doors down.

"What happens then?" I had to jog to keep up with her, so eager she was to get home as she must have recognized her neighbor's houses.

"She has long, curved claws and she grabs them," Lorelei made a gesture with her free hand, like a raptor snatching its prey from the air. "Then, her mouth is full of pointed fangs, and she eats them, face first."

"That is scary," I noted as we passed another mailbox and then we stood in front of her house.

It didn't look any different from any of the other houses in the subdivision, one of the four or five different designs that had been hastily built in the latter half of the last century, this one a single story, with a recessed entryway, hidden from the street,

"Come on," Lorelei gave my hand an encouraging squeeze. "She'll be so happy to meet you. She likes nice guys, like you."

The intimidating image of a tall, blonde runway model gave me pause, but I took a deep breath, steeled my nerves, and followed her towards the front door.

There was no light on the patio, and I was submerged in inky blackness. From inside the house, I thought I heard the muffled bubbling of flowing water. A faint stench of decay touched my nostrils. My forehead began to perspire at the same time my hands became numb.

Despite the solid gloom, Lorelei found the doorbell with little effort and a lively chime rang out. She gave me a reassuring smile, nothing but her gleaming white teeth visible in the gloom, "my mommy's going to love you."

I was about to ask Lorelei her mother's name when the door opened, and a strikingly beautiful woman stood before me. Before I had a chance to introduce myself, she opened her mouth and sang. Her song was the cry of unfathomable anguish and forlorn hope. It reverberated in my skull and shattered my eardrums. Then, I felt the pierce of long, curved claws and I was drawn to a mouth full of pointed fangs.

Summoning Candles

Fay Jekyll

"To summon a demon requires a three-part ritual; a summoning rune, a candle to light the path and lift the veil from the otherworld and the true name of your chosen demon...On Hallows Eve, the veil betwixt worlds lifts its shroud. On this night, demonic forces be at their strongest and in their masses.
-Demons and Their Corporeal Uses, 1223 AD.
"-And for goodness' sake, don't light the summoning candle on a shagpile carpet."
-Summoning Demons for Dummies, 1991 AD.

"We can't have a Halloween like last year. We simply can't," Charon insisted, drumming his skeletal fingers on the grey slab tombstone, which had been heightened to form a conference table.

The spirits beyond the castle ruins, he thought, were restless, and *not* in a good way. He was under strict instructions from the Big Man downstairs to encourage the troops for their next haunting.

Charon eyed the thinning veil nervously, for it was him alone who could see its shimmering façade between the haunting hordes and reckless living. Halloween would be upon them in mere hours.

"Yeah, did you see those haunting stats?" the Red Lady asked, appearing silently in a fine mist of crimson blood by his side. With a black sleeve, Charon nonchalantly wiped away a speck of blood from his minutes. "Not one of our boys from the zombie horde made it out in a full corporeal form. They're going to be *so* tedious. We should never have put them in charge of the D.R. department."

"D.R?" a familiar voice asked, appearing before them.

"Demon Resources," Charon clarified to his old friend, Mephistopheles, to whom he extended a hand of welcome. He felt the squelch of sloughing skin slap against his exposed phalanges. "Welcome, Mephisto."

"I hope this plan you've been implementing is a solid one, Charon," he sighed, heaving his rotten mass into what Charon assumed was a sitting position around the tombstone. "We can't have a Halloween like last year," the blob grunted, mirroring his sentiments. "I've got twenty-six legions out there itching to give a Halloween haunting."

"Don't you worry," Charon said. A fourth member of the board meeting had yet to arrive. He was the most terrible of all, and apparently, Charon thought while griding his dry teeth, the most tardy.

"Ah, *here* he is!" Charon cried enthusiastically. "Everyone, welcome the third Eldrich Terror. He specialises in Modern Humanity Studies, don't you know?"

The many legged eldritch terror slunk in under then crumbling stone archway and perched himself considerately beside Charon, crossing ankle over ankle over ankle.

"Here's been our problem," Charon said, leaning in and launching right in with the nitty-gritty. "Look right here. The humans use these things on their computers called 'hashtags'... Hash?...am I saying that right?"

The eldritch terror nodded it's horned head solemnly.

"What is this thing?" The Red lady inquired, lifting a tattered wedding veil from before her empty eye sockets.

"They call it... The Void," Charon said ominously.

"Actually, it's called the internet. And it's on a *phone*," The Eldrich Terror clarified. "See how the hashtag 'Halloween,' has declined these past five years?"

"What? Why? Where's it gone?" the Red Lady demanded, her voice creeping an octave higher. Charon interjected before it reached the infamous banshee wail.

"The hashtag taking over our Halloween market has been replaced with, and I know this may seem alarming...hashtag 'Fall Girl Aesthetic.'"

Charon took the black screen from the tombstone slab, tapping his fingers on the screen. His bone clicked against the glass, repeatedly and with growing frustration.

"Why doesn't this infernal device do anything when I click it?" he hissed.

"Oh! Um, sorry." The Eldritch Terror sucked a breath in and scrunched his nose with the dawn of an awkward realisation. "It's fingerprint activated," he muttered.

166

Charon nodded solemnly as the Eldrich Terror typed for him. "Jeez, this thing is *really* evil. You outdid yourself, Barry."

"His name is *Barry*?" Mephisto asked, obnoxiously loud; his flabby, sloughing lips unable to drop to a subtle whisper. Charon wished he had eyes so that he might roll them.

"No, my proper name is Baralaxidegon, Evil Incarnate and Destroyer of all Men, The Third. But it's too long to write out in the minutes," the Eldritch Terror said politely, as the blank screen of the cellular device acquired from the living realm sprung to life on the tombstone. "Barry will do."

"Thanks man," Charon muttered appreciatively, flexing his wrist. Writing was deceptively difficult without tendons. Writing *and* typing.

Mephisto sat back in his throne and raised the two wiry hairs which formed a single eyebrow.

"Didn't have this modern problem back in my day. Just turned up in some random Spirit Cabinet and shook a few tambourines to scare the willies out of them- devil bless those Davenport conmen. Loved popping out of one of those cupboards on Halloween for a classic Séance. Who was going to actually believe them once I appeared?" Mephisto snickered, reminiscing fondly of Halloweens long past. The 1850's had been his prime. "Let me take a look at that new fangled thing," he said, reaching an oozing hand towards the loading phone. Charon had not anticipated the connection requirements. It took all his learned subtlety to reach through the veil beyond for the precious and elusive, '4G.'

The Red Lady's withered claw smacked Mephisto's hand away while the social media app loaded.

"Devil's sake, get your ectoplasm off the screen," she snapped.

"Sorry. It's been so long since I've been out at Halloween. No one calls for the slime these days. Physical manifestations take too much energy to summon so I'm all *pent up*."

The Red Lady scrunched her bloodless face in disgust at her colleague.

"If you're going to talk about bodily fluids then I'll eat my own words and call in the zombie D.R."

"What's a bit of slime if you get to spray blood? It's only a little fun. Which reminds me," the old dog said wryly, leaning forward, his goop leaking into the R.I.P etched into the stone. "Did you hear the rumour about The Headless Horseman? Summoned by some horse girls on ranch for a slumber party. Just ten little girls he scared with no one trick or treating for *miles*. He only got back through the corporeal barrier by the skin of his teeth."

"You can't say that, it's offensive," The Red Lady snapped, folding her deathly pale arms from underneath flowing lace sleeves of a tattered gown. Charon thought it was a proper knock off from Bloody Mary, but he did well to keep his jaw fused shut, unwilling to add fuel to this particular fire, despite it being his prized pastime. They were already off track as it was.

"What? How?"

"Well, he hasn't got teeth if he hasn't got a *head*. A bit insensitive to his condition and all," the Red Lady scoffed.

Charon's hollow ribcage contracted with relief as the screen at last loaded, and he interjected the beginnings of friendly fire with a wholly offensive photograph that stopped all four nightmares in their tracks.

The 'feed,' as Charon had heard Barry refer to it, was full of photographs of uneaten pumpkin pie in quaint cafés, crisp orange leaves and woolly hats with coordinating scarves. There was not a ghoul nae a goblin in sight, replaced instead with overtones of warm orange and neutral beige.

Sickening.

"Who is this blonde lady leading the revolution against Halloween?" Mephisto asked, his chins wobbling with rage as he examined the blonde-haired human who unrelentingly beamed up at the demons with neat pearly whites.

Barry leaned forward excitably, the year of research and planning piquing their interest at long last.

"She calls herself, FallGirl. Her real name is Alyson McGuire, of Massachusetts, Boston. This is her with her 'long term life partner,' Bryant McCormon. Both with Y's. Both with Mc's. And you best believe that everything they do is matchy-matchy."

Charon cringed. Mephisto shuddered, sending flecks of slime scattering across the barren room. The Red Lady dropped her veil back over her empty eye sockets.

"That's a Fall Girl?"

"That's a Fall Girl."

"Wow, just look at all those coloured candles. And none of them used for summoning. What a loss. I bet they're scented with vanilla," the Red Lady observed mournfully.

"I'm allergic to vanilla. I come out in hives," Mephisto grunted.

"Would anyone be able to tell?" the Red Lady muttered.

"Ah, well I'm pleased you brought the candles up, my terrible lady!" Charon announced, reaching into the endless depths of his black cloak.

"Behold, my dastardly plan."

The vanilla and pumpkin spice candle, retrieved from a particularly dank pocket dimension Charon stored in cloak fold, began to permeate the stale room with its warming overtones.

"Oh god put it away!" Mephisto said, his voice muffled having shoved his face underneath his own arm to escape the real thing in its complete form. "Here comes the rash. Why in the devil's name would you offend our sight with such a *thing*?"

Charon gave Barry a nod to go ahead; after all, he was the one qualified in Modern Humanity Studies.

"Ah well, our human puppet Alyson is what they call, an 'influencer.'"

Mephisto let out a sarcastic barking laugh and the Red Lady, a high pitched yowl of frustration which made Barry wince. He scratched his horns nervously, waiting to finish his pitch.

"No, listen to this part, this is the good bit," Charon jabbered, shushing her with the dismissive wave of a skeletal hand.

"It wasn't difficult to convince Alyson and her…ehem… 'long term partner' Bryant to accept a 'trial' batch of Halloween themed candles to offer out to her followers. 'Like this Halloween post and receive a free, bespoke pumpkin and vanilla spiced candle,'" he read from the latest post on her feed, quoting verbatim.

"And here's the nifty part," Charon jumped in, practically bouncing in his seat like a little human baby. "As we are all too aware, the ritual to summon a demon involves three things."

"Lighting a candle," the Red Lady said, dully.

"A drawing of the summoning rune," Charon added, clicking a phalange against the branded label on the candle before them, where it became all too clear that the Halloween theme, as Charon had aptly called it, was indeed the ancient summoning rune, disguised as a company logo.

Barry, in his deep baritone voice, solemnly added the last rite of law.

"A request for the chosen demon by their true name."

"Look at the name printed on the candle," Charon said, pointing at the fine print. This one read 'Furfur.' "Each one has the name of a different demon!"

The Red Lady shrieked with, what Charon hoped was, delight.

"How many likes did the post get?"

"500,000," he said smugly.

"Flipping heck, Charon. That's 500,000 summonings in one night! That's my 26 legions sorted right there!" Mephisto said, slapping his thigh dully.

"And all the zombies in Demon Resources!" The Red Lady cried, shooting a spray of cursed black blood into the sunless sky.

"So, I'll be a busy ferryman tonight, if everyone lights their summoning candles," Charon reckoned, scratching his skull underneath a black cloak.

All the humans had to do this Halloween was light the damned candles…

"Damnation, I'd better get my good cloak on," he said discarding the smooth silk shroud for his moth-eaten best.

In fact, Charon observed, the unusual notion of joy seeped through Limbo's beings like a poison, for each of them had a candle bearing their name…

Each, except…

"Ah," Charon said flatly, hesitantly placing up a single bony finger to halt a premature celebration for *one* of them, at least.

"I'm afraid you may not be going through the veil, Barry."

The Eldrich Terror's many legs froze and his horns scraped loudly on the crumbling castle ceiling, sending fragments of stone cascading down as he snapped his head around in disbelief.

"What? Why?" he asked, wringing four hands together nervously. Under his cloak, Charon's skeleton quaked.

No, he could not die, but it would be an awful inconvenience should it occur to the Eldrich Terror to throw him into the River Styx, in a fit of rage.

Instead, Baralaxidegon, Evil Incarnate and Destroyer of all Men, The Third, sat down again dejectedly.

"I'm sorry, Barry…it's just, well." Charon cleared his throat. "Your name was too long to print on the candle label."

It was on that note, Baralaxidegon, Evil Incarnate and Destroyer of all Men, The Third, was forced to watch as Mephistopheles and The Red Lady were pulled by invisible forces of Charon's hand through the lifted veil between worlds. The night was Halloween. The veil was lifted. 500,000 demons were summoned by the lighting of influencer candles, and despite Barry's yearlong efforts of completing a tedious course in 'Modern Humanity Studies,' he was the last demon left in Limbo.

"It's not fair," Barry said to no one in particular, for even Mephisto's 26 legions and the DR zombies had been invited unwittingly for a Halloween soiree and the harrowing land was empty for one night only.

The efforts were wasted. Sure, he was happy that it would be a record-breaking successful haunt, but who would remember *his* demon name in the mortal plane?

Yet, before Barry had the chance to ask himself, 'what now?' amidst his self-pity, he felt a familiar skeletal hand take one of his limbs, and a shudder as his corporeal form was navigated by the busy hand of Charon to the plane of the living.

He had been summoned!

"It's your time to shine, friend!" his skeletal comrade whispered, before continuing his duties as ferryman, leaving Barry alone…in a strange dwelling. A *human* house. It was full of beige furnishings, and the startling ambiance which he'd read being described as 'cosy,' threw him into disarray, the cavernous desolation of a crumbling castle perched on the edge of time replaced by…Live, Laugh, Love signs.

"Dear devil," he uttered. "Modern Human Studies did *not* prepare me for this," he observed, his yellow eyes wild and frantic, searching for the powerful human who summoned his presence on this Halloween night.

But how? Charon had not placed his name on a summoning candle.

It was then, he heard a sniffle and looked four feet down to the blonde-haired woman. She was *crying*.

"Alyson McQuire?!" Barry cried, startled by the influencer's presence. But his question was rhetorical. It was undoubtedly her who had summoned the Eldrich Terror to her home.

"You... know my name?" she snuffled. She craned her neck up to look at him, while he wringed his many hands together awkwardly. They were drenched in sweat.

"Uh...I mean. I am an all-powerful demon, I know all."

For devil's sake, he sounded so out of practice.

"But *are* you a destroyer of men?"

"Uh, yes?" said Baralaxidegon, Evil Incarnate and Destroyer of all Men, The Third. "It is in my name, I suppose. Is it important?" he asked, tentatively. Usually the Halloween objective were 'hauntings of a sinister nature,' or as Mephisto liked to describe it so eloquently, 'scaring the willies out of the humans.'

The Eldrich Terror, cramped into the tiny living room inside a crudely drawn summoning circle surrounded by jasmine scented tealights, realised three things.

This woman had summoned him the good old-fashioned way. *Intentionally.*

She was neither haunted nor scared.

Alyson summoned him for a *purpose.*

Finally, for once this dreary year, Barry felt a rush of electric excitement, which was immediately crushed by another wracking sob from the self-proclaimed FallGirl.

"He left me! On Halloween!"

"What? Do you mean your 'long term life partner' *Bryant?* Is that relevant?"

"We're in couples costumes!" she wailed dramatically. "It's like having mac with no cheese!"

"I...I don't know what any of those things are."

As the blonde haired human sobbed face down onto her taupe crushed velour bedspread, the eldrich terror rubbed his eight arms together nervously, minding his horns on the tinkling glass chandelier.

"You know, Alyson...you really shouldn't leave naked flames burning on your carpet like that," he said, blowing the tealights out with the gust of a gale force breath, sharper than the frigid wind across the Caspian Sea.

Thankfully, she ceased crying and twisted her body curiously. Her make up smudged into some terrible ghoulish mess. The sight relaxed him.

"You're not what I expected a demon to be."

"I've been a little out of practice," he admitted.

Gosh, if Baralaxidegon, Evil Incarnate and Destroyer of all Men, The First and Second could see him now. They would scold him for not taking complete advantage of the situation! On Halloween nights of all, summoned for nefarious reasons, it should be his time to shine!

"But Halloween isn't over yet," he said aloud, a steely resolve entering his thunderous voice. If Alyson summoned him, then by the devil, he would do this strange little human proud. "You wanted a man-destroyer, right?"

"Right!" she nodded dumbly, and then, with fire in her eyes, added, "abso-freakin-lutely. Come on, pumpkin," Alyson said, taking one of his many hands. "We've got one last stop for trick or treat."

"And just to clarify…I'm doing the trick part, right?" the Eldrich Terror asked, before following the tiny, scorned woman out into the Halloween night for a very overdue haunting.

Halloween Horror

Austin Muratori

Sam found himself standing in front of an old, decrepit mansion. He had no recollection of how he got there, but he felt a strange connection to the place. He stepped inside, the eerie silence overwhelming him. The mansion seemed familiar, yet alien, like a forgotten memory struggling to resurface.

Sam wandered into a room. The room was filled with antique furniture, the air heavy with a sense of melancholy. As he touched the dusty furniture, a sense of *deja vu* washed over him. He had been here before, but when?

Drawn to the grand staircase, Sam began ascending. Each creak of the old wooden stairs echoed through the silent mansion. He reached the top floor, the darkness greeting him like an old friend. An inexplicable chill ran down his spine.

A ladder leading to an old attic caught his attention. He made his way slowly up the rickety steps. A pungent scent of mold and decay punched his nose. The attic was filled with old trunks and cobwebs. A sense of dread settled in his heart.

His mind raced with an odd sense of nostalgia. This place felt so familiar, but he just could not recall why. Investigating further he opened a trunk and found a newspaper clipping from the Haddonfield Gazette. At the top the date read: *'November 1st, 1899.'*

The headline caught his attention, it read: *'Halloween Massacre: Man found beheaded outside of mansion.'* Below the article there was a picture of the man who was identified. It was Sam's own face that stared back at him from the paper.

In a daze, Sam descended the grand staircase. The mansion had taken on an ethereal glow. The realization hit him like a freight train. He was in fact dead. His thoughts immediately went to the fact that he couldn't remember anything. Something had been off today, as if waking from a coma, groggy and out of touch.

Haunted by the truth, it all became clear. Sam's throat quelled and he felt that fight or flight response. He wandered through the mansion. Why was he feeling anything if he were dead? So many questions rushed his mind at the same time.

His home was now his prison, a chilling reminder of his past. He could remember it now, the Halloween party, the laughter, the man with a large knife and then... nothing. He had died here.

Sam stepped out into the moonlit yard. The world seemed to have moved on, but he was stuck, forever trapped on Halloween night. His death had been a mystery, the case unsolved. The killer never caught.

Sam roamed the silent town in a daze. The world was oblivious to his presence, a ghost lost in time. He was a shadow, a whisper of a life once lived.

He found himself at the town's graveyard. His tombstone stood there, a stark reminder of his forgotten life.

In loving memory of Samuel Strode, November 10th, 1869 - October 31st, 1899

A lone tear cascaded down his pale cheek. Thunder boomed in the distance as the wind picked up. Darkness loomed overhead. Sam realized that he will never see his beloved Elly again. He will never see his family again.

He is doomed to wander alone, forever trapped in the past. His death was his eternal Halloween horror.

The Jawbreaker

Bernardo Villela

It was hard for Connor to stop smiling long enough to get his grease paint on. His mummy costume turned out better than he hoped. Having just turned eleven, he felt it was important to show his mother he could follow through. She'd given him that hopeful yet doubtful nod of approval when he'd asked.

There was a knock at his door. Connor reached for an alcohol pad to clean his hands. Fingers tingling, he clicked the light-switch on. The switch connected to a hallway light for some reason. Connor's father had the idea to leave that wiring quirk in place. Due to an onset of selective mutism a few years prior, Connor didn't speak, his controlling a light outside his room allowed him to close his door and say, "Come in" without texting.

Seeing the light flicker on, Connor's older brother, Paul, entered.

"Wow," Paul said seeing his makeup. Then in ASL he added: "Where are the wrappings?"

Connor indicated a side-table where they were laid out to dry after having been smeared with some Plaster of Paris, then tea-stained them.

Paul was genuinely impressed.

Connor had received many halfhearted "good for yous" for completing basic tasks since he fell silent, but he knew there was no acting here. He beamed with pride.

"Alright," Paul said, remembering why he'd come in, "The guys will be here at six. Be ready."

A few years ago, when Connor's silence was still a new phenomenon, he had his older brother lobby their parents to let him trick-or-treat with Paul and his friends without parental supervision.

Their mother resisted at first, arguing, "I don't know why Connor wants to do scary Halloween things after—".

"Mom, I don't either," Paul said. "But he does."

"Saying no might do more harm than good, Lynn," their father said.

Eventually Lynn gave in, though she second-guessed herself, at least until Halloween arrived and she saw Connor in his hand-made costume next to Paul's store-bought zombie get-up. Seeing her son smiling, laughing at his big brother's outfit, made her realize that her husband had been right.

"I'm so impressed, kiddo," his dad said smiling.

"It's adorable, Connor."

Connor shot daggers at his mom.

"I mean scary, it's terrifying." Seeing she'd appeased her son, it was back to business "Connor, you got your phone?"

He showed her.

"House key?"

He showed her it, then flashed his laminated card that explained to sticklers why he wouldn't say "Trick or treat?"

"OK, he's ready," Lynn said grudgingly and let her boys go.

That Halloween was a perfect fall night; the cold didn't wane and chilled only so deep, so unlike the dead of winter which grips one by the bones. Connor felt cozy in his wrappings, like he was buried in a pile of fallen leaves. They trick-or-treated for hours and at many houses without incident, filling their pillowcases with candy as the orange sky burnt its way purple then pitch. Nevertheless, he always showed his card at every house they visited. It was perfect until, during a long gap between houses, Connor felt a sudden, sinking feeling.

I lost my card, he thought.

He closed eyes and clenched his fists, hoping he was dreaming. The crisp night air told him he wasn't. Connor tugged his brother's sleeve. Paul turned to see his younger brother's hands trembling as he signed desperately, as if everything was falling apart.

"Don't worry, I got you," Paul said, taking Connor by the hand. That settled him for a moment. Connor held his pillowcase tight to his body. They were so far from home, without his card, people here might think he was being a punk when he refused to speak.

Those anxieties haunted Connor as they approached an expansive house. The only light that shone emanated from a jack-o'-lantern glaring through a window to the left of the door. Paul rang the doorbell while Connor clutched his hand.

The door creaked agape, and an old man greeted them.

"Trick or treat," the group said as soon as they'd seen him. The elderly man handed each of them some jawbreakers but stopped at Connor.

"And what about you, Mummy? What do we say?"

Connor's throat constricted. He bit his lip and tasted oily, chalky paint.

"My brother doesn't talk, sir," Paul interjected.

Garrity raised a bushy eyebrow and looked at Paul askance.

"First an uppity neighbor threatened to sue 'cause I handed out peanut butter candies last year, now I have to buy that a grown kid that can't talk."

"But—"

"Hit the road!"

Paul turned to his brother. "C'mon, I'll give you mine."

Connor didn't want Paul's jawbreaker. He was hurt, and his big-eyed glance back at Garrity as they left let the old man know just how he felt.

"No use making puppy-dog eyes at me. Get lost, brat!"

Connor looked ahead, and they managed the remainder of their trick-or-treating without further incident. Still Connor fixated on the old grouch chasing them off.

That night, Connor couldn't sleep. While that was normal on prior Halloweens, this year he'd hardly touched his candy. It was rage keeping him awake. When they'd arrived home, Connor had refused his brother's jawbreaker for a second time. Paul didn't understand that the candy was beside the point. The old man had shamed him, not only unnecessarily but cruelly too. Neither of which he deserved, being denied his basic human dignity on this holiday, Connor obsessed.

Well past midnight, Connor gave up the pretense that he'd sleep anytime soon. So he snuck out to get what he deserved.

Not long thereafter, Connor arrived at the sprawling, dark house. He glanced around expecting motion-activated lights to spotlight him like he was making a jailbreak. There were none. When he touched the doorknob, he inhaled deeply and exhaled slowly, anticipating alarms from a home security system. Again, there was nothing. The knob turned. Connor pushed the door inward, petrified by the door-hinges' squealing. All his nerves anticipated an ambush.

After a few moments' terrified silence, he noticed the bowl of jawbreakers on an end-table to the right of the door. Connor grabbed one.

A floorboard squeaked.

He looked up. Atop of the stairs stood the old man, teetering. His eyes sleep-glazed.

All Connor's nerve-endings told him to run. He didn't, though, out of fear his heart might burst if he did.

The old boy started down the stairs. Connor tried to run, felt his legs flinch, but his feet held firm. Unable to move, he only knew of one way out.

Connor screamed, which was no small feat when his mind wouldn't let him speak. The octogenarian man was roused from his stupor. Both their eyes went wide as the old man tumbled. The first thud a quarter of the way down the staircase flung Connor into the past. It was the last time he'd ever walked to school. He'd diverted from his usual path, come to an intersection, waited for the light to change. Something had distracted him. A bird maybe; he hadn't had a phone yet. All he was sure of was that he'd peered into the trees and clouds a little too long; he hadn't walked as soon as he should have. If he had, then he wouldn't have borne witness to that gruesome scene.

He'd heard it first, air brakes exhaling forcefully. There'd been a crunch, a thump. A man—maybe older than his Dad named Mr. Featherstone—had been thrown by a city bus and rolled through the intersection.

Connor's consciousness pushed back into the present to see the senescent man rolling down his stairs—just as Mr. Featherstone had ragdolled across the street—now he saw the old man slamming face first onto the hardwood mere yards from him. A hollow, plastic pop compounded Connor's fear. He saw a fractured, bloodied set of dentures, skitter across the floor. Puncturing his eardrum was a sickening snap, which he recalled from the chorus of crushed bones when he saw Mr. Featherstone hit. It was the sound of a neck cracking.

Connor's jaw he scraped his throat raw and put his screams into a word.

"HELP!"

In tears, he knew he'd not speak again that night. He called 911 on his cell phone and would let the police find him. The jawbreaker remained in his left hand uneaten.

The Devil Wears Dockers

Bill Freas

A crisp, cool autumn breeze swept through the picturesque campus of the Heart of Grace Academy, an all-girls Catholic boarding school tucked away in a pristine enclave of dense forests and rugged mountains in upstate New York. It was the day of All Hallows Eve. A solemn, uneasy shroud fell upon the campus every year on this date. Once a decade, on Halloween, the school suffered the tragic and ominous death of a student or staff member. Today, a special prayer vigil was underway in the campus cathedral. Only thirty or so students were in attendance, including a feisty foursome of eleventh-grade friends: Kristi – the sassy leader, Violet – the good girl, Zoe – the clueless one, and Dora – Kristi's sidekick. The four knelt in a pew far in the back of the sizable yet cozy cathedral, gossiping at a whisper volume instead of praying on this somber and mysterious day.

"I'm beginning to think that this place isn't as fun as I thought it was going to be," Kristi said.

Dora chimed in, "Tell me about it. All this praying is making my knees hurt."

"And a curfew? Gimme a freakin' break," Kristi added.

"You guys better start praying, or we're gonna get nailed," Violet said.

Kristi replied, "I *am* praying. Praying that the boys' school moves closer."

"I thought this was going to make me a better person," Zoe said.

"Yeah, maybe if you wanna be a shriveled-up, middle-aged virgin librarian," Kristi retorted.

A stern nun in the front of the church became aware of the girls' soft chattering.

"Shh!!"

"I told you we'd get caught," Violet said.

Kristi rolled her eyes. "Get a grip, Violet. Little miss goodie two-shoes here is afraid she might tick off one of the fine police nuns patrolling the cell block."

Zoe interceded, "Maybe we should start praying."

"In your case, Zoe, I'd recommend it. In fact, go light a candle," Kristi replied.

Zoe smiled and departed for the votive candles up near the altar.

"Maybe I'll go light one, too," Kristi added.

"A candle?" Dora asked her.

"No, a cigarette."

"Not a good idea. We need to be serious in here. This will look really good on our transcripts. Let's not screw it up," Violet said.

Kristi chuckled softly. "Transcripts? Ha, please. Keep your straight As. I'll take the two Bs: boys and beer."

Farther ahead in the pews, another student seemed to be suffering from a very strange coughing spell. Helena, a quiet loner of the same age, was the source of the odd hacking, and she appeared quite restless in her seat.

"Oh, boy. Freakshow's at it again," Kristi commented.

"What is wrong with her?" Dora inquired.

"A mystery that has plagued us since we were good, little acolytes."

The nun was once again agitated by the murmuring.

"Shh! Ladies, please. This is a vigil of silent reflection."

Helena peered around the church bizarrely while scratching her skin, as if she was covered in fire ants.

"Look at her. Helena is a total nutjob," Kristi said.

Helena abruptly sat still and turned around slowly in her seat to face the three gossiping girls several pews behind her. Her expression was cold and grim. A voice to the girls' right side snapped their attention away from their peculiar classmate.

"Are you young ladies using this time as an opportunity to cultivate your spirits, in holiness?"

The three girls looked to their right and observed Father Matteon, a confident and respected residing priest, standing near them at the end of the pew.

Violet answered, "Yes, Father."

"Yes, Father," Dora followed.

"Good. Strong prayer will bring you redemption. Continue your Rosary, girls," the priest said.

"Yes, Father," Violet replied.

The priest strolled ahead, passing Helena on his way. Her offsetting appearance and weird behavior struck him as noticeably odd, but he continued on without addressing it.

The day moved along, and the sun eventually faded behind the mountains before the shadows of Halloween night took their rightful place among the young inhabitants of the campus. The foursome of friends threw on their pajamas and settled into their candlelit dorm room. Kristi retrieved the group's trusty bottle of cinnamon schnapps, taking a big swig and then passing it along to the other girls.

"Now, *this* is what I call a day's-end devotion," Dora said.

"I am fully devoted to finishing this bottle," Kristi added.

Zoe spoke up, "Save me some, Dora."

"There's plenty. Remember, Violet won't drink any. She's a delicate and devout Catholic flower," Dora replied.

"And tomorrow morning, you all will be wilting Catholic flowers with major hangovers. Good luck explaining that to Father Matteon," Violet retorted.

"Oh, lighten up, Mother Theresa," Kristi said to her.

Suddenly, there was a pounding on the door.

Kristi perked up nervously. "Oh, crap! Nun patrol! Put it under the bed!"

"Whose bed?" Dora asked.

"I don't know! It doesn't matter!"

"Mints! We need mints!" Zoe exclaimed.

Zoe rummaged through her bag, for breath mints, as the pounding occurred at the door again.

"Uh, just one minute! We'll be right there, Sister!" Kristi called out, buying time.

Zoe retrieved the mints, and the girls threw some into their mouths. Swiftly, they composed themselves and prepared for the impending inspection. Kristi then marched over to the door and opened it, only to find no one there. She poked her head out into the hall. Not a single being was anywhere in sight.

"Well, that's funky."

"Who was it?" Zoe asked.

"Probably Gina and the other skanks with a lame attempt at a Halloween scare prank."

She closed the door, and to their surprise, the pounding instantly went off yet again.

"What the hell?!"

Kristi yanked open the door once more to find nothing.

"Okay, this is getting old."

Violet spoke up, "Maybe it's not a joke. Maybe it's a sign."

"A sign?" Dora asked.

"From you-know-who," Violet answered.

Kristi scoffed, "Oh, stop, please."

"What person could knock on our door and be able to get away that fast, Kristi? It's not possible," Violet said. With no answer, Kristi simply sent her a frustrated glance.

"Think about it," Violet added.

Zoe was quickly growing anxious. "You guys, I'm getting really freaked out."

Their conversation was interrupted by the intermittent sound of small stones lightly smacking the outside of the room's main window.

"What is that?" Zoe asked.

The edgy girls hurried over to the window and peered down at the courtyard outside their dorm, where a dark, shadowy figure jetted around in an abnormal and inhuman fashion. This ghostly figure below them almost resembled their peculiar classmate, Helena. Although, it moved far too fast and erratically to confirm that.

"What the hell are we watching?" Dora asked.

"I don't know," Kristi replied.

"Kind of looks like Helena," Violet added.

Shockingly, the door, left open by Kristi moments ago, slammed closed by itself with force. The startled girls screamed and whipped around toward the door, staring at it, frozen and terrified.

"Let's get our asses to bed. Now!" Kristi said.

The four friends raced into their respective beds and hid under the covers. Before long, they dozed off to sleep, soon entering a dream state they wish they never had experienced. Each girl floated through a dark nocturnal fog that led her to the surface of a creepy lake long forgotten in an abandoned state park deep in a vast forest up at the New York-Canada border. Each girl was slowly pulled beneath the surface into the murky waters, drifting deeper and deeper into the uncertain, unnerving aquatic environment. The desolate darkness soon broke as a menacing glow of supernatural origin, greenish gold in color, appeared and illuminated the grim, frightening silhouette of what looked like an otherworldly creature, a demonic entity perhaps.

186

It raised its inhuman arms and let out a sinister growl that seemed to make the uncanny glow around it stronger. Soon, a force gently pulled each girl in closer toward the figure, and the macabre glow began strobing. The conclusion of this terrible confrontation was uncertain because none of the four friends ever spoke of their nightmare, a nightmare they unknowingly shared. Its residue lingered and was palpable upon waking – a presence they couldn't shake.

Morning finally broke, and a fresh day was ushered in by some early sunshine, attempting to dissolve the chilling atmosphere that veiled the school yesterday and on every Halloween each year. The foursome of friends sat in theology class, weary and still disturbed by the haunting events of last night, while Father Matteen taught his daily lesson. The nun from the prayer vigil sat next to the priest's desk, assisting him with paperwork and other classroom duties.

"It's important that we understand the sacraments and the role they play in our daily faith," the priest lectured. "The beast himself, along with his hellish disciples, will challenge your hearts and souls and test your very beliefs in the Holy Trinity."

Several seats down from the four friends, the strange girl, Helena, struggled while taking in the religious lecture. Every time the priest mentioned a holy name, she writhed in torment.

"But do not ever take the power of the Lord God, for granted. For He shall have the last say over the wicked and evil of heart," he spoke.

Helena's behavior did not go unnoticed by the four friends, who stared at her silently and with great concern. Helena's unsettling motions were soon accompanied by a soft, foreboding chanting that poured out of her mouth insistently.

"And the beast will be defied and will lose its malicious grip on the good of heart before it is cast back down into the bowels of Hell, where it belongs!" the priest declared.

The friends were met with a terrifying sight when Helena turned to look at them. Her face was pale and scarred, and her eyes were rolled over white. The nun sensed something amiss and scanned the room, with her eyes, expecting to validate her keen awareness.

"There is a pall over this school, a threatening cloud. It comes once a year. Yesterday was its homecoming. Its roots lie deep in the earth here, in the soil and nature on and around our campus. Its origins are ancient, but our faith is constantly new and fresh, which will always render us the victors over its wicked powers and malevolent influence," the priest said.

Zoe let out a scream, which seized the attention of the entire classroom. Helena sprung up from her chair and bellowed a cryptic phrase loudly in Sumerian, her voice gravelly and demonic. The nun cried out in shock as Helena went ballistic, attacking her classmates violently. Then, the girl stormed over to Father Matteon, wrapped her hands around his throat, and choked him with an unnatural strength and the full intent to kill. With the assistance of several other girls, the nun wrestled Helena off the priest. The man of the cloth swiftly gathered himself and boldly recited a special Latin prayer while spritzing the possessed student, with holy water from a small bottle he retrieved from his pocket. Within mere moments, Helena calmed and appeared to return to normal again. The frightened, traumatized girl wept in the arms of the consoling nun while the four friends clutched one another and gripped their rosary beads tightly.

Father Matteon caught his breath and wiped the sweat from his brow before finally addressing the shocking incident. "Evil appears in many forms, my children. This Halloween, it decided to come in person."

Make Your Claim

Chris Blinn

"...So Peter finally gets to the top of Calvary. Beaten, bloody, no arms, no legs and Jesus says; Peter I can see your house from here."

The punchline caught the rotund Celt mid guzzle. Ale sprayed across the table. He slammed his mug, foam spilled over the sides.

"Disgusting." A nun in full habit said. She was the only female at the table.

"I'm sorry Sister." The Roman jokester apologized. "But I love that one."

"Heard it before." A man complained. Thick English accent.

"Well, of course you've heard it before Rodney. You're almost two hundred years old and dead for a hundred and fifty of those." The Roman said. "You never miss a chance to complain."

Rodney sipped tea and snarled at the Roman over his cup.

The Celt spoke. At two thousand he was just a bit older than the Roman. "I wanna make this as short as possible. We all know I have the most legitimate claim to the spoils of Halloween."

The group grumbled. The usual bickering followed.

A sudden flash silenced all. Lighting crashed blinding the group. The room shook.

"Bloody hell." Rodney's tea fell on his lap.

They wiped their eyes and looked for the source. A hazy form appeared. Humanoid. Reddish.

The giant Celt stood. A studded leather belt stretched to accommodate his indulgence.

The nun fingered a rosary and prayed quietly.

"In the name of Rome I demand you identify yourself."

Rodney was the last to speak. His sight clear. "Who in King George's name are you?"

"I am called many things. Satan. Beelzebub. The Prince of Darkness."

"Wait." Rodney said. "I thought that count fellow from Transylvania was the Prince of Darkness?"

"I think you're right for a change, Rodney." The Roman added.

"Not sure myself." The Celt said. "Sister you're the freshest of us dead here. What say you?"

The nun finished her prayer. "I think Rodney is correct. I believe The Transylvanian called himself the Prince of Darkness but I wouldn't bet my soul on it."

"Silence." The red figure pounded. Flames singed the middle of the table. "I am the Devil. The ruler of the underworld. Torturer of the damned."

"Well, Devil, can I call you Devil?" Rodney asked. "You've made a mess of this fine furniture."

"Obedience or you shall all burn." The red one shouted.

The Roman cleared his throat. "May I speak for the group." He waited for permission. They nodded. "Mr.Devil. We have gathered to decide who has the greatest claim to the profits of Halloween."

"I know why you're here General Octivius Julius Gemanicus."

"You can call me O.J."

The group snickered.

"Sister Mary Margaret Katherine Eunice Ellen Sybil O'keefe." He stared at the nun. "Mac Macnamacmac." He turned to the Celt. "And Mr. Rodney Charles Barrows."

"Barrow." The Englishman corrected. "Singular. Bar-row." He exaggerated the last syllable.

A bolt shot from the intruder's hand smashing Rodney's tea set.

"I've had quite enough of your behavior sir." Rodney whined. "That serving was a gift. Priceless and irreplaceable. Now state your business or be gone so we can get on with ours."

"My business is the same as yours. I seek my slice of the Halloween pie."

"Alright then." Rodney allowed. "Make your case."

"I am Lucifer the fallen angel I will make no case but merely take what is mine."

"That hardly seems fair." Rodney said.

"Yes." Sister Mary agreed. "Pope Benedict instilled All Souls Day inspiring the children to dress as angels or their favorite saint."

"True as that may be Sister, Halloween is clearly a turn on the most ancient Celtic tradition of Samhain." Mac argued.

"Yes, but it was the English who began leaving food on their doorsteps for the wandering dead which leads us to today's trick or treating, therefore the Kingdom should be awarded the profits." Rodney said.

190

"We've been over this." Mac jumped in. "I can tell you because I was there. My clan would dress as animals or spirits to avoid the dead during Samhain. Gifts were also left for appeasement long before your ancestors did Rodney and I'm sorry sister but it was also before your pope decreed All Souls Day. Not to mention he waffled a bit on the matter if I recall."

"Remind us of your claim, Roman." Rodney asked.

"I have nothing. We were just a greedy bunch." O.J. chuckled. "Besides we're all dead. What are we gonna do with money anyway?"

They all thought for a moment. The devil drummed his clawed fingers on his chin.

"I confess." Mac began "I can't think of anything."

"Nor I." O.J. chimed in and turned to the Englishman.

"Don't expect me to follow suit because you're too daft to come up with a use for the money." Rodney said. "I would open a museum in London expounding on the Kingdom's great contributions to the tradition of Halloween."

"I would do the Lord's work and use the money to open an orphanage." Sister Mary said.

"Oh, how original." Rodney scoffed.

The red one's head spun. "Insolence." He swore and whipped his tail lassoing the four bickerers, lifting them off the floor. "Get this through your thick skulls." He tapped their foreheads with a pointy finger. "I am the mighty mischief maker and I do not recognize any of your claims. I will take what is mine."

"To use the modern vernacular. Whatever. Just please put me down." Rodney said.

The Devil inhaled deeply. A building tirade was cut off by a knock on the door. He released the group from his hold. They landed in a pile. "I will fry the interrupter." He snarled and tore the door open.

"Cool costume, dude." A trick or treater awed.

The devil howled. Fire shot from his mouth. Smoke curled from his nostrils. Great wings appeared from his shoulders and a wind sent the children tumbling down the walkway. He slammed the door. "Now." He turned back inside.

"Sorry." Rodney dusted himself off. "We specifically chose this house for its dilapidated state assuming it would keep the children away."

"Musta came up on a dare." the Roman said. "Spunky kids. I like that."

"Shhuuuuttt uppp!" the Devil was at his wits end. "Prepare to die!"

"We're already dead." Mac's belly rolled.

The Roman tried to suppress a laugh and snot shot from his nose.

Another knock sounded. The devil looked like he was going to explode. "I pity the soul on the other side of that door." He said and ripped it from its hinges.

A small child dressed as a mummy stood on the stoop. "That was mean what you did." He said.

The Devil was stunned.

The little pharaoh looked at the devil unafraid. "We say trick or treat and you give us candy." He explained. "The tricks are for the older kids to play on each other."

Mac and the gang fell in on either side of the Devil.

"Nice costumes, you having party in there?"

"Ah yes, yes..." Satan stuttered, his dark heart melted by the child's innocence. He didn't understand. Normally he would drool over the prize of such a young soul. He turned to the others "Did any of you think to bring any candy?" He asked.

They all shrugged.

Sister Mary produced a couple of butterscotches from her sleeve.

The Devil shook his head at the nun's offer. Gross. He closed his eyes and whispered an unheard spell. He clenched his fist and opened it producing a stream of candy.

"Wow." The child said. "What're those?"

"Atomic hot balls. What else?" The little red balls continued to shoot from the Devil's unrolled fingers into the mini mummy's bag. "Go and share those with the others and tell them I'm sorry I scared them."

"Thanks." The child said and ran to his friends.

The Devil secured the door the best he could and turned to the group. Their heads hung in unspoken embarrassment.

Profits or not, Halloween didn't belong to any of them.

It belonged to the children.

Buffering

Roo B. Doo

Death materialised out of thin air at the front of the coach, just as the vehicle had started to career off the icy road. The screaming passengers, however, were not yet aware of the arrival of the diminutive grim reaper and nor was the driver, who convulsed violently in his seat, even as he gripped the steering wheel, trying to prevent the coach from crashing through the barrier that separated the road from a steep embankment.

Death remained immobile, silent and serene as the vehicle first tipped onto its side and then onto its roof, rolling over and over, down the embankment. The same could not be said for the rest of the coach occupants. With a sickening crash of glass, metal and bones, the coach finally came to a shuddering stop, its large wheels slowly rotating against the cold, night air. All was silent for a moment, save for the ticking engine and the soft hiss and crackle of flame. Then the moans and screams began in earnest.

Coach party, Death thought dully, *I hate coach parties.* He pulled his Psi-Pad from the folds of his robe and flipped open the cover. The glowing screen showed a list of thirty-two names, some of which were coloured red. Soon enough they all would be red.

Bing! the Psi-Pad chirruped.

The sudden explosion was loud, engulfing the broken wreck and its unhappy passengers in blooming fire and black, acrid smoke that reached up into the dark, starless sky.

"Oh man!" the zombie cried unhappily. "This is the worst Halloween ever!"

He stood in a group of other zombies, staring at the burning coach with wide eyes and open mouths.

"Excuse me," Death called, trying to get the horde's attention. He'd never seen so many zombies together in one place. "When I call out your name, I'd like you to step forward."

"Who are you?" the lamenting zombie asked. His blackened eyes stood out against his pallid face, except for his lips, teeth and chin which were all stained blood red.

"I am Death," Death replied gravely.

The lamenting zombie wasn't convinced. "Are you sure?"

Death had experienced doubt before from those he'd reaped. On the whole, the newly departed expected to be met by a Grim Reaper that was somewhat taller. Actually, a lot taller. It was best to ignore any scepticism, Death had found, and to just plow on. "Yes, I am Death and I have come for you."

"Really? 'Cos you look more like a Jawa."

Death didn't answer; he didn't know what the zombie was talking about.

"You know, a Jawa. From Star Wars," the lamenting zombie explained. "Utinni!"

Death was at a loss. He'd been mistaken for many things, including a child, a hobbit, a dwarf and a munchkin. Being likened to a Jawa was a new one for him. "Star Wars?"

"Yeah," another zombie interjected excitedly. "Episode four, A New Hope. 1977. The original and the best film, in my opinion."

"Nah, nah, nah," the lamenting zombie replied. "The Empire Strikes Back is far superior in every way."

The excited zombie was having none of it. "Wrong, Graham. Granted, entombing Han in carbon was a stroke of genius, but—"

"Excuse me," Death said firmly. His telescoping scythe shot out of sleeve of his robe, the sparking electric blade finally grabbing *all* the zombies' attention. "I AM DEATH."

The change of tone worked; the horde fell silent. In the distance, sirens wailed mournfully as emergency vehicles raced to the scene of the crash.

"Now," Death continued, "there are quite a lot of you to process, so I would be grateful if you would step forward smartly when I call your name."

He retracted his scythe back up the sleeve of his robe and pulled out his Psi-Pad. He checked the list on the screen. "Alison Dawkins."

A dishevelled female zombie pushed through the horde and faced Death. "That's me. Utinni!"

Behind her, the lamenting zombie called Graham sniggered.

The night sky now pulsing with blue lights as the fire engines, stationed on the road above, streamed foam down onto the burning coach, and Death had finally processed the horde. They weren't really zombies, Death had gleaned, but merely a group of cos play enthusiasts returning home from a Halloween Zombie sponsored walk. Their spirit souls were still adorned in the clothes they wore upon their demise, including the make-up and fake gore that they had assiduously applied and now enhanced by their ethereal appearance.

"So, what happens next?" Graham asked. The horde behind him was starting to get restless.

"I will now escort you all to The Other Side," Death replied.

"What's on the other side?" the excited zombie, who in life had been Chris Waterman, a small business adviser for a high street retail bank, asked. "Is it heaven? Hell?"

"Tatooine," Graham smirked.

Death ignored the jibe. "It is The Other Side. Please, follow me."

"Well, what about him?" Alison asked, pointing toward a weeping figure sat alone on the embankment.

"Who?" Death turned to look in the direction that Alison was pointing.

"The coach driver," Alison said. "Don't tell me he got out alive and we all perished, because that would really not be fair."

The zombie horde moaned in agreement.

Death checked his Psi-Pad. He had ticked off all of the 32 names on the list, and 32 freshly processed zombies stood in front of him. "Hmm. I will check."

He glided toward the weeping coach driver, closely followed by the horde, who shambled along behind in true zombie fashion. Even in death, they remained in character.

The coach driver looked up at his former passengers surrounding him, his face contorted with grief. "I'm sorry. I'm so sorry. It wasn't my fault," he wailed.

"Don't worry," Alison stated in an effort to comfort the man. "We all know. It was an accident."

Death agreed. "Indeed it was."

He flipped open his Psi-Pad then turned and glared at the surrounding horde, who were craning to see what was written on the screen. "Could you step back, please? I wish to speak confidentially with the driver."

The moaning horde shuffled back a step.

"What is your name?" Death asked the distraught man.

"Phil," the driver croaked. "Philip Bland."

Death tapped the screen of his Psi-Pad. "Do you have a middle name or names?"

The horde inched closer behind Death.

"No," Phil said, wiping his sleeve across his eyes.

"And your date of birth?" Death asked. He quickly spun round and glared at the horde, who shuffled backward somewhat abashed. "Thank you."

"25th December 1968," Phil with a sniff. "Mum always said I was her Christmas gift from Santa."

As one, the female contingent of the horde cocked their heads on one side and sighed. "Ah."

"It's not great having your birthday on Christmas Day though," Phil confessed. "Everyone else gets two days a year for presents. I only had one."

"Aww," the male portion of the horde responded, shaking their heads. "Mate, that stinks," Graham said.

Death continued tapping the Psi-Pad screen. He tapped it some more, hunching over it to prevent the prying zombie eyes that were now right over his shoulder. The horde waited in hushed expectancy of what Death would say next.

"Philip Bland," Death proclaimed, flipping the cover to his Psi-Pad closed. "Unfortunately, I cannot take you to The Other Side at this present moment."

"Why not?" Graham asked indignantly.

"Yeah," the horde agreed.

"Did I do something wrong?" Phil asked plaintively.

The horde moaned louder.

"No, no, not at all." Death tried to calm the situation. "Well, maybe but that's not what's important. Philip Bland, can I ask you if you were a recipient of the Rona vaccine and a participant in the subsequent booster shot programme?"

"What?" There was general confusion amongst the horde. "What's that got to do with anything?" Chris demanded.

"Of course I did," Phil answered Death. "Everyone did."

196

"I didn't," Graham stated loudly.

"You lied!" Chris was most aggrieved. "Graham, you knew it was mandatory in order to participate in the Halloween Zombie Walk in 2021."

"And 2022," Alison moaned. The rest of the horde agreed.

Graham shrugged his shoulders. "Pfft. Sorry, but there's no way I was letting the bloody useless NHS pump an untested drug into me."

The horde stared back at him.

"What?" Graham sneered defensively. "All that you lot were doing was fluffing some mega pharmaceutical company's executive's massive bonus. Fuck that."

"Wait, wait." Phil reached out a hand to Death. "What does that mean?"

"It means," Death said gravely, "that you, Philip Bland, were murdered. You must remain here until you either avenge your death or until we can reschedule you for a later collection. I'm afraid it might be some time. There's rather a large backlog."

"What are you saying?" Alison demanded. The mood of the horde was becoming more aggressive.

"What I am saying," Death said, pulling himself up to his full height and shooting his scythe from the sleeve of his robe, "is that he's not on the list."

"You're just going to leave him here?" Alison was aghast.

"I must," Death replied firmly, turning his back on Phil. He addressed the zombie horde. "Now, would the rest of you will please follow me."

"Now wait a moment." Chris stepped out of the horde. "You're saying that the Rona vaccine killed Phil, here." He gestured toward the driver. "Murdered him, but not us. But we all took the jab."

"Again, I didn't" Graham said, holding up his hands.

Chris shot him a dirty look. "If we're all vaccinated the same as Phil, then why aren't we considered as murdered?"

"Because you died as a result of an accident," Death explained. "The late hour, the icy conditions, your driver suffering a catastrophic seizure at the wheel all contributed to your death being categorised as an accident. Tragic, but an accident nonetheless."

The horde quietened into sombre silence.

"Well, I'm not going." Graham puffed his chest out. "I'll stay here with Phil."

"You will come with me," Death asserted.

Graham moved out of the horde and sat on the grass next the driver. "I don't think so. I'm not going anywhere with a Jawa peddling a bad motivator. I'm staying right here."

"Thanks mate." Phil turned to his new friend, his bottom lip wobbling. "Appreciated."

"No problem, Phil," Graham said, placing his arm about his shoulders. "I could do with some avenging."

"You'll be a ghost," Death declared.

"Wrong, Jawa!" Chris blurted out. He too broke from the horde and sat next to Phil. "We'll be *zombie* ghosts!"

"Yeah," Alison shouted and the rest of the horde agreed. "Zombie ghost avengers!"

They shambled past Death and surrounded Phil, Graham and Chris.

"Will none of you come with me to The Other Side?" Death cried. He was confounded; he'd never experienced a mass declination before.

"No!," the horde replied as one. "Utinni!"

"Very well." Death stowed his Psi-Pad inside the folds of his robe and turned away from the horde. "Coach parties," he said with disgust, and disappeared back into thin air.

Halloween on Mars

Ginger Strivelli

"We are going to celebrate what?" The Mayor of the third Mars colony city asked in disbelief.

"Halloween!" Stella said brightly. "It's an old Earth holiday. Well, it was called Samhain first by the ancient Celts of Europe but in the twentieth century they called it Halloween. It was very popular in the old North American countries."

"Like Christmas?" The Mayor asked.

"Yeah kinda."

"So we decorate the city. You think that will improve morale?"

"Yes, we decorate but also there are parties. Costume parties and we give out chocolates and other sweets to the kids." Stella said.

"Not the kinda thing I had in mind when I charged you with finding a way to boost morale when the Earth was destroyed last week. Sounds like it might help get people's minds off of the tragedy, at least though." The Mayor had left his desk to peer out the big picture window that overlooked the main square of his city.

"Yeah, it also has an aspect of ancestor worship in the original Celtic holiday traditions. The Day of the Death it was called in Mexico. It was a time to honor the dead and mourn them but happily in a fun way." Stella said, checking her notes on an old fashioned pad of paper.

"Okay. Sounds perfect. You are in charge. Make it happen."

Stella almost ran out of the Mayor's office. She was glad he had approved her idea to help the floundering morale of the city since the tragedy back on Earth. Everyone on Mars had sunk into a depression over the loss of their home world. She headed to the cloth maker's shop and ordered meters and meters of black fabric with embroidered pumpkin designs. She let the bakeries know they needed to make cakes and candies in the shape of spiders, owls, and bats. She had the street lights all changed to orange light and posted actual paper flyers about town announcing the costume party on 'Halloween' the following Sunday. She made the announcement on the web of course also but she thought the flyers on the street lamp poles were a quaint old fashioned part of the decoration as well as a means to spread the word.

Stella was dismayed to hear very little excitement over her Halloween celebration the following day. There was more confusion related to her decorating and announcements than excitement. She returned to the Mayor's office with another idea.

"Mr. Mayor, I'd like to offer a prize for the best costumes at the Halloween party…to ya know, increase participation and generate some more enthusiasm."

"What kind of prize? I have heard some grumbling about the Halloween party being weird. Not everyone seems keen on it."

"A really big prize! That will get everyone on board. We could offer a private home for the family with the best costumes. Everyone wants to move into the new private homes out of the dorms."

"They aren't done yet and there will only be twenty to start with." The mayor said.

"I know." Stella admitted, "and they'll go to you and the other city leaders…but you are married to the city engineer, Mr. Stein. So you two won't need but one. So that extra one we can award to the family with the best Halloween costumes."

"True." The Mayor sat back in his chair. "If it will get everyone out of this funk they are in…it will be worth it."

Stella left the Mayor's office and made up new flyers announcing the costume contest. She also put out words again on the web. It wasn't fifteen minutes later when she started hearing positive feedback. Everyone in the city was all the sudden all gung ho for Halloween then.

The city had only six days to prepare for Mars' first Halloween. People from the two other Martian cities even contacted her asking if their citizens could come and join in. Stella advised them to both hold their own Halloween celebration with the same best costumed family prize as both those cities were also in the process of building new private residences to replace the dorms the cities had been using for fourteen decades since colonization of Mars.

Stella had no family and certainly wouldn't want to take up a whole private home for herself and someone had to be the judge of the contest so she told the Mayor she would to keep him from being the bad guy for all the people who didn't win. Nevertheless she wanted to dress up too. In her research she had found that witches were a favorite costume of the holiday but she feared the religious Witches in the city might take the ancient silly caricature of their

200

people as an insult so she decided to dress up as a fairy instead. She laughingly told herself there were no modern fairies to insult.

Sunday morning before sunrise, the city was bustling with people all out walking around happily in fancy costumes. There was one family all made up of cats. Another family had dressed as ancient sea pirates. The bakers bringing out all the sweets to the city community center were dressed as different types of loaves of bread.

Stella was so proud of herself seeing all the creative and fun costumes and mostly because of all the smiling faces she saw as no one had seemed to have smiled in two weeks since the Earth tragedy had unexpectedly occurred.

At noon the party officially started and almost every city citizen was in the community center enjoying ancient earth music that Stella had selected for the Halloween theme. The huge room was filled with so many different types of strange looking people that no one noticed the three aliens that had landed and followed the crowds into the community center.

The aliens were very tall and should have instantly been recognizable as not human. However, on that first Halloween on Mars, everyone just assumed they were a local family wearing stilts under their strange copper colored jumpsuits. Even their bushy yellow hair was just assumed to be wigs. Their snow white faces with over-sized yellow eyes and over-sized mouths were just assumed to be masks.

The aliens were just as confused. They thought this new species they had discovered came in a hundred different forms. They thought the costumes were all just different subspecies of humans. The aliens asked many people to take them to their leader. They didn't understand why everyone they asked just laughed and laughed. They didn't get the joke. They wondered if their translation machine was malfunctioning and they were accidentally saying something else that was for some reason hilarious.

Stella was wandering through the crowd looking over each family's costumes. She was rather impressed with their creativity and more impressed with herself having devised a way to cheer up an entire city. She took to the podium and drew everyone's attention with a bell.

"I am so happy to see my fellow colonists all embracing this first Halloween on Mars." She said into the microphone. "I am delighted to announce the three top families as judged by myself. I am asking them to come forward, then all their peers may vote on them by applause. That top family will get one of the first private homes in the city when they are completed next month."

There were lots of murmurs and then the crowd went deathly silent. They all looked about at each other wondering who had caught Stella's eye. She had paused for dramatic effect but finally stepped back toward the microphone.

"The three finalist families are: the vampires, the aliens, and the goldfish! Please come forward so we all can vote."

The family dressed as four goldfish came forward fist all crying tears of joy. The vampire couple with their vampire baby swooped forward with capes raised as if they were flying to the front of the crowd. Then everyone turned to face the three aliens who were standing perplexed at the center of the room.

"Come on aliens!" Stella called, waving them forward.

The threesome looked back and forth between themselves then slowly approached the front of the room where Stella was waiting with the other two finalist families.

Stella walked in front of the aliens and asked for votes by applause, The crowd thundered with wild clapping. She moved to stand in front of the vampire family. The Vampire mom held the baby up and flew him about the other two families as if he was a bat. The crowd rewarded her with almost as much applause as the aliens had gotten. Stella moved to the goldfish family and gestured to the audience who applauded politely but with less gusto as they had clapped for the other two groups.

"It seems clear, the aliens are our winning family!" Stella returned to the alien's side and reached to unmask the shortest of the three as she could barely reach that one's chin. "Who's in these costumes? You have won a private home!"

The tallest alien was the one who spoke. "I do not understand your words clearly. We wear no costumes."

Stella stopped grabbing at the alien's chin and stood dumbfounded staring up at them.

The Mayor was all the way across the crowd, dressed as an octopus. He ran through the crowd who were all either fainting, running out of the room, or frozen like statues. When he got to the front he pulled Stella away and took his place in front of the aliens he now knew to be real live aliens.

"Sir...ah Madam. I'm the Mayor, the local leader here in this city." He stuttered.

"You are the leader of this planet? We have been asking everyone here to take us to you."

"Not, the whole planet, just this city but the other two mayors and I do run the planet's government together. Why are you here? Do you mean any harm? We are prepared to defend ourselves." He said straightening his back which made his six fake arms fall slack below his two real arms. "These are all costumes. It is a party. We don't normally look like this." He was pulling off his mask and costume arms.

"We do not understand the costumes. We mean no harm as you ask though. We only came to help any survivors from the planet that exploded." The tallest alien said, making a strange gesture of respect that looked more like a seizure to the humans watching.

"Oh, thank the Gods," the Mayor said. "We have been looking for aliens for generations. We always worried if we did finally meet aliens they would be hostile. Many people had started to think we were the only people in the universe."

The aliens all laughed at that remark, though it looked like more seizures to the humans.

A hundred years later both humans and that one alien race told the story of Mars' first Halloween to every other alien race they both met. It became something of a folktale for the whole Milky Way Galaxy.

Jacqueline Esmerelda and the Troll

Katherine Kerestman

Without a doubt, Jacqueline Esmerelda, the Mitchell family house cat, was a beauty. When in motion, she epitomized an elegance which was entirely feline, a four-pawed ballerina gliding through the aether on a flying trapeze. When still, she could easily have been mistaken for a totem of polished onyx. An extraordinary shade of ebony, dark as the deepest inscrutabilities of the universe, her coat was soft as the Babel of nimbus clouds which was, at that very moment, roiling overhead in the storm-pregnant sky. The whites of her almond eyes contrasted with the pair of stygian wells, the gateways to mysterious realms, which were her irises and pupils. The black orbs had as many phases as the moon – full round, elliptical, parabolic – and as many variations as her mood. Long black whiskers radiated outwardly from her small black nose and rounded cheeks, feeling the air for invisible signals. Rearranging herself upon the four feet which she had tucked up under her belly, Jacqueline Esmerelda closed her eyes and lowered her chin, conscious of being admired.

Julie Marie had entered the room. She was six years old and she adored the black kitty, whom she had christened Jacqueline Esmerelda when she had first discovered her on the back porch. Jacqueline Esmerelda had been only a tiny puff of fur then, but, after two years of mothering by little Julie Marie, she had grown into a fine feline. It was Julie Marie who lovingly brushed Jacqueline Esmerelda's coat every morning, which task, now that she was in first grade, she had to perform earlier than she had in her pre-scholastic days. Her love for Jacqueline Esmerelda had much to do with her early acquisition of a sense of responsibility. Just to be on the safe side, though, Julie Marie's mother, Frances, would ask her every day if she had fed and groomed the cat, but her interrogation was merely a matter of protocol, for she knew that Julie Marie would as soon forget to eat herself as to feed her beloved puss. Jacqueline Esmerelda loved Julie Marie as much as Julie Marie loved her cat.

"It's Halloween, Jacqueline Esmerelda," Julie Marie said, punctuating her remark with kisses on Jacqueline Esmerelda's velvet head.

"It's Halloween, and today I learned at school that black cats are Halloween cats. I'm going to be a princess tonight when I go trick-or-treating, but you're already a Halloween cat, so you don't need a costume." Julie Marie giggled at her own drollery.

Jacqueline Esmerelda rose to her feet in unhurried stages, and she then lengthened her body, raised her spine into a sinuous arc, and finally settled into an Egyptian-cat pose. She gazed into the girl's eyes and then blinked her own. Twice. Julie Marie hugged her kitty to her heart, and Jacqueline Esmerelda purred into the girl's embrace.

"Julie Marie, supper's ready! We have to eat early so that you can put on your costume and go trick-or-treating when your brother gets here." Julie's mother and father were going to dress up as ghosts, in white sheets with cut-out eyes over their heads, bestowing M&M's and red licorice upon the little ghouls and goblins who came to their door, while Julie Marie canvassed the neighborhood with her college freshman brother, Jeff, who would look after her before he went off to his own Halloween party.

Julie Marie scampered to the dining room, the cat trotting in her wake; and, once the princess-to-be had taken her place at table, the feline jumped up on her lap and twisted herself into a purring pretzel for the duration of the family meal. The reader may be pardoned for supposing that the girl shared a morsel or two of her tuna fish casserole with her friend.

When Jeff opened the front door and entered the foyer, he let in the low sound of rumbling in the distant mountains. Frances and Wil (Julie Marie's father) whisked Julie Marie to her room to get her dressed, while Jacqueline Esmerelda secured herself a place on a soft hassock in the living room, whence she could observe all the flurry.

"Oh... It's beautiful," breathed the princess, as she made a regal entrance into the living room and spied her cat on the hassock.

Around Jacqueline Esmeralda's neck sparkled a collar of blue and green stones.

"Well, she is a Halloween cat, and today is Halloween," said Wil.

"And our little princess is a real princess today," said Frances.

"Well, I don't have a coach, so the princess will have to walk today," her brother added. "Just don't even think about kissing any frogs."

Julie Marie giggled and kissed Jacqueline Esmerelda on her black nose. She picked up her plastic orange Jack-o-Lantern, fully anticipating bringing it home weighted with candy.

Frances and Wil kissed their daughter good-bye and sent her, hand-in-hand with her brother, into the growing procession of youngsters in borrowed finery. Then they donned their own ghostly attire and assumed their station at their door.

Bearing buckets and bags, hordes of short people, dressed in strange costumes colored ashen by the grey light of the harvest moon, filled the steep and narrow sidewalks, so that a contingent of juvenile devils were compelled to walk in the street for lack of room, and some trolls trod upon people's lawns.

A pirate wearing too-large boots and a skewed eye patch ascended the three steps to the Mitchell's front porch and demanded some booty in lieu of walking the plank. A demon came next, who merely brandished his pitchfork and spake, "Trick or Treat."

"The wind is really starting to blow," Wil said to his wife. "Look, honey, at the way the clouds are moving across the face of the moon – they're creating moving shadow-pictures on the Catskills. I hope the rain holds off until the kids have come home."

"Makes me think of Rip Van Winkle and all those strange little men playing nine pins in the mountain crevices," she replied. "It's getting chilly – I hope Julie Marie is warm enough. Would you like a cup of hot chocolate, dear?"

Frances went to the kitchen to prepare the hot beverage, leaving Wil to distribute the candy.

"MMRrwsxtfmrrw," snarled a gruff voice from under a curious costume. "Snrrfff. Fffrrw."

The child was dressed in a ruffled "fur" onesie with long sleeves that terminated in mittens with claws and pant legs which ended likewise. Its mask featured a long, bulbous nose overhanging a pair of wide, thin lips above a triangular jaw. Straw-like and straggly brown matted tresses descended from its crown to its elbows.

"What a clever costume! What are you supposed to be – a gnome or something?"

"FFFRRRRRmwrrrrrrrssssss!"

The candy bowl crashed on the painted floorboards of the porch, its contents strewn into the grass. His mouth agape, Wil looked at his scratched and bleeding hands. He sought his infantile assailant – the wayward creature was behind him.

"You're no kid – *you're a monster!*"

All at once, the troll was riding his back – as if he were a horse.

"Hel –"

The troll sank its claws into Wil's throat.

"Wil – *my God!*" Frances was standing the doorway, a mug of chocolate in each hand. She hurled one of the steaming cups at the troll. It howled, but hung on. She threw the steaming contents of the other into the red, trollish eyes. It let go of her husband, covering its eyes with its hands.

"GROOOWWWWLLLL!" The weird creature emitted a guttural shriek – Jacqueline Esmerelda had leapt onto its shoulder – and had bitten off a hairy, pointed ear! The ear in her mouth, the Amazonian cat bounded back into the house, Frances and Wil close behind.

Frances attempted to attend to her husband's hand, but he insisted that they secure the house first. After the pair had made a hasty circuit of their home, checking every door and window, they locked themselves in the master bedroom, watching as Jacqueline Esmerelda deposited the bristly ear under the bed and then began patrolling the perimeter of the room, pacing back and forth in front of the windows, stealthily watching the space under the door, her ears en pointe, her whiskers twitching, and her tail erect.

"Geez, Julie Marie, do you know any of these kids?" Jeff asked his little sister.

The trick-or-treating crowd was tremendous. Was this Halloween in Littleville, New York or New Year's Eve on Time Square? Not only was the foot traffic overflowing the sidewalks, but the costumes were beginning to creep him out. Here and there, he spied a Barbie or Spiderman costume, and a number of ghosts and vampires. But the brown shaggy onesies preponderated. He wondered if he had missed a new hit movie or television series: he could not place the sinister character.

Julie Marie glanced up from her plastic Jack-o-Lantern. She had been totaling her take. Scanning the street, up one direction and down the next, she tried to identify neighbor children, classmates.

"Nope."

She began to feel a bit nervous.

"Ever seen those hairy characters before?" Jeff asked her, trying to appear unconcerned. "In a new movie or TV show, maybe?"

The leaves whirled by their feet, skittered along the sidewalk and across the shorn, end-of-summer lawns, somersaulted in the road, propelled by the intermittent gusts of cold autumn wind. Julie Marie pulled her sweater closer.

"Uh-uh," she replied, shaking her head as she uttered her response. "I don't like them."

"Me either. I like princesses better than little hairy monsters."

A large gust blew between the brother and sister, catching the skirt of the girl's princess gown and wafting it in the breeze.

"You must be getting cold now. It feels like it's going to rain. How 'bout heading home?"

"Okay," his sister replied, nodding her head.

A few minutes later, they were startled by a commotion across the street – several people were screaming – and then *they all* ran away screaming, taking off in every direction! Trembling, Julie Marie drew closer to her brother.

"Just some morons playing a practical joke, I'm sure. You don't have to be frightened, Julie Marie, sometimes on Halloween people like to scare other people for fun. Jerks!"

"*Ow! Get away from me!*" he cried, spinning around to see what animal had bit his ankle. He picked up Julie Marie. "I don't know what bit me, but we better get going."

"One of those kids," she answered, sobbing. "One of the ugly kids."

The rain started to fall, and Jeff walked more briskly, his sister in his arms.

"Jeff – there's one!" she screamed.

He looked around. A little brown troll was running on its short legs after them. Jeff was running now, and Juliet Marie remained quiet in his arms, despite the tears streaming over her cheeks.

When they reached their house, their parents were not at their post. Setting Julie Marie down on the porch, Jeff tried to open the door. It was locked. He knocked.

"Damn. I didn't bring my keys."

They looked through the windows. No one was in sight.

"They have to be in there. They wouldn't have gone away and locked us out."

Taking his sister's hand, Jeff walked around the house and tried the back door. It was raining steadily now, and the thunder was louder. As they peered into and knocked on all the first-floor windows, Jeff called to his parents, raising his voice so that he could be heard over the storm. A face appeared at their bedroom window, opened the sash – his father answered:

"Is that you, Jeff? Are you okay? Is Julie Marie okay?"

"Yes – please let us in out of the rain."

Moments later, the parents were letting their bedraggled children in the kitchen door.

"Daddy! Daddy!" Julie Marie screamed. *"It's got me!"*

She was being pulled out the door.

Jacqueline Esmerelda came flying through the kitchen, leapt valiantly into the aether, landed gracefully upon the ugly, bulbous snout of the troll – and rent its face into shreds. Purple trollish fluid ran all over Jacqueline Esmerelda's shiny fur and the linoleum kitchen floor, and ebony cat fur wafted through the air.

As Jacqueline Esmerelda battled the troll, Wil snatched Julie Marie from its clutches. Frances tried to lead her into the living room.

"Jacqueline Esmerelda! Don't let it hurt her!" Julie Marie cried, refusing to allow her mother to take her from the kitchen. *"Help Jacqueline Esmerelda, Jeff! Save her, Daddy!"*

Galvanized by the child's cries, the stunned men joined the fray. Jeff pulled the battered feline from the troll and gently handed her to his mother. Father and son felled the waterlogged and cat-worse troll. The evil creature ran from the house and into the gale, leaving a viscous purple trail.

Thunder thrummed – thrummed, and boomed – in louder and louder celestial drum rolls, roll upon roll of booming bass percussion, while red and white lightning inflamed the sky, setting the firmament afire. The troll sizzled, fizzled into purple vapor. When they looked outside the next day, the Mitchells would discover a purple puddle in the lawn, where the troll they had slain had fallen. Soon, everyone living in the quiet village at the base of the Catskill Mountains would discover purple stains upon the earth. Villagers would long discourse on what had drawn the creatures down from the mountains on that fateful Halloween, and what had vanquished them at last. From that day, Jacqueline Esmerelda and Julie Marie were seldom apart, and Littleville lost its taste for trick-or-treating and for old Rip Van Winkle.

Shenanigans

Mark Dozier

"Ha! Brilliant!" Allison said pointing to the plaque on the building where they were standing.

"What?"

"The bar you were going on about last night. The Rathskeller. Right there in front of you."

Seemingly transfixed, Chuck remained rooted in the middle of the sidewalk while he stared at the tavern's large neon sign and dark-timbered exterior. Craning his neck, he peered up at the huge, turn-of-the-century skyscraper spearing the heavens above.

"Well, I'll be damned," he muttered with a grin. "This is prophetic."

"I'll say," Allison said, "after all your whining over the ten dollars you paid for a beer yesterday."

"I bet the plaque you're looking at says something about Prohibition, just like Jenkins told me," Chuck said, more excited than Allison had seen him all trip.

"One of the first barrooms to re-open when Prohibition was lifted," she paraphrased aloud.

"I knew it!"

Snapping his fingers, he bounded up the steps. "Let's see if they really do have one-dollar German beer."

Allison flashed him a bright smile when he glanced back holding the door. She had always thought that her extremely bright fiancé was in many ways – like most men – simple. Even his name conveyed a great deal about the man. Chuck. A down-to-earth, cards-on-the-table jokester who loved a good time. A real contrast to her own urbane, more reserved demeanor.

But as opposites often do, they got along well enough. As long as Allison could keep her incorrigible rascal of a boyfriend's enthusiasms in check. Particularly this time of year, with Halloween looming next week.

Inside, they found the bar separated from the restaurant by a long divider garishly decorated in orange and black streamers and masks; a young, gum-chewing woman strategically anchored at the point of separation.

"Two for dinner?"

Chuck shook his head, giving her a broad smile.

"No thank you. We're here for your dollar beer."

"Sorry, but that's only during happy hour on Tuesdays," she said.

"Damn," he swore theatrically, "and we came all the way from Virginia for your beer."

Rolling her eyes, Allison gave Chuck her look while the young woman shrugged.

"Why don't you tell Jason, the bartender, you saw his video," the hostess suggested. She nodded toward the bar. "He might help you out."

"Yes, why don't you?" Allison said with a smirk, but to her surprise, Chuck had already rounded the antique divider and was heading for the bar.

"Who's Jason?" Allison heard him call out.

The twenty or so patrons gathered around the bar looked up.

"Hey Connors, fella wants to see ya," a lanky bartender wiping down a stool yelled over his shoulder.

From the back, a burly man a few years younger than Chuck, with sandy hair and thick forearms, came out carrying a keg of beer. Setting down his heavy load, he straightened and stretched upright, a hand on either kidney.

Seeing Chuck and his pretty date, he smiled.

"Can I help you?"

"Are you Jason?"

He nodded.

"Not the Jason who made the video about Chicago's finest bar?" Chuck said, pivoting his awestruck expression from the young bartender to Allison.

"You've seen my video?"

"Hell, Jason. Everyone in Richmond, Virginia's seen your video. You're a goddamn legend."

"*My* video?"

Allison nodded with feigned enthusiasm when Chuck shot her a look.

"*They've seen my video!*" he exclaimed, yanking the cord on the cast iron seaman's bell next to the register. The loud clang of the bell brought several of the patrons off their stools and overpowered the televised baseball game overhead.

"It's 'bout time," one of the men sipping a beer chortled.

"Ya been whining 'bout it long enough," another said.

Jason clanged the bell again and ran back and forth behind the bar high fiving the regulars and repeatedly clapping the other bartender on the back.

"What did I tell ya?" he said to no one in particular. "And they came all the way from Virginia!"

Glancing at Allison, Chuck caught a flicker of alarm in her stare. She could put up with practically any of his nonsense as long as she was not publicly embarrassed.

"Say Jason, think we could have a couple of those dollar beers?" Chuck asked when the bartender's wild back and forth slowed to a trot.

"Dollar beers? Hell no."

He charged around the bar, and Allison saw Chuck flinch from the anticipated punch to the jaw. Instead, Jason locked a meaty fist on their elbows and directed the couple past the other patrons to a table overlooking the room.

"You can have anything you want." Pushing Chuck into a chair, he held out the other one for Allison. "We normally don't serve dinner over here but tonight's an exception. I'll get you a waiter. Dinner and everything else is on us. Just sit back and enjoy. I can't wait to get your personal reactions to every part of my film. I'll be right back."

"Holy shit," Chuck said. "Can you believe this guy?"

"Just brilliant," Allison muttered in exasperation. "And I thought the South was supposed to have all the yokels in the country. What are you going to do?"

"Whatdaya mean?"

"When Jacob starts asking…"

"Jason," Chuck corrected.

"When that bugger wants your critique of his cinematic masterpiece, what will you say?"

Chuck gave his fiancée a hard look. Ever since her return from six weeks in England, anything out of the ordinary was "Brilliant" and every rube they encountered was a "Bugger"; the limited addition to her otherwise extensive vocabulary constituting her takeaway from what was supposed to be six weeks by herself to figure things out.

"I guess I'll…."

Chuck's whispered reply was interrupted by two ridiculously enthusiastic waiters circling their table with silverware, plates, wine glasses, and an orange cardboard box illustrated with a carved pumpkin's twisted grin.

"What's with the box?" Allison asked, making a face,

"A case of souvenir glasses from Rathskeller's!" one of the waiters beamed, while his associate vigorously nodded.

When one of the waiters handed each of them a menu, Chuck protested.

"I'm just going to have a cheeseburger."

"Oh, not likely, sir. Everything's on us," the waiter explained. "I suggest the filet mignon. It's divine."

Chuck gave the man's discolored teeth, his rummy's nose, and stained Lederhosen a quick glance. His speech did not jibe with his appearance. He sounded schooled. How could one trust a waiter who had to be trained? One either had the natural skills to wait on others or he didn't. They'd have to keep a watch on this fellow.

He glanced over at Allison to see if she had picked up on it too, but to his horror, realized that her earlier look of alarm had transitioned into one of contrite capitulation. She was about to spill the beans.

"Before this goes too far," she said to the waiter, "maybe we should explain that we've never…"

Blocking her comment with a raised menu, Chuck gave the waiter's sleeve a firm tug.

"Two medium rare filet mignons sound perfect. Thank you."

"And the wine, sir?"

"A Bordeaux. Why don't you surprise us with something hearty. Really earthy and full-bodied."

"Very good, sir," he said, obsequiously backing away.

"You were about to give us away," Chuck scolded in disbelief as soon as the waiter was out of earshot. "I could see it in your eyes."

Allison shook her head.

"I feel terrible leading these poor buggers on like we are."

Chuck gave her hand a warm squeeze.

"It's only a lark. The joke of the ages. I had no idea it would mushroom into something so…," he waved his hand around them and laughed, "so preposterous. But think what a great Halloween story we're going to get out of it."

216

"Ahhh–," Allison all but screamed. A primeval emission of frustration and fear he had never heard. "You and your stories. Everything's a lark. Or a prank. Or… Oh, what the hell. Why do you always put me through these things? You're thirty-years-old. Why can't you just be normal?"

Because normal is boring, Chuck started to say. But given the circumstances, he knew better than to antagonize her. It wasn't the first time they had had a row over one of his antics. But Allison was right about one thing – he could not wait to tell the boys back home about this latest.

Within minutes the steaks arrived. Two generous cuts of delicate tenderloin perfectly prepared.

"This looks wonderful," Chuck said, cutting into his steak with relish.

"Brilliant," Allison agreed. "Didn't know how hungry I was until this gorgeous food arrived."

"By God, I'm famished."

For the next quarter hour they consumed the delicious meal in silence, washing down each bite with the incredible Bordeaux the disheveled waiter continued to pour.

Sated at last, they sat back from the table while the dishes were cleared.

"And for dessert?"

"Oh no, no thank you, Lawrence," Allison said with a glance at his name tag. "That was one of the most incredible meals I've ever had. Let's not ruin it with dessert."

"You have to admit," Chuck said, smiling at his fiancée when the waiter left, "sometimes my shenanigans pay off."

"Now how 'bout that photo?"

When they looked up, Jason had squatted down between them, beaming. Before they knew what was happening, Lawrence the waiter snapped their picture.

"How 'bout a vertical one," Jason suggested. Before they were finished, the waiter had snapped a half dozen startled portraits of the celebrated pair.

"I'm just dying to know. Cannot wait any longer," Jason said, pulling a chair to their table. "What part of the video did you like the best?"

Even flush from the wines, Allison's face blanched. Chuck coughed into his fist and turned up what was left of his glass.

"That's a tough one, Jason," he replied, wiping his mouth with the back of his hand.

Jason nodded, waiting.

"I liked the entire production, the way each segment was followed by another. But if I had to choose, I would have to say the ending. Yep, I think the last few minutes were my favorite."

Jason slammed his palm on the table, spilling wine over the tablecloth and rattling the silverware.

"*Me too!*" he cried. "By golly, I knew we were kindred spirits. You felt the ending brought everything together, didn't you."

"Exactly," Chuck said in relief.

"What's your occupation, Chuck?" he asked, although Chuck could not remember introducing himself.

"Believe it or not, I'm a stockbroker, and Allison's one of the best dang hairdressers in Richmond," he replied, although in reality Allison was the principal of the high school where Chuck taught social studies and coached the debate team.

"A man of the financial world and his lady," Jason nodded. "I asked because we don't put just anyone on our email list, isn't that right Lawrence?"

"No sir," Lawrence confirmed. "We're a tight little group here at Rathskeller's."

"One has to have the right... How should I phrase it?"

"Pedigree?" the waiter suggested.

"Exactly. One has to have the proper credentials. Like Lawrence here. Right Lawrence?"

"Aw," the waiter blushed, "you're going to make me tear up."

And exchanging looks, the two men shared a disconcerting giggle.

"We like to keep the riff-raff out."

"No pretenders in Rathskeller's."

"When I heard that faint but beautiful English accent," Jason said, turning to Allison, "I knew the two of you were something special."

"I spent some time outside London last year," Allison explained, obviously pleased.

Waving for a pen, Jason refilled their wine glasses. Although they had not given their surnames, the young bartender asked, "Now how do you spell your names again?"

As though in a dream, Chuck watched himself carefully jot own their real names and email addresses beneath a list of others in an old ledger. Reading over what he had written, he heard Allison let out a nervous sigh. Startled, he realized too late that she was about to confess.

"I feel like an idiot," she said in such a way that for the first time, Jason gave them a doubtful stare. "I'm afraid we've misrepresented ourselves. None of this is true."

Chuck looked from Allison to Jason. When he smiled and rolled his eyes, Jason smiled too. He padded Allison's hand.

"Now not to worry. We've had others express similar feelings. I'm afraid our Midwestern hospitality can be overwhelming at times. But look how far you came to share your feelings with us. Both of you deserve everything you get."

He looked over at Chuck and grinned.

"Just think of all the publicity you're about to receive. Why the two of you will look like real troopers on Facebook."

"You've been on our Facebook accounts?" Allison asked in shock.

"On your accounts?" Jason laughed. "No. Of course not. I was talking about *our* Facebook account. Lawrence just gave me a thumbs up. We posted your photos on Rathskeller's Facebook page while Chuck was writing down your email addresses."

"On Facebook?"

"Within the next few minutes we'll have your happy smiles on a half dozen other social media sites that will circle the globe. Don't you worry."

Before Chuck or Allison could respond, large steins of beer were placed on their table. All the customers walked over from the bar and the other tables and gathered around them, beers in hand.

"It's a Rathskeller tradition that we sing an old German beer song of friendship to our special guests, so if you'll join us…"

"Ein Prosit, ein Prosit
Der Geremutlichkeit
Ein Prosit, ein Prosit
Der Germutlichkeit"

They sang, swinging their mugs with great cheer. At the end of each stanza, a waiter would shout,

"Oans! Zwoa! Drei!"

Followed by a robust,

"G'Suffa!"

And everyone would drink up.

At the far end of the bar a Congo line was formed and hands pulled Chuck and Allison forward.

"A Congo line in a German bar?"

"It's another Rathskeller tradition," Jason said laughing, taking their hands. "Come on, let's have some fun."

Each time they circled the bar, Chuck caught Allison's troubled expression. A look that reflected his own. When would this insanity end?

A half hour later, people began dropping out, collapsing with a laugh at their tables or stools.

At length, Jason escorted the frazzled couple back to their table to gather their belongings, including the box of beer glasses.

As they were saying goodbye, Chuck asked the young bartender, "Why did you need our email addresses?"

"To stay in touch until next year's Halloween, of course."

"What happens next year?"

"Our special guest status ends, right?" Allison asked, perking up.

"Oh no. That's forever. But next year you'll be invited to Rathskeller's Halloween Party. You don't want to miss that. It's deliciously decadent," he added with a leer. "Even the mayor will be there."

"Chicago's Mayor?" Chuck said in disbelief.

"Of course. Traditionally we've had almost 100% of our special guests participate every year."

"No fooling?"

Jason nodded, whispering surreptitiously, "Most of 'em wouldn't dare miss it."

"Why?" Allison asked.

"Because it's so much fun." Jason laughed before suddenly growing serious. "And then, of course, there's the curse."

"What curse?"

"Sounded like the two of you were a big hit," the hostess said, interrupting Jason's reply as they reached her podium.

Glancing at her, Allison experienced the ridiculous feeling that even the young, gum-chewing girl had an evil glint in her eye. Staring, she felt the hackles tingle her neck and cold sweat run down her sides. But once they were outside, the cool, fall air quickly shook Allison out of her inexplicable panic.

"Thanks for everything. Jason. And congratulations again on that video of yours."

"Thank you for your feedback. And remember," he said pausing for just a beat, "be real careful for the next few days 'til things settle in."

Chuck and Allison looked at each other.

"What things?"

"What's that mean?"

But Jason only smiled and waved goodbye before disappearing inside.

"Say, what'd he mean by that?" Chuck asked, but before he could start back up the steps, Allison pulled him down the sidewalk.

"Let's get the hell away from here. It's just too... What are you doing?"

Taking out his cell phone, Chuck had started savagely punching buttons.

"I'm googling to see if that video is as bad as I fear."

"Step it up, Chuck. Forget that stupid video. I want to put as many blocks as possible between us and those Rathskeller weirdos."

"Wait a sec," he muttered in a distracted voice. "I'm pulling it up now."

Allison never broke stride. Every ten feet she felt a little better. Stopping to catch her breath, she turned to see Chuck almost a block behind her, still peering down at his phone.

"Will you come on," she screamed.

The next time she looked back, she heard her fiancé yell something, the faint light of his cell phone illuminating his frantic waves.

"What's the problem?" she yelled back in irritation before realizing that there must be something desperately wrong or her fiance was drunker than she thought.

Allison watched Chuck stumble toward her. Then felt her entire body go cold when she heard the fear in his high-pitched scream, "The video, my God, take a look at this video."

A Scream That Wouldn't Come

K. T. Booker

The skeleton hung above Eric, noose lashed over a sprawling oak tree. Black pitted eyes stared down. Just like—

Be a good boy, Eric! I will always love you!

No, he wouldn't think about that.

The corpse wearing a 49ers jacket rose up suddenly out of its lawn chair, reaching with grimy hands.

Eric knew it was coming, gave a fake scream, lifted his hands in mock fright. The corpse sat back down, played dead again for the next trick-or-treater.

Looking down the street, Eric didn't know when that would be. The neighborhood was deserted. If you could call it that. The streetlights hadn't been installed. Still under construction, the partially built houses sank into deep shadows further down the street.

James and Amy were in that darkness somewhere. Things were getting heavy between the two of them, so Eric decided to give them space. He grabbed a cast-away construction hat, shoved it on his head. It was Halloween, might as well get some candy.

But he hadn't trick-or-treated, nor celebrated Halloween one bit, not since his father…

Without thinking, he looked back at the skeleton hanging there, moving slightly with the wind. He turned away, knocked on the door. It swung open.

"What are you supposed to be?" an old woman asked him, gazing up and down doubtfully. He was startled by her eyes. Catlike and piercing. Contacts, he thought. You can get them cheap at the Halloween store. She was wearing a short black dress, thin fabric like silk, cut high, revealing an obscene quantity of her spindly thighs, thin as spider legs.

"Construction worker, ma'am," he said, tipping his hard hat. "Trick or treat."

"Aren't you a bit old to be trick or treating?" she asked, her voice a haggard imitation of an old crone. Behind her was a huge table. It was stacked with vials, bottles, a huge witch's cauldron.

"Aren't you a bit old to be wearing *that* dress?" he retorted.

He heard the corpse in the lawn chair give a short, clipped laugh. The old woman glared at him. Eric snatched a fistful of candy before the witch could pull the basket away.

"Just one," she shrieked at him.

But he was already striding away. "It's for my friends," he called back.

"I curse you," she howled.

He laughed to himself at the genuinely witchy way she spoke. He lifted his middle finger as he tramped across her crab grass. Intentionally keeping his eyes away from the oak tree, he looked again at the corpse in the lawn chair with a strange sense of melancholy. He'd probably never be scared again. He was sixteen now. Too old.

"I'll cook you and your friends in a stew," her cackling voice lifted once more into the night.

The dumb lush, he thought.

Where were his friends anyways? They usually weren't gone this long.

The next house, the only other one that looked occupied, was much nicer. Painted a deep olive green, it looked almost black in the night. The sidewalk smooth and bright, a perfectly round pumpkin sat at the edge of the manicured lawn, face lit with a small shaky flame.

A floodlight flicked on as he walked up to the house. When he knocked, no one answered. There was someone inside. He could hear heavy footsteps moving away from the door, as though they had been looking at him through the peephole. The sound moved away deeper within the home. He knocked again, louder.

He was being discriminated against. Because of his age. Petulantly, he kicked over a plastic dog skeleton, then left. When he reached the pumpkin, he looked around, picked it up, then hurried down the street.

After he heaved it over his head, he watched it floating in the air, momentarily backdropped by stars. It exploded with a hollow, wet *smack!* then flattened and broke into pieces. He kicked one of the pieces with his foot.

Maybe he should call for James. Have him collect more pumpkins—

A door slammed shut. At the house that he had just grabbed the pumpkin from. The flood light kicked on again. A man, a very large man, in a dark jumpsuit, wearing what looked like a silver mask came sprinting across the lawn. He was holding something and, from a distance, the man's movement and physique, and even his strange Halloween costume, reminded Eric so much of his father that he almost called out to him.

But that was stupid, his father was dead. Been dead for five years.

The man was holding a bat. And the distance between them was closing fast. Startlingly fast.

"*Shit*," Eric mumbled as he turned and ran down the street. He wanted to call out for the man to chill out, that it was just a pumpkin, but nothing came.

The night was strangely silent save for the man's heavy and rapid footfall. He must have been wearing engineering boots, just like his father. The sound of them thundered on the asphalt, getting closer.

A sound, like a fluttering bird, shot past Eric's head and made him duck. The bat skipped like a stone along the road ahead of him at an astonishing speed.

"What the—" he groaned.

That would have done real damage if it connected. Anger welled up inside him. He turned to shout but froze. The man had nearly caught him, his mask shining in the moonlight, his strange stiff movements bearing down.

He remembered a mask like that...

Eric turned sharply into one of the empty lots, crashing through a thick wild hedge of manzanita bushes. They clawed at his shirt, his pants, his face, but he pressed through, a whimper escaping his mouth as the sounds of pursuit remained close.

He burst out of the bushes at the top of a cul-de-sac and stumbled across the road. He ran up a driveway and crawled behind a cluster of trash cans, crouching there, panting, his heart racing, his nose filled with the scent of refuse. He hid a long time, listening, waiting, but the man seemed to have quit the chase. The street was quiet.

Why were there no trick-or-treaters here in this section of the new suburb? The street was well lit, the houses large, all finished. This was the type of street that might give out full sized candy bars.

His father would also give out full sized bars on Halloween. His father's favorite holiday. The only time he seemed to enjoy himself. Eric thought of the haunted house he'd created in their garage for the neighbor kids. It made him feel uneasy.

And what was this? Near him, a black sheet was draped across the entrance to a garage, streaked with dust from the road. Red paint splattered across it. Thin ribbons of fog leaked out the edges. A fake plastic skeleton sat in a chair, a sign in its lap. *Enter If You Dare!* in dripping blood.

A movement in the bushes made him duck in fear. He darted under the black sheet and into the garage. Was it the man in the mask? Maybe. Or it was just the wind in the bushes. He couldn't tell.

He steadied his heart rate, his rising panic. The man wouldn't come here. Maybe he should just go knock on the front door, call the police. Okay, yes, he smashed a pumpkin. He'd cop to it if needed. But the man tried to bludgeon him with a bat. And Eric was a kid still, technically. Although he hated to think of himself as that. But when it worked to his advantage, he would use it.

The small room of this modest haunted house was filled with fog. He swatted at it, but it was like trying to part muddy water. It was almost suffocating how thick it had accumulated. The owner probably expected kids tramping in and out of the place, just like his fathers. He couldn't have expected for it to be barren of children.

The low rattle of a machine on concrete played in the corner. Odd shapes floated like black smears in the hazy white fog. He touched one, sending it swinging like a pendulum. Rubber bats. How closely this resembled what his father had done. Or was it just his memory playing tricks on him? He had learned that half-forgotten memories latched onto the present and could permanently warp what you understood of the past.

He shook the thought away, but he knew where the fog machine would be. He put his hand behind the plastic witch's cauldron and shut it off, already knowing where the switch was. The rattling hum faded, but now the silence in the fog was almost physical.

He walked through a door. The walls were covered in white sheets. Something was in the corner. A little girl, in a hospital gown. The white sheets were meant to represent a padded room, a psych ward, he realized. There were drawings on the wall, hard to see with the fog that had seeped in. But there was something familiar in the drawings. He stepped closer, peering, before something grabbed his foot.

He yanked back, startled. The little girl was crouched near him. How she'd moved so quickly and quietly he didn't know. She was hunched over, her hands clasping her legs. Hands that were long and bony, wrapped around feet with hideously overgrown nails. Repulsed, he stepped away. The girl laughed, but he couldn't see her face, her greasy matted hair was draped down. She wheeled about in little hopping circles. Her rotten feet tread on her hair and with each step she ripped out patches of the dirty blond strands.

Stop that, he wanted to say at this display of self-destruction. But it was probably a wig, he convinced himself. Stupid. But the sight of the hair being torn out, the patches snaking about on the floor, unnerved him.

The girl had scurried back to the corner. She was creepy alright. She had done her job. He had performed something similar for his father's haunted house. But it was only as a zombie, lumbering out, groaning. He remembered enjoying it. That fear. The eyes on those few kids he scared. It was power. Intoxicating.

A closed door was on the other side of the room. He'd go in and ask to use their phone. He had no intention of going back outside at this point. His nerves were too keyed up.

When he grabbed the door handle, the door seemed to swing open on its own. The room was completely bare save for a large wooden box made of plywood. A hole was cut neatly in the center of the top. The side facing Eric read: *Reach In If You Dare!*

He smiled at this. Another similarity to his father's haunted house. He'd even sat in one of these sensory boxes during one Halloween. Crouched in the dark, waiting for kids to reach their hands in. He'd touch them with different things, brush against their quivering hands, claw at them. They'd scream and laugh.

Eric reached his hand in. His nerves fluttered with anticipation. Nothing. He moved his hand around, searching for a small kid. He'd grab them, tussle their hair. But there was no one.

As he pulled his hand out, there was a thunderous crash that exploded through the room. Something latched onto his hand, something terribly strong, with fingers that were almost scaly. The flaky, blistering skin rubbed on his, then something warm and wet enveloped his fingers.

Inside a mouth. His fingers were inside a mouth, he realized with revulsion. The teeth scraping his knuckles felt too large, sickly, like fungus-covered stones. He tore his hand out with a cry of disgust to jittering cackles.

There was a horrific smell coming out of the box now, and off his hand. He wiped it on his pants. Didn't help.

He realized the crashing sound he heard had been the door slamming behind him. It must have been the girl. Part of the trick, to make him vulnerable and to signal to the person in the box. But there had been nothing in there. It was not that big. He had reached around, scooping out the whole area for discovery. They were playing tricks on him. What kind of haunted house was this anyways? Who would put their mouth on some stranger's fingers. He flushed with anger and kicked out at the box savagely. "Bastard!"

He grabbed at the door that had shut behind him. Locked. It wouldn't budge. He might as well have put his shoulder to a slab of granite.

He wouldn't panic. No. They wouldn't terrify him. They wanted him to finish the haunted house. Fine. Let it be, he'd go on.

He stepped around the box, and up a small flight of steps where a door lay open, waiting for him. The door entered a hallway, dimly lit.

The door softly clicked behind him. Locked again, he knew. He walked along the hall. The further he went in, the paltry light faded. The air was stagnant, thick. He called out weakly. No one answered.

Had he been here before? All of this looked familiar, but from where? He couldn't remember.

The light continued to die, slowly, until there was only a sickly yellow aura. Four doors hung in that jaundiced half-light. He tried one door, then another. Locked.

But what kind of place was this? Had they changed the whole damn thing into a haunted house? He thought of his father then, that dark descent. How each year, their house gradually had gotten more consumed by his grand designs. Designs that became more and more unhinged. The obsession with the perfect haunted house. Until finally, unable to fight the depression anymore—

Eric tried another door. Locked. He banged until his knuckles ached. The smell from the box remained on his fist. A raw sewage smell that made him queasy. Sweating, mouth dry and faintly tasting of cheap chocolate, he wanted the haunted house to be over. It was dredging up memories. Memories buried deep, very deep.

The fourth door was unlocked. His hand flinched when it opened. He peered inside. Deep shadows. Six figures hunched in the bulk darkness. He recognized them instantly. A shudder went down his

228

spine like a cold slithering snake. The six dolls. His mother had painstakingly sewn these over one summer to make his father happy, for his haunted house. Six child-sized dolls. Eric had loathed them. The dolls sat in the rafters the rest of the year. When he took the trash out at night they would stare, their gazes following him. On Halloween, they were placed primly on chairs, at old antique student desks, smiling their insane idiot smiles. Now all six were facing the wall, as if in prayer.

Was this a dream? His mind felt fevered, his breath weak.

All at once, the dolls turned their heads, their crazy smiling faces rat-chewed and pouring out stuffing like fish guts. He slammed the door, ran down the hall, into the clinging darkness, panting, feeling as though he would burst open with the pestilential flow of terror. His quivering hands groped, reaching for anything. A door handle. It swung open so violently he tumbled headfirst into the room. And he knew, instinctively, before he even looked up, what was in this room.

Hanging from the ceiling fan, a note in his hand, was his father.

Be a good boy, Eric! I will always love you!

The door slammed shut behind him. Locked. His father's room. Trapped in here with him. *Be a good boy, Eric!* Terror iced through his guts, spreading through his limbs. His body felt sluggish, as though he was at the bottom of the ocean.

He remembered. The crawlspace. In the closet. As he swung his father's closet door open, he heard a sickening thump as the body crumpled to the floor. But what was that scratching sound? Was it heaving toward him?

He ripped the crawlspace hatch up, dove into that shadowed square cutout, headfirst, hands desperately clawing at the cold packed dirt. A gray pewtered light spilled from an agonizingly distant window.

There, deep on the other side of the crawlspace. What was he looking at? The space seemed to extend downwards, opening into a vast darkness. And in that vista, he glimpsed hellish things. Things, hazy in shadows, that his mind recoiled from. Wailing, stuttered cries filled the cramped space, as though prey was being eaten, torn apart. His eyes, blurry from tears, focused on the fractured dim light as the scampering of claws in the hardpacked soil closed in on him.

He jammed his thin frame through the small window. His pants caught on a latch, he yanked with all his might, hearing the jeans tear, not looking down into that choked darkness. He scrabbled through the lawn, the sounds of broken glass behind him. Running up the street, he saw, with stupid fascination, the smashed pumpkin in the road.

But how was that possible? Had he gone in a circle? He passed the olive-green house, not caring about the man with the bat. The skittering of wobbly hooves on asphalt and wet heavy grunts followed him. He dared not look back. The sounds made his legs rubbery, his bowels cold.

The skeleton hung from the oak. The corpse-man gone. He pulled at the front door. Locked. He pounded the wood so hard he thought it would splinter. The lock turned. He shoved it open, slammed it shut, fell panting on the floor.

He looked up, confused at first, then his bladder released.

The man with the silver mask held the heads of James and Amy. He tossed them into the witch's cauldron. A scream that wouldn't come died in Eric's chest as the witch's long bony hands came to rest on his shoulder.

"Welcome," she said. "Stay for dinner."

230

Bad Things Happen to Good People

Paul Northgraves

"Bad things happen to good people…"

"Now, I ain't starting any rumours about what happened and what kind of people they were. I can only tell you about what I saw with my own two eyes. Say it's bright in here isn't it? Can you turn down the lights a little or something? My eyes hurt. What? No, no am fine, just a little tired, I guess, not surprising with all what's happened. Where was I oh yes!

"If I ain't of seen any of it for myself then I wouldn't have believed it. Sorry say that again… Oh sorry, yes please… thank you. I haven't smoked in thirteen years. Gave them up after I had a health scare with pneumonia back in 2011. I couldn't even get up the stairs without wheezing or a coughing fit. I know I shouldn't but after the last twenty-four hours or so it doesn't to matter anymore I guess. Seems like a good time to start again doesn't it… Thank you. Filthy habit my wife use to say. Dragging on another coffin nail there Harold she would say, they're no good for you and all that. She was glad when I gave them up bless her soul, but you haven't come here for my life story have you so I will proceed."

"The first I knew of anything was when I was awoken by shouting and screaming in the street. Someone was pounding on my front door. It was the Whites from opposite shouting in the street, lovely family, moved here three years ago from North Lincolnshire… um pardon? No, Mr White, Patrick is his first name, he was already in the street by the time I looked out of the bedroom window and it was he who was calling the fire brigade, or you guys I guess. He was hammering at my front door at the same time. Well I opened the window to see what all the commotion was about and I shouted down to ask what the hell was going on but all I could hear was Kathy White screaming FIRE! FIRE! And waving her arms frantically as if she trying to signal a passing plane for help."

"This cigarette, is it Silk Cut? I thought it was… now, where was I, oh yes! Anyways, when I finally got on my dressing gown and started making my way downstairs, I could feel the heat radiating through my wall and I prayed to God that it wasn't coming directly from next door but when I stepped into the street my worst fears were confirmed, next door was engulfed in flames. I mean it was an inferno. Even from standing on the other street it felt like I had my head in an oven. All I remember thinking is good lord I hope the poor woman had gotten out in time."

"Whoa, I shivered then, chills all down my spine, felt like someone had walked over my grave. Did you turn down the heating down in here or something? No am ok to continue, I feel a bit funny but am fine, I will continue."

"Now I know there has been some strange going on's in that house. Nothing I could quite put my finger on but she never introduced herself. Not to me, or the Whites or anyone else who live in the street. She always seemed distant and even though I said my morning's and evening's to her, just to be polite, manners cost nothing and all that, she would just look at me with this vacant stare. She looked at you in the sense she acknowledged your presence but not exactly looking at you, but more was looking straight through me, like if I were made of glass or something. If you catch my drift."

"Come to think of it. Her skin was always pale as if she had not been getting enough sunlight or something. Emaciated is the word I would use to describe her. I just thought there are certain folks who like to keep themselves to themselves. Ain't nothing wrong with that but you have got to understand. I been living in that house down Crescent Lane for the past thirty-three years and I ain't never seen anything as awful as this happen but, since she moved in next door last summer that house just seemed to deteriorate overnight. Every time I walked by, either coming back from the shops or from the pub. I always felt an unease when she was around. Never saw her in the daytime. I just assumed she worked nights or something but I tell you when on the odd occasion I did see her, my skin use to crawl. If I even so much as looked up at them windows with them big blackout curtains she had hung up it had reminded me of those old Hammer horror films. It always felt like she was trying to hide something and well... now we know what."

"Could I have a glass of water please, umm yes thank you, nice and cold, tastes good. Refreshing. Can't seem to quench my thirst lately, but I seem to be having trouble keeping my food down."

"I'll tell you a story, you might think at my age I was been a silly old fool and a little bit senile but after what happened last night I will tell you it anyways, doesn't seem to matter much now but I always took pride in my back garden. It weren't the Chelsea flower show or anything as fancy as that but it was my little slice of the Garden of Eden. My wife god bless her soul always said I cared more about them bluebells and primroses then I did about her but I knew she was just pulling my leg. She had an amazing sense of humour did my Lizzy. I do miss her."

"Anyways I digress. One day I heard a scratching noise coming from the other side of the fence, like something was scraping on wood, so naturally I popped my head over to see if I could see anything and well I wasn't prepared for what I saw. The grass and weeds had grown so tall they started to block the sunlight to my greenhouse, but in spite of their size and that they had grown considerably during the spring, all the plant life seemed to be… *dead*. I was going to ask her if she would consider trimming it all back a bit and if they she needed any help I was only too happy to oblige, but something gnawed at me not to, like a warning sign telling me not to. This thing that my wife would have called a 'panic rat' rose up in me. For two days I thought about how to approach the matter. Finally, I worked up the nerve to knock on her door but something in my brain – that panic rat again- told me not to stir up that nest of snakes. Call it what you want. Intuition, cowardice or just blind luck but I lost my nerve and returned home."

"I will tell you the rest and then I think I need to lay down for a bit. My gums feel sore. Tender to touch with my tongue. Such a strange sensation as if a new tooth is coming through and the taste of that water has left a copper taste in my mouth… anyways nothing could have prepared me for what I saw next. Look at me, am still shaking even now."

"As I looked through the bay window I saw a figure calmly walking through the front living room. Walking through the fire, now I can tell you straight and with no doubt in my mind because I know I am of sound mind but I saw her… yes Alison… you say that what her name was?. Just goes to show you. She lived next door to me for just over a year and I didn't even know the woman's name. Well she… yes Alison was walking through the inferno as if her skin was made of asbestos but I can tell you it was not. I could see her already charred skin and the blister red twisted skin. The pain must have been excruciating, unimaginable. Thankfully the flames blocked most of what I could see. The fire was ravaging the house by then but I could

233

not stop thinking of the way her skin blacken and contort in ways no skin naturally should. There was no screaming, no emotion… no nothing. She simply just resigned to her fate. I think she welcomed it, I could tell she seemed at peace as the conflagration raged. A blessing if you will. I knew then that even if she survived her life would just be pain and suffering. Misery, if you will. Am glad to hear that you found her body in the ruin. I can't image what that must of looked like, or smelled like for that matter. Ain't no way to live when you're just a burned out husk."

"Look, outside the window, look at that beautiful sunset. You don't appreciate the beauty of everyday life, things we take for granted. Only god or something beyond our comprehension could create such magnificent beauty."

"Anyways you'll be wanting to hear the rest of my story so I shall continue. By then the Cowells had come out of number twenty-seven and they was they asking me what on earth was going on. I explained I had just come out of the house myself only a minute ago. Lenny Cowell, a good man. Have known him for a long time; asked me has anyone tried kicking the door down and getting in to rescue her but after what I saw I told him there was no use. By then the rest of the people started pouring onto the street, gawking at the bonfire that was three-seventeen Crescent Lane. We all just stood there helpless. We could hear the fire engines getting nearer at that point but the damage had already been done. The fire was coming through the black slate tiles on the roof. Even if she was still alive she would have been crushed to death.

"What happened next, everyone saw with their own eyes. The front door to three-seventeen opened, like a coffin lid opening at a wake we was all startled. At first it was just a small figure, I knew it was a child but I couldn't understand how she had gotten out. She calmly walked forward and stood there was the sorriest, palest little girl you ever set eyes on. She walked out of that house untouched and seemingly undeterred at the chaos going. Apart from the blackened soot that covered her face and dirtied her clothes she looked relatively unharmed. It was a miracle."

"It shocked us all, we all were rooted to the spot. None of us knew she even had a child. Well I was the first to react and I ran straight to her and pulled her away from the fire. Good job I did because the front window had just blown in and sent shards of glass flying everywhere and a big shard whistled by where we had stood. Taking her hand, the first thing I noticed was how cold her skin was. I mean she had just appeared from a burning house and she felt like she just come out of a meat freezer. She looked at me as if she had just woken up from a deep sleep. A questioning look that asked 'what's going on'. I talked to her but she did not say anything to me. I asked her if she was ok and was she hurt but she just looked at me in that faraway gaze that children have. She had the same vacant look to her as Alison when I saw her. God rest her soul.

With her been so cold I took my dressing gown off and wrapped it around her, to try and warm her up. We had just gotten to other side the road when the first fire trucks had just arrived. I asked her again if she was ok. She just looked up at me, her pupils were like pin pricks, and her faraway vacant eyes assessed me. Then she spoke... It was as light as the air and it took me back a bit as I studied the gravity of the question.

"Is my mummy dead?"

"I was tongue-tied. I did not know what to say to the poor kid. I just managed a fake smile and said nothing, then the most peculiar thing happened, as if she read my mind. She smiled at me and said something I couldn't quite hear so I bent my head down and asked her to repeat what she said. It chilled me to the bone what she said and then... well you know."

Harold Kinman gulped and looked straight into the eyes of Officer Maloney. Maloney, now suffering from a numb arse, finished the sentence for him.

"Then when she attacked you?

Maloney sat on the opposite side of the table and neatened the stack of papers in front of him.

"Right." Harold nodded. In front of him, poised on top of a clear plastic tub was his cigarette which had just extinguished itself.

Harold, for the last hour or so had told Maloney the police officer his story of what happened the night before. He moved his chair back. Scraping the tiled floor with its skinny metallic legs, stood up and straightening his back. He moved a hand up to his neck to feel for the two tiny puncture marks that now marked his skin. They were both raised slightly but the swelling had gone down since she first bit him.

He had his tetanus shot, just a precaution and since midday he had never felt better. In-fact he felt better than he ever did in his whole life. Just over twenty-four hours ago the man who lived at Three-fifteen Crescent Lane was just a normal law abiding citizen with a bad pair of lungs and was a widow of nearly five years. Now he could feel the change. He could feel her 'magic' coursing through his blood. He knew officer Maloney would be dead soon as the sun went down. It would be his rebirth and he would seek out the little girl who after biting him escaped from the blaze by climbing the walls and scurrying over the tiles of the houses that lined Crescent lane to disappear into the night.

Now the day was in its final throes and the sun's influence was nearly over. As the sun went down behind the river, which gave it a golden steel look. Harold looked behind him and saw what he presumed was a large two-way mirror filling one end of the room up. He smiled to himself and turned back around.

Methodically, he leaned across the table where Maloney was thumbing through his paperwork.

"When I said bad things happen to good people… I meant it."

Maloney looked up quizzically at him, as the last of the day's sun disappeared behind the golden steel river, he saw Harold's reflection disappear too.

Last Walk Home

Paul Northgraves

Apprehension gnawed at her like some ravenous mental crow pecking at her intrusive thoughts. Standing at the entrance at the all-but abandoned park, she shuddered at the howl of the wind, almost shrieking as it whistled past her ears. It was a bitter winter's night and all she wanted to do was to get home, and get into her comfy, warm bed.

Shuddering, she put her iPhone into her bag, along with her earphones -they were almost dead anyway- and decided then and there, to take the shortcut through the park.

The big monstrous gates gaped like a black mouth, as if it was in a big yawn. The long-rusted railings looked like giant jagged blackened teeth waiting to swallow anything whole that dared to enter the park.

Normally, she would have driven to work and back but this week her sister had borrowed the car from her. She was moving into her boyfriend's house. Amy had promised her that it would only be for this week, and as a thank you, she would wipe out the 'secret loan' that she asked her sister for three months ago. Begrudgingly she accepted, as financially, she was in no such position to manoeuvre.

Clutching her handbag tighter to her chest she crossed over the entrance's threshold and began walking through the park.

She cursed herself for missing the last bus home. It was that God-damn Andrew Smith's fault. He would never leave her alone if he saw her leaving late. She always felt that underneath that boyish bravado there was a creep.

Her heels clicked and clacked on the uneven paving slabs that jutted out seemingly in random places, as if assembled by some drunk labourer. Frosted weeds had settled and taken root in the cracks. A light fog had descended. It swirled around her. Teasing and twisting.

She had reached the edge of the children's play area. All that remained of it were the husks of what once were slides, swings and climbing frames. Now forlorn and hollow, these rusted ruins were once conduits of joy and happiness. Now they stood waiting for the inevitable. A sobering reminder that all things are ephemeral.

The sound of hushed teenager talk emitted from the direction of the bandstand opposite, a quick glance up confirmed this was the case. Three youths, two in grey hoodies and one in black Adidas hoody stood with their backs to her in a kind of semi-circle. She quickened her pace; they were obviously up to no good. Some illegal paraphernalia of some kind. She had no interest in what they were doing or what they were up to. She tightened the strap of her handbag even tighter over her shoulder as carried on with her journey.

She had made her way to the narrow path that snaked through the rest of the park. The path itself was a long S shape. It looked like it was participating in a demented game of snakes and ladders. The path, which nearly stretched the length of the park exited at Malvern Street. She was only a couple of streets away from where she lived and the thought of collapsing into a newly made bed gave her a renewed sense of vigour. Biting her lower lip, she started to walk down the path.

She noticed the further she wandered down the path, the more poorly lit it became. Occasionally, there would be the ethereal presence of a streetlight. Dim sodium lights that stained the fog a kind of gassy yellow.

The grey-metal monolithic streetlights emitted next to no light, alongside the lights were the things that partially obscured their existence. Horse chestnut trees glowered their gnarly knotted skin that overlooked the path.

A debris of dead leaves fluttered by her feet, making her jump a little, Brittle and fragile, they rustled by as if they didn't notice her or were too busy going someplace else.

She glanced up at the trees, ghost-like branches swayed in the wind. She watched them dance. They all boogied to the macabre rhythm. Their ash-coloured branches hung down like brittle skeletons from an anaemic trunk. An unnerving feeling came over her, she felt like she was being watched, not by someone but something. Which was stupid of course. It was impossible. The stuff of kid's nightmares. She shook it from her mind, but she could not escape the feeling that something lurked in the shadows.

The moon was at half crescent, looking like a leering lazy eye that was winking. It had all the black canvas of the sky to itself except for a few lonely grey clouds that scuttled by.

The wind had picked up even more now and she felt the chill it brought with it. Bringing the collar of her jacket up to her face, she buried herself deep in. A mini tornado of dead rotting leaves whipped up around her feet, this time she did not jump.

She knew that she left the hooded youths far behind now, they were engrossed in their 'activities'. To busy getting high to notice her. She thought that no-one in their right minds would be walking through the park at this time of the night but when darkness surrounds you, you feel exposed and alone. She had that intangible feeling of being watched.

The cut through to Malvern Street started to appear through the haze of the fog. She looked behind her and saw nothing but the empty poorly lit path. When she turned around to face forwards again, her heart leapt up her mouth and she stopped in her tracks.

A silhouette stood motionless at the other end of the path. Blocking the exit to Malvern Street. She felt suddenly vulnerable. Clearing her throat, she told herself that she was just being silly. She was taking a cut through and maybe, just maybe this individual was doing the same.

Her legs felt heavy, but she willed them on to start moving again. Walking at a slower pace, she kept her eyes firmly on the silhouette that had begun moving towards her.

It might have been thinking the same thing as she was. 'What idiot would be walking through the park at his time of the night'? She gave out a nervous chuckle.

The figure started to approach, its stride steady and strong. She could hear the footsteps now. She noticed a small flash of amber light burning bright, recede for a moment and then shrink down to almost a pinprick.

The figure slowly ambled its way towards her. The small circle of light growing bigger as the figure came closer. It could not be more than twenty feet away now. Smoke drifted up and appeared to merge with the thin veil of fog. It had lit a cigarette. That would explain the flash, it came from a lighter. She could hear its heavy breathing now. The footsteps steady, never losing its timing. Ten feet away now and her stomach churned, she clutched on the strap on her handbag.

They were almost side by side now. She tried not to make eye contact as they passed by each other. She was about to breathe a sigh of relief when a cold touch clamped around her left arm, instead of a sigh, all that came out of her mouth was a shriek. It had grabbed her arm and just as she was about to scream, she heard her name being spoken.

"Jennie, Jennie, calm down, calm down it's me. Andrew, it's me, Andy from work, it's me."

Confusion, panic, fear all flooded her internal systems in a matter of seconds, then a slow, dawning realisation took hold of her as her fear dissipated. She began to recognise the figure's features in the dull sodium light. She was shaking, and it was nothing to do with the cold. It was the creep that was now holding her arm.

"Andrew, Jesus, what the hell are you doing? What the hell is wrong with you?"

It came out in a register that was a pitch higher than her usual voice. A mixture of anger and nausea swept over her.

"I could say the same thing"; he gave out a little laugh and finally let go of her arm.

Taking a drag of his cigarette he blew the smoke to one side and smiled. He looked like the cat that had gotten the cream, but he was no tom cat she thought. he was a wolf in sheep's clothing. She did not like his nicotine-stained smile, not one bit, it made her stomach churn, and she could still feel her heartbeat hammering in her chest after the scare he had given her.

He continued to stand there grinning and smoking, she looked at him dumbfounded. What was he doing here? Had he followed her? All she wanted to do now was get away from him.

"What do you want Andy? I'm really tired and all I want to do is get home. What are you doing here?"

He took another deep drag of his cigarette and threw it on the floor. With his shoe she crushed it into the ground. Not once taking his eyes off her, she could feel him undressing her with his mind.

"I just wanted to see you."

"Jesus Christ Andy, can't it have waited until tomorrow?"

Shaking her head in disbelief, she began to walk, and as she tried to brush past him, he took hold of her arm again, more tightly this time, she saw the change in his eyes.

"Let go of me now, let go of me, please."

He pulled her up rigidly. Straight into his face with such a force that she nearly wetted herself, she could smell his smoky breath. He was a vile human being, she never wanted to think badly of a person, but she knew that Andrew Smith was a nasty piece of work.

Sneering, Andrew grinned at her, licking his lips like he just about to delve into a bargain bucket of Kentucky fried chicken. He held tightly on to her arm. He began clicking his tongue on the roof of his mouth. *Click, Click, Click*, like a lizard smelling the air with its tongue.

"Let GO OF ME NOW PLEASE! You're hurting me, Jesus Andy let go."

He didn't let go. The more she struggled the stronger his grip became. Now she was starting to panic. She wanted to scream for help but all that came out of her mouth was a dry scratchy sound.

"I know you've wanted this for a long time, I've seen you staring at me when you been talking to your friends around the copier and or in the staff canteen. Giving me the eye, the old come to bed eyes."

"You must be out of your crazy mind"

This angered him and he hit her face with the back of his hand. Her head flew back. She rose her free hand to her face. Jennie tried to pull away but all she succeeded in doing was tightening his grip like a Chinese finger trap. It was only now she realised what his intentions were. He began to pull her away from the path and into the direction of the bushes.

She dug her heels in and started to cry. This was not happening.

"No… you're wrong, you're wrong! I've never sent out any signals to you. I'm sorry Andy I never meant to give you that impression."

He just laughed in her face.

"You're the same as the rest of them, just teasing a man because you think you can."

She pulled them both back, with all her weight, back to the edge of pavement. Her strength weakening but the urge to fight back was stronger. It surprised Jeanie how she could resist a man double her size in the strength department. Jennie felt her flight or fight mechanism click into gear just at the right time, spitting in his face, it was instinctive. A desperate measure to try and get a reaction out of him. She didn't know the effect it would have on him, she hoped in the disgusting act of the gesture he would have let her arm go but he did not, it only angered him further, she could see the menace in his eyes as the spit ran off his cheek. She thought he was going to strike her again, her jaw stinging fresh from the first blow.

At that moment, Jennie disconnected from reality. Something caught her attention. Just above her vision she witnessed the shadows of the tree moving, not moving because of the bitter wind but moving as if it had mass. A muscular system made up of muscles, joints, tendons, and ligaments. The darkness had cocooned them somehow, stealthy and quietly. It was a stupid childish thought that came to Jennie, but the dark seemed to have taken on an insidious agenda.

She registered the look of confusion in his face first, then the look of panic as his feet lifted off the ground. His feet kicking out at nothing but empty space six feet off the ground, Jennie stepped back and stumbled backward, she broke the heel of her shoe. Only her hand saving her from falling on her backside completely.

Andrew screamed, his feet and legs still kicking out desperately, ash-coloured bony skeleton fingers bent and curved around his skull in a vice like grip. The intensity of the pain rattled through his whole body. Panic seized his throat as something rough and scaly covered his mouth, then entered his mouth, it tasted of soil and bark.

'It can't be true' she told herself. The tree with its white and gnarly long ash-coloured fingers had reached out from the darkness and seized Andy in her hour of need.

Her mind could not comprehend what she was seeing, already traumatised as she watched helplessly from the ground. The wires in her mind short circuiting and disconnecting from her rational thinking.

The tree had turned into a living, breathing monster. Her daddy told her monsters weren't real, even though she knew the about the one that lived under her bed when she was in year three or the one that she worked with for the past eight months. The one who was now being dangled in mid-air like a puppet.

In a sickening thud, Andy dropped to the ground and moaned, blood covered his thin brown hair, and it ran down his forehead and neck. He was still alive. Jennie wanted to see if Andy could still move and to try and get him away but as she shakily got to her knees the shadow above her blackened, blocking out the dismal glow streetlight.

A long thin branch with five smaller branches attached to the end of an arm, a gruesome representation of a human hand grabbed his right leg. Andy screamed again. He pleaded, more in terror then pain this time. His jeans ripped and she could see he had wetted himself. Nails snapped off the ends of his fingers as he desperately clawed at the concrete. The hand started dragging him back into the darkness that was the trunk.

It toyed with him; Jennie was slowly inching herself away from the horror that unfolded in front of her eyes. The visceral mutilation of Andrew Smith before her was something no human should see.

Half of his body was now submerged into the gnarly, twisted trunk of the tree. A tree hollow which acted as its mouth. It began to devour him. A few seconds of silence followed by then a tearing sound. She saw his legs spasm one last time and then grow still, as his body gave in. He then vanished into the mouth of the tree, like someone was slurping a piece of spaghetti. The few remaining leaves left on the branches of the monster had fallen to the ground, they began to frost over, then wither and die.

Her breath charged the air, massive frantic gulps of ice-cold panic filled her lungs. She looked up at the place where his body had vanished into and then wished she hadn't. Deep within the knotted bark of the tree, two malevolent red eyes pierced her very soul and scoured her sanity.

From inside the tree, she heard the sound of snapping and gurgling. The two red eyes had sunk back into the gnarly trunk.

She thought the nightmare was over, that it was just a horrifying dream, and she would wake up at any moment safe and sound in her bed. She still remained on the floor. Too paralysed with fear to move.

All she could hear was, what sounded like the sound of the monster eating and the wind as it blew down what was now a wintry graveyard.

Then she heard something.

A long, rakish ash coloured arm snaked out onto the path from the bottom of the trunk. The long bony fingers clicking on the concrete like dry bones. It reached up to her face and by some miracle her flight mechanism kicked in again and she began backing away.

As she turned, the hand took a swipe at her. The bark fingers scraping the side of her face which Andy had struck. They snagged the handle of her handbag, and she went screaming into the air, both of her high heels came off and fell to the ground.

By some luck, the handle of the bag snapped, and she hit the ground, winding herself in the process. In between sobs and screams she started to crawl away. She heard the monster snarl, and she was just in time as the long bony hand tried to take another swipe at her.

Leaping out of the way, she dived onto her side on to the softness of the grass, which thankfully was soft after the rain earlier that day.

Staggering back to her feet, tired and weak she watched as the human like arms of the tree retreated back into its normal position. She started to cry and as she cupped a hand over her mouth to stifle the sobs, she saw the eyes of the monster glow from the dark. She ran screaming across the grass, her feet bare. Running as fast as fast as she could. Never looking back.

Dummy

Kelly Piner

Daisy groaned as she entered the dank basement with its muted lighting and stale smell of trash. She sidestepped puddles of coffee that someone had spilled. Monday! The weekends never lasted long enough. Some career, too; CPR instructor when she'd dreamt of being a nurse practitioner, doing medical rounds at an esteemed hospital alongside revered physicians. But her plans had changed after her husband, Rob, and her best friend, had swindled her out of every cent she had. Unbeknownst to Daisy, the two had been seeing each other for over a year, scheming to empty her bank accounts. They'd even ran up her credit cards to the limit before disappearing. She hadn't heard from them since. With the surge in crime, under-staffed police departments didn't exactly have the time to comfort a distraught wife.

No longer able to afford the pricey tuition at the prestigious Clara Barton Institute, she'd been forced to drop out of school. For now, she'd have to be satisfied with her RN degree. Not exactly the acclaimed career she'd hoped for, but she was lucky to have a job at all. She'd been so upset over her financial ruin and Rob's betrayal that she'd made a medication error by giving old Mrs. Landis someone else's morphine, a mistake that sent the elderly woman to the ICU for a week. She supposed that she should be happy that she'd only been banished to the dungeon. Maybe she'd see the light of day sometime, but not anytime soon.

At the end of the hallway, when she flipped on the overhead lights of the lab, a gasp caught in her throat. She'd never get used to it, the dummies in the darkness, all lined up on tables, stumps, as if they'd been sawed in half. Their dead eyes stared up at the ceiling, privy to some other-world reality inaccessible to living humans. She swallowed her fear, and as if on automatic pilot, she removed the alcohol wipes to clean each one before the 8 am class. Another day of the same old routine, teaching chest compressions and rescue breathing to mostly burned-out employees who'd rather be elsewhere.

Daisy cared for the mannequins so much better than the nurses before her had. When she'd first been transferred to the lab, the dummies were grimy, and most wore a sad expression from years of neglect. But to Daisy, they were like silent friends and family. If she could, she'd breathe life into each of them. Sometimes in the early morning hours, alone with the mannequins, she had thoughts of a dark factory, an assembly line of plastic body parts all waiting to be assembled. She shuddered as she recalled the images, so real they almost felt like memories. She needed to spend less time in the basement and more time among the living.

Daisy leaned down to the infant dummy, "Good morning," she said, and gently cleaned his body as she would a human baby. This one looked so real that she wouldn't be surprised if it came to life.

She was sanitizing the child dummy when its eye moved. She could have sworn it did. She stepped back and watched, but the dummy lay still, an emotionless piece of plastic. Perhaps she'd imagined the movement – just the stress of the past year getting to her. She turned off her thoughts and moved on to an adult mannequin without incident. Fifteen minutes later, she calmly sipped coffee from a Styrofoam cup as she greeted a class of nursing students from the local university.

Daisy forced a smile. "Welcome to the American Heart Association's Lifesaver training. Today, you'll learn a series of intervention techniques that could save not only a patient, or a complete stranger, but possibly even a member of your family."

She watched the youthful faces staring back, so eager to learn, so unconscious of how many disappointments awaited them in life.

After the standard 20-minute instructional video, Daisy walked to the front. "Break up into pairs. I'll give feedback as I observe."

Curious chatter filled the room as the students practiced chest compressions. "Push harder," the electronic monitor told a perspiring woman.

When Daisy stepped in to give her some tips, that's when she heard it, a distinct, "Ouch," coming from the child dummy. When she looked around, no one else seemed to have noticed, so she watched his mouth closely. She'd recently watched a documentary about AI that had left her wondering about the dummies' level of consciousness.

"You hurt me," she thought it said.

She gaped, but once again, no one else seemed to hear the voice. Maybe she'd been working too many hours. She tapped the student's arm. "That's fine. You passed."

Distracted by the talking dummy, Daisy rushed the class's progress and let the students out early. As soon as they left, she locked her office door and leaned her head down to the mannequin's chest. He was breathing shallowly. Someone or something had breathed life into him. This was real. She hadn't imagined it. She caressed his head. "Are you okay? Are you okay?"

His head tilted slightly toward her and his mouth moved. "Danny," he said.

She backed away. She'd definitely heard him. She wasn't crazy or prone to seeing or hearing things. She examined the other mannequins, who were all quiet, just stiff mechanical medical devices.

She walked back over to the child. "I'm Daisy. I'm here to help you." But he only looked straight up at the ceiling as he had for the past year that she'd been doing the training. If anyone saw her now, she'd certainly be committed to Unit 12C, the psychiatric floor. When she'd worked that unit, despondent patients lay stiff, staring up at the ceiling, just like the dummies.

Before her next class arrived, she'd have to put him away. She wouldn't risk someone else hearing the child and reporting it, so she carried the tiny dummy to her small private office in the back, where she lay him on her desk and covered him with a soft blanket. She'd tell Medical Supplies that he'd malfunctioned and ask them to order another.

By the time her 10a class arrived, Daisy felt lightheaded, as she had when she'd first learned she was pregnant with Connor. But she'd only held her son in her arms twice before he'd died. She'd never recovered and still visited his tiny grave weekly at Baby Steps Cemetery. His death had driven a chasm between her and Rob that she could never repair. But now with the child dummy, could she finally have someone to love; someone to end her loneliness? More than anything, she wanted a child. Had Connor reached out from his tiny grave to reunite with her?

"Listen up class," she said to the weary employees. "Think of this as a refresher. I'll get you out of here soon."

Several students cheered, and thirty minutes later, Daisy sent them on their way.

Then she rushed into her office and leaned her head down to be certain that Danny was still breathing. She held him in her arms and gently rocked him, as she looked into his eyes.

At the end of the day, she nestled him in the bottom of her gym bag and quickly carried him down the long hallway, past hand-drawn pictures of witches and creepy jack-o'-lanterns from the pediatric unit.

On the drive home, she wondered what she'd do with him. He wasn't just a piece of plastic. Something had instilled life in him, and it was her responsibility to keep him safe. How quickly things had changed. Only that morning, she had been living a marginal existence, teaching CPR in an ancient hospital with no prospects of her own. Now, she had a breathing child whose name was Danny.

Inside her tiny bungalow, she rolled Connor's crib from the unused nursery into her bedroom. Connor hadn't gotten to sleep in it even once, but she couldn't bear to part with it. She lay Danny inside and arranged a handmade blanket, a gift from her mother, around him. "Danny," she called out, but the mannequin only lay motionless, a stiff medical device. She pulled the crib next to her bed so she could check on him throughout the night.

At midnight, Daisy leaned over the crib. Danny's chest rose with each breath, and his eyes were closed. She tightened the blanket around him and smiled. He'd be the child she'd never have.

The next morning, Daisy lay Danny's plastic torso into a warm basin of water and ran a soft cloth over his body. His eyes were now open. Was it really so far-fetched that he had been brought to life when AI robots were found in every corner of life, including hospitals and restaurants? Just last week, she'd seen a robot assisting the pharmacist refill prescriptions.

She dried Danny with a soft towel and cradled him in the crib with a blanket and a stuffed dog she'd bought for Connor. She hated leaving for work, but she'd run home during her lunch break and check up on him.

But she'd been scheduled for two extra classes. At half past noon, hungry and frazzled, she slipped her canteen card into a vending machine and pulled out a pimento cheese sandwich that she wolfed down at her desk. With no time to check on Danny before her next class, she struggled to breathe.

That afternoon, students in the 1 pm class grumbled when the mannequin software malfunctioned.

"Let me take a look." Daisy felt all eyes on her as she punched buttons on the laptop. "I'll reboot," she told them, but after five minutes of the computer wheel turning and turning, she spoke over a growing lump in her throat. "Give me a minute to call IT."

"You are tenth in line. Please hold," the operator said.

Nervous chatter filled the room. And on today of all days, when she needed to get home early to Danny.

By the time the technician had applied a necessary update to the laptop, it was already 1:30 pm and the class was half over. And with that setback, one class overflowed into the next, so by 4 pm, a group of angry employees stood in the hallway, looking at their watches. "I get off at 5 pm and can't stay a minute longer," a red-faced man told Daisy.

She nodded. "I'll get you out as quickly as possible."

Daisy eyed the clock continuously as she wandered around the lab, barely glancing at the students. "That's fine. You pass," she told a struggling young man.

She kept her word and forty minutes later, after the last student had left, Daisy rushed to the parking lot.

Her head throbbed as she drove home, and she pressed the accelerator harder. What if he'd gotten injured, or worse, had returned to his original plastic stiffness? What she'd do with her new baby, she didn't know. She couldn't take him out in public, not during the daytime anyway. But he'd be waiting for her at the end of each day. They'd have dinner together, and she'd read him bedtime stories, and cuddle with him on snowy winter nights. She'd finally have someone to tell her troubles.

When she raced inside to her bedroom, she reeled when she saw Danny clinging onto the side of the crib. His facial features had softened, were less mannequin-like, more human. His previously vacant eyes now moved slightly and had turned a muted grey.

So this is where she'd landed after the medical error she'd made last year, in the basement of a faltering hospital where someone had breathed life into a dummy named Danny. She couldn't tell anyone about this, not even her coworker and friend, Meg, who always covered for her when she was out of town. But she couldn't resist the urge to touch his face, now smooth, like baby's flesh.

He smiled and cooed when she stroked him, and he wobbled on his torso, like a toddler attempting to walk.

He'd need legs, so she sorted through some old dolls she had stored in the basement, examining one after another until she settled on a lifelike doll named Maribel that had belonged to her grandmother. She felt bad, sawing off its legs, but they were the perfect size for Danny.

Upstairs, she used superglue to attach them, careful to press them hard against the plastic torso until the pieces dried together. She then secured the legs further with strips of packing tape.

She balanced him on his new legs and held his hands. "Come on, Danny, come on. Just one small step."

But he stared far away, expressionless.

"Please, Danny. I know you can hear me."

Disappointed and uneasy, she placed him back inside the crib and searched for any sign of movement. Was she becoming ill, like her grandmother, delusional with a total break from reality? Grandma Sally had died inside a roach-infested state mental institute when she'd been just sixty-two.

Daisy massaged her temples. Enough with the morbid thoughts. Call her crazy, but for now, she had to think of Halloween, Danny's first Trick-or-treat. Maybe being out among the living would accelerate the life process for him.

The next day, avoiding people and cameras, Daisy pushed a portable wheelchair to her Honda Element during lunchtime and loaded it into the back. She'd need it for wheeling Danny around the neighborhood. It wasn't like she was stealing it; she'd return it tomorrow. Danny deserved this, and so did she, given how she'd been robbed of raising Connor.

After work, feeling like a kid, Daisy thumbed through the leftover costumes at The Halloween Superstore and settled on a clown costume with facial makeup, a green wig and red nose. She'd hide Danny's plastic body inside it, and no one need know that he was a dummy.

At home, she held up the costume. "See what I got for you?"

Danny's eyes moved back and forth, and Daisy was certain that he whispered, "Mama."

Her heart fluttered. "Yes, I'm your Mama." She carefully placed his body into the clown costume and fastened the red ruffled collar around his neck. White facial makeup, a green wig and red nose completed the look.

She stepped back. "You look just like a real-life circus clown." When she held a mirror up to him, his eyes moved, and his head nodded slightly, as if he approved.

She hooked a jack-o'-lantern candy bowl around his arm and tucked a crocheted blanket around his legs. She snapped a picture of him before leaving the house.

Outside, Daisy tightened her wool coat to ward off the frigid wind. Not even winter, and a few snowflakes already sailed through the air. She was entering unfamiliar territory. What did she expect? That at the end of the evening, Danny would emerge as a full talking, laughing child? Or would she return home with nothing more than an inanimate piece of plastic?

She pushed him toward a streetlight that illuminated the south part of Beckley Lane. Its trees looked gnarled and menacing in the night, not at all the welcoming Maples that shaded her home in the summertime. Orange Halloween lights cast shadows and made the otherwise safe, quiet neighborhood feel surreal. In the distance, black capes and ghost costumes flapped in the wind of the approaching local children.

When Daisy arrived at her favorite neighbor's house, dozens of bugs swarmed around the yellowish porch bulb. In the muted light, Danny looked like any other toddler, clutching a candy bucket.

Still, she flinched when the front door opened and Dora stepped outside, offering the same flowered candy bowl from years past, filled with miniature candy bars.

"What on earth?" Dora adjusted her glasses. "Where'd you get this child?"

"He's my nephew, Danny, from Alabama," Daisy lied.

When the elderly woman leaned down and peeked at Danny' face, Daisy's heart pounded so hard that she feared her neighbor could hear it.

Dora held out the bowl. "Take as much as you want, Danny."

"Let me help," Daisy said as she dropped two tiny bars into the bucket. "Thanks, Dora. I'll stop over soon for a visit."

Daisy rolled Danny to the next house where Mrs. Barrett greeted him with delight, "Hello, Danny. Are you enjoying Halloween?"

"Oh yes, he is. It's his first." Daisy dropped a bag of M&Ms and a chocolate bar into his bucket.

With each passing home, Daisy's anxiety lessened. No one had acted the least bit suspicious.

At the end of the cul-de-sac, something moved under Danny's blanket. Daisy clearly saw a movement by the light of the full moon. But then, a flurry of leaves blew across her path. Maybe just the wind, she thought, as she pushed Danny toward a nearby tree to escape pelts of freezing rain. Then she heard a sound coming from him—the unmistakable rattling of a candy wrapper.

"Danny? When she peeked down, he held a chocolate bar to his mouth, munching on it.

Daisy froze. He was alive. It wasn't her imagination. On legs as unsteady as twigs, she pushed the wheelchair to her house, and then she struggled to get it inside as she held the door open with one hand and attempted to push the chair through with the other. She panted as she rolled the chair into her bedroom.

She lifted Danny and placed him on her bed. "Danny, talk to me."

His eyes moved back and forth, first looking into her eyes and then focusing on her lips, as if he understood her. Candy crumbs clung to the side of his mouth. She couldn't deny that he was becoming more and more lifelike. Maybe within a few weeks of concentrated effort, he could pass for a real child. Then, she could take him with her shopping and out to eat.

When Danny didn't speak, Daisy lay him in the crib and covered him with a warm blanket. Tomorrow, she'd only work half a day so she could spend more time with him, teaching and nurturing him. As she prepared for bed, a thousand questions raced through her mind. Would Danny become a full-blown child that she could claim as her own? Would people question where he'd come from? Would the authorities get involved? Or was this God's answer to her prayers, to ease her pain and show her a new path after the lousy couple years she'd had? Exhaustion gripped her body, and soon she dreamt of visiting Connor at Baby Steps.

In the early morning hours, Daisy felt Danny crawl into bed. She didn't dare move at first lest she scare him off. A fast learner, he'd obviously used his new legs to crawl from his crib. In a matter of a couple days, he'd advanced to a whole new level. Soon, he'd be walking around the house or even accompanying her when she went to the grocery store or to the park.

Wondering what feelings dwelled deep inside him, she drew him closer to her chest. She hadn't felt such love since she had held Connor in her arms.

By morning, Danny was grasping Daisy's hand in his. He kicked his new legs into the air, just like a new-born and stared up at her face.

She kissed his forehead. It wouldn't be long now before she'd be carrying on a real conversation with him. She smiled at the thought as she carried him into the bathroom. There, she ran a warm cloth over his body and sang, "Hush, little baby, don't say a word, Mama's gonna buy you a Mockingbird."

After, Daisy propped him up in her bed against a fluffy down pillow and tucked a quilt around his frail body. "I won't be gone long. I'll leave the TV on for you. Don't be scared." Before she left, he turned his head and looked straight at her.

From her Honda, Daisy phoned her supervisor, Kathy. Her first two classes had been scheduled for weeks, but her heart ached at the thought of being away from Danny for even a few hours. She'd shorten the classes and tell the students it was just a refresher course.

When Kathy answered, Daisy coughed into the phone. "I'm so sorry, but I don't feel well. My allergies are acting up. I'll need to go home after the 9 am class."

"Just remember to put it in the computer," Kathy said. "Get some rest."

Daisy sped to the hospital and fumbled with her keys as she struggled to unlock her office. Then, when she at last flipped on the lights, she involuntarily squealed – the same sound she'd made when she'd nearly stepped on a Diamond Back Rattler.

The mannequins were all lined up, sitting upright on their stumps. Their eyes shot daggers at her.

"Dear God," she heard herself say. Had they all come to life? She slammed the door behind her and dropped her purse onto the floor.

"Bring him back," the larger male dummy said.

"He doesn't belong to you," another one said.

Daisy pressed her hand to her mouth and backed against the wall. She searched the menacing faces of the mannequins, first one and then another.

The larger male used his hands to propel himself forward on his stump. "You broke the rules, Daisy. Who do you think you are?"

She struggled to understand. "What rules?"

"Don't play dumb," a female mannequin said. "You know who you are. You've always thought you were smarter than the rest of us. You broke The Golden Rule: *Thou Shall Not Take Human Form!*"

"Yeah," said another, "You stole Danny and went off into some make-believe world. You split up the family."

"But you don't understand," Daisy explained. "With time, I can bring all of you to life, just as I did Danny."

The male moved closer. "We don't believe you. Prove it to us."

"I wouldn't lie to you. And I'm not one of you. You're trying to drive me crazy."

As if trapped in a surreal portal, Daisy felt paralyzed, unable to speak or move as she tried to digest the nightmare unfolding in front of her. In a brief moment of sanity, she fled the room and ran through the dark hallway. Why were they so hateful? Jealous of Danny, perhaps? And what crazy accusations. Wouldn't she know if she were one of them? Or had she totally lost her grip on reality? She shook off the thought. She had never joined with coworkers who referred to the mannequins as *Stiffs*. She'd always treated every mannequin with respect, sanitizing them daily and even talking to them. Given time, she had hoped to bring all of them to life.

Daisy stumbled outside as images washed over her, those same dark images of a factory where the mannequins had been assembled, each a doll-like creature waiting to have life breathed into it. Had she dreamt about this, or perhaps one of her patients had told her about such a place? Still....

She got into her car and drove. As she sped toward her house, she had trouble remembering the route, making one wrong turn after another. Now, she could no longer remember her husband's face, and she only had a fuzzy memory of nursing school. My God, she no longer knew her last name. Had she completely lost her mind as her Grandma Sally had? Or were the mannequins right? Maybe she'd never been human at all.

Finally back home, she charged to the bedroom where she found Danny watching TV. Unable to contain her panic, she dove under the covers and pulled him close to her trembling body. "It'll be okay, Danny. I won't let them take you. I won't."

He squeezed her finger and cried out, somehow understanding her fear.

What recourse did she have now that the others were out to get her, kill her even? The idea of them entering her home and snatching Danny away from her in the dead of night—she couldn't bear the thought. She climbed farther under the covers and hugged Danny tighter.

When Daisy opened her eyes, she lay on a table, staring up at the ceiling. She tried moving, but she couldn't feel anything below her waist. Danny lay to the left of her, a motionless piece of plastic, no longer the evolving child she'd brought to life.

Then, she heard her coworker, Meg, speaking in the background. But what was Meg doing here? And where exactly was she? She tried calling out, but no words would come. Had she been committed to the psychiatric floor? That must be it.

She'd likely lose her nursing license over this. Meg must be speaking to staff on her behalf. She could always count on Meg.

As Daisy struggled to make sense of the past few days, Meg leaned over her and started performing chest compressions for the on-looking CPR class.

Too Few Surnames

Robert Bagnall

Too few surnames.

That was what my husband said was wrong with people from the countryside. Something tip-of-the-tongue odd about them, as if they played life to a different set of rules, possibly one with a few pages missing. To him, it boiled down to too few surnames.

He also thought there was something weird about their eyes.

It may not have explained why we lived in the city for so many years—a King's Cross flat, a Crouch End maisonette, then a Brent semi-detached which could have been anywhere if the urban tinnitus of four lanes of traffic beyond the double glazing didn't prove otherwise—but helped justify why we never considered leaving.

And then he died, and I moved to a hamlet in the wilds of Devon, one of those places reached only by crevasse-like hedge-lined byways, where a journey beyond the village curtilage carries the accomplishment of a jailbreak. Just like that. Others fall back on ill-judged and empty love affairs or work their way through compendia of cocktails, but my release from grief was Boveyhempston-in-the Moor.

I don't know what I expected. Not open arms and open doors, but maybe the odd cheery greeting as a minimum. I'd been there a month and Boveyhempston-in-the Moor was proving hard to crack. It was like I couldn't get them to see me. Never one to make friends easily, I'm always the one standing on the outside of the circle, watching for the slightest parting of shoulders so I can ease in, say *Hi, I'm Wendy*. I suspect I was seen as being from London. Which I was, I suppose.

Which was why the addition to the parish noticeboard by the churchyard lychgate was such a godsend. *Boveyhempston-in-the Moor Art Club – Life Drawing*. An untutored two-hour session for a nominal sum to cover the hire of the church hall. And hopefully a contribution towards the heating, I thought. This was, after all, Halloween night.

I shook the October drizzle off my coat, hung it in the vestibule, and pushed open the inner door. It was my first time within the church hall. The size of tennis court, it had a 1950s austerity aesthetic, exposed wooden roof trusses, pastel paintwork, and polished parquet, offset by twenty-first century dayglo safety signs, like clowns at a funeral, imploring me to only use in case of emergency, push at doors and exit. Curtains covered a raised stage at one end, decorated with toy spiders and cut-out paper pumpkins. Next to the cricket team's honors board, a corrugated metal roller covered a serving hatch. In the middle sat an empty chair surrounded by six tall wooden easels, each loaded with paper and armed with pots of charcoal, chalk, and soft pencils.

Three men stood, head bowed, chatting in low voices. They continued talking just beyond the point where the balance of probabilities suggested they were ignoring me, then turned in unison and suggested that, ah, I must be the new girl.

New girl? I'm fifty-seven.

Like something from the days of gentlemen and players, it was all Mr. this or free-floating first names, as if the lesser members were pets or servants. Older than the other two and the one they took their lead from, hawk-like Mr. Allan sported a knitwear and corduroy farmer aesthetic, though I'd seen him in his garden farming nothing more than hydrangeas. He introduced Mr. Carlisle, who ran the village shop. He'd served me with suspicious civility, like a dragon guarding its hoard. In contrast, Toby had an eager to please face and sausage fingers. In recognition of the date, he sported an incongruous Harry Potter-style wizarding gown. From both accent and the state of his nails I suspected he dug drainage ditches, but I'd overheard him discussing chiaroscuro, so what did I know?

Then two others arrived, a woman about my age and a man with the ashen look of the long-married. I tried my best welcoming smile, made to speak, but Mr. Allen introduced me as if I were a newly acquired specimen, already pinned to a board or drowned in formaldehyde. In London I would have said something, but upsetting the social order of an English village is like trying to change the direction of the clouds. And, in any case, the moment was lost as a lanky man in a dressing gown scissored into the hall as if sleepwalking and placed himself on the chair at the center of our easel circle.

Mr. Allen called us to order with a clap. Our nameless model jutted his chin and shed his robe as if under duress, his thousand-yard stare fixed somewhere out towards the graveyard. Well-chosen, he was all freckles and birthmarks and protruding bones, like his skeleton was metric but his skin imperial. My view was of left flank and a lot of the back of the chair. The nameless wife had made a beeline to the easel with the best view of his cock. As I charcoaled and chalked the drooping curve of his back, I wondered what her tired husband thought of it.

I was engrossed in my work, lost in time, when Toby came around with a mug for contributions. I could see Mr. Carlisle eyeing me warily as I put in a tenner and took out five, but Toby smiled encouragingly, even if his eyes looked askance at my work. Rusty, I may have been, but I thought I had captured the shoulder blade's shadows, the flop of hair, the swirl of the model's ear quite well. What level of competence did they expect?

To my left, Mr. Allen shaded furiously, little charcoal strokes. I took a step back, feigning assessment of my own work, and glanced at his. *Oh, Christ.* I felt my stomach drop, a cold sweat break out followed by a glow of shame. He'd gone for *interpretation.* The model had become some sort of sea creature, an octopus with multiple tentacles and suckers, his head an obsidian eye with a huge chalk-white teardrop pupil, the chair lost under flaps of flesh. Was that the rule? Why had nobody told me? I'd drawn the man *as a man.* I would never be able to live this down.

What could I do in the last few seconds to rescue my work? Perhaps put my figure within a giant but feint translucent polyhedron, claim it was symbolic of man's inhumanity to man or suchlike. Mr. Allen, perhaps sensing my stalling blush, clapped again to bring the class to a close and, at once, they were on the move, examining each other's work, clucking with appreciation. I already had Nameless Husband on my shoulder with Mr. Carlisle approaching. I choked back an explanation, an apology, and shuffled sideways to do my own circuit.

I can only hope my expression at seeing Nameless Wife's effort gave nothing away. What I'd taken, seen obliquely in Mr. Allen's rendering, to be an octopus was, in Nameless Wife's work, more formless, shapeless, like viscous dripping liquid bestowed with life, fighting to retain its form. If it had a penis, it was lost in its folds. I drifted onwards. Mr. Carlisle's drawing showed a somewhat concertinaed rendering of the same creature, but with more sparkle, as if oiled. Toby's was the first to show a mouth below the single malevolent all-seeing eye that formed the top of the beast's head. He, too, had tried to capture iridescence with little chalky scratches but made it look oddly furry instead. Nameless Husband had gone for straight lines where others had emphasized bulges, bubbles, and boils, but straight lines worked for its rows of small sharp teeth in its slit-like smile. Which brought me back to Mr. Allen's, which I could see now wasn't a cephalopod. Not really. At least, not of this world. Not unless this world held a monster of the deep that ate corpses in your nightmares.

The six of them, the re-gowned model having joined them, were by my picture, studying it with apparent confusion. Nameless Wife leant in, muttered something to Nameless Husband, who mumbled something to Mr. Carlisle who shook his head. Then, as one, they turned and studied me as if for the first time. Mr. Allen blinked, an ever-so-slightly asynchronous blink, each eye closing almost-but-not-quite together, like two fingers drumming. Then Nameless Husband did the same and so did Toby, who continued to smile disconcertingly.

As we stood and stared at each other I realized what my late husband had meant. This is what you saw when the mask slipped. But it was what was behind the mask that froze me to my core. Their paintings were not interpretations of the scissor-limbed model. They were renditions of what they really were, what I would see if the scales were lifted from my eyes. Was it just them? Or was everybody in Boveyhempston-in-the Moor—on Dartmoor, in Devon, in England!—one of the lizard people?

They were between me and the door. If I just pretended none of this had happened, would they do the same? Would they let me pass, through the door and out the hall, into the October rain? Perhaps I was wrong, perhaps this was what passed for humor out in the sticks, a carefully rehearsed cosmic joke at the expense of the city-type. Some sort of initiation ceremony, a rural hazing. Perhaps my husband had dredged a distant memory of this, heard about it in a friend-of-a-friend way. Perhaps this only happened on this night of the year.

Somehow I doubted it.

My safest bet, my icy stomach and pounding heart told me, was to follow the dayglo signage and bolt for the emergency exit into the autumn night, like a mad middle-aged woman. That was my only guarantee that I would live. But if I had misread the runes and this were all a practical joke, the question then became: in a Dartmoor village, could I ever live it down?

Things I Found in Samhain Forest

Tanya Delanor

When the police carried out the body bag, I moved forward with my camera. A medium-sized, medium-ranked officer, stuck out an arm, and said, "That's as far as you go, pal. This is a crime scene, and the likes of you need to wait your turn."

"I'm a friend of the cottage owner," I lied. "What I have to tell you could help you to solve this case."

The officer sighed, fixed me with cold grey eyes, and said, "If I could have a pound for–"

"I know, I know," I said, handing him my business card. "If you could have a pound for every time-waster, you could have retired a year ago and built a mansion on the moon."

"Now that's a new one." He smiled a thin smile, pocketed the card, and motioned me away.

Six months earlier, on 31st October, my mother said, "Isn't it time you got yourself a proper job?"

"Of course, you're right," I replied, then scoffed down the last of the delicious cooked breakfast, grabbed my anorak, and headed for the area marked on the map as a place of antiquity.

On the drive to the professor's rented cottage, I switched on the radio. David Bowie announced that all of us could be heroic. I recalled Dad's funeral six weeks earlier, and the promise I had made to take care of Mum.

I drove past a newish housing estate that skirted the old weapons factory—hidden within woodland—along a narrowing country road surrounded by sheep-filled fields, and across to the 12th-century church. Parking outside the Roman wall, I locked the car and headed towards the yellow cottage that perched on the edge of the amphitheatre. A breeze swept up, scurrying the first fallen leaves of the autumn. I zipped up my anorak, heard a call of "You found it OK," and turned to see the professor hurrying towards me.

"Just in time for coffee," he said, a tad breathlessly. "Follow me."

Before entering the low-ceilinged cottage, I said, "Wow, that amphitheatre is quite something. I had no idea–"

"Yes, yes," he said, fussing around with white mugs and a percolator. "It's all quite exciting to the novice. But there's so much more to tell you about, and I don't have much time."

The professor had been summoned by his sister regarding the care of their elderly parents. She had to go into hospital for a minor op, and needed him to "provide his share of the care."

He ushered me into the sitting room where every chair was stacked high with books and files. "May I?" I indicated shifting some of the paraphernalia.

"Yes, yes, yes. There's no order to this chaos. That's what you're here for."

"When was the last time anybody worked on the dig here?" I said, sipping my coffee.

"Hmmm." The professor had squeezed himself into a book-laden chair, was templing his hands, and opening and shutting his mouth as if deliberating over how to break this all to me gently. "The truth is, we don't know why they suddenly abandoned the dig. We think it was a few years before that plague."

"So it wasn't plague that brought it all to a halt?"

"No. Hand me your mug and I'll top it up."

"Lack of finances?" I handed the mug over.

"Well, Brexit didn't do much for research projects. You'll come across a small volume, with the photo of an eagle on its cover, which will tell you about the dig in 2014, and after that zilch. They closed it down, and we think the Ministry of Defence took over the area for um…"

"Target practice?" I nodded my thanks as I took back the refilled mug.

"Not exactly. You see, the area was going great guns for a couple of thousand years. Then it was abandoned for seemingly no reason."

"Any chance the archaeologists might get the funding to get going again?"

"Sadly no. Just try and archive and index as much of this as you can. I've been given notice to move out. I think our good friends from Defence want to um…"

"Ramp things up a bit?" I offered, placing the mug on a coaster on an amazingly book-free small walnut-wood table.

"Precisely. Look, I need to get packing. You've got my contact details. Get what you can done, then lock up and post the key back through the letterbox. Oh, and another thing."

"Yes?"

"The car park to the site is locked at four in the autumn and winter months. Best not hang around outside after then, if you get what I mean."

"Is there a pub near here?"

"Oh, no, no, no. They shut it donkey's years ago. Plenty of booze in the fridge. Just help yourself. Good luck, young 'un." He paused, then turned back and said, "One more thing. You might bump into Angela while you're here." He grinned. "They'll probably want to lend you something."

I tried to ask what that might be but he was already strapping himself in and had turned the radio up full blast.

As the professor screeched off in his black people carrier, I stared after him. Before I turned to re-enter the yellow cottage, a person in a long, black hooded coat shuffled towards me from the direction of the churchyard. "Sorry if I made you jump," they said and handed me a birdcage covered in a green cloth. "Percy will keep you company." They turned and waddled back towards the old church, arms held out from their body.

There was a squawk. I peeked under the cover expecting to find a parrot. "Thank you very much, *Angela*," I said.

"Thank you very much, *Angela*," said Percy. I laughed, and Percy laughed. A talking, laughing penguin. Fair enough.

The next morning, Percy and I shared a breakfast of dried seeds, fruit, and nuts. I walked around the amphitheatre, and descended into it from the entrance opposite the cottage. It was a perfect circle, banked up by flint and grassy walls. Opposite each other on either side was a semi-circular niche. The small volume about the dig suggested at one time they were vaulted. In my amateur opinion, they seemed too tiny to have any use other than to house an altar. Again, I referred to the volume, and it speculated that there might have been an altar to Nemesis, the goddess of fate. My studies revealed this goddess, of Greek origin and adopted by the Romans, enacted retribution against those who succumbed to hubris or arrogance before the gods. Alternatively, these niches may have served as refuges for participants in the games held in the arena. Another possibility was execution. A chilly wind blew some leaves in a semi-circle.

I climbed back up to the cottage, checked on Percy, who squawked happily enough at me, packed some sandwiches along with a can of pop, and headed off towards the church, rucksack on back, whistling away as if I hadn't a care in the world.

"Morning!" It was Percy's owner, Angela. They pulled back the hood of the long black coat, revealing a large head and short neck. Angela stood very straight and upright. "Anything doing?"

"Just taking a look round. Any shops round here?"

Angela shrugged, wrinkled their beaky nose, and said, "The few folks left around here shop online. I can let you have a pint of milk and a loaf of bread. The prof asked me to keep an eye on you. I'll be back to collect Percy tomorrow morning if that's OK with you."

"Yes." I smiled. "I'll be leaving in the afternoon. Don't worry about the bread and milk." But Angela had gone.

I planned to photograph the surrounding area while it was still daylight, and then attempt the archiving in the evening. I walked towards the car park at the north gate. The car park was empty save for a man with a couple of large grey dogs. He was locking his van.

"Good morning," I said. "Lovely day for a walk."

"Yes. Thought I'd get these two out a bit sooner. By the looks of it, it's going to get dark earlier today."

He was in a hurry, so I didn't bother asking him questions. One of the dogs dashed off towards the fields where sheep hunkered down.

"Alice!" yelled the man. "You leave those poor things alone."

After the man and his dogs had disappeared, I headed further along the Roman wall, taking pictures all the way. Part of one of the flint walls looked like a dragon head. I sat near it, ate my sandwiches, and drank my pop. A pale, weak sun ushered itself through the soft grey clouds, providing snug warmth in the sheltered spot I'd secured, and I must have nodded off for a few hours. My phone battery was dead, and it was now far too gloomy to take any more photos. I sped up the pace, and sploshed through the mud, cutting through a field to get back to the cottage. A jackdaw's high-pitched "Jack!" sang out in the chilly late afternoon. I had read something in the volume about the ritual burial of ravens and fixed my mind on this to assure myself I wasn't lost. I cursed, looking all around to see if there was anybody out there to call on for help.

"Hello?" I said.

Nothing.

I stomped along the muddy ground, swearing at my absence of a sense of direction. Then joy of joy, I saw the yellow cottage ahead, and dashed towards it, running straight into the middle of the amphitheatre. "This is not where I want to be," I said aloud, turned, and clambered up the hill, moaning at whatever muck I must be trampling in when I heard a familiar voice, say, "Tut, tut, you townies." It was Angela, and I was so relieved that I tripped and almost fell on them.

"Come inside and have a drink," I said.

"I just might do that," they said.

Inside, when I switched on the light, Percy was doing an up-and-down dancy thing on his perch.

"He seems pleased to see you," said Angela.

"Yes," I said, pouring us both a drink. My hands were shaking as I handed them the glass. "Tell you what, why don't you take him back tonight. I think I'll make an early start in the morning."

"You don't seem to have got much work done here," they said, eyeing the mass of books.

"No. Perhaps I should stay up a little and get some archiving done, otherwise the professor will think I've been skiving."

Then Percy went crazy on his perch. First, he staggered along, neck bent as if someone had a noose around him, and then he hung upside down, clinging onto the side of the cage with one claw. Do penguins have claws? I thought they usually had flippers. I must make a note to remind myself to pay more attention when I am watching the next David Attenborough programme.

Next thing, Percy began shaking his cage like a crazy beast. He must be missing all his other penguin friends. Perhaps he wanted to go for a swim to catch some fish.

"Christ, Angela," I said, spilling my beer. "Whatever is the matter with the creature? I think you should take him out now. I'm not good with birds. Sorry to be so blunt."

Angela snatched up the cage and was out of the door before I could say "Blue murder."

Blow this for a game of soldiers, I decided, and packed my gear into my car, and drove off like the very devil were after me.

Seven months later, on the radio David Bowie was singing about the prettiest star he had ever seen, when the officer rang me.

"I owe you a quid," he said. "Tell me what really happened that night you stayed at the yellow cottage."

"I'll forward a photo I took earlier on in the day." I ended the call and referred to the picture gallery of dozens and dozens of photos I had taken of the Roman wall, the amphitheatre, and the semi-circular niches. The professor had recommended I apply for a grant to complete my studies. One particular photo had captured his imagination, and until now only he and I had seen it. The post mortem revealed he had died of a heart attack, so I shared the terrible secret with another person: the image of a body hanging from the gibbet in one of the semi-circular niches was zipping through cyberspace.

Tigers in Red Weather

S.W. Duffy

I was in the passenger seat and Lena was driving, coming home to Cambridge from a weekend away, late one Sunday night in October.

'Tell me a story,' she said.

'Let me see,' I pondered, 'Is a ghost story all right?'

'Yes, but not something horrible.'

Inspired by our current situation, in a car on a dark night, I made this up as I went along.

I was alone in the car, around eleven o'clock on a moonlit Autumn night. I was driving south from the North Norfolk coast. I occasionally passed a vehicle travelling northbound. Very few people seemed to be going in the same direction as me. No red rear lights ahead. No headlights in my rear view mirror.

But then I did see something in my rear view mirror. In the moonlight there seemed to be a human figure running in the same direction as my car. The road wound and I lost sight of the figure. Travelling at fifty or sixty miles an hour, that would be the last I saw of him or her.

But I was wrong. On another long straight section of road, there the figure was again, and it seemed a little closer in the mirror. God, he was thin. Of course, it couldn't be the same person. I drove on, paying little attention to what was behind me. I switched on the radio, but the reception was dreadful, I would catch a few sentences of news, then crackling and rushing would take over.

I was driving through forest, and my headlamp beams glanced off tall trees on either side. The figure in the rear view mirror was closer still, and definitely the same painfully thin person. And now I realised who he was. I drove faster, to try to shake him off. There are people from my past that I do not want to meet again.

I reached the outskirts of a town, with a dual carriageway bypass endowed with orange street lights. The figure in the mirror was no longer visible. I breathed more freely and drove on, at some speed. The bypass ended and I was back on country roads. And there was the emaciated figure in my mirror again, running so fast that he was gaining on the car. And I could see his face. I accelerated recklessly, driving faster than I could ever have imagined doing on this sort of road. After a minute or so, the figure was no longer in the mirror. Thank heaven. Is revenge such a strong motive?

Then I realised why the figure was no longer running along the road behind the car. He was sitting in the passenger seat beside me.

'That's scary,' said Lena, 'Don't you dare go to sleep now, and leave me on my own.'

I stayed awake and tried to talk of cheerful things. We got home close to midnight and the following night found us at a dinner at Fisher College, Cambridge.

I've always felt that celebratory dinners in Cambridge colleges were characterised by striking ancient surroundings, excellent wines and institutional food. On this occasion I was right about the first two but wrong about the third. The food was as impressive as the centuries-old banqueting hall and the Montepulciano.

We were attending a dinner in honour of a distinguished professor, Dame Caroline Macgregor, who had just retired. Lena and I had walked the half mile or so through the mist across Jesus Green and up King's Parade. The magnificent college and chapel buildings loomed indistinctly on either side, and the fine drizzle dampened what's left of my hair.

After champagne in an ante-chamber, we were ushered into a highly ornate dining hall, with a vaulted roof painted colourfully, roof-beams adorned with carved angels reminiscent of figureheads on wooden ships. Smoked bream with pepper salad, saddle of lamb, then an ornate dessert which I cannot name, but which was delicious. Various witty speeches, accompanied by a welcome last glass of wine.

After the speeches and before the coffee, I went to the lavatory, which meant stepping out into a cloister and following it round a small lawn on this damp and misty night. Despite the antiquity of the buildings, the lavatory facilities were clean and modern.

I was washing my hands beside a frosted window, open at the top at a level just above my head, when I overheard a conversation outside, as clearly as if the speakers were standing beside me at the washbasin. These old colleges have labyrinthine paths and passages, with modern additions such as the gents in which I was standing, slotted in where planning laws and preservation orders will allow. The acoustics of these old buildings can be surprising. A man and a woman were speaking in the dark outside.

'You don't need to worry about it. It's a shoo-in for you,' said the male voice.

'But Murray might say-' the female replied, but was interrupted.

'Murray Twigg won't be in a position to say anything. He'll be pushing up the daisies by the time the appointment committee meets.'

'For God's sake, this is so risky.'

'We'll be careful. You got the most shitty treatment all those years ago. Payback is long overdue.'

'But we can't-'

'But nothing. This time next year, the holiday will be in your street.'

'All right,' I heard footsteps and the voices started to lose volume. Evidently, they were walking away. I heard, 'So when do we...' then they faded.

I rushed out of the lavatory, turned left, in the opposite direction to that of the banqueting hall and left again into the next court of the college. There was no-one to be seen. I ran up the path which I estimated passed under the lavatory window, and followed it into yet another medieval court, deserted and appearing haunted in the poor visibility. No-one again. I returned to the banqueting hall and wondered what to do.

'OK, I understand that you didn't recognise the voices as anyone you knew,' said Detective Sergeant Ripley, 'But was there anything about the voices? Any particular accents or mannerisms?'

'Not really,' I replied, 'I'm from Scotland, and south-eastern accents all sound the same to me. They all sound like London accents. That's what these were like, although quite educated. I don't know about posh, but proper, you know?'

'Yes, all too common round here,' the sergeant sighed, 'Look, we will find this Murray Twigg- you're sure that was the name?'

'Yes, I heard that very clearly, and it's an unusual name,' I said.

'Well, we'll find him and have a word. You don't need to do anything unless we get back to you. And we might, since what you heard sounds serious. But don't worry about it until then.'

I was impressed that the police at Parkside had not simply dismissed me as a nutcase. I had felt obliged to tell the police, as it had seemed to me that there was a serious risk to the life of this Murray Twigg, whoever he was. The detective sergeant had listened to my story, asked a few pertinent questions, and undertaken to follow it up. I left the station feeling that I had done my stuff, and although curious, determined to leave it at that unless the police came back to me.

But... There's always a but, isn't there? How could I leave this alone after overhearing such a sinister and intriguing exchange? Lena told me in no uncertain terms to leave it alone. She felt that for me, this was just a distraction from empty nest syndrome, now that both kids were away at university, but it wasn't necessarily a harmless one. However, from my point of view, what harm would it do to find out who Murray Twigg was? It might give a clue to which of the other guests at the dinner were linked to him.

'Listen, you're not Inspector Morse, you're not even Inspector Clouseau or Inspector Gadget. Forget it,' Lena was scathing.

'All right, all right,' I said meekly but with a hint in my tone that I thought she was overdoing the scepticism. Then I surreptitiously looked him up, first in the telephone directory, unsuccessfully, then on the internet, successfully. He was professor of feline endocrinology at The White School of Veterinary Medicine. His Wikipedia entry was strangely guarded, mentioning controversial remarks at after-dinner speeches and contested appointment decisions in his department, but with no details. There was also a footnote to the effect that the University was an equal opportunities employer and did not discriminate in any way in academic or other appointments.

So, the two speakers were vets, in all probability. I had no access to the guest list for the dinner, and I had been unaware of any vets present. I presumed that the police would have been able to obtain the guest list and investigate accordingly. The fact that they had not recontacted me suggested that they had ruled out a murder plot. However, I couldn't shake off my curiosity, so I called up Archie Waterson.

Archie was a good friend of mine who had been a particular colleague of Professor Dame Caroline, and had been on the committee which had organised the retirement dinner. I met him on a Sunday evening in a dark and quiet pub on the south side of town. We sat over two pints and exchanged pleasantries, comfortable old jokes which were only funny to the two of us, as our families had frequently observed. Then I told him my story.

'So what do you want to know?' he asked.

'Well, for a start, were there any vets at the retirement dinner for Caroline Macgregor?'

'I know of only one, a Dr Jane Morton. She's a partner in a city practice, and has some sort of associate position in the vet school. Small animal specialist, I think, but I may be wrong.'

'I bet you're right,' I thought of Twigg's speciality, which must surely be mostly to do with domestic cats rather than lions and tigers, 'But are you sure there was only one vet at the do?'

'Ninety-nine percent. I could find out. But look, if the cops haven't got back to you, surely there can't be anything in it?'

'Yes, that's right, but wondering about it is driving me mad. I have to find out a bit more. Do you think you could check if there were any other vets there?'

'Yes, I will, but I don't think so,' said Archie.

'What do you know about this Murray Twigg guy? Or can you find out? Being in the university, you can get the faculty gossip. On the web, any material about him is cagey but suggests he has some sort of past.'

'I have heard of him. I think officially retired, but with some sort of honorary position, and still holding grants and bossing people around, very active in research. As far as I know, he's harmless, but one of these old buffers that think a woman's place is in the home. I don't know for certain but, I think he's quite a toff, ex-public school, very plummy accent, and all that. Thought to be a brilliant veterinary scientist, and a great character, but a bit of a loose cannon. He's occasionally had to be told off for sexist remarks in speeches, and bad attitudes when selecting and interviewing candidates.'

'So not that bleeding harmless, then?' I reflected, 'And he could certainly have enemies.'

'Yes, but he doesn't have the reputation of a schemer or manipulator. You have to work the system or at least work with it to get on, as in any organisation, but his reputation is of someone who got where he is on merit and in fact, with his old-colonel attitudes there goes a certain naivety.'

'Aye well, I don't like the sound of him, but I don't want to see him pushed under a train or something. Did this Dr Morton bring a partner to the dinner?'

'Against my better judgement, I'll try to find out. But don't be surprised if I can't. And I really think you should drop it. Don't email about this. Email is about as non-confidential as it's possible to be. Same again?'

'Yes, go on then.'

I could not keep it a secret from Lena that I was trying to find out more. She thought this wrong-headed, as of course she would and as of course it probably was, but she didn't just tell me not to be silly.

'Listen, love,' she said in a gentle and concerned tone, 'The cops haven't been back in touch, so the chances are there is nothing in it. But suppose you're right, and there is something there- if they're not above bumping off this Murray Stick or whatever he's called, what might they do to someone who's interfering?'

'Twigg,' I said, 'Well, I'm not interfering, I'm just being a bit nosy.'

'If they found out you were asking around, that would count as interfering in their book, I bet.'

'OK, I'll trust the cops to handle it. I'll be content with whatever Archie digs up and tells me. No further, honest.'

My next meeting with Archie was in a busy city centre pub. I cycled across Jesus Green on another night of mist, on this occasion, lying in patches and drifts on the Green, sometimes only up to my shoulders, so that it seemed like swimming through a murky sea. The pub was cheerful and bustling, the premises large and rambling. I found Archie sitting at a table in a corner of a back room, nursing a large glass of red wine and looking very serious. I bought him another glass of wine, along with a pint for myself, and joined him.

'I found out a couple of things. First, Doctor Morton was the only vet there. Second, she did bring a guest with her, and it was Jim Garrison.'

274

'Who's Jim Garrison?' I had never heard of him.

'He's an oncologist in the hospital, about to get a personal chair in the medical school, and a great machinator and worker of the system. Unlike this Twigg character, he has a reputation as a manipulator and schemer, and I had to be very careful not to let it be known I was enquiring about him. You don't want to make an enemy of him. Less of an issue for you as you don't work for the university, but I have to be circumspect, even though I can look after myself in office politics.'

'That fits with what they were on about,' I reflected, 'It sounded like they were talking about a job for the woman, and that maybe she'd been done out of one in the past, possibly by Twigg. But the bloke said that this time, Twigg would be pushing up the daisies. There's a difference between being a slippery customer and doing someone in.'

'I found out something else,' said Archie, 'There is funding for a group leader in some specialist area of small animals, sort of translational research, you know, bringing lab results to clinical practice, and Dr Morton is up for it. Probably the bookies' favourite.'

'Any history of her being turned down in the past?' I asked.

'I don't know, but Twigg has a reputation for thinking of female colleagues as girls and male colleagues as men, so it wouldn't surprise me.'

'When do they make the appointment in the vet school?'

'The search committee has shortlisted, and they are talking to three people. They will have the candidates give seminars between now and Christmas, and they'll have formal interviews in January, making the decision towards the end of January.'

'Is Twigg on the committee?'

'No,' Archie replied, 'But they might ask him his opinion along with other faculty members who attend the seminars.'

'So what do I do now?' I mused.

'Drop it. Do nothing. If the police haven't done anything it's just dirty politics in the workplace. You don't want to be involved in that, particularly if you're up against the expert, Garrison.'

'You're right of course,' I acknowledged, 'But I feel someone should warn this Murray Twigg.'

'Leave it to the cops,' said Archie, 'They're not stupid, and that detective took you seriously, you said.'

'Yes, all right. Nineteen, twenty, my plate's empty,' I waved my empty glass at Archie and he went to the bar.

I telephoned Detective Sergeant Ripley, and he too told me to mind my own business. However, it was implicit from our conversation that he had already identified Dr Morton and soon-to-be-Professor Garrison as the people I had overheard, and had spoken to them. He did say something that rather alarmed me.

'I can no more tell you anything about others in this business, than I can tell them who was listening in the lav. Sorry, forget I said that.'

My enquiries about whether Morton and Garrison had asked him to identify who had overheard them were met with a stone wall, but he had really already given the game away. However, he did emphasise that he had investigated and found that there was no crime, committed or planned. He suggested that I had misheard the phrase about pushing up the daisies. I assured him that I didn't think so, but since he had gone into this with the persons involved, I should accept that I must have. DS Ripley made it clear that he was not asking me to let it drop but telling me. I agreed to do so.

But I still felt I should warn Murray Twigg, even though it was likely that DS Ripley had already done so. Lena was still discouraging, this time angrily so.

'Archie has told you, the cops have told you. This is not a good idea.'

'I know, love,' I said, 'But how would I feel if something happened to this Twigg guy because I had done nothing about it?'

'You've done plenty about it. You've told the police, whose job it is, and they've looked into it. For God's sake, let it go.'

In any case, I didn't let the issue go because it didn't let me go. Archie phoned and said that Jim Garrison had got hold of the guest list for Dame Caroline's retirement dinner, and had been making enquiries about others interested in the list.

'The chances are that he's found out that I've been asking questions,' said Archie, 'I can look after myself, though. With a bit of luck, he'll not identify you, since you don't work for the university, and in any case, even if he did, there's not much he can do about it, because, again, you don't work for the university. But for heaven's sake, give it a bloody rest, will you?'

'OK,' I said.

Then there was a complaint about me at work. An anonymous note sent to the director of the lab accusing me of jiggery-pokery in some of my experimental work. The allegations were vague but sufficiently specific that I could establish that they were nonsense. But now it was clear that I had made an enemy. A further scare came when a policeman turned up at our front door, stating that someone had seen what appeared to be violence towards a child taking place in an upstairs bedroom window. The police officer didn't say so, but again, it sounded like an anonymous tip-off. It did not take long to convince the officer that this accusation was also unfounded, since our two children had grown up and flown the nest in the last few years, and since at the time of the alleged incident, both Lena and I could establish that we had been out at work.

Lena's anger was now incendiary, and like DS Ripley, she wasn't asking me but telling me to give it up. But given that someone, presumably Garrison, was taking this trouble, I felt I had to take the threat to Twigg seriously. I went back to the internet. Searching for Twigg again, I discovered that he was a member of a local preservation pressure group or committee in the affluent area of southern Petersfield between Fenner's cricket ground and Station Road. Big, million-pound-plus town houses, some of them split into flats or bedsits, but others occupied by individuals, very rich individuals. High windows that give you a glimpse of a life unachievably cosy and luxurious as you cycle past on an Autumn evening. A little more internet research and I found minutes of this committee which included a list of those present with the streets they represented. Now I knew that he lived in Lyndewode Road.

The following Saturday, in the middle of a dull, late October day, I went around the doors in Lyndewode Road, and found a bell with the name Twigg beside it. I rang the bell. The door was answered by a middle-aged lady.

'I wonder if I might speak to Professor Twigg,' I asked, 'He doesn't know me, but I have some news for him. My name's Tom Mackay, and we have some friends in common in the University.'

'I just look after him,' she replied, 'I'll ask.'

She closed the door on me, but reopened it perhaps twenty seconds later.

'Come in to the front room.'

I was shown into a luxurious sitting-room. As I said before, a passing glimpse of a lighted room from a dark street in these houses suggested impossible luxury, and that sort of thing can be deceptive. If you were inside the room, it would be as cluttered and shabby as your own living room. In the same way, on the London Underground round about Aldgate East, you often get a good look into another tube train travelling in the same direction as yours. It always looks cleaner and warmer than the draughty, littered carriage in which you are travelling. But on this occasion, even from the inside, the room looked impossibly cosy and luxurious, furnished with sumptuous armchairs with no coffee stains on them, rosewood console table against one wall, and a matching rosewood coffee table in the middle of the room. The walls were adorned with large numbers of oil paintings, of a quality and an antiquity that put me in mind of some of the Dutch rooms in the National Gallery in London. A tall man with wild grey hair sat in an armchair, his long legs stretched out, his feet resting on a low stool. He was dressed in pin-striped trousers and a white shirt, with a colourful cravat at his neck.

'Forgive me for not getting up,' he said, 'I'm not as sprightly as I used to be.'

The voice reminded me of someone. It took a few seconds before I remembered. Jack de Manio on the BBC Home Service when I was a kid, every morning before I went off to catch the school bus. Upper class twit, I thought. In fact, I was wrong about de Manio, although I'm not so sure about Twigg.

'What was it you wanted to tell me, my boy?' Nobody had called me 'my boy' for nigh on fifty years, 'Have a seat. Would you like some tea? Or something stronger? I often have a sherry at this time of day.

I had a sherry with him and told him my story. When I had finished, he looked amused rather than concerned.

'I think there are wheels within wheels, but I can tell you one thing, dear boy: no-one is plotting to bump me off. You don't need to worry at all on that score.'

'What's all the stuff about an appointment committee and all those years ago?' I asked.

'Not really your business, but I think it's that delightful little popsy Jane Morton and the new translational job. It may be that they think that I would block her appointment. I have a reputation as a male chauvinist pig, completely undeserved I assure you, dear boy,' the expression male chauvinist pig had a certain antique charm.

'So you would have been all right with her appointment?'

'I would support her appointment, although they won't be asking my opinion. Nice to have a pretty face around the place. And she is very clever for a lady. Lovely bedroom eyes.'

'What about the reference to all those years ago?'

'Yes, I think the lovely Jane was in for a fellowship soon after she qualified, but someone else pipped her to the post. But I didn't put a spoke in her wheel. I think they must have jumped to conclusions because of my MCP reputation. I admit I have had my metaphorical backside tanned for unguarded remarks in the past, but I can put my hand on my heart and say I have never opposed a pretty girl's appointment in the lab.'

I tried not to have a mental picture of his metaphorical backside. I reflected that he had an interesting way of asserting his non-sexist credentials.

'And I don't need to worry about you being in danger?'

'Very kind of you, my boy, but no need to worry about a plot to do away with me. I can promise you that.'

'So what was the thing about you pushing up the daisies?' I asked.

'Nothing for you to worry about. In any case, I won't be on this appointment committee. I hope I will be up at my country bolthole on Little Ore Farm when they are deliberating.'

'I know Little Ore Farm,' I said, 'Place out in North Norfolk near Holt, with all these farm buildings converted into holiday homes? We had a lovely holiday there a few years ago when the kids were still at home.'

'Yes, and I own one of the converted buildings. It's my dacha, dear boy. Most weekends, I am up there enjoying the quiet of the Norfolk countryside. You were lucky to catch me on the one weekend I didn't go.'

I went home soon after, this time determined to forget the whole business.

And then the phone calls started.

The first one was on the last day of October, Halloween. I am quite fond of Halloween. The kids who come trick-or-treating round our street are mostly young and polite and only call at those houses with a pumpkin lantern in the window. Here in the south and east of England, we often hear the remark that Halloween is an import from America. That's not strictly accurate. Halloween has been celebrated as long in the UK as in the US. Trick or treating is an import to England from the USA, but trick or treating is itself an evolution of guising, a Scottish and Irish tradition. When I was a child, we would wear fancy dress, and usually a mask, and would go from house to house in our neighbourhood. When the door was answered, rather than saying 'Trick or treat?' we would ask, 'Wantin' ony guisers?' If the answer was yes, the guisers would have to perform in some respect, usually singing a song or telling a joke. Girls would almost invariably sing 'Queen Mary, Queen Mary, my age is sixteen...' Boys would be more likely to tell a joke. Then the householder would reward the performers with sweets, fruit or money.

One American import of which I am all in favour is the pumpkin lantern. A pumpkin is soft and easy to scoop out. When I was a child, we used to make turnip lanterns, which seemed to me to be an ordeal akin to picking oakum, as Oliver Twist and his fellow workhouse inmates were forced to do. A turnip's flesh (so to speak) is as hard as a brick. Once you had made the turnip lantern, after hours of attacking it with spoons, breadknife, meat cleaver and so on, you were tearfully nursing blisters from the effort and self-inflicted wounds from the dangerous utensils you had used for the vegetable surgery. And the finished product looked stupid. A pumpkin is much easier to deal with.

Anyway, I like Halloween, as I say, with the little groups of trick-or-treaters making their nervous way round the houses. I always buy in a couple of big drums of cheap chocolates to distribute to the callers. Whatever is left at the end of the night I will hoover up over the next few days and feel bloated as a result.

On this particular Halloween, the visits were over and it was around half past nine. We were sitting in front of the television, me with a beer in front of me and the telephone rang. I answered it and there was silence, apart from what I thought was someone breathing at the other end. After a few seconds of my asking who was there the caller hung up.

In the days that followed, there would be similar calls, but usually around four in the morning. As with the first call, the caller would hang up a few seconds after Lena or I answered it. The caller always withheld his or her number. The experience was unnerving. After the third or fourth time, I contacted DS Ripley again. I reported that I had taken his advice and dropped the matter (leaving out the bit about going to see Professor Twigg first), and these phone calls were occurring despite this. DS Ripley was getting rather fed up with me by this time, but he promised to look into it.

The other person I told was Professor Twigg. The phone calls made me worried that he would now be a target again, despite his assurances that there was nothing to worry about. I called him a few times at the Vet School and eventually caught him. He was sympathetic and sublimely confident.

'Leave it with me, my boy,' he boomed down the telephone, 'As I say, don't worry in the least about me. I shall try to look after you, however. I shall speak to some people in the near future, and the various bothersome things, including the phone calls, will stop.'

And I am sure you are thinking, Here we go again. You're right of course. Something did reawaken the issue. A week or so later, I was down at the hospital, giving a pal of mine a lift to and from his oncology follow-up appointment. Fortunately, Bobby's tumour showed no sign of recurring, so that was all right. The appointment had been for four o'clock, but as often happens, he was not seen until six o' clock, by a registrar whose youthful features suggested that he was just out of short trousers. The all clear more than compensated for the wait.

Then, just as we were leaving, I recognised a plummy voice behind us.

'Well, thank you, Doctor Garrison. I hope to see you at a future appointment,' it was Murray Twigg, 'No, hold on a minute. I think I need to trespass on your time a little longer. YOU! DEAR BOY! MISTER MACKAY!'

I turned to see Murray Twigg, looking fatigued. With him was a white-coated man, aged around forty, handsome and powerfully built, who looked very confident, even arrogant.

'Hello, Professor Twigg, I am sorry I have to rush off, chauffeuring a friend of mine. Bobby Holton, this is Prof Twigg, and I don't know...' I turned to the doctor accompanying Twigg, 'I don't think we've met.'

'Well, you have now,' said Twigg, 'Mister Holton, do you think you could wait for a few minutes in the café at the outpatients entrance? We won't keep your driver long.'

Bobby agreed and walked off down the corridor.

'Doctor Garrison, can you find us a room, please, where the three of us can have a quick few words in private?' asked Twigg.

After a token protest, the doctor complied. The three of us were soon in a small consulting room, containing two chairs, a washbasin, a light box for viewing X-ray films, and a trolley. Doctor Garrison perched on the trolley, and Twigg and I sat on the chairs. The doctor's face was dark with anger. I had the very uncomfortable feeling that the runner in the rear-view mirror was now sitting in the passenger seat beside me.

'Now then, Doctor,' said Twigg, 'This has got to stop.'

'I don't quite get you,' said the doctor, and I immediately recognised one of the voices I had overheard in the lavatory in Fisher College, 'I realise we can only offer palliative care...'

'Not my life,' Twigg interrupted, 'I know that has got to stop, more's the pity. I mean your campaign against Mister Mackay, here.'

'I don't know what you are talking about,' said the doctor, not looking at either of us, but glaring at the floor with an expression of rage.

'Listen to me,' Twigg's tone was friendly but firm, 'This man heard you telling your delightful little popsie, Miss Morton, that I would soon be pushing up the daisies. I am sure you are right about this, but you had no right to tell anyone else about my prognosis. If I hear about any more harassment of Mister Mackay, a single more phone call or complaint, I will report you to every professional association to which you belong. And I will tell that very personable police sergeant who came to see me. Do you understand?'

Again, Doctor Garrison said, 'I don't know what you are talking about.'

'Even if you don't know what I am talking about, do you understand what I am saying?'

'Yes, I understand, but I do not accept that it applies to me.'

'Go on not accepting, but no more nonsense with Mister Mackay. I think we understand each other?'

The doctor said, 'I understand what you are saying.'

Murray Twigg continued, 'And here is something else. I was never against your little girl's appointment, never blocked it. Some more critical souls than myself had previously favoured a more academic candidate, but I would have been on her side. Less sure now, but no one is going to ask me. So she is almost certain to get this new post. If she does not, it will be nothing to do with me or Mister Mackay, here.'

I wasn't used to being called Mister Mackay. I was beginning to feel like the prison officer on Porridge.

'So it all stops here?' asked Twigg.

'I don't know what you mean by 'it all', but I can assure you that I will have no contact with Mister Mackay.'

'Good. So we are all friends, then. Give the lovely Jane a pat on the behind or an improper remark from me. Mister Mackay, squire me to the outpatient entrance, will you?'

We walked down the long hospital corridor. Professor Twigg had the slow and deliberate gait of someone who is not at full strength.

'You see,' said Twigg, 'He knew I was going to be pushing up the daisies not because they planned to murder me, but because he was my oncologist and knew I had terminal cancer.'

'I am so sorry,' I said.

'No need. Not your fault, and I've had a good innings. He had no business telling Jane Morton that I was not long for this world, but he won't have been the first doctor to do that sort of thing. The little lady thought that there were wheels within wheels and that I was against her appointment, but she was wrong. She had the bad luck to be up against a brilliant and irritating achiever the time before.'

'Well, thank you for calling off the Doctor's attack on me.'

'Not at all, dear boy, I should thank you. Although I was in no danger, other than from my tumour, you thought I was and did your best to protect me, at some inconvenience and unpleasantness to yourself. Golly, look at that,' his head turned an almost one hundred and eighty degree angle to follow the walk of a Junoesque nurse who had just passed us.

'Here we are.' We arrived at the outpatients' entrance with the café just inside, Bobby sitting over an enormous paper cup full of coffee, 'There's your fare. My driver will be just outside. Good luck, young man.'

'I'm nearly sixty. Young man is overdoing it.'

'Wait until you're my age. I am off to Little Ore Farm. Get as much time in as I can there.'

We shook hands. Professor Twigg walked slowly and carefully through the automatic doors. I never saw him, Jane Morton or Doctor Garrison again.

An Eye for Taste.

Yvonne Lang

"She's out there already – polishing her skeletons! At this hour. Doesn't she have anything else going on in her life?" Nikki scoffed as she peered out her curtains.

"Whereas you have a husband, a new house to decorate and lots of unpacking to do. You'd never be caught wasting time doing something so trivial as spying on a neighbour setting up her Halloween decorations."

Nikki turned to shoot playful daggers at her husband Mike, who was happily working his way through a bowl of cereal so large he may as well have served it in a bucket. She cast one last glance over the road, to the house her neighbour was busy decorating, then turned back to a smiling Mike. She sighed and began opening kitchen cupboards, not able to remember where they had unpacked the mugs to.

"Third along!" Mike chimed in, sensing she was hunting for a caffeine fix.

Nikki grabbed a mug and stuck the kettle on.

"Why don't you go introduce yourself? Make a friend. She'll be retired so home all day like you while you job hunt."

Nikki snatched up the boiled kettle and poured a mug for her and Mike.

"You know, that is a good idea. She may know someone who needs a party planner, or at least I can pick up some decorating tips. Halloween is really taking off and it would be nice to have new ideas for that season. Nice idea, I knew there was a reason I put up with you. Now, I'm going to unpack the kitchen and get baking. If I go over with some of my cookies that will be an excellent first impression. So start unloading boxes or get out of my way."

Later that evening, Nikki nervously made her way across the street to her new neighbour's house. She clutched the Tupperware of Halloween themed cookies and was uncharacteristically nervous as she made her approach. The house was midway through being decorated, but it already looked spectacular. Nikki had worked with professional decorators back in New York who wouldn't have met this standard with a generous budget and a whole team. She could not help but be impressed. Nikki could have really used a decorator like her on her team. She rapped the shiny black knocker, which was a raven holding a ring in its beak. She wondered if this was her year-round door ornament or if she even changed that with the holidays.

"Coming!" A voice called from inside.

Nikki waited patiently, then the door creaked open and she was face to face with her new neighbour.

"Hello?"

"Hi. I'm Nikki Masters. My husband Mike and I have just moved in across the street so I wanted to come over, introduce myself and offer up some home-baked Halloween cookies."

Nikki was gabbling. A month or so out of work and her brain seemed to have lost the art of conversation.

"How thoughtful! Would you like to come in? I can provide the tea since you brought the biscuits!"

"That sounds lovely, if it's not an inconvenience?"

"Of course not. I'd be glad of the company. I'm Ethel Sprite by the way. If we become friends, you can call me Ettie. Hopefully we do, I have a sweet tooth!" Ethel laughed, a glint in her faded blue eyes twinkling behind her purple rimmed spectacles. She spun in her slippers, which were 3D black cats, and strode off, beckoning for Nikki to follow her and her bright orange cardigan that was adorned with beads and sequins. Rather like a pumpkin had bred with a disco ball. Nikki had a feeling, and she was usually quite good at gauging people, that despite the age difference, Ethel was a character she was going to enjoy becoming friends with.

"Take a seat, and excuse the clutter." Ethel gestured behind her in the vague direction of a kitchen table that was heaped under a mountain of clutter. Nikki handed over the biscuits, sat on the closest seat not swathed in fabric samples and looked over the pile. It was all arts and craft supplies. A pumpkin and skull lantern sat open, waiting for new batteries but looking as if its jaw had been broken. A string of marbles painted to look like eyeballs was lying coiled next to a velvet bat with ruby red eyes.

"You have an eye for decoration," Nikki observed as she looked round the cosy, cluttered kitchen.

"How kind of you to notice. People barely do. It's like you get handed an invisibility cloak with your pension. Even in my quirky outfits people barely give me a second glance. They notice my house and my art though. They're my way of making the world a better place and feeling like I'm still making an impact. Anyway, enough about me. You can tell I'm not used to guests. I'm not the only one with an eye for decoration. It almost seems a shame to eat these divine looking biscuits. You shouldn't have gone to so much trouble. Fruit tea or regular?"

"Regular will be fine, with two sugars please. It wasn't any trouble. I used to make things for a living, and considering how exquisitely decorated your house was, I thought you may appreciate them."

"Well I do, and thanks for the compliment. I was a dressmaker before I retired. Then I ended up making a few props for films to keep myself occupied once I was widowed. My crafts have expanded even more since. Nice to keep the mind active and the fingers nimble. So, what do you do?"

Ethel cleared some materials off a chair and brought over a plate of biscuits and two cups. None of the three items matched each other. The plate was hidden by a spread of Nikki's biscuits but the deep blue background had gold images and lettering seemed to be representing the signs of the zodiac. Nikki's mug was jet black with cat's yellow eyes on. Ethel's was fire engine red with a huge pair of lips outlined on it. She waited for Ethel to take a biscuit and then helped herself to an iced pumpkin cookie before answering.

"I was an events coordinator. A party planner on a massive scale. Especially good at themed parties, balls and murder mysteries. My husband was offered a huge promotion if we moved here – like triple his salary huge. So we took the plunge and I'm hoping to re-establish myself here."

Nikki didn't share she had also been keen to flee New York to escape a certain client. Who was wrong and who was right didn't seem to matter as much as who was richer. She wasn't going to think of Troy now though. She was here for a fresh start, away from his sexist face.

"How do these taste better than they look?" Ethel exclaimed.

Nikki glowed at the compliment, nothing like a self-esteem boost when you were somewhere completely new and unemployed.

"Thanks. I started out doing most of the novelty pieces for themes myself as I'm a bit of a control freak," she admitted as she sipped tea.

"Good on you gal. If you want a job doing properly, do it yourself. I was much the same. Good help is hard to come across. People are tricky and customers hard to satisfy. They want the world on a plate for a few cents!"

Troy's smirking face came to mind before Nikki pushed it out and distracted herself with a second biscuit, a ghost sprinkled in coconut with liquorice eyes. Ethel studied her for a second, as if she could read the uncomfortable memory just by Nikki's expression.

"Anyway," Ethel continued, "Onto happier subjects. I'll keep my ears open for any opportunities for you, and you're welcome here any time. I see a lot of people out and about, but rarely get visitors here. I like my privacy, people don't like my clutter or I worry they'll disturb a project. And of course, there's Cerberus."

"Cerberus?" Nikki asked.

"My rescue hound. Poor thing had so many tumours it looked like he had three heads when I adopted him. They're better now but he'd never win any beauty contests – everyone overlooked him at the shelter just like the elderly, always in the background, never noticed. He's got his forever home now though. People have treated him so poorly he can be grumpy to the point of unwelcoming to any visitors. I locked him in the lounge before I answered the door. Unusual he's not howling his little head off. He must like you."

"Well I adore animals so don't keep him locked away in his own home on my behalf."

"We'll risk an introduction," Ethel decided as she pottered off.

Nikki heard a door open and the scrabble of claws before a black and grey scar covered mutt with a wonky jaw and nose and a shortened tail came flying at her. The stumpy tail was definitely wagging though.

"Hello there little guy. I'm Nikki," Nikki cooed as she patted him.

Cerberus then launched himself into her lap.

"Cerberus no! I am so sorry. Is he too heavy?"

Nikki giggled as she avoided sloppy kisses,

"No, he's fine. Looks like I've made another friend around here. If you exclude my husband, that's doubled my friends in this area!" She hugged the dog who seemed to settle onto her lap.

288

"Well, you should be very honoured. I've never seen anyone he hasn't growled at. You'll definitely have to come back."

Nikki decided to take a risk, "Any chance you want a hand with your decorating? I bet I can learn a few things and it will be nice to keep the creative juices flowing whilst I job hunt."

Ethel had a long drink and Nikki sensed she was stalling for time. She wondered if she had pushed her luck.

"You're on. There are some specialist techniques I'm very particular about so will probably continue to manage those myself. But another set of hands and an entire head full of ideas would be most welcome."

A few weeks later Nikki was settling into a comfortable routine with Ethel and Cerberus. Ethel was delighted about the company and having a spare person to walk Cerberus. Ethel's baking was improving as she and Nikki exchanged skills and Nikki almost felt qualified to create film props she had learnt so much in such a short time. Halloween was tomorrow so they were working away furiously for finishing touches in time for trick or treaters. Then it would be onto plans for Christmas, a favourite of Nikki who had learnt a lot about ice sculptures and LED displays in her last job. Ethel was firmly Team Halloween though and loved all the spooky and quite macabre props.

"When do you want to fill the cauldron up?" Nikki asked as she manoeuvred the bulky thing round heaped crafts and a meandering Cerberus.

"Let's get it out there now, check the lights work and we'll put in the severed hand, eyeballs and liquid tomorrow. The hand should be dry now. I'll go check."

Ethel hurried away as Nikki negotiated the black cauldron out to the porch. As she heaved it into place her elbow caught the prepared eyeballs and a few rolled off the table and made a dash for freedom. Nikki cursed and took after them. Cerberus thought it was a fun game so joined pursuit.

"Cerberus no!" Nikki hissed as she ran after him, arms outstretched.

She did not want him to gobble one up. She couldn't cope with the guilt or the financial hit of an unexpected vet trip. She managed to snatch one up before he got his slobbery chops on it, but the other three picked up speed as they fell down the stairs to the cellar. Cerberus shoved his way through the open cranny, his body forcing the door to swing wide open and reveal the wooden steps. Tiny silver studs lined the end of each step and they glinted in the light. Nikki frowned. Ethel was quite protective, almost secretive about her cellar. Nikki hadn't wanted to pry, she didn't want to ruffle feathers so early in a blossoming friendship. Her curiosity was piqued though.

Nikki hovered on the threshold, uncertain whether or not to venture in. She had a genuine reason for going down. She wasn't snooping. She crouched to look closer at the stair edges. The silver studs were pointed, like needles, not just grips. Surely that was dangerous for Ethel? They could pierce right through her slippers and she'd be in a right state if she fell down these stairs. It was almost as if the entrance to the cellar was booby trapped. Then a horrible thought struck her, Cerberus had probably cut his paws scrambling downstairs. Nikki looked for a light switch but found none.

"Cerberus?" She called, "Ettie, Cerberus has got down into the cellar, is that safe?"

"What? Oh no!"

Nikki could hear the worry in Ethel's voice. God, the cellar must be a death trap.

"Don't worry, I'll get him!" Nikki called and gingerly picked her way down the steps as fast as she could without cutting her foot or falling. She got to the bottom and her senses were assaulted a weird mix of decay and chemicals clawing at her nostrils. Something, it sounded like a generator, was humming away and Nikki could hear the snuffling of Cerberus. Her eyes hadn't adjusted yet so all she could see were vague shadowy outlines, and Ethel's cellar looked as cluttered as the rest of her house. Nikki didn't dare move.

"Cerberus!" she called again, "Treats!"

She was relieved to feel him pawing at her knees, "Good boy, let's get you upstairs," Nikki soothed as she scooped his wriggling body up. She hoped she could ascend the stairs OK carrying him, but she didn't want him walking up them. She paused with her feet at the foot of the steps. Had she heard a muffled voice? She turned around slowly,

290

"Hello? Is someone down here?" She called softly, feeling daft as she did so.

Suddenly the place lit up and Nikki held onto Cerberus tightly as she blinked. She looked up to see Ethel at the top of the stairs, who obviously knew where the light switch was.

"I've got him," she held her arms out, "I don't think he's injured himself but obviously we should check him in the light to be sure."

"Is that really what you want to talk about?" Ethel asked as she descended.

Nikki was flummoxed and found Ethel's expression hard to read. Ethel took Cerberus and deposited him at the top of the stairs, then turned to face Nikki. Confused, Nikki turned around and saw a bizarre makeshift morgue cum laboratory. Bodies, some with flesh, some in pieces, some reduced to skeletons, were piled all over. Some were attached to drips. One man was tied and bound in a giant bird cage, struggling feebly against his restraints. It was his eyes, wide with terror, that really showed to Nikki that he was real and still alive.

"Sorry you found out this way," Ethel offered, still stood a few steps above Nikki.

"Is there a good way to find out?" Nikki breathed as her eyes roved round the room, taking in the horrors.

"No great ways, but better, planned ways when we've known each other longer."

"So, you rob graves or kidnap people?" Nikki asked, trying to make this scene fit with the eccentric but kind grandmother figure she had been enjoying getting to know.

"Now you know my secret. Humans, their body parts and pieces touched by their souls really do make exceptional decorating pieces. Not just for Halloween, although that is the easiest and most obvious fit. They're not random, if I may?"

Nikki stepped aside, speechless, confused and happy to be led as her brain scrambled to make sense of this. Ethel started pointing out people, or parts of people.

"These kneecaps belonged to a thrice convicted paedophile who was about to be sentenced again for another offense. Obviously beyond reform. The tinsel is from some soldiers who used war to cover up brutality against civilians. That arm is from a mother who poisoned her own daughter for attention. Those skulls that still have some flesh to be stripped are of parents who prostituted their daughter. The man in the cage is a rapist. A serial rapist. Scum."

Nikki locked eyes with him. She could see the plea but it only brought someone else to mind who never paid for their wrongs against women either.

"How on earth do you overpower them? Or never get caught?" Nikki breathed.

"They are from far and wide, sporadically spaced and as I said when we first met, no-one notices me. The elderly, especially women, are almost invisible to society, and almost always underestimated."

"Are you going to kill me?" Nikki dared to ask, acknowledging the elephant in the room.

"I'd really rather not. I'm very fond of you and you are my first real friend in years. And Mike knows you were coming here."

Nikki wasn't sure if the last part was a joke, or if they were ready to laugh yet.

"Will you keep my secret?" Ethel asked when Nikki still didn't answer.

Nikki didn't have to think long. She was surprised by the way her gut went whilst looking at other guts strung out.

"Can you teach me? This will really give me an edge in decorating? And, do you do requests? I'm quite keen for you to hear about Troy."

Ethel nodded as a smile spread across her face. She picked up one of the errant eyes that Nikki had run down here chasing.

"Marvellous, another partner who has the same moral compass and," she passed over the eye, "Another woman with an exceptional eye for taste."

The Witches' Bridge

Max Jason Peterson

Halloween turned the Eastern Virginia amusement park into a carnival of frights. Each year felt scarier than the one before. Susan stood on the bridge that led into the witches' camp, where the trip-trap of human feet triggered bloodcurdling screams. The tree-lined bridge spanned a stream whose gurgling depths disappeared into darkness. Occasionally, the ribbon of Halloween revelers snapped, leaving Susan alone on the bridge where her friend Holly had died six years ago today—Halloween Sunday, 2004.

Susan leaned out over the rail, gripping it tightly. She stared intently at the glistening tips of protruding stones and the froth of the waterfall sliding past. From the slope above, running feet emerged from the witches' woods. "Hey, lady, are you going to jump?" Two teenage boys loped past, laughing. As they crossed the right point, the bridge shrieked. One kid laughed a curse. Susan stood alone.

"Holly," she whispered. "Holly, can you hear me? It's tonight, sweetheart. It's finally Halloween Sunday again."

The trial had been agonizing. As the only witness to the crime, Susan had burned with shame as the defense team dragged out secrets and speculated about motives, accusing her of everything from being jealous of Brant to being jealous of Holly. The defense lawyers had pointed out how plain Susan was, even ugly without makeup, and accused her of both bitter envy and lesbianism. They'd even dissected her divorce.

It was true, of course, that she'd loved Holly, but not that way. Since the divorce, Susan had cherished her friends even more. Since second grade, Holly had been the best of friends, someone whose love and loyalty Susan could trust when her husband's failed.

Since they were girls together, they'd made special plans for Halloween—parties and haunted tours, spooky poetry readings and ghost hunting. They'd first met at the school Halloween party, and it was this enthusiasm that cemented their friendship after school at each other's houses as they created books of ghosts and drawings of black cats. They loved witches best of all—black silhouettes against the moonlit sky, riding twig-crooked brooms, their black cats arching to spring and scratch out eyes. At eight, the girls' highest ambition had been to become witches themselves, with crooked hats to mirror the sickle moon they flew beside. They'd written witch haiku and limericks that they called spells, and even made a witches' pact of friendship, dripping blood from pricked thumbs into a pot of boiling water over the stove's gas flame. This, Holly's idea, felt dangerous, rash—thrilling and scary with forever.

They'd shared more than Halloween, of course: dancing to Holly's mom's '70s LPs, playing in the tree house, acting out their favorite television shows, and, later, laughing about boys. They remained best friends through high school, despite Holly's growing mania for makeup and making out with jocks who never treated her right. But Susan loved Holly enough to put up with all the embarrassing public displays, though she far preferred the time they spent alone.

Six years ago tonight, when Holly told her that Brant would be joining them at the park, Susan had tried to object.

"It's Halloween. Our special day."

To include Brant in their private moment felt like a betrayal. She knew what Brant was like—what an evening in his company would mean. She'd gone to the park with them a few times. For Holly's sake, she'd put up with Brant's aggressive and possessive shenanigans, his extremely public displays of affection and sexual ownership. Privately, Susan had urged Holly to kick him out. But Halloween meant too much to squander on Brant's macho tomfoolery. He did his best to spoil the fun for everyone.

But Holly had been adamant: "He goes where I go." And the evening had quickly gone sour, between Brant's teasing antics and harassment of the costumed staff and Holly's deliberately sexy shrieks. The monsters went out of their way to scare the beautiful girl with the round, laughing cheeks and eyes that gleamed with each new thrill. They wanted to see the lusty swell of her breast as she threw back that long chestnut hair and screamed. Sometimes Brant beat them to the punch, yelling in her ear to make her jump or goosing her as he laughed wickedly. When a bloody vampire surprised her and she cowered against Brant, he shoved her protectively aside and roared threats till the monster melted away.

It disgusted Susan, who walked behind them through one wasted maze after another. At last, they emerged from another haunted house ruined by Brant's sarcastic, cajoling wisecracks. Holly's laughter goaded him on.

"I'm going to explore the park by myself," Susan said. "I'll meet you later at the witches' caravan."

Holly shrugged as if it didn't matter. As Susan walked off, she thought she heard Holly say with a low laugh, "Thank God we got rid of Ms. Sourpuss." But the warped carnival music, revelers' shrieks, and growls of the spooks were so loud, she couldn't tell for sure.

Susan put it behind her and threw herself into the Halloween spirit, cringing so the spooks would jump out to get her. Sometimes they passed her over for pretty girls, but it served the ghouls right when, as often as not, the beauty laughed or made bored comments to her boyfriend. Susan did it right; she shrieked and scampered at a skeleton's sudden lunge. Once they caught on, they followed her through the maze, more and more of them. They tilted their eyeless skulls, their movements stiff with lack of cartilage. Their finger bones clutched after her, till she ran screaming into the night. Sometimes she stumbled in surprise, lifting one leg like a pawing horse before starting to run, their deep chuckles following her into the darkness. Only under the arc lights did her grin escape.

Alone, Susan could slip through the crowds in half the time, weaving around clumps of friends and families with strollers. She toured maze after maze, again and again. Near closing time, her regret caught up with her. Halloween was almost over, and she'd spent most of their favorite holiday without her friend. Remembering their first Halloween as kids when they'd pretended to be witches, she made her way toward the Witches' Bridge.

Susan passed other stragglers whose leisurely pace said that they, too, wanted to milk the final moments. Trees darkened the approach to the bridge, and a blind curve meant hidden monsters could scare a screamer twice. Tired home-goers grew sparse on the paths. The creepy music sounded louder as the park emptied, that eerie music piping into the dim, dead place.

The boards of the bridge were smooth from many crossings. The sides dropped away into a moist, gurgling darkness. As Susan neared, mist shot up over the bridge, accompanied by a sepulchral laugh from underneath. As the mist parted, Susan saw Holly and Brant embracing on the bridge.

Brant's back was to her, and Holly didn't seem to see her. Holly laughed at Brant's mutter. The curling ends of her long chestnut locks swung freely, brushing her shoulders, while his crew cut was so short it was hard to see the color of his hair. Her round hips pressed his narrow ones, both of them in jeans. His biceps bulged under a thin, green T-shirt.

Susan stepped back. Holly looked up. Holding Susan's eyes, she whispered in Brant's ear.

Her own ears burning, Susan started walking away. Then Holly shrieked. Susan glanced back. Brant had lifted Holly into his arms like a bride and tossed her up. Staggering slightly, with a nasty chuckle, Brant crooned, "So you want to go home? Without me?"

Holly screamed—a pleased, haunted-house squeal. "Let me down!"

"You think you're getting off that easily?" he murmured tenderly.

Holly kicked the air. He staggered a little under her weight.

Susan froze. For a joke, it was too dangerous. With each toss, he lurched closer to the rail. Holly clung to his neck and started pleading, "Brant, let me down, oh please God, let me go!"

Susan looked up and down the bridge. No one else was in sight or within hearing range, with that blasted music. Far ahead, the last walkers didn't look back.

Holly stopped kicking; she clung to Brant's neck. "Please, baby, put me down!" Her hair fell over his shoulder.

"Come on, you know you like it," he chuckled. His waist pressed the rail. Through the thin shirt, the muscles bunched visibly across his back.

"Help!" Holly shrieked. Over Brant's shoulder, her eyes sought her best friend.

Susan took a step toward them, arms outstretched, readying herself to make a grab—could she catch Holly without making things worse? There were guards in the park—even a few local police. But they'd never get here in time.

Holly's back hung over open space. Susan checked her fists to be sure her thumbs were outside the way Daddy taught her. She ran toward Brant's back.

"Hey!" she bellowed.

Brant whirled. His face convulsed as he saw Susan. With a spastic jerk, he dropped Holly over the rail.

Holly's gasp hung in the air. No time to scream. In an instant, the splash ended in a terrible crunch. Susan thought inanely of trolls grinding bones.

She ran to the rail. Brant stood there, frozen, his face an unreadable mask. Holly was gone.

Susan cursed him and ran for the cops. When they returned, Brant still waited on the bridge, staring over the rail at the water with glazed eyes. It took the rescue team some time to retrieve Holly's remains.

At the trial, Brant's defense lawyers painted Susan as an obsessive stalker who'd figuratively suffocated Holly and hated Brant for his influence on her. According to Brant, Susan would have accused him of anything; she was always badmouthing him to Holly, trying to turn her against him. Susan clearly had a chip on her shoulder, and Holly was sweet as pie unless she'd been talking to Susan, after which she'd suddenly come home with a laundry list of complaints. Brant had claimed he hadn't seen Holly since they entered the park—that she'd gone off with her friend. He'd finally caught up with them just in time to see Susan push Holly off the bridge.

But security cameras showed Holly and Brant walking toward the bridge, wrapped in each other's arms. Staff and attendees from haunted houses all over the park remembered Brant's obnoxious behavior and Holly's beauty. They remembered the way the couple had been all over each other. Then Brant tried to claim it was an "accident," that Holly had been so startled by the recorded screams on the bridge she'd tripped and fallen over the side. In response, the police proved the railing was chest-high on Holly and difficult to climb.

Gruesome crime scene photos showed Holly's body shattered on the rocks, her bones poking through twisted limbs. The medical examiner described lungs filled with blood and water. The grisly evidence silenced Brant and cemented the case in the jury's mind.

And then, in the eleventh hour, the police had found the email Brant sent Holly a month before her death, threatening to kill her and himself. He said he'd had enough of interfering friends and family who sapped her time and attention and swayed her against him. He said that he was only happy in the moments when she truly loved him, when she was focused only on him; so, in some unsuspecting moment of happiness, he'd make sure they died together like Bonnie and Clyde, together forever, proof of their love. That it would look like an accident, but he wanted her to know how deeply he cared—"I'd go to the grave with you, baby." Holly's answering email sounded truly scared. She'd demanded he stay away from her. In dozens of wheedling, insistent replies, Brant laughed it off as a joke, said she'd made too much of it, and promised if she gave him another chance she wouldn't be sorry.

But events proved otherwise.

In the end, Susan got justice for Holly at the risk of her dignity, her reputation, and possibly her life if Brant got free. But Brant's conviction, even his execution for premeditated murder, couldn't bring Holly back.

Each year, Susan returned to the park, wishing with all her heart for an impossible reunion with Holly, oppressed by the thought of what she'd failed to do. Halloween itself had fallen during the week when the park was closed until Halloween Friday in 2008. Brant was still making appeals.

Susan found herself at the bridge rail, talking earnestly to Holly while the spooks swirled all around. She felt as though her friend were listening, a ghostly presence as faint but real as the wind upon her cheek.

For Halloween Saturday in 2009, Susan had done her research. Her voice trembled with excitement as she spoke the words that should free her friend. Fog rose to surround her; the green lights from the foot of the bridge shone through it in a blurry haze. In the blindness, she felt Holly's cold, clammy hand upon her wrist. But the fog blew away with the same acrid aftertaste as that generated by the park's machines. Susan stood on the bridge alone, feeling useless and lost, as bewildered as she'd been when Holly first went over the side.

But 2010 brought new hope. Halloween fell on Sunday once more, just like when Holly died. Though the fall in Eastern Virginia had been warm and bright as usual with cheery blue skies, Halloween dawned crisp and cold, with fog shrouding an orange sun in a visible reminder of the powerful change in the year. Susan felt calm, certain. The conditions were right. This time, she would free Holly's spirit. *Third time's the charm,* she thought. And within moments, Holly's killer would be dead.

"His last appeal fell through," Susan told Holly. "I guess he finally accepted what he did to you," she choked, then continued raggedly, "He never did say he was sorry. But he asked to be executed tonight at the same time you fell. His request was granted. They told me I could watch, but I'd rather be here with you."

Brant's execution alone couldn't bring Holly back. But Halloween had its own magic and power. And tonight she had a whole park full of Halloween believers to back her up, lending strength with their screams. Even the scoffers added weight by participation.

"We'll be witches at last," Susan told Holly with a shaky laugh. When the moon was high, she performed the simplest ritual of all. One nick to the thumb, and blood fell into the roiling water where Holly's blood had pooled six years before. Their childhood spell revived with all the strength of a friend's belief and the wild magic of Halloween.

Susan leaned over the dark water.

"You're free now, Holly! He's dead!"

Her eyes filled with tears. The park's generated mist coalesced under the bridge and rose, glowing purple in the Halloween lights as it engulfed the walkers around her. Their startled protests sounded muffled. They bumped into one another and laughed.

Susan put her head down on her arms on the wooden rail. Her long hair tickled her arms. Why was she such a coward? Why hadn't she saved her friend?

The wind brushed her neck. Her arms felt wet. When she wiped her eyes, she felt dizzy.

Why was the ground so far away?

A new fog crept up over the railing. Susan felt stretched between earth and heaven—like a bridge, her soul spanning a road born of witches' blood. *Holly?* These last few years, she'd felt her friend's presence, slumbering, waiting for the right moment. Now, her chest hurt as Holly drew breath inside her. The fog formed a phosphorescent face—not decayed, not broken, but dark with pain.

Susan opened her arms to Holly.

"At last," Holly whispered, her breath as cold as mist. "I've waited. To tell you."

The green-shot fog embraced Susan, filling her sight. Thrilled, Susan felt her feet lifting from the ground. "Holly—I've missed you—"

The mist vanished. Susan's stomach dropped with terror and fluttering delight as she hung suspended—flying!

Then Brant's face leered up at her, his crew cut so close she could see his scalp through gold stubble. She yelped and clutched his neck, the only thing to hold. He murmured soothingly, "I got you, babe," with a wicked smile.

She shrieked; he laughed. He tossed her again, his arms strong and solid, though he pretended his knees buckled under her weight, and let her fall a little more. She sobbed, terror like a knife at her throat, but the thrill in her belly was expansive and warm.

Across the bridge, she saw her friend Susan—her old self—standing like a ghost, her face shocked and pale. Watching over Brant's shoulder, Holly-Susan laughed inside and ratcheted up the screams, putting a new note of terror in her voice. True to form, Brant smacked his lips at the lusty quaver in her cries.

Brant didn't know Susan stood there. Holly pleaded with her eyes. Susan thought so little of Brant. This would be amusing. Let the big lunk be scared for a change!

Susan. Best friend for so long. Suffocating devotion. Yet Holly had regretted the instant when she'd let her annoyance slip into mockery. Susan could be cloying, but that was due to them being as close as sisters, so close Susan felt she had a say in how Holly lived her life. In truth, Holly did feel humiliated sometimes by the public ownership Brant demanded—their lascivious spectacles. But he was exciting and dangerous to deny. His recklessness was a breath of fresh air after Susan's overprotective cocoon. For one nasty moment, the imp of the perverse had seized her outside that maze. Playing up to Brant, she'd insulted Susan *sotto voce*. She saw the pain in Susan's stiff back and hated the deed. But Susan would get over it. She'd forgive, without ever admitting she'd heard. Holly blamed Brant for inciting the whole thing.

So, when she'd seen her friend hesitating at the edge of the bridge, she'd whispered in Brant's ear, "I'm riding home with Susan."

Inside Holly, Susan's heart swelled with joy. She cried out in Holly's mind, "Yes!"

Holly's back crawled where Brant held her so near the edge. He bent his knees suddenly and she felt her heart stop. He caught her, chortling, "Oops!"

"Help!" Holly screamed.

Susan watched from Holly's eyes while that other, past-Susan's mouth hardened with determination. Past-Susan's eyes flashed. Riding inside her friend, now-Susan saw that Holly knew her friend would battle demons—go to the ends of the earth. That past-Susan would fight Brant.

In that instant, from Holly's vantage point, Susan saw it. Breaking through the fog in her head and the light, ghostly pressure of the wind on her neck, Susan sobbed, "Holly, no! I didn't."

Behind her, a whisper trailed her neck in dewdrops.

"Yes. You did. But it's too late now for regrets. My boyfriend's dead. And so am I. You killed us both."

Trapped inside Holly—in Brant's arms—Susan shrieked as her determined past-self ran up purposefully.

"Witch sisters," Holly crooned. "Halloween night. You said you came for a reunion. Our special day."

Past-Susan yelled. Brant shied like a colt. His burden slipped. He whirled, his arms lifting, providing accidental boost.

Holly-Susan flew—hung for a moment, buoyed up in cold, dead arms.

Behind her, the bridge shrieked lustily, then burst into maniacal laughter and dragged them over the side and into a watery embrace.

They tumbled down, shrieking along with the bridge, in perfect harmony with Halloween.

Be Careful Dennis

Kevin Ground

"Be careful Dennis, don't try to take too big a slice." The words were hardly out of Helen Proctor's mouth, when a shrill cry of pain alerted her to the fact that her eight-year-old son, Dennis, had sliced into his fingers with the supposedly child friendly safety knife he was using. The bright orange pumpkin he was carving sat amongst a pile of scooped out flesh and seeds on the plastic covered kitchen table. The splash of blood running between his fingers dripped off his wrist onto the table cover, and onto the pumpkin. In stark contrast, all the colour drained from her injured son's face as he slumped sideways in a dead faint. His mother caught him by the shoulders just as he was about to fall sideways off the kitchen chair and onto the unforgiving tiled floor below.

The next hour, everything Halloween was forgotten as the frightened little boy endured the pain of having his injured fingers cleaned and inspected by his concerned mother. The knife blade had nicked two fingers and cut across another, leaving superficial wounds in its wake. Which none the less required plasters and some serious mummy cuddling to restore Dennis to something like his usual self.

All the while the pumpkin sat silently on the blood-splashed kitchen table. The droplets of blood from Dennis's wounded fingers congealed around the openings carved out to denote the pumpkins facial features. More bloody droplets slowly soaked in the fleshy inner part of the pumpkin, staining the orange flesh a rusty colour as it dried.

Not that Dennis was interested, pumpkin carving had lost all its appeal, it was left to his mum Helen to clean up the mess on the table and run a cleaning wipe over the tabletop and kitchen floor. Ironically, Dennis had almost finished when the accident happened, so as far as his mum was concerned the pumpkin was as Halloween ready as it was going to be.

Later that afternoon, as night began to fall and trick or treating youngsters began to dress up and take to the streets, Dennis was allowed to light the three candles placed inside the hollowed out pumpkin with a smoking wax taper. The yellow glow illuminating the features Dennis had so carefully carved before cutting his fingers, the heat of the candles warming the blood soaked into the pumpkin flesh, causing a sticky patch of bubbling blood to give off a strange vapour. This reacted with the yellow candle flames, making them burn with a purple glow that wavered back and forth as the light evening breeze blew across the small front garden.

It didn't take long for the dancing purple light to attract the youngest of the trick or treaters, out and about early under the watchful eyes of their parents. Knocks on the front door and shouts of trick or treat soon filled the air, as Dennis held a small tray of assorted sweets and chocolates for the would-be ghouls and ghosts to choose from. His own trick or treating was on hold due to his injured fingers. Not that he minded, his injuries marked him out for sympathy from other parents and no little admiration from some of the youngsters.

All the while the candles burned, and the blood boiled, and the vapour filled the air with its strange almost sickly-sweet smell. The pumpkin's face glowed ever brighter as a succession of young children and toddlers drew close to accept the proffered Halloween treats.

It seemed to Dennis's mum that more children than ever before were making their way to her front door. Ghosts and ghouls and pointy hatted witches rubbed shoulders with bandaged mummies and undead zombies, all rattling collecting buckets for the treats on offer. Dennis was happy and laughing as he recognised friends from his school under their Halloween disguises. His injured fingers were all but forgotten in his excitement, until the pumpkin began to smell even stronger, and the flickering purple candles began to burn ever brighter and change colour to a fierce blood red. The flesh inside the pumpkin melted into a gooey mush as it cooked, the candles floated upwards as more and more of the pumpkin flesh dissolved.

Dennis's mum didn't know what to make of it, but the children loved it, and their parents, thinking it was all supposed to be happening, looked on as the pumpkin put on a show all of its own creation. The candle flames writhed and rolled as the candles floated higher, and the pumpkin began to lose its shape. The orange skin slowly collapsed in on itself as the flesh inside cooked and dissolved. It was then that the parents began to realise something was wrong and called their children back to a safe distance from the bubbling pumpkin.

Dennis's mum reached out to guide Dennis away from the melting mess oozing over her front doorstep, but she was too late. With a loud popping noise, the pumpkin fell apart, and the candle flames jumped head high up in the air, leaving the burned-out candle stubs lying amongst the dissolved pumpkin flesh, bubbling, and boiling on the doorstep. The red flames joined together in the air to swirl around, chasing their collective tails until, blown by the light evening breeze, they hovered over Dennis's head and, without warning, fell out of the air and covered the mesmerised boy in a shower of burning red fire.

For a heartbeat no one moved. The only sound was a sharp intake of breath from the parents and scattered 'oohs' of surprise from the children. Then, just as quickly, everyone moved at once and the night air was full of screams and cries of alarm. The strange smell faded, and Dennis's mum tried desperately to beat out the fire engulfing her son. Another parent hurriedly ripped off his jacket to throw over the flames in a desperate effort to smother the blaze, but the fire burned unabated, forcing the would-be rescuers to retreat from the heat and smoke.

Beside herself with concern for her son, Dennis's mum yelled his name at the top of her voice and tried to wrap her own jacket around him but to no avail. The fire seemed to have a will of its own and flared brighter and hotter to push her away. To those watching on as others struggled to save the burning boy, the most bizarre part of the drama unfolding in front of them, was the fact that Dennis stood within the smoke and flames, seemingly unconcerned, his head and shoulders obscured by the ball of red fire. He showed no sign of any discomfort, the fire seemed to be around him, but not on him. Flickers of red and smoke moved this way and that around the standing boy until they began travelling down one arm towards his injured fingers. The carefully applied plasters fell from the cuts as the fire weaved its way around the injured fingers, a glowing furnace, hot for a few seconds before all of the swirling fireball slowed and steadied itself. More and more of its red glow travelled down to Dennis's injured fingers, until with a final shower of red sparks the ball was no more than a red haze around Dennis's hand, before it too disappeared completely.

Dennis reappeared from the clearing smoke seemingly unharmed, save for the fact that his blonde hair and eyebrows were now completely orange apart from three thin red streaks running from his fringe to the back of his head.

The next hour was the strangest anyone could ever remember, as the emergency services arrived in a dazzle of blue lights. The fire brigade damped down the smouldering front door and door frame. Paramedics checked over an amazingly unharmed Dennis, and the police who were taking statements from the assembled crowd of bemused parents and children, began to wonder if they were dealing with an elaborate Halloween hoax that had gotten wildly out of hand.

Dennis's mum didn't know what to make of it and she was beyond caring. Her son should have been burned alive, but he wasn't, he was sat by her side as the paramedics checked him over. He smelled of smoke and his hair looked ridiculous, but he was safe and unharmed. even down to the cuts on his fingers which had miraculously healed. If anything, she felt nauseous after being frightened out of her wits, and enduring the horror of watching her only child supposedly die horribly in front of her, but other than that she was okay, in fact the other parents who had tried to rescue Dennis from the fire were all uninjured, which, given they had wrapped their jackets and coats around the burning boy, and tried to beat at the flames with their bare hands was unexplainable.

The mobile phone footage caused an internet sensation with most dismissing it as no more than an entertaining Halloween trick, but for Dennis and his mum, this Halloween had certainly been a night they would never forget, neither would anyone else for that matter. One of Dennis's school friends, dressed in a smoke smelling zombie outfit, summed it up perfectly.

"That was great Dennis. Can we come again next year please?"

Not the Cutesy Café

Annie Knox

Diana folded her arms and used every ounce of her strength not to quit.

Stacey, the short, plump, middle-aged assistant manager stared up at her with earnest eyes, as if she hadn't spent half an hour patronising the fuck out of Diana. She had a pair of whiskers drawn on her face and orange furry ears poking out of her hair.

"Ask any questions," she nodded, eager, bossy, irritating - but more frustratingly, nice, therefore making Diana feel guilty for her thoughts. "I'd rather you asked. Even if you ask ten times. Better than doing it wrong, eh?"

How, Diana wanted to ask, *could I possibly manage to pick up plates from a table wrong?* That was what Stacy had spent thirty minutes 'training' her to do. As if she hadn't hired Diana because she had five years of waitress experience.

"It gets really busy in here," Stacy eyed the room apprehensively. "Today's been crazy, hasn't it? Halloween rush!"

Diana pursed her lips, regarding the nine tables, five of which had customers on them. There were five members of front of house staff. A table each. No wonder half the waiters were smoking whilst she got a lecture on how to spray a surface and wipe a microfibre cloth over the top. The other waiters were teenagers, earning money around school, and the rest of the team was management. She was the odd one out, the twenty-five-year-old who didn't have anything else going on in her life. Except mental health issues.

"So," Stacy gave her a pat that had Diana fighting the urge to pick up a steak knife from the nearest table and tear off the older woman's face with it. "Do you need five minutes? That was a lot of info, I know."

The reality of her situation suddenly overwhelmed Diana; her shitty new job, her shitty new countryside bumpkin town, the crisis team appointment waiting for her on her next day off. A terrifying future stretched ahead of her: being endlessly patronised by Stacey, collecting pathetic tips from gross pervy old men, and sitting alone in her flat while she tried to rebuild from her suicide attempt.

Bitter tears stung her eyes.

"Yes," she blinked desperately. "Yeah, I need to pee."

"Of course, love," Stacy fumbled at the keys hanging from her belt. "I think Liam took a shit just now, but there's some air freshener in there." She handed the keys over, catching sight of the vacant, distressed look on Diana's face. "Don't worry, sweetheart, it's a learning curve. You've only been here two days! You'll get the hang of clearing the tables in no time."

"Right," Diana prayed for her voice not to wobble. "I'll just take five. Ta." She grabbed the keys and scurried out, head down, aware that the old men on table three were staring at her butt. Hurtling through the corridor to the kitchen she dashed outside, snivelling snot up, pretending not to notice the smokers watching her.

The staff toilet was a weird little hut across the car park out the back of the kitchen. Someone had taken the time to string a lump of ugly orange lights across it. A shitty pumpkin with a coffee carved into it greeted her on the steps up to the peeling door. She struggled to find the right key to jimmy open the latch.

"Hey, you need help?" Trey, the most irritating of the smokers, called out.

"No!"

"You sure? You got the keys?"

"Yeah, thanks!"

"Want me to come?"

God, *no* - she cracked the door open through sheer desperation, face crumpling, and slammed it shut behind her. Sinking to the floor - Liam had definitely shit in there not long ago - she put both hands over her eyes and grappled with her emotions. It was a quasi-panic, an explosive ninety seconds of struggling to breathe, before she took her hands away, back in control, looked to the cobwebbed ceiling, and prayed for the strength to get through the rest of the shift.

Her phone buzzed in her pocket. She pulled it out to see a message from her maybe/maybe not boyfriend Harvey. Harvey, who was back in London, being handsome and funny and a good person in front of all the sexy, not-mentally-ill girls at his office. Whilst she, his probably-not/likely-deluded girlfriend, sat crying on the floor of a hut toilet, getting paid minimum wage to do so. Eczema all over her pale face from crying too much. Cracked lips. Bags under her eyes. A bit of a mess, in summary.

'Hope your day is going good babe x'

Followed by a photo of him at his desk, giving her the thumbs up. Cassandra, his gorgeous secretary, was visible in the background with two mugs in her hand. She was probably about to hand him a coffee, all smiley with her red lipstick and her nice self.

Diana could throttle her.

Pulling herself together, she got up, peed on the manky toilet - so low was her sense of happiness, she sat on the seat instead of hovering above it - and then washed her hands and splashed cold water in her face.

Looking in the mirror, she wondered when she had stopped recognising the girl looking back.

Sighing, seeing the sickly creature in the reflection sigh too, Diana turned to leave, grabbed the toilet handle, and felt something hairy jerk under her palm. Yanking her hand away in horror, she looked at the handle, and saw a fat spider sitting there.

"Oh shit—" she tried to breathe, and her lungs said no. "Not now, oh shit, shi-shi—"

Her eyes rolled and Diana fainted to the ground, passing out on some upsettingly suspicious stains.

When she peeled her sore eyes apart again, wincing at the pounding in her skull, Diana gingerly sat up and tried not to panic over the fact that she couldn't see. Had she broken her eyes? If she was blind, it was fucked. She wasn't learning Braille, she was too dumb and depressed. She'd take it as a sign from the universe that she should have done a better job of killing herself. She'd fuck right off and -

Half of the hut lit up bright white. Her phone vibrated by her butt.

Okay. She was fine. It was just night-time, apparently.

Fumbling the phone up, Diana squinted at it, the brightness hurting her. A message from Harvey. Actually, a tenth message. Perhaps a drunk message, judging from the typos. She scrolled through them, all approximations of *'you haven't tried to kill yourself again, have you?'* and fired off a, *'you wouldn't believe what's happened to me! No death today xx'* before using the phone light to find the handle and open the door.

Stepping outside, the cold made her shiver. The car park was empty. The moon was full in the sky above.

Scurrying unsteadily across to the kitchen, Diana pushed inside, happily surprised that the backdoor was unlocked. She had left her hoodie with the keys to parents' flat in the staff room. Her parents usually rented their holiday home out, but upon hearing of Diana's latest (and greatest) menty B they had emptied it so that she could stay somewhere rent-free.

Creeping through the kitchen, Diana passed the humming walk-in fridges, the hulk of the oven, the flat surfaces of the island where Stacey violently kneaded dough for pastries in the morning. Everything was illuminated by moonlight, shrouded by shadows.

Passing into the hallway something creaked so suddenly that she shrieked, clasping her hands over her mouth, heart pounding, before she realised it was actually the floorboard under her own foot.

"Oh fuck," she whispered, laughing quietly, wiping at a bit of fear-sweat on her forehead. "I'm so stupid - AHHHHHH!"

Leaping back from the figure who had appeared at the end of the hallway, Diana clutched her phone to her chest and tried to control her bladder. The figure, small and stout, stepped into the moonlight.

"Stacey!" Diana slumped. "Why are you still here? It's like, eleven!"

"Diana?" Stacey looked uncomfortable, glancing over her shoulder back into the cafe. "We thought you'd gotten diarrhoea and run home or something. You vanished."

"I fell in the loo." Diana held out the key for the staff toilet. "I was knocked out for ages. Do you think I should call for a doctor?"

"I don't know." Stacey's usual motherly persona was gone. "Listen, it's late. It's Halloween. Get out of here so I can lock up, okay?"

"Right but… "

Diana glanced into the cafe.

"Why are you still here?" She looked back at Stacey. "The cafe closed at eight, you should have been gone by nine."

"Why aren't *you* running home to get your head checked?" Stacey countered with an almost-warm smile. "I think you should do that, sweetheart."

Okay, whatever. Diana was trapped out here in the countryside while the non-committal love of her life partied it up in London. She had just survived an attempt to end her own life. She didn't care about this shit. Stacey was probably having some orgy with the book club in the cafe.

"I need my hoodie." She started to walk towards the cafe. Stacey did not move out of her way.

"In… the staff room, Stace. My hoodie. Staff room's that way."

"Do you really need your hoodie?"

"Yes," Diana struggled to cling to the remains of her tattered patience. "Seeing as my key is in it. May I pass?"

There was a long, awkward beat.

"I'll get it for you," Stacey said, finally. "Health and safety, you can't go in… after hours. It's the law."

Diana bit back the urge to call bullshit. "Okay, I'll wait here."

"Okay. Wait here."

"Yeah, I just said - okay."

Stacey vanished into the cafe. Her footsteps bumbled across the old swollen floorboards. Diana checked her phone. Harvey had sent back a row of question marks.

'Passed out at work! crazy manager is here… think some kind of book club orgy'

She tucked her phone in her pocket. It started to buzz incessantly as a call came through, but suddenly Stacy popped up in front of her, hoodie held out, practically shovelling Diana back through the hallway to the kitchen.

"I got it. Time to go, love."

"Alright, alright! I'm going, thank you." Diana half-walked, was half-pushed out of the back door and turned to say goodnight, only to find the door already locking behind her.

She was calling Harvey back, phone beeping in her ear, when something caught her eye. The backdoor was largely glass, so she could still see into the kitchen. Stacey's shadow was gone, back to her shadowy sex party. But when she had used her hand to press against the glass while struggling with the stiff lock, she'd left a blood-like handprint against the glass.

Diana moved closer. Could Stacey's sex party be Halloween-themed? Gross!

"Babe!" Harvey's drunk voice exploded into her ear. He was in a pub, the sound of glasses and crowds in the background. "I miss you. What happened, why didn't you message me today? Did you fall in love with someone else?"

"No, Harvey," Diana whispered, squinting at the handprint. Something felt off.

"Why are you whispering then?" His voice got sad. "You live alone."

"I'm outside work," the moon burst out from behind a cloud and lit the handprint red. Yeah, fake blood. These guys were maniacs. "It's really weird Harv, I think the assistant manager is having some secret Halloween sex rave in the cafe."

"What are you talking about? I love you. You passed out and you didn't even tell me, what the fuck."

Sex party momentarily forgotten, Diana sighed, sad. "*I love you*, Harvey. I miss you." Tears welled up in her eyes. "I got upset and hid in the toilet, and I touched a spider by accident."

"You hate spiders."

"I do," she laughed a bit, despite her tears. "And I passed out. I just woke up five minutes ago. I probably got like, ten STIs from the floor."

"I want you to go home," Harvey sounded more sober. "You could have really hurt your head. Who cares if the weird lady is fucking half the village. I don't care about her; I care about you. Walk home, Diana. I'll stay on the phone until you're in."

Sniffling, Diana wiped her nose on her hoodie. "Just until I'm in? That's only ten minutes." Her hoodie was damp on her face, and she pulled it back. Had Stacy gotten fake blood on it? She sniffed at the patch. A hint of copper was all she detected. Fake blood was normally syrupy.

"Well… I'm out, Di. So, I'll make sure you're home, and then I'll go, and then I'll call again before I go to bed. We can sleep together. How's that?"

She snivelled a bit more, starting down the drive towards the front of the building. "I hate this place, Harvey_"

"I know—"

"I know I have stay to get better for a bit—"

"You do —"

"But I hate it, and I hate being away from you, and I hate this job, I'm so overqualified for it—"

"I bet you're the best one there -"

"I'm so tired, I just want to be where I'm supposed to be in life—"

"It's going to work out, I promise—"

"Like, this isn't where I'm meant to be—"

"Diana relax, don't get stressed and upset again—"

Diana paused at the edge of the driveway and looked up into the night, trying not to get overwhelmed. The sky was full of stars and empty of pollution. She longed for a dirty sky. She loved her city pollution. She had loved her life, and she had thrown it away.

"I'm not even celebrating Halloween, Harvey. I love Halloween."

"If you stop dawdling like a dickhead, and get yourself home and showered, I'll leave here, and we'll stream a scary movie on Facetime together. How does that sound?"

Before she could eagerly accept, someone booed in the background. A woman, close to Harvey. Their words carried down the line.

*"Are you seriously leaving Harvey? Is your girlfriend crying **again**? She's not even here, why are you going home?"*

"Cassandra!" Harvey barked.

"It's true! Is she even your girlfriend!? You guys weren't official when she left. Just tell her you're busy!"

"Back off," Harvey hissed before his voice got loud again. "Did you hear that, babe? You didn't, did you?"

Diana swallowed hard.

"Diana, yeah?" Harvey sounded stressed. "We'll watch a movie?"

"Um," Diana cursed herself as fresh tears filled her eyes, her heart sinking. "Um," she searched for words. "You should stay out and have fun."

"Diana." He got firm. "Ignore what Cassandra said."

"Goodnight Harvey." Fuck, her voice was shaky and pathetic. She took the phone away from her ear and hung up. Her face crumpled and she started to bawl, both hands fisted in front of her eyes.

Something smashed in the cafe. A man screamed in pain. The scream cut off, there was a series of loud thuds, and then quiet.

Diana stood frozen; breakdown forgotten. Slowly, she twisted to look back at the cafe, which sat in darkness.

That wasn't a sexy scream, that was a murder scream.

"What the fuck," she whispered. "Who the fuck..." Maybe it *was* a sexy scream. A sexy murder scream, some kind of killer role-play situation. It couldn't be actual trouble. Not Stacy of the table-clearing police. Not the cutesy cafe where everyone knew everyone else's names and kids' names and grandkids' names and grandkids' dogs' names. Surely not.

Anxiously peering through the window, she couldn't make out any movement inside. Tiptoeing around the plants by the entrance, she cupped her hands around her face, and pressed her nose against the door.

Nothing.

Scooting around some more, she headed towards the side of the building where the kitchen window was. They always left it open because otherwise a strange rotten smell filled the building overnight and took hours to clear in the morning. On her way there, something else grabbed her attention. Rounding the corner, she saw a slither of light snaking across the grass. A basement window lined the wall, facing out to the garden area. Diana got on her hands and knees and crawled as close as she dared, then lay on the ground, near enough to spy in.

A wine cellar lay before her. Below the window was a sharp drop of roughly two metres to a concrete floor. The walls were lined with thick dusty racks piled with alcohol. The room was dim, golden brackets sprouting from wooden beams, each holding a candle with a flickering flame on top. None of that really took Diana's attention though; what she immediately latched onto were the three teenage staff sat in the centre of the space, bound, gagged, and crying. Stacey, along with Jeanie the manager and Liam the supervisor, were standing around casually in long purple cloaks, sipping wine and waving dirty great knives around.

It didn't look like a Halloween sex party. It looked like a straight-up torture scenario.

Diana held in the urge to gasp and decided that the best course of action was to crawl to a safe distance, get up and walk to a safer distance, and call the police.

What happened instead was that she started to crawl, felt her phone vibrate in her pocket, took it out, dropped it, gasped out loud, fell over her own foot, and thus was lying with both feet planted right in front of the window when Liam darted over to open it and yank her inside.

A pair of hands wrapped around her ankle. She scrabbled for her phone, sitting inches away. Managing to clasp it she picked up the call, kicking as much as she could, trying to free her feet.

"Diana, don't be upset, I want us to watch a movie —"

"HARVEY CALL THE POLICE IT WASN'T A SEX PARTY - *OW FUCK!*"

Spinning around, she saw a blade poking out of one calf, blood blossoming into her jeans. "*THEY'VE GOT KNIVES!*"

The window ledge ate into her thighs as Liam hauled her in, Stacey grabbing her thighs to help.

"Diana?! What's happening?!"

"*CALL THE POLICE! **PLEASE!***"

Her butt was through the window. Gravity as well as one tremendous tug slammed her hard to the concrete floor. The impact thumped the air from her body. Her phone was plucked from her hand.

"Diana? Where are you? DIANA?!"

Liam and Stacey looked at each other, panicked. "What do I do?!" Liam whisper-shouted. "I don't know!" Stacey whisper-shouted back. Diana stupidly started scrabbling at the wall, trying to spider-crawl to freedom.

Jeanie, a tall, scary, slender woman whom Diana had avoided since day one rolled her eyes, stepped across the space, hung up on Harvey's pleas for an address, and turned off the phone.

"Relax," she told them, taking a classy sip of wine. "We'll throw her off a bridge in the morning. Everyone will assume she jumped."

"Oh." Liam's face broke into relief. "That's why you're the manager, Jeanie. You always find solutions."

"God, I *knew* you were a bum licker," Diana wheezed, clutching at her lungs. "Please, Jeanie, I'm perfect, nothing's my fault. I didn't forget to mop, that was Trey."

There was an indignant grunt from one of the gagged three. It turned out, with a quick glance, to be Trey.

"You should watch your mouth," Liam scowled. "I can stick my knife in plenty of places other than your leg."

"Liam," Jeanie admonished.

"Sorry, Jeanie. Sorry."

Diana accepted defeat against the attempt to get back up to the window. Looking around, she tried to keep her reaction in check. The three victims - Trey, Stuart and Katie - looked back at her with terrified eyes. Blood trickled out of stab wounds littered across their bodies.

"What is happening here?" Diana tried to sound angry but missed the mark, voice shaking. Liam and Stacy looked down at her, Liam wrinkling his nose like he was looking at shit he'd narrowly avoided treading on. Stacey shook her head.

"Why didn't you just leave?" She asked. "I bought you your hoodie so you wouldn't be involved."

"I heard someone scream."

"Fucking Stuart," Liam kicked Stuart. "This has been the most complicated year. Lucy quitting, having to get Katie to take her place, Stuart getting free like the little rat he is… and you." He scowled at Diana. "I never liked you, bitch. You're a city snob. Turning your princess nose up at us all."

"At least my nose isn't up Jeanie's butt."

Liam started towards her and she flinched away. Stacy stopped him. "Jeanie's right. We can get rid of her easily. No one will doubt a suicide, but a suicide who's been beaten around first?"

"I've already stabbed her leg," he grinned nastily. "It could be a mugging gone *tragically* wrong."

"Stop." Jeanie's voice was sharp. Everyone stopped. "I said we are going to throw her off a bridge. No more discussion."

"We can't even drink her blood," Stacey rolled her eyes. "I could have sworn she was a teenager when I did her interview."

"I get that a lot," Diana tried to think if there was any way to alert the neighbours to the situation. "I've got a baby face."

"You've got a stupid face." Liam poked his tongue out.

"Wait." Something said sunk into Diana's brain. "You… you're drinking their blood!? That's rank! What the fuck!? You aren't vampires!"

"Obviously," Stacey went over to the bar running along one of the bays, picked up a glass and her knife, and crouched by Trey. She casually sliced open his arm and caught the blood with her glass. "Vampires aren't real."

"Why are you drinking it then?! It's not tasty!"

"We don't just drink it," Liam sipped from his glass. "We use it for other stuff too. Like face cream."

Diana's mouth dropped open. "That's why your skin is so smooth. That's why you laughed at me when I asked if it was vitamin C serum."

"Bitch," Liam laughed at her again, "if we weren't going to kill you, I'd offer you some. That dry skin is nasty."

"It's eczema! I've been stressed!"

"God, we fucking know. I see you dash out to cry in the toilet a hundred times a shift."

Diana's eyes flickered back to the teenagers. Katie was looking woozy, flopping against Stuart. Stuart, who was already unconscious, leaning on Trey. Trey, who... looked a bit like he was constipated.

She squinted at him. His shoulders were shaking.

He was trying to wiggle free.

She had to keep their attention.

"Why these guys?" She blurted out. "Why them?"

"Cause they're the worst workers." Jeanie was irritatingly elegant, even in the setting. "We spend a year filtering through school children until we find the ones we think most deserve death."

"Deserve death for what? Having too many cigarette breaks?"

"And never doing pot wash." Liam took another sip of his wine, shuddering at the taste.

"You don't do pot wash!"

"I'm a manager, I don't have to."

"Why do they have to be young?"

"We aren't drinking blood for fun," Jeanie looked at her derisively. "We aren't insane, Little Miss Overdose. It's how we keep everything running so perfectly. These idiots aren't going to make anything of their lives, so what difference does it make if we sacrifice them? You might look down on our cafe because we aren't in a city, but we are the only thing keeping this village alive. The only attraction for outsiders, the only income. The only source of employment for the youth. The ones who work well leave with valuable experience. The ones who don't..." She eyed her victims. "They contribute differently."

"But..." Diana tried to wrap her brain around the issues with that explanation. "But... how are you sacrificing them? You're just drinking their blood."

"Well, *somebody* interrupted us!" Liam scowled at her.

Trey's shoulders were starting to shift with more urgency. He met Diana's eyes, and she knew he was almost free. If she could keep them talking, maybe the two of them could somehow overthrow the captors.

"It's part of the ritual," Jeanie finished her drink. We're in our fifties, Diana. The blood treatments help us stay young. We wait until midnight to begin the sacrifices, which is... in five minutes."

"How do you sacrifice them?"

"It's a bit boring," she laughed, genteel. "We stab and bury them here. It's been the tradition ever since our cafe was founded by my grandfather. Their bodies keep the ground beneath us happy, and in return, we have good custom for another year."

Diana grappled with what to say. The managers waited expectantly. Trey kept wiggling from one bum cheek to the other.

Stacey looked irritated. "Don't you have any questions?"

"Well... just..."

"What?"

Diana bit her lip. "It's... so you're not like, sacrificing them to a specific thing? To... a demon, or anything?"

"It's a *tradition*," Jeanie emphasised impatiently. "It's how my grandad got the business on its feet. He kept the ground happy."

"The ground."

"Yes. It's worked for generations."

"But..." How could she phrase it? "But... you guys are the only cafe for like, five miles. So, it's not like... it's not like the sacrifices are doing anything. Your good custom is just... there's nowhere else for people to go. And you're barely busy."

"Hey!" Stacey moved closer, threatening. "We make a thousand a day!"

"That's... not that much. And like... you guys do have good skin but... I can totally tell you're in your fifties."

"How *dare* you?" Liam dropped down, stuck his fingers into the gash in her calf. Diana screamed, trying to pull her leg away. He clamped it to the ground with his other hand. Vision blurry, she broke into a sweat, struggling to sit, agony where his fingers were diving down to her bone, tearing the muscle and skin.

"There's nothing wrong with it!" She moaned, voice weak. "There's nothing wrong with being fifty!"

"I am barely forty-seven!" he hissed back and rammed his thumb into the wound as well. She used what energy she had to shriek in agony and then the pain was lessening. His hand was gone from her leg. She clasped her trembling hands over the bleeding skin.

318

"It's midnight," Jeanie was saying excitedly. She had barely looked over for Liam's little torture break, busy getting herself a fresh glass of Katie. "Get them ready."

Diana forced herself to focus. Stacey was yanking Stuart away from the trio. Trey's side revealed, Diana saw he was working through the ropes around his wrists using cutlery from the cafe. He sawed feverishly at the thick, durable rope with a blunt butter knife. No wonder he was taking ten years. Liam started to reach for Katie. If he moved her, he would see Trey's knife. They would have no hope.

"You're all idiots!" Diana shouted.

The managers paused. Trey's eyes widened with the opportunity he was being given. He ducked his head, focusing all his efforts.

"You're fucking idiots!" Diana laughed. "You realise you aren't doing anything magical or mystical, right? You're just serial killers! You're not sacrificing them; you're just killing them!"

"Don't be stupid," Jeanie scowled, but Diana detected a hint of panic under her anger.

"You already know that," Diana accused her. "You know you're killing for fun, but you didn't want Liam and Stacey to realise, so you've made up some story to get them to join in. I bet if you get caught, you've got a plan to pin the whole thing on them and wash your hands of it, haven't you?"

"Enough!" Jeanie ushered Liam and Stacey towards Trey and Katie. "It's past midnight already."

"So what?!" Diana yelled, louder. "It's not like Satan will get mad, you're not even offering them to him!"

Stacey was hesitating.

"What *does* happen if it's not Halloween when we do it?" She asked Jeanie, curious. "You said it must be on Halloween every year. Why?"

"Because we must follow the tradition."

"But…why?" Stacey sounded confused. "Why does it have to be Halloween?"

"It doesn't!" Diana shouted. "You're sacrificing them to a pool of mud in a wine cellar, the day doesn't fucking matter!"

"That's not true." Stacey sounded reasonably firm. "… Is it?" Less firm.

"Think!" Diana pleaded. "Why are you drinking it? Jeanie gets Botox!"

"No, she doesn't," Liam laughed. "No way."

"You can literally see it! You guys have wrinkles because you don't have Botox, not because she drinks more blood!"

"You don't get Botox," Liam was in disbelief. "Do you?"

"You can kill her," Jeanie avoided the question, fury building. "Do it however you want. Hurt the bitch."

"Jeanie." Liam didn't move, betrayal in his voice. "Promise me that you don't get Botox."

"*I don't get Botox.* Are you really listening to her? She's working here because she ate two packs of paracetamol. She's crazy!"

Diana tried not to take the words of the middle-aged serial killer too personally. Stuart, Trey, and Katie, all of whom had been unaware of her situation, looked at her over their gags with surprised, sad eyes.

"Just kill her, Liam," Jeanie walked to Katie, reached down, and started hauling her to lie next to Stuart. "We haven't got much - HEY!"

Trey leapt up from the floor, tried to bunny-hop away, and completely failed, smashing face-first into the floor. Liam and Stacey charged over, both failing to notice that his hands were now magically bound at the front, not the back.

Seeing the trap, Diana threw herself onto her hands and knees, crawled for the nearest bay, grabbed a bottle of wine and smashed it against the wall. A 1998 Rioja sloshed all over her. Hearing the noise, Liam stopped halfway to Trey and started towards her instead.

"Back off!" She brandished the glass wildly, leaning against the shelving as her stabbed leg wobbled traitorously. "Stay back, Liam!"

Stacey wailed from across the room. Diana caught sight of her backing away from Trey clutching her face. The butter knife protruded proudly from one of her eyes, blood pouring down her face, splattering the dusty floor.

"I can't see," she howled at the ceiling. "Jeanie!"

"Don't be so dramatic!" Jeanie snarled from where she was wrestling Katie. Katie was wriggling and squirming mindlessly, flinging her bound torso from side to side.

"Fucking stop moving," Liam snarled at Diana, trying to lunge around the bottle at her.

"You're an idiot," she snarled back, "you're drinking blood for no reason!"

Outside, somewhere in the distance, sirens. Everyone froze for a second, straining their ears. Stacey stopped wailing, the knife still sticking out of her eye.

The captors looked at each other in worry.

The captives looked at each other in hope.

"That's not for us… is it?" Liam asked Jeanie.

Jeanie looked around at the scene in front of her. The sirens got closer. Seemingly making a decision, she drew herself up to her full height, graceful.

Then without a word she dashed up the stairs to the cafe and was gone. A second later, they heard keys upstairs rattling, the front door opening, and then slamming again.

Stacey and Liam turned to look at each other with horrified eye(s).

"What do we do?" Liam asked Stacey. Stacey gestured at her face speechlessly. The sirens got louder. Liam looked at Diana, who wiggled the bottle in her hand.

"Fuck this," he muttered, and sprinted across the room, thudding up the stairs and out of sight.

"LIAM!" Stacey shouted. "LIAM?!"

Silence.

She looked around, bottom lip trembling.

"I can't run very fast," she told Diana, fearful.

"You'd better get a move on, then."

Stacey stared at her for a second, as if expecting some kind of aid, and then started across the room, stumbling over Katie's head, struggling up the staircase. She was barely out of sight before the sirens pitched, blue and red lights snuck through the basement window, and car doors outside started slamming.

The four remaining in the basement all sat and breathed heavily. Diana dropped her broken bottle, which smashed, and sniffed her hand, wrinkling her nose. The Rioja smelt rank. Trey was sitting on the floor, white with shock, pulling out his cigarettes. He held out the pack silently to Diana.

"No, thanks," she waved it away. "I quit a while ago."

"Oh," his voice was faint. "Good for you."

"I guess we know what that rotten smell was now." Diana glanced up at the kitchen. "I thought that cabbage story didn't make sense."

Katie made a slightly irritated noise behind her gag.

"Oh shit, sorry!" Diana scrambled to untie her. Katie sat up, coughing. Somewhere above them, Stacey could be heard screaming, and a bunch of voices shouted for somebody to freeze.

"Are you okay?" Diana helped Katie undo her feet. "Are you badly hurt?"

"Just cut," she started to cry. "Thank fuck you were here, Diana. They would have stabbed us. We would already be dead by now."

"Um…" Diana struggled to know what to say. "They did stab you, a bit. And it was just… I was crying in the toilet and passed out, so… it wasn't like. Heroic."

"I don't give a fuck," Katie got up. "Who cares if you were here by accident or not, you saved us. We would all be dead. I always hated this stupid job, I *never* thought of you guys as family, no offence, it's a shitty cafe, I only did it cause my mum said…"

She carried on rattling away as she limped for the staircase. Diana stayed crouched, holding the rope she'd pulled from the other girls' ankles. What if she hadn't been there? What if her overdose had worked and she'd died? If she hadn't taken the paracetamol in the first place, of course, she wouldn't have been there at all, and the guys would still be dead. But she had survived, and she'd been there at the exact right time to rescue them, whether she'd been heroic or not.

Freaky.

Stuart was in the process of following Katie up the stairs. Trey went over, still smoking, and got an arm around him, supporting him.

"Yo," he called over to Diana. "City girl. Are you coming?"

"In a minute."

The two boys started up the stairs. Diana squeezed the rope in her hands, suddenly overwhelmed with a feeling of life that she hadn't experienced in many months. Letting it go again, she crawled to where her phone had been left by Jeanie and switched it back on.

It was crammed with texts and missed calls from Harvey. She called him back.

"DIANA?!"

"Woah!" She moved the phone away. "Yes, stop shouting! I'm here!"

"Oh, thank God you're alive! Are the police there?!" His voice was terrified. "I found the address on google, are they there?"

Her heart warmed. "Yes, you did great, Harv. They're here. We're safe."

"Are you hurt? You said there were knives!"

"Ah... there was a little stabbing, but only a bit. On my leg. You sent them just in time. I'll explain —"

"I'm getting the last train. If I get a taxi to the station, I'll make it. I'll be there in just under two hours."

"You're... you're coming? Here?"

"Yes, Di." His voice wavered. "Fuck, I thought you might be dead. I love you, you idiot. I'm on my way now. I want you to stay on the phone as long as you can. If the police want you to go with them, tuck your phone somewhere and keep it on, okay?"

"I love you too." She put a hand over her eyes as they watered, blocking out the basement for a second. "Harvey, I fucking love you. I know I cry all the time—"

"Fucking Cassandra, don't listen to her—"

"But I love you, I feel like I can come to you—"

"You can, always come to me when you're sad, I want to help—"

"Harvey, something really important happened—"

"Tell me."

"I'm glad I was alive tonight."

Silence for a second.

"Did you hear?" She took her hand away, looked at the basement, stinking of corpses, covered in blood and wine. "I'm glad you realised something was wrong and called an ambulance that night. If you didn't, three people would have been murdered. They're alive because I was here. I'm glad I'm alive right now. Not glad. I'm happy. I'm happy I'm alive, even if things are hard."

"Oh..." He sighed. "Diana. I love you. It's... that's... I'm happy too. I'm coming, alright?"

"Alright."

Diana looked up as several officers came into the basement.

"Miss?" One of them asked. "Are you okay? Are you hurt?"

Diana smiled down at her phone, tears in her eyes again, but not tears of despair this time.

"I'm a bit hurt but... I'm okay."

The Halloween House

Liam Hogan

Tammy watched the trick and treaters pass by, resting her head on her arms, which lay on the sill of the upstairs window. Dressed as princesses, dinosaurs and superheroes, and even the occasional white-sheeted ghost, the children didn't stop, didn't wander up the mossy, unkempt path to her door. If the very youngest of them hesitated, if they lingered, wide-eyed, staring up at the spooky moonlit house beyond the rusty fence, then their in-tow parents would soon hurry them along. But most didn't even do that. And why should they?

There was no pumpkin on the front step. No welcoming light from the windows or the porch. No fake cobwebs or crime-scene tape or plastic gravestones propped up on the overgrown lawn. No help-yourself tub of candy for when the adults got tired of answering the door and cooing over costumes, trying to remember the neighbourhood kid's names despite the face-paint disguises.

No-one ventured beyond the stuck-open, leaf-trapping, paint-peeled gate, *ever*. The older kids—aged fourteen, fifteen, some in costume, some too cool—who would come along later might try some half-hearted tricking from the safety of the pavement. The unravelling rolls of toilet paper never quite reached, the house set back further than others on the street, but the eggs often did, leaving a yellow smear against the walls, or even the windows, to eventually be washed away by autumn rains.

Older kids still might have thrown rocks, or dared each other to creep along the neglected path, to ring the bell that didn't work before running away, and then to return, giddy with transgression, to try the front door.

They would have found it unlocked, if reluctant, which was probably better than having them seek an alternative way in. The house they explored would be echoey and empty. The invading teens might be emboldened to engage in mindless petty acts of vandalism, whilst getting drunk on illicit booze and smoking contraband cigarettes. They might have lit trash-fires in grate-less fireplaces that, unguarded as they fumbled with one another's clothes, could easily have gotten out of hand.

But those kids, on the cusp of adulthood, a little too old for Halloween really, raised on a diet of horror films they shouldn't have been allowed into the cinema to see, still tame compared to what they watched online at home, they never saw the house. It wasn't *for* them. And so it stood, largely unmolested except by time itself, disappearing from mind as well as view for all but a few chilly autumnal nights.

Tammy sighed. The youngsters had thinned out, returning home with their pails and pockets full of sweets, to be counted and redivided, and, perhaps, rationed by parents worried about getting sugar-overdosed kids to sleep. The excitement was over for another year.

She was about to turn away when she spotted the straggler. A lone kid, who couldn't have been any older than she was, twelve, possibly thirteen, but definitely more a tween than a teen. Dressed in a cowboy outfit, a sheriff's plastic-tin badge glinting beneath the street lamp, red caps on the end of his six-shooters, an inside-out canvas tote from a local bookshop, the dark logo showing through and somewhat spoiling the effect.

What was he doing out alone? Tammy frowned, but she thought she could guess. The earliest of the older groups, *sans* adults, was already abroad, the lull between dusk and night proper being a short one. No doubt some harassed parent, possibly a single mum, had entrusted an older brother to look after the younger. Except that was social suicide with his mates. So they will have chased the younger sibling home, maybe even pulled pranks to reduce him to tears, proof positive he was too young to be out with them.

And the older brother—it couldn't be a sister, could it?—would watch as the cowboy, battling to be brave but trailing tears and snot, headed back the way he had come, certain the younger brother would be snug in his PJs by the time he returned, ideally having forgotten the whole ordeal, even if the older kid knew he'd probably catch hell from his parent or parents. And the parent was no doubt just as certain the youngest kid was safely out with the older, and could relax, for maybe the first time that week, pour a generous glass of wine or call a friend. They'd compare parenting notes, laughing at the whole vicarious ordeal that was Halloween, how it really hadn't been much of a thing when *they* were growing up.

Meanwhile, the cowboy with his empty bag of swag wasn't giving in quite so easily. He wasn't the baby his brother called him, and he'd show them; he'd return with more sweets than *anyone* else on the whole street!

Even if it meant starting at the scariest house not only in the neighbourhood, but perhaps the entire town.

Tammy held her breath (the breath that never misted the grimy windows, no matter how cold it got outside), as he hovered by the gate, the canvas bag dangling from one shoulder. And then he turned, and marched *through* and down the path, trampling weeds. She hiccupped, and leapt from her perch, before coming to an abrupt halt as caution bit.

"Hello?" a voice came haltingly from below. "Is anyone there?"

"Hello," she coyly replied, from the top of the stairs that led to the double-height hallway, leaning over a balustrade that really shouldn't have taken her weight.

His smile was as bashful as hers. "I wasn't sure...?"

"I'm Tammy," she said as she began her descent.

"George," he replied, cocking his head to watch her. She halted on the last step. They were about the same height, but with her small, stolen elevation she felt more confident. Until his next words, anyway.

"Are you a ghost?" he asked.

"Are you a cowboy?" she snapped back.

He looked down at his outfit and shrugged. "I don't mind if you are."

"*Really?*"

"So what's keeping you here?" he asked, ignoring the scorn in her voice. "What thing did you leave undone?"

"Excuse me?"

"That's what people say," George said. "Ghosts are spirits with unresolved issues. That's why they won't go quietly."

Tammy felt vaguely annoyed, as though someone was trying to decide her future for her. Why could she not simply be a ghost? Why did she need some sort of motive, or backstory, a path to redemption? Something that left her dependent on somebody else? Why couldn't she be master of her own fate—whatever that might be?

"I dunno," she said, before changing the subject. "This isn't even my house."

"It isn't?" He looked surprised, glancing around as though searching for evidence that would catch her in a lie, some gloomy family portrait hanging askew on a wall. But of course the walls were bare. There was hardly any evidence the house had ever been lived in.

"No," she affirmed. "But it's where I ended up, after..." Funny how, even after all these years, it was difficult to put into words. Not that she'd had much practice.

"You weren't... you weren't *murdered* here, were you?" George asked.

She eyed him with something like contempt. "I was ill. Very ill. This is my death-day. Just my rotten luck to die at Halloween! But then, you're a bit of a *ghoul* yourself, aren't you George?"

"I would be if I could," he said, darkly.

"I'm surprised you ended up a cowboy."

He blushed at that. "It's a hand-me-down. My brother—Kevin's. Mum said she couldn't afford to buy a new costume, not with a chest full of dress-up clothes."

Tammy nodded, smiling. So she'd been right about the older brother, and maybe the single parent as well. But George didn't seem pleased by her reaction.

"It's not fair!" he protested. "Kevin gets all the new stuff, and I get his battered bike and his scuffed shoes and his *rubbish* Halloween outfits!"

"What would you have dressed up as instead?" she asked, attempting to placate him.

"A vampire," he said, the smile returning as fast as it had fled. "Though... not a cartoon one, y'know? With a sword."

She nodded, though she wasn't entirely sure what he had in mind. Was over-elaborate collars and a sharp widow's peak cartoonish? And since when did vampires carry *weapons*?

"So... why *here*?" he persisted, a dog worrying at a bone.

"I don't *know*. I think... there was a vacancy."

"A vacancy?"

"Yes. This house... feels like the sort of house that *needs* a ghost, doesn't it?"

He laughed at that, though she hadn't meant it to be funny. She pointed at his inverted bag. "Any luck with the trick or treating?"

His hand flew to his side, suddenly protective. "Not much..." he admitted, with a small frown. "I'd barely got started." Then he tugged the tote from his shoulder and opened it wide. "Do you want one?"

Inside, there were a half-dozen sweets, slender chews of some sort of another, along with the unfavoured chocolates from a selection box.

Tammy reached in, picked up something pink and shiny. She managed to get it almost to the neck of the bag, before it slipped through her fingers.

"How did you do that?" George gaped.

"I don't know." She tilted her head, peering up to where moonlight flickered through the night's clouds and lit the arch window above the front door. "I think when you're here, I'm a little more *real*, somehow?"

"Oh wow... We should conduct experiments! Read up on the supernatural."

"I loved to read, before..." Tammy said, wistful. "Went to the local library all the time."

"Me too. I mean, I still do. Do you know Percy Jackson?"

She shook her head, not recognising the name. Was that an author? "Do you know *The Famous Five*?"

It was his turn to shake his head. He scuffed a shoe—a trainer, rather than cowboy boots—in the thick dust, sketching a half circle picked out by the moonlight. "I'm reading a book at the moment about how, in the Greek underworld, the souls drink from a river, the *Lethe*, to forget."

"To forget what?"

"Their lives."

Tammy shuddered. "Why would they want to do that?"

"I dunno. I think it's meant to be a kindness. All the things they can no longer have?"

She turned away, and then, a moment later, back again. "My parents moved away, after a few Halloweens."—How many Halloweens ago was *that*?—"I don't think they could cope with the annual reminders. Maybe the living should be the ones to drink the forgetting water?"

"Maybe." He looked deep in thought. "It's a good book though."

Tammy pondered for a moment. "Aren't Greek myths all about innocent young women being changed into trees?"

He blushed again. "It isn't *all* about that, no..."

"Just mostly, then," she said, with a grin.

"Kind of." The grin wasn't matched and he looked nervous. "Tammy, I'd better get going. Can't stay too long, you know?"

"Will you come back?" she asked, hating the plaintive note.

"I will," George solemnly promised, before putting the pink sweet on the step by her foot.

But once he had left, stopping briefly beyond the gate to wave, Tammy was hit by sudden sadness. A year was such a long time to wait! And what if he forgot? He wouldn't even need to drink from some mythical Greek river to do so. What was half an hour spent in a spooky house, compared to all the other stuff he'd get up to before then? School, and friends, and battles with his brother. Christmas, and birthdays. He'd be a year older, a year more mature. Edging towards not seeing the Halloween house at all. And he'd be taller than her, when, or if he ever returned. The problem with not growing older, she realised, was that when she met someone her age, it wouldn't, couldn't last.

She left the sweet where it lay, not trusting herself to even try and pick it up. She hadn't exactly been happy being so alone, so forgotten. But had anything changed? What, exactly, did she want? A little company, *sure;* though probably not all the time. She was kind of used to being on her own.

And a few creature comforts, definitely. The house had been in a better state when she'd first arrived, hadn't it? The woodwork a little less rotten, the wallpaper less washed out. It had once been an easier task to imagine the rooms furnished, and occupied. Now, even the patches that showed where pictures had once hung, where wardrobes had once stood, they too were faded. It was all so... *bleak.*

Except for that splash of unexpected colour on the bottom step.

Tammy crawled into the small space all the way up in the attic. It wasn't furnished either, other than by some offcuts of long forgotten wood, but it was a *smaller* emptiness than the other rooms. It was still dark, and cold, and lonely. Except, when she awoke sometime late at night, she was surprised to find herself clutching a pillow, the faint pink flowers distantly familiar. She drifted back to sleep, curling herself around it.

The pillow was just a memory when she emerged from her lofty space. But then, in the bright autumn sunlight of All Saints Day, the house itself pretty much vanished. Even the youngest of kids didn't give it a second glance, yawning as they headed to school or to playgroups, and the thin, gangly man posting junk-mail flyers offering the services of a psychic medium, didn't even break step as he marched awkwardly up the paths of the houses on either side.

So she was surprised to hear a repeat of that "Hello?"—braver, this time—just as the sun was beginning to set and the temperature started to drop. There was George, in his school uniform, a backpack (hand-me-down, no doubt) instead of his bookshop tote. He waved at her as she descended the stairs once again, and swung the backpack from the shoulder it dangled from, undoing the zip one-handed.

"I brought you something," he said, with a smile.

She wondered if it was another sweet. Wondered how long it would take him to notice the one that he'd left—or had a mouse, or rat, already made off with it? She was too busy looking at the ground around and beneath her feet to see as he slid a chunky looking book from the bag, holding it towards her.

A Treasury of Greek Mythology, it read, the cover astonishingly colourful. *Classic Stories of Gods, Goddesses, Heroes & Monsters.*

Before Tammy had even thought the thought, her fingers had lifted the cover and rifled through the first half-dozen pages, pausing on an illustration of Gaia: Mother Earth. It was a bit *young* for her, it had been a while since she'd read books with illustrations, even if these were more like artwork. But there was comfort in such easy texts, and she imagined spending a lazy afternoon curled up on a comfortable armchair, and, for just a moment, thought she glimpsed just such a piece of furniture out of the corner of her eye, to one side of the bay window where the light would be best.

"I can get you more books, if you like?" George said, a little shyly. "When you finish this one? From the library."

She wrapped her ghostly arms around him, and gave him a hug.

The Reluctant Ghost

Paul Lonardo

She heard the laughter of the trespassers as they made their way across the lawn and headed up the walkway. The three boys who mounted the steps to the front porch were not wearing costumes, but she knew instantly that it was Halloween. She strongly disliked the annual pseudo holiday and avoided it at all costs, but it caught her by surprise this year. It had been a milder and wetter autumn than normal, and even the ash trees were still holding onto their leaves.

"Let's go inside and divide up the take," said the boy carrying two pillowcases filled with candy.

"Just as long as you divide it equally this time," another boy spoke up.

"I'll decide what's even," the first boy shot back.

A sudden pounding on the door rattled the walls and ceiling, dislodging a layer of standing dust inside, which drifted down around her like dirty snow.

"Trick or treat, Dead Girl," the boy shouted.

She quickly ducked behind the couch when a shadow appeared in the window across the living room.

"I think I saw her," the third boy screamed.

"Where, where?"

"I don't see anything."

The window filled with silhouettes.

"Over there. Behind the couch, near the fireplace. See her ponytail?"

There was a tapping on the glass as cell phone camera lights penetrated the pitch-black interior. It was the only window in the entire house that wasn't broken. Because it was entirely concealed by dense, overgrown hedges, it was protected from the stones that the local teens frequently hurled at the old house for fun. She had plugged up the other windows with some cardboard, though it was more for privacy than as any sort of hindrance. Anyone could access the vacant property if they really wanted, but the children in the neighborhood had always been too afraid to set foot inside the abandoned house. Halloween was different, however. It had a way of making some kids brave, or at least daring enough to act on things that otherwise scared them, just for the thrill of it. On this particular night of the year, mischievous children, and even adventurous adults, would wander closer to the house than usual, walk around the grounds, and occasionally knock on the door. They wanted to see a ghost. However, if anyone of them had ever found themselves in the presence of an actual ghost, she couldn't be sure how they might react, so she would always spend Halloween night locked in the basement. That's why she hated Halloween.

Now, she felt trapped. She would already have been in the safety of the cellar behind the steel-reinforced door if she had realized that it was October 31. Her only hope was to make a run for it before the teens got inside. There was a large open space between her and the door in the kitchen that led to the basement. She was sure to be seen, but she didn't have a choice. She dashed toward the kitchen, hoping the shadows would conceal her movement.

"There she is. Come on. Let's get her."

As she entered the kitchen, the back door started to open.

Oh, no, she thought, remembering that she'd left the door unlocked after coming in from the backyard that afternoon. She stopped and quickly dove under the kitchen table as someone entered the house.

"Is anyone here?" The soft whisper was followed by the sound of the door closing and the *click* of the deadbolt lock.

She crawled on her hands and knees across the floor to the far end of the table as the intruder came further inside. The legs of the boy stopped directly in front of her, between her and the cellar door.

"It's okay. You can come out." The boy's voice was kind. "I don't mean you any harm. I just want to meet you."

She didn't move for a moment, then she slowly crawled out from under the table and stood facing the boy.

"Hi," said the tall boy with a gentle smile. He had on a white robe with a separate oversized hood that was pulled down behind his head.

"Hello."

"My name is Roger. What's your name?"

"I don't remember."

The house was dark, but she was glowing with a low, throbbing luminescence. "You don't seem surprised that I can see you."

"This is the only night of the year that just about everyone can see me," she said. "I'm not really sure why. I think it's because people

334

expect to see ghosts on Halloween, and their minds are more open to it than any other time of the year."

"I see you all the time," Roger told her.

"You do?"

"Yeah. Out on the back porch. Sometimes in the back yard."

"There used to be an old tire tied to the branch of a giant sycamore tree that I used to like swinging on," she said. "It's gone now, but I still like to go outside and try to remember what it was like then."

"What else did you like to do?" Roger asked.

"I don't know."

"You don't look like a ghost," he told her. "You seem like a regular girl."

He smiled at her and she blushed.

"What's it like to be..." he began. "You know?"

"It's not bad," she said.

"Aren't you lonely? Do you miss being with your friends?"

"I never had any friends when I was alive," she said.

"I don't have any friends, either."

"What about those boys outside?"

"Oh, that's Dennis, my older brother, and his friends, Jaden and Alex. I was out trick-or-treating with Dylan. He's my little cousin, so I don't think that even counts as a friend. Those big boys came along and took our bags of candy. Dylan ran home crying and I came here to get our candy back from them. I thought maybe you could help me."

"*Me*, help you?"

"Sure."

"What do I have to do?" she asked.

"Do you ever scare people?"

"I try not to scare anybody."

"But you could? I mean, if you wanted."

"I guess so." When Roger smiled at her, she couldn't help but smile back. "And you'll be my friend if I help you?"

"We're already friends," Roger told her. "Besides Dylan, you're the only other kid that will talk to me."

"What do you want me to do? she asked.

When he finished telling her his plan, the sound of shattering glass from the living room caused them to look up.

"Okay," Roger said. "It's time. Let's go." He paused briefly and looked her in the eyes. "Thanks."

A moment later, they disappeared into the basement together as the three teens entered the house through the broken window.

"Whoa!" Dennis exclaimed, shining the light from his phone around the vast living room. The sparse furnishings were festooned with cobwebs and covered in a half inch of dust which rendered the room colorless, like an old black & white TV show. "This place looks like it belongs in one of those bad horror movies you like, Alex."

"Yeah," Alex agreed. "I don't think anybody's been in here for years."

"Except for the ghost," Jaden added. "Let's just divide up the candy and get out of here."

"Don't wimp out on us now, Jaden." Dennis stepped in front of him, looking down on the boy who he had a half foot advantage over in height. "I don't see any ghost. Do you?"

"I *did*," Jaden told him. "It was right over there." He pointed toward the faded antique camelback sofa.

Dennis reached into one of the pillowcases and removed a candy bar, tossing it behind the sofa. There was a shrill squealing as it struck the floor followed by the sound tiny nails *clicking* on the floorboards as a rat scampered off into the darkness carrying the chocolate in its mouth. Jaden jumped and let out a shriek as Dennis and Alex laughed and mocked him.

"There goes your ghost," Dennis said.

"This place is giving me the creeps," Jaden said. "Just divvy up the candy between you two. I don't want any of it."

"Fine by me," Alex said.

"Me too. Give me some light here."

Alex fixed his phone on Dennis as he opened one of the bags and reached a hand inside. Suddenly his eyes widened as something attached itself to his hand. He would have looked pale if everything around him wasn't already a monochromatic moonscape. The LED lighting revealed the lower part of his arm swarming with cockroaches.

"What the…" he began as he withdrew his arm from the sack and shook it vigorously to dislodge the vile insects before they made it above his elbow.

Dennis dropped the pillowcase and the roaches spilled out, disappearing under the sofa and into the nearby walls.

Just then, a small figure in a white robe appeared out of the gloom and stopped near the boys. The hood was pulled up, concealing the identity of the wearer, but Dennis recognized the homemade costume as the same one that his younger brother had been wearing.

"Roger?" Dennis stepped closer to the hooded figure. "What are you doing in here?" He reached down and pulled the hood back. When it dropped down, there was no face, no head, nothing at all inside the costume. It was completely empty. Then the robe fell to the floor and there was nobody inside.

"What's going on here?" Alex asked.

Dennis was too shaken by what he had witnessed to respond.

"Can we get out of here now?" Jaden begged.

Something moved inside the other pillowcase Dennis was holding and he released it from his grasp. It struck the floor with a heavy THUD and out rolled a bloody severed head. It came to a stop face up, and when Dennis saw his brother grinning up at him, he took a step back and yelped. "Let's go," he said breathlessly and set out quickly in the opposite direction. The other boys followed.

"Where's the window?" Jaden asked, his voice shrill and full of panic.

"It's got to be here," Dennis said, more of a demand than a statement. But as they continued along, there was only an endless dark wall.

"We must be going in the wrong direction," Alex suggested. "Let's double back."

They headed back the other way, but there was still no window to be found. Their frantic movement released clouds of dust particles into the air, which swirled all around them, diminishing their vision even further.

"We're trapped," Jaden bellowed. "We never should have come in here."

"You better shut up," Dennis warned him. "We must have missed it, that's all. Keep looking."

All at once, the lights on their phones went off at the same time and it became as black as a tomb inside the old house.

"My phone battery just died," Alex said.

"Mine too." Jaden shook his phone vigorously and struck it with his other hand to try to get it to work. "What are we gonna do?"

"We're gonna stay calm," Dennis said evenly. "This house isn't that big. There are other ways out."

A loud bang, like the tailgate of dump truck opening was followed by the sound of some granular substance being emptied nearby. All around them heavy, damp soil began to pile up rapidly. It ran over the tops of their feet and continued pouring in.

"We're being buried alive," Jaden croaked.

They maintained their position atop of the rising tide of earth, riding it like a dense wave. Higher and higher they went, well beyond where the ceiling should have been. Completely blind and terrified, their pleas and cries for help did not resonate. It was as if they were underground, and no one could hear their anguished screams. Soon, they were at the peak of a high mountain of dirt, where they were no longer able to maintain their balance. One by one they fell, tumbling down the steep slope. In an uncontrolled descent, their faces impacted the dirt and chunks of soil lodged in their ears, noses, and mouths. Sputtering and coughing to keep from suffocating, the boys thought they would continue to fall forever. Then, without warning, they rolled to a stop, their bodies collecting in a heap. It took a moment for them to get their bearings, and to their collective astonishment they found themselves lying on the ground in front of the abandoned house. It was a moonless night, but there was considerable ambient light for them to see that they were not in any danger whatsoever. No one said a word as they surveyed one another's faces, which were caked with mud and blood.

Dennis was first to get to his feet. "We don't tell anyone about this," he warned his friends. "Ever. Or you'll answer to me."

Alex and Jaden nodded and then all three boys quickly strode away from the house at a brisk pace, almost running.

Watching from the broken window, she and Roger laughed.

"That was awesome!" Roger said. "You're pretty good at that. Especially for never having scared anyone before." He looked down at the pumpkin lying on the floor and nudged it with his foot. "I really liked that trick. Did you see the look on my brother's face when he thought it was my head?"

"It was nothing," she said.

"*Nothing*? It was nothing short of spectacular."

She blushed.

"Thanks again," he said.

"I should thank *you*," she said. "That was fun. I probably used to like Halloween a lot. I do now, at least."

"I meant, thank you for being my friend." He stepped close to her and gave her a hug, and even though she did not have a physical body, she felt his embrace.

The Erebus Incident
Part 3 – In the darkness, hope is a luxury

Adam D. Stones

Aboard the *Erebus*

Helena Tyche and Knight Luke Reinhardt moved slowly along the corridor being careful to make as little noise as possible. With no engines providing thrust, the ship was floating inert allowing them to drift along in zero gravity using only minimal contact with the walls for directional correction. Helena was impressed with the Templar Knight. Even with his armoured gauntlets, he barely made a sound as he pushed along. She was envious of his armour as well. While her own pressure suit had heavily worn standard padding around joints and along the back to mitigate bumps and knocks, his armoured assault suit gave much more protection. It was also in a much better state than her ageing and patched equipment.

As they approached a junction, he signalled they should stop. She had suggested she lead. Having spent a few hours alone on the bridge while waiting for the Templars to come and rescue her, she had studied the layout of the ship extensively and had their route memorised. He had politely but firmly declined, taking the lead to allow him to check branching corridors for any Crazed. *Crazed was the right word*, she mused. Anyone infected seemed to have lost any grasp on reality, first becoming disoriented and forgetful before aggressive and short-tempered. Finally, they degenerated into extreme animalistic aggression with a much-reduced pain response. There was no reasoning with them at that point, no rationality. They were crazy.

"All clear." Reinhardt said softly, bringing her out of her reverie as he pushed off from the wall, leading the way. It was about the only conversation they had. He didn't seem to be much of a talker.

"Can we rest for a minute?" she asked further down the corridor, transmitting only to him. He looked back for a moment and she could feel him appraising her, probably resenting her slower pace, before nodding and coming to a stop near another four-way junction.

"Thanks," she said as she stopped nearby. He had adopted a semi-crouch, sleek suit braced against a wall allowing him to check each way in the corridor every few seconds. He gave the impression of a hunting falcon perched on a branch, waiting for sign of a potential meal before launching a strike. By contrast she felt like a puffer fish pulled from the water and dumped on the floor, unwieldy and out of her element.

She should have been handling this better, she thought. The vast majority of her time was spent in zero or low gravity on a rickety old spaceship where death could come in any number of ways. A breach in a fatigued Reaction chamber. Carbon Dioxide scrubbers failing. Pirates. Micro-asteroids. Hazards were both legion and common, and could easily put an unexpected end to life. Yet for some reason, here she was finding it hard going. Maybe it was just that random half-dead psycho crazies weren't an everyday occurrence or something she had prepared herself for.

"How are you so calm?" she asked. Reinhardt responded without looking at her, maintaining his constant checks of their vicinity.

"I learned a while ago to accept the inevitable."

"That's… a little bleak. You don't think we're getting out of this?" It was worrying to her that a clearly hardened warrior had no expectation of survival.

"Oh, we might survive. It's just that you won't leave here." His tone was flat as though it was all a foregone conclusion barely worth talking about.

"I don't follow. Are you planning on shooting me or something?" Helena's confusion was clear.

"Experiences like this change you. You killed someone. You'll be under constant threat for hours to come. Whoever you are now, isn't who you're going to be after."

"I've destroyed pirates before…" she started.

"Not the same. That's remote, distant. You ignited a welding strip that you stuck a to a person and then bludgeoned her to death with a spanner. That's visceral, personal. Like it or not, you're not going to be the same."

"I hope not. Besides, I don't feel any different." she said dismissively.

"Too soon. You're still in the fight really. Give it a few days or weeks. It'll come after the adrenaline has gone and you have time to reflect."

"*Knight Reinhardt, respond.*" Came a voice she didn't recognise over their intercom. From the way his shoulder's sagged, she could guess the call was unwelcome. At first she thought he was afraid of the conversation – a superior officer could quite easily lay the blame for the team being all but wiped out on the Knight. But he didn't seem to be afraid, on second consideration she judged it more likely to be the resigned exasperation of someone dealing with an annoying office manager.

"Reinhardt, here. Identify yourself."

"*Inquisitor Francisco, here Knight. As I think you know.*" The voice exuded arrogance and self-aggrandisement even through the tinny connection.

"I'm a little busy, Inquisitor."

"*We have established a channel into the communications network, Knight. I require a full update on the situation.*"

"I haven't got time for this. You can view my report when we're off here, alive and intact." His voice was hard and full of suppressed anger.

"*What do you mean alive? Has there been a problem?*"

Another voice came onto the channel which Helena recognised as Frederick, the Templar Security Guard who had remained on the bridge and was monitoring their progress. He had been quiet since they had left for the engine room to restore power, with little more than perfunctory responses to open doors or requests for information and direction.

"*Yes, there's been a problem! Most of the team are dead and we're stuck on a zombie ship from hell being chased by mad science experiments got loose! Call for help and get the cavalry here to rescue us!*" He was borderline panicking, stress evident in his voice. Detachment and sudden irritability, Helena thought, the security guard was exhibiting signs of Post-Traumatic Stress, something both she and her sister had had to deal with in the past.

"*Say again and identify yourself. A proper status report! Casualties? How many?*" Luke ignored the Inquisitor's strident demands to focus on Frederick.

"Hey, Frederick. Take a breath. What's going on up there? How are you and, uh…" He broke off, glancing at Helena to see if she knew the name of the other guard on the bridge. She shook her head and shrugged as much as is possible in zero gravity, she couldn't remember either. "How are you both doing?" he finished somewhat lamely.

"Oh, just fucking peachy, you twat! How do you think we're doing? Trapped on a hostile vessel and all we can hear are murderous fucking zombie experiments prowling the corridors hunting for us! I don't know about you, but I'm having a whale of a time. All I need is a cup of tea and a biscuit and it'd be a regular fucking tea party!"

"Hold it together. We've got a hundred metres to go until we get to the access shaft and it's two decks down to the engineering section. Then we can power back up then get off this hell ship." Reinhardt reassured the guard. He sounded genuinely concerned about the man at the other end of the radio who was clearly struggling with the horrific events unfolding around him.

"So, there's clear evidence of Syndicate wrongdoing? That's perfect! A good outcome!" Inquisitor Francisco sounded actually happy. Helena could tell Reinhardt was controlling his anger from his body language, clear even through the somewhat bulky armour he was wearing, though the real giveaway was the way he flexed his hands open and closed around his carbine. Frederick on the bridge was less controlled.

"A good outcome!?!" the guard was incredulous. *"Most of us are dead! Fuck you!"* Helena decided she didn't much like the Inquisitor, though the Security guard was growing on her a bit despite their earlier antagonism.

"Their sacrifice was not in vain. It will allow us to strike a powerful blow against the Syndicate!" The Inquisitor sounded positively happy. The way the Inquisitor spoke of sacrifice reminded Reinhardt of how he had also recently referred to their deaths as sacrifice, creating an uncomfortable similarity between the two men that the Knight would rather not exist. A female voice came onto the channel.

"Knight Reinhardt. Bishop Marielle. Have you had any luck in locating the crew of the Jackdaw? What is their status?" Her concern for the civilians contrasted with the Inquisitor's coldness. Luke didn't respond as quiet metallic clunk came from around the corner, as if something had been knocked over. Not wanting to make any sound and without taking his gaze off the corner, the Templar Knight slid his carbine into a receiving slot on his back, holding it firm and freeing his hands. In the same motion, he drew a knife from the small of his back where a sheath held it secure. With a blade seven inches long,

sharply pointed tip and a razor edge, the weapon looked to be as efficient a dealer of death as its wielder.

"Bishop Marielle. Helena Tyche of the *Jackdaw*." Helena whispered, "Knight Reinhardt has found me. We are on our way to the engine room to restore power to the ship." Reinhardt motioned for her to be quiet without looking back. A Crazed floated around the corner, eyes widening as he took in the sight of the Knight and Helena. He opened his mouth to emit a warning shout only to have the Knight's knife shoved unceremoniously through his neck just above the gap between his collar bones. The Crazed opened his mouth to scream but could barely manage a gargling sound as he found his throat and oesophagus severed. A second crazed came round the corner, also opening their mouth to scream as it launched itself at the Knight. Helena couldn't tell if the Crazed was male or female under all the blood it was covered in. Not that it mattered. It opened its mouth to scream only to have the Knight's armoured forearm jammed in hard, sending shards of shattered teeth spinning off in the zero gravity. The two went tumbling back slowly as they tussled, tangled up into a mass of writhing limbs and armour.

A third, heavily muscled Crazed barrelled into the fray, clawing and swiping with abandon at the two entwined combatants as they span in the air, however its initial trajectory wasn't quite right and it failed to brace itself resulting in the violent swings sending the bloody figure floating into the bulkhead. At that point it finally noticed Helena. Using the bulkhead as a brace it snarled and launched itself into her, grabbing her bodily and flailing wildly, hitting her body, helmet, legs, everywhere it could. Helena's world contracted into a buffeting whirlwind of fabric and flesh that kept spinning her around, disorientating her completely. The thuds and impacts on her helmet were loud enough to drown out any communications while making the already existing cracks in her faceplate grow larger. Attempts to reach her tool belt to grab something, anything, she could use to defend herself just resulted in more wild impacts. Several blows landed on her ribs and wrist, already injured from a previous fight, sending sparks of pain searing through her consciousness. It was all she could do to curl up into a ball. She might have been screaming, she couldn't tell. Time became meaningless. It may have been a minute, it could have been years until suddenly it stopped.

She didn't realise at first, head still ringing from the onslaught. Reinhardt pulled the now inert body away from the beleaguered engineer, sharply twisting and pulling his knife from the back of its neck as he did so, allowing the corpse to float away down the corridor with the other two. Wiping the blood from his blade, he sheathed it on his back. As her wits returned her breathing became steadier and the world regained focus, though her ears were still ringing. She shook her head, trying to get rid of the sound until she realised it wasn't in her ears and it resolved into the panicked shouts of her son, Chase.

"MUMMY! MUMMY! MUMMY!" came the desperate cries over the radio.

"I'm here, Chase. I'm ok." She gasped out, unsure of she was trying to convince him or herself as she winced at the pain.

"MOMMY! ARE YOU OK?!?"

"It's ok, Chase." She took a breath which turned out to be a bad idea as several of her ribs protested forcefully at the motion. "I'm ok. Don't worry."

"I was so worried! I could hear you screaming and…"

"It's alright, young man. The Templar protected me. I told you they're good."

"I want you to come back now Mummy!" Helena sometimes forgot how young he actually was but his childish nature was evident in the whine. Clearly the danger was too much for him to handle, but there wasn't much she could do about that right now.

"I'm on my way. We just have to make a stop first…" she reassured.

"Can't you come back right now?"

"I'll be back before you know it, young man," she said.

"We've got to move." Reinhardt said calmly, pulling his carbine from its holster mount on his back. He scanned around the corridors. "Now." Helena nodded, and they pushed off quickly towards the access shaft.

"I'll have to speak to you later, Chase. Look after the ship and Ophelia for me, okay?" she whispered into the radio, trying to distract him with responsibility. Receiving an unhappy but positive response allowed Helena to focus on the current task. They had moved a short distance down the corridor and were approaching the shaft which would take them to the Engineering section. She saw the hatch ahead, a small maintenance panel built into the wall, designed for access to the service systems by repair crews. It would be a squeeze to get down to the lower levels – as with all things, maintenance seemed to be an afterthought for the design engineers – but unlike taking the main pathway, the maintenance access routes should be empty. Luke activated his mag-shoes and braced to pull the hatch open, but it didn't budge. Helena activated her own mag-shoes as she pointed to the numerous cap screws holding the plate in place. Without looking she pulled out a mini-ratchet from her tool belt and after snapping on the correct head, set to work opening their route. Reinhardt kept watch as before, glancing each way down the corridor every few seconds.

"What section was this?" He asked softly.

"Ah, I think it was microbiology experimentation." She replied absent minded, focussing on undoing another screw. Whoever had specced the plate had clearly been a fan of bolts. There were far more than needed. "I think the outbreak started near here, actually." She said, more to distract herself while she worked than desire to have a conversation.

"Fantastic." He replied, clearly unhappy at that little bit of information. He wandered a few steps away to check a windowless door hatch, to see if it was locked. The handle turned slightly, emitting a piercing squeal which chilled the bones. It wasn't loud, but any noise would give their position away and that was less than ideal. Reinhardt took a step backwards, mag shoes clicking softly in the silence. Helena hurried the rest of the bolts out, allowing them access to the shaft.

"It's open." She said redundantly. Reinhardt didn't move. He was staring at the label above the door. "Come on!" she urged.

"I thought you said this was the experimental area?" He whispered.

"It is." She replied, floating down the corridor to stand next to him, wondering what he was looking at. Above the door, written in incongruously playful letters for the setting was the word *Kindergarten*.

"May… maybe they had a day care for the scientists' children?" Helena said, trying to come up with a plausible reason why there would be a kindergarten on such a ship. Reinhardt didn't respond. His thoughts were filled with much darker probabilities.

"We have to check for survivors." He said to nobody in particular before he moved forward and took hold of the handle. Again it squeaked, stopping rapidly as the Knight flung the hatch open and stepped through. Helena followed quickly. She didn't want to go in, afraid of what might be inside, but the fear was overpowered by the even more intense terror at the thought of being alone again on this ship of horrors even for a few moments.

On the other side of the hatch, bunk beds stretched the whole length of both sides of the long room, like an army barracks. Small, child size bunk beds with simple metal frames. A monitor for each bed was built into the bulkhead, with sensor modules on retractable cables underneath. Everything was dark without power, only a few red emergency lamps scattered sparsely around the room provided any meagre illumination.

"What in God's name were they doing here?" Helena asked, before flinching slightly at the minor blasphemy in front of the Templar Knight. She hoped he wouldn't be upset. Luke didn't even seem to have noticed. He was staring down the room, to the far end and had raised his carbine to a low ready.

"What is that?" Helena asked. She couldn't make it out clearly in the gloom. It was a mass of something, writhing, convulsing. "Is that...?" she continued. Luke switched on his carbine mounted torch allowing a spear of bright light to pierce the darkness, a slender finger of purity to reveal the truth amid the oppressive corruption all around. It spiralled around, searching for its target before zeroing in and settling on the mass which bucked at the imposition.

A small head poked out of the mass, under the bright glare of the light. Suddenly a high pitched scream filled the air, audible even through their suit audio filters. A scream of anger and pain, not of fear. The engineer and the Knight watched in horror as the mass broke apart into dozens of small figures which rushed towards them, screaming horrible banshee wails. They moved quickly in zero gravity, leaping from surface to surface, from ceiling to bed, to wall, to floor. They flew between bunks, under floating objects and around frames. It seemed like aliens had appeared on the *Erebus* and wanted to feast on their bones, but both knew the terrifying truth. On an instinctive level, humans can recognise other humans and how they move. These were definitely humans, despite their animalistic movements. They knew what they had found. Children. Crazed children.

Half the distance had already been covered in only a few short seconds and they were getting closer, their small, blood covered bodies a nightmarish sight, a horrific accusation of lost potential and human inhumanity. Reinhardt reacted first as his training took over – don't freeze, act. Grabbing Helena's suit, he swept her feet clear of the deck to break the mag shoes' hold and launched her unceremoniously through the hatch just behind them. Without waiting to see where or how she landed, he pulled the hatch shut behind him slamming the lock mechanism home and turned to face the horde. His carbine slotted into his shoulder in a perfect firing position, an extension of his body primed and ready for action. Lost amid the screams and noise of the approaching nightmares was the soft click as he switched the safety off and chose his first target.

Helena waited in the hallway, fraught with worry. She didn't like being alone and it was far too quiet as she stood next to the now open maintenance access hatch. After being thrown through the hatch, Helena had recovered her feet and tried to open the doorway back into the Kindergarten of nightmares to no avail. The handle wouldn't budge. She hadn't put too much effort into opening it, a large part of her recoiled at the thought of going back into that horror. It seemed that the room was well soundproofed though, the booming report of the carbine had been damped down to nothing but a faint coughing sound accompanied by some high-pitched squeals almost below audible levels. What had started as a continuous and rapid but irregular beat had petered out after a couple of minutes until there was only a depressing silence broken three times by single muffled gunshot sounds that sounded different to the staccato beat of the start.

A squealing sound filled the hallway, frightening Helena and causing her to look around in fear for one of the Crazed children who must surely be already pouncing on her... before she realised it was the Kindergarten lock opening and the hatch swinging open. She prepared to dive into the access hatch and pull it closed behind her if necessary. Knight Reinhardt stepped through, his armour glistening darkly in the red emergency light, covered with what she guessed was a large amount of blood. He walked slowly towards her in an automatic manner, his gaze fixed into the distance of the corridor behind her. He was holding a pistol in his hand, his carbine loosely floating from the strap on his shoulder. She couldn't see his face behind the goggles and combat mask, but was willing to bet a year's supply of fuel that he had a thousand-yard stare.

In a manner that spoke of years of training and practice but reminded her of an automaton, he reloaded and holstered the pistol, retaining the used magazine. With one hand he clicked the half-spent magazine into a holder and the other slotted the carbine into its holder mount on his shoulder blade.

"Aren't you going to reload that one?" she asked, hoping to try and snap him out of his vacant state. His head turned slowly to look at her.

"It's empty." He said, with all the emotion of a plank of wood.

"Want me to pop over to your ship and get some more bullets?" Helena asked flippantly.

Without giving a response, or giving chance for further enquiries, the Knight went into the access shaft and began to descend to the Engineering level. Helena followed closely, worried by the man's demeanour. She didn't know him well but even through all the layers of armour and pressure suit, it was obvious he was suffering with what he had just had to do.

Silence reigned as they both drifted down, he was clearly suffering and she wanted to help but realised that she didn't know how to. The last thing she wanted to do was to make it worse by saying the wrong thing. She was grateful for the silence in a way, it meant the Crazed hadn't heard the Kindergarten slaughter. Clearly the soundproofing had been efficient.

The rest of the journey to the main engineering section was uneventful and they reached the department control booth without incident. It was a small room, bulkheads and walls covered in control interfaces, readouts, indicator lights and electrical cabinets. One wall had a large window along the wall above a control console, looking out over a series of reactors and generators connected by a veritable three-dimensional maze of piping all spookily illuminated by sparse emergency lighting.

"What's next?" Knight Reinhardt asked tersely as he surveyed the mechanical complexities through the window. Helena had crossed to an electrical cabinet and was examining the contents.

"Let there be light!" Helena responded, flicking a breaker to its on position. A few white lights came on in the control room, with a few more scattered around equipment through the engineering department, above status indicator boards. A lone screen began to run through a loading process near to Helena anticlimactically.

"No fireworks for bonfire night it would seem. I thought that would be more impressive." Helena admitted sheepishly, smirking at Reinhardt who didn't respond or even seem to pay attention. She sat by the screen for a few minutes feeling awkward in the silence until the load sequence finished. If Reinhardt felt any discomfort, it wasn't evident. The militaristic religious order warrior just hung in the zero-gravity, watching the access hatch and occasionally checking through the window. Finally, the screen switched to an industry standard interface, detailing various system statuses, alarms and messages.

"Right. We're getting somewhere." Her fingers hovered over the controls as she scanned the messages, tapping a few buttons to clear some of them. Then she pushed one marked *'Power on'*. Deep in the bowels of nuclear machinery, a fuel pellet was ejected into a chamber before being ignited into a nuclear reaction by a laser. Another one followed shortly after, then some more in a specific sequence. Each one ignited, the system began to generate significant amounts of power. Lights and systems began to come online as their electrical lifeblood began to flow once more. Sub-reactors took some power and began their own ignition sequence. The *Erebus* began to hum with energy, indicator lights turned green to show outputs had reached specification.

"Can we set the ship to fly into the sun now?" Reinhardt asked.

"Not from here. Not easily at least. Our ducks aren't lined up." Helena looked at Luke, he didn't respond, simply stared in her direction. With his combat helmet enclosing his head completely, she couldn't see his face. "Command and navigation systems are on the bridge." She explained, reaching up to unhook an intercom handset.

"Bridge, this is Helena. Power is back on. Can you hear me, Frederick?" A few moments of silence preceded the response.

"I can. Lights are back on. Command systems have finished booting up. I can't believe you made it." said the clearly strained voice, made tinny by a cheap intercom.

"Thanks for the vote of confidence. How are you both doing?" She enquired, glad that they were still alive.

"I'm ok, all things considered. I'm worried about Jimmy though. He went quiet a while ago. I don't think he's handling it well."

"He can deal with it with a shrink later. Right now, I need you to plot the course into the sun for me. Gotta light it all up!"

"Er… Already on it." The room filled with only background noise from a multitude of fission reactors in combination with their ancillary systems as they waited for Frederick to input the requisite commands. They didn't have to wait long. With advanced navigational aids, it was as simple as selecting the desired destination and clicking accept. Sure enough, an acceleration alarm blared through the entire ship followed by a gentle increase in gravity. Unlike small vessels where acceleration could change sharply, the Erebus massed tens of millions of tons. Direction changes were slow and gentle. Knight Reinhardt gradually lowered to the floor, knees absorbing a gentle bump on contact. Helena, already sat in the chair, didn't move as the gravity changed but waited for the strange sensation to pass before contacting the bridge again.

"Well done. We'll meet you at the airlock and transfer over to *Jackie*."

"*Jackie?*" came the confused response.

"Oh, yeah, right. It's my ship, the *Jackdaw*. Holding position on the port side, we have a transfer line to cross over. Meet us at the airlock."

"Will do. Can't wait to get off this ship." Frederick replied.

"Amen, Brother." Luke said somewhat under his breath.

"A sentiment we all share, Freddie." Helena transmitted, "Are you guys going to have any trouble getting there?" A reply wasn't immediately forthcoming. Helena glanced at Luke as the silence stretched out. His helmet was inscrutable, but from the way he shifted his weight and hoisted his weapon, Helena thought he was starting to get concerned. The intercom crackled again, Frederick's voice was soft, like he was whispering.

"I should be alright, but my friend here isn't looking good. He seemed a little... distant. Wasn't always saying the most relevant things. Been quiet for a bit now."

"Alright, try your best. It'll be a walk in the park. Just take care and don't stop for pancakes." The handset crackled as the conversation ended. She reached up to put the handset back into its holder. Suddenly a hand grabbed her arm, holding it above her head, eliciting a startled shout from her. She felt a gentle tug on her side and turned to see Reinhardt looking down.

"Your suit is ripped." He stated matter-of-factly, with the emotional content of a robot. He backed away, not quite pointing his weapon at her, but it wasn't quite away from her either.

"What?!?" Helena exclaimed. She tugged at her suit, feeling cooler air coming in through on her side. "How? When did that happen?!?" Panic began to gnaw at her, threatening to send her into a spiral.

"Probably when we had the fight in the corridor." Reinhardt said, dispassionate. His calmness was infectious, calming her down a little. "You know what this means, right?"

"I'm probably infected," she said softly, body deflating at the inevitability it implied.

"For what it's worth... I'm sorry." It was the most genuine affection she had heard from the Knight. Helena sat back, considering. She knew that she couldn't go back to *Jackie*. Reinhardt would never let her off the ship, the risk of letting the virus spread would be too high. Nor would she want to put her family at risk.

"We've still got to get you off this ship," she whispered.

"Don't worry about me. I'll get to the nearest airlock and eject out. The *Judas' Kiss* can pick me up before I run out of oxygen. That'll give your ship a chance to get clear so Inquisitor Francisco can't go after them so easily."

"And your other two guys up on the bridge?"

"I'll take care of them as well. Just tell your people to get clear."

"I can't." Helena stated flatly. She could tell that Luke wasn't happy with that from the way he flexed his hands on the pistol grip. "I need to see my son again. One last time. One last chance at..." she tailed off, words stuck in her throat.

"I can't let you leave the ship." Back to robotic mode it would seem.

"Wouldn't dream of it. But I have to say goodbye to my son, even if it's through a viewport. I promise I won't leave the *Erebus*."

"How can I be certain you won't leave the ship?"

She thought for a moment and then started to undo her helmet. Tossing the cracked headpiece away, she quickly shrugged out of the suit itself in a practised way. Clearly it was an action done thousands of times. Under Reinhardt's watchful gaze, she bundled up the suit and wrapped a welding strip around it before pulling the activation tab. Its tough, thermally resistant material put up a strong resistance but was no match for the concentrated heat. Metallic and para-aramid fibres melted away amid flickers of flame as the rubber-like coating vaporised. Reinhardt understood, without a suit she wouldn't be able to go into the vacuum of space. Sure, there were probably other suits onboard or her ship might have the ability to dock directly with *Erebus*. It was a statement of intent, one that he could either trust her on, or take action now…

He chose to trust her. Reaching past Helena, he unhooked the intercom.

"Bridge, this is Reinhardt. Change of plan. Meet me on the starboard side, opposite the Jackdaw. Acknowledge." Static filled the air as they waited for a response.

"Bridge, Reinhardt. Acknowledge." More static came out of the radio, the white noise made the time seem longer.

"Do you think they've started moving already? Keen to get off this ship? They did seem the type to go pre-emptively…" Helena asked.

"No. I'll have to find them. Or try at least…" He tailed off as he saw an expression pass across her face. She was staring at one of the screens. "What?"

"Coolant temperature is on the rise. Going past what I would expect." She said, frowning. A few button presses took the display through several screens, flicking up and down some that looked like a ladder and through many tables. Luke couldn't keep up, let alone figure out what she was looking at.

"So what? What does that matter?"

"Well, given the standard temperature limits for the coolant system and the auto-shutdown procedures were passed a while ago, I'm guessing that either there was some incredibly specific system damage during the shutdown. Or…" she trailed off.

"Or what?" he asked, suspecting where it was going.

"Or it's a post-quarantine security measure. The system is reading correctly and the ladder is responding appropriately. You can see the output coils here and here are high," she tapped a few points on the screen, "yet the CNC isn't returning the alarms that should have come up already. The question is why? This system should be in an automatic e-stop. It isn't. There aren't even any alarms."

"And that means... what?" Reinhardt asked, not understanding what she was talking about.

"It means that the system is actively suppressing the alarms."

"Can we pretend like I'm five and don't have a clue what you're talking about?" A tone of irritation underlined his voice. Helena sighed, exasperated. Clearly thinking this was simple knowledge.

"The ladder controls the equipment. It's specific to the system, programmed by whoever built the ship. The CNC is what runs the ladder. It has control over everything. Whatever is suppressing the alarms is happening there. Which means high level."

"Alright. What are you getting at?"

"That the reactor isn't going to shutdown. It's going to keep getting hotter until something fails. And when that happens..." She let the statement hang in the air. It didn't need to be said.

"So... why don't you shut it down? Override whatever they did."

Helena sighed theatrically, feeling as if she was explaining this to a slow child.

"I can't. It's hard coded in the system architecture. I'd need a laptop with the right software just to even look at the code. And I'm fresh out of laptops."

"Couldn't you do something manually, in there?" his hand waved at the mass of pipes through the window.

"On *Jackie* I could. But here? I don't know their reactors or tolerances. I could shut it down, or I could quite easily pull the wrong lever and blow us all up. The first sign would be a reactor overload to the face."

Reinhardt absorbed this, analysing the situation tactically. He keyed his radio.

"Reinhardt to *Judas' Kiss*. Situation update. The *Erebus* will detonate in..." he glanced at Helena who mouthed *'Two hours max'*. "Two hours at most. I'm moving to the Starboard side airlock, halfway down the ship. Get ready to pick me up EVA."

Helena couldn't hear the response, but she could guess from Reinhardt's next comment.

"Two more possibly. We got separated. I'll wait as long as I can, help them out if they need it, of course."

She wasn't expecting the next part.

"Fuck you, Inquisitor. There's nothing we can do. Lives are more important than evidence and I'm not risking anybody to get what you want. We're getting off." He seemed annoyed.

"Problems?" she asked.

"Not right now. Something to deal with later. Bureaucrats with teeth." he scoffed dismissively.

"So what's the plan?"

"Power's on, so we take the elevator up to where your ship is. You say goodbye to your family and I'll go starboard, prep to EVA."

She frowned, she'd figured that his combat suit could survive in space, at least for a short time. It would seem sensible for a combat suit to be able to, in case of unforeseen ejection into vacuum. Maybe he was just being polite.

Chase hung in space a few feet from the airlock into *Erebus*, attached to the transfer cable from the *Jackdaw*. He knew he was meant to stay in the airlock, but he thought his mother might need help. He didn't know what help he could provide, at ten years old his bravery far exceeded his capability, but he was ready for anything. Several tools hung off his belt, clanking soundlessly together in the vacuum of space as he fidgeted with them nervously. Several times the thought of opening the airlock and going in to help his mother had crossed his mind, considered and discarded. It was likely his mother and Ophelia, his aunt, would already tell him off just for being here – the instructions had been to stay in the *Jackdaw*'s airlock to make sure no unauthorised people came across. Yet after listening to the transmissions, he had decided to come over. But if he actually went aboard the *Erebus*? Both Auntie Ophelia and his mother would probably confine him to his quarters for a century.

Suddenly the radio crackled in his ear, destroying the silence filling his helmet. It made him jump, inducing a slight spin requiring a few gentle tugs on the tether rope to stop.

"Chase, Ophie, I'm nearly at the airlock. How are you doing?"

"Mum!" Chase yelped, "We're fine! I'm waiting here for you! Outside the *Erebus* airlock. I attached myself to the tether." There was a pause as Chase waited, excitedly seeking approval while simultaneously half-expecting admonishment for leaving their ship.

"That's great, Chase! I'm nearly there. What's the situation, Ophie?" she asked her sister.

"All quiet. Holding relative position steady as before one hundred metres off the port side. Transfer Tether attached. Might have been nice if you'd given a bit of warning before turning their engines on." Ophelia gently chided Helena.

"Didn't want you to get bored. Thought you might want something to do." Helena chuckled. Ophelia frowned at that. Helena wasn't usually quite so cavalier when it came to... well, anything really. But especially concerning safety.

"Everything ok, Hels?" she asked.

"Just fine. Chase, if you look in through the airlock viewport, I'll be appearing soon."

He glanced with trepidation at the window that had been continuously glowing red since he had first crossed the tether. It reminded him of scenes of hell in the holo-films that his mother wouldn't let him watch but that he occasionally managed to sneak out of her collection without being noticed. Plucking up some courage, he moved himself over to the thick glass with the ease of someone who was growing up experiencing zero gravity regularly and nervously peered in.

Red light filled the airlock and the corridor beyond the far side stretching off to the distance. There was no way he would have been able to get aboard, he realised. With the internal airlock door open, the external one wouldn't have opened. As he watched, a couple of figures emerged halfway down the corridor. One tall and imposing, even from this far away. The other he instantly recognised.

"Mum!" he yelled, waving excitedly. She turned and waved before having a short conversation with her companion. That must be the Templar Knight Reinhardt, Chase thought. He had been listening to the radio broadcasts with curiosity. He had never seen a Templar before and they appeared to be as intimidating as their reputation suggested. Helena turned and started walking towards the airlock, the Knight started to walk away to the other side of the ship. As she approached, something seemed off. Something he couldn't place immediately. As Helena reached the airlock, it clicked in Chase's head.

"Mum, you aren't wearing a space suit!" He exclaimed.

"I know, young man. It's alright. It's not a problem."

"But, how are you going to get across without one?" Confusion was scrawled across his face, evident in his voice.

She took a deep breath, marshalling her effort to say the hardest thing she had ever had to say. "I'm not, young man. I'm afraid that I'm infected. I have to stay here."

"NO! MUMMY! You can't stay! You said the ship's about to explode! Get another suit!" Anger almost caused his voice to crack.

"I can't, Chase. I have to stay. I just wanted to see you one last time." Resignation in Helena's tone was diametrically opposed to the desperation in Chase's.

"Hels?" Ophelia chimed in.

"Yes, Ophie?"

"Are you for reals?"

"Unfortunately. It's my time." She replied simply.

"But Mummy! I want you to come with us!" Chase wailed as he started to hyperventilate. Tears had begun to flow which he tried to blink away. Without gravity to pull them down his cheeks, they pooled in his eyes making everything blurry. "PLEASE!!" Automatic monitoring systems in the suit detected the imbalance in exhaled gases and began to restrict the oxygen flow to compensate.

"Chase. Take a deep breath for me. I want to say some things to you both."

He blubbed a few more times, but managed to get his breathing under control with the assistance of the suit. Helena was up by the glass on the other side, placing her hand on the window. Chase mirrored the gesture. Even though it was only a few inches of reinforced polycarbonate, it felt like a million miles between them.

"Ophie. I want you to know, you are the best sister in the solar system. I wish our lives could have been different in a lot of ways. We got through so much together, had so many good times as well as the bad. But no matter what happened, it was all okay, because I had you with me. And damn, girl. You can fly!" Ophelia grinned at that through the tears which were also making her vision blurry. "But I need you now, Ophie. I need you to look after Chase for me. He needs you now. Needs you to teach him how to survive, how to live and most importantly, how to stay one step ahead."

Ophelia could barely keep her voice from breaking as she responded.

"I'll take care of him for you, Hels. Don't worry. Love you, sis."

"Love you too, Ophie." Helena's voice was more measured than Ophelia's. She had had time to come to terms with the inevitable. She turned her attention to Chase.

"Young man. I'm sorry I won't be there for you growing up. Listen to your Auntie Ophelia. She'll look after you. But you have to be there for her as well. Help her out and help keep *Jackie* running. She's an old ship, but strong and will serve you well if you take good care of her."

"It's *not FAIR, Mummy!*" Chase interrupted, tears coming freely.

"I know, Chase. Life never is. All you can do is try and play the hand life gives you. Sometimes you'll win. Others you'll lose. No matter what happens. You just have to keep fighting, always keep going, keep struggling. Even when its hard, especially when its hard. Choose your friends and crew carefully, people that you can rely on. Fight for them, be there to help them and they will be there for you when you need them. But most importantly, remember that I love you."

"I love you too, Mummy!" he could barely speak and with the tears in his eyes, could barely see. The inside of the airlock was a red blur, his mother a dark shape. Behind her, another dark shape appeared, standing in the inner hatchway. Black and fuzzy through the tears, its only defining feature within the silhouette was two eyes shining gold and what looked like a Templar logo on it's shirt breast.

"MUMMY!! Behind you!" Chase screamed. Helena turned.

"Ophie. Get out of here!" She yelled. A split second later and a hundred meters away, all the manoeuvring thrusters on the starboard side of the *Jackdaw* fired, pushing the ship away from the *Erebus*. Designed to hold onto surfaces to allow people to transfer between ships, the switchable magnet couldn't withstand the load of eight thrusters designed to push a hundred-thousand metric ton ship through rapid combat manoeuvres. It popped off easily, incapable of resisting such force. Motors switched on to reel the Transfer Tether in, pulling Chase away. He kept screaming "No! Mummy! No! No!" at the top of his lungs as the *Erebus* airlock shrank away. Shadows were cast across the airlock viewport, fast moving, blocking the red light intermittently. It was obvious there was a big struggle going on, Helena fighting the shape he had seen.

As he approached the *Jackdaw*'s airlock, Chase reflexively activated his mag-boots to secure onto the floor. He was meant to close the outer hatch before heading up to his acceleration chair on the bridge. But he couldn't. He couldn't move, couldn't take his eyes off the ever-shrinking hatch on the ship of nightmares. Ophelia saw him frozen through the ship monitor, but said nothing. There was nothing she could say, her own grief was threatening to overwhelm her. They had grown up together, spending their entire lives working and living in close proximity, first on a space station as virtual slaves then after their escape aboard the *Jackdaw*. Now her sister was gone. It felt like a part of her had been chopped off. *And all because Chase was bored and had wanted to come to a distress call for some excitement. It was his fault...*

She pushed the thought down. It wasn't right to blame him, he was a child. But still the thought lingered at the deepest recess of her mind. As they reached twenty kilometres from the larger ship, a small explosion erupted from the hull. Far in advance of predicted timescales, the *Erebus* reactors were going critical. Unable to shutdown or stop, they had now reached a temperature that caused fuel pellets in their feed tubes to start to first meltdown, then contribute their own nuclear fury in an unstoppable chain reaction. Several more explosions erupted near the first, then from other parts of the ship.

On the opposite side of the *Erebus*, Knight Reinhardt ejected himself from an airlock to be picked up by the Templar ship nearby. As soon as he was aboard, the *Judas' Kiss* ignited its engine to get clear.

Ophelia closed the airlock from her pilot's console on the bridge and checked Chase was braced then pushed the main thrust to its maximum rated output. The nightmare vessel that was the *Erebus* shrank rapidly as punishing g-force tried to squash Ophelia and Chase into the floor. It had become a small star, indistinguishable from the many others when the chain reaction hit the fuel pellet silo. A thousand tons of nuclear fuel detonated in an almighty explosion, vaporising the entire ship to leave nothing but a dense cloud of excited gas dispersing into the immense vacuum of space.

Thomas' Last Day

H. K. Hillman

In the quiet corner of the town once called Cincinnati, now called US 455-12B, in that space of a few streets still patrolled by law enforcement, the last safe space in town, Thomas 31653 walked to work with his head in the air. He had worked diligently since he was fifteen years old and now, after fifty-five years of obedience and hard work, he was to finally get his reward. He was to be retired.

Oh there was a new word for it. There was a new word for everything these days. Now it was referred to as 'decommissioning'. Thomas 31653 was old enough to remember the old terminology. One of the few remaining who remembered it. It was retirement, and he had been looking forward to it for a long time. Finally, now, at the end of this October, he could retire. No more work. Well, just this one more day to finish up any loose ends.

He opened the door to the office building that had become a second home to him and entered. On his way up in the lift, he wondered how much his pension would be. The administration had never given him a figure, they just smiled and said he'd never have to worry about money again. Thomas allowed himself a little smirk. That must mean his pension would be substantial.

On the way to his desk, he was intercepted by his manager, Mr. 74322. Thomas had never known the man's first name, even after working under him for the last seventeen years. Truth be told, he had never had any interest in finding out. Socialising had been made socially unacceptable decades earlier, especially at work.

"Unit 36153," Mr 74322 said, then coughed, smiled and started again. "Thomas. Can I call you Thomas? I mean, we'll only be working together for a few more hours so there's no need for deep formalities any more."

Thomas gaped. This kind of intimacy had been considered assault for many years. Even those he regularly met on the way to work or home only ever referred to him as Mr. 31653, and he had only ever referred to them by their unit numbers too. "Uh…" He made a sound as his mind tried to comprehend what was happening. Eventually he decided that Mr. 74322 was his manager, a superior, so he should accept this intrusion on his privacy. Still thinking it might be a trap, he answered. "Of course, Mr. 74322. Whatever you say, sir."

Mr. 74322 laughed. "Oh, Thomas, you're old enough to remember when calling people by their first names was normal. I know it's not considered polite these days, but it's not actually illegal." He took a breath and smiled. "You can call me Brian now. You'll be decommissioned in a few hours and it's very unlikely we'll ever meet again so it really doesn't matter."

"I suppose you're right, Mr 74322." Thomas looked at the floor.

"Call me Brian. It'll soon be a much more relaxed world for you. Best get used to it." Brian said, smiling.

Thomas pressed his eyes shut. This was a lot to take in and it broke every taboo he had been taught. Yes, he remembered his childhood when he called his friends by their first name and often didn't even know their unit numbers. He pressed his eyelids together harder. They didn't have numbers. They had names. Second names. Surnames. That meant something. Thomas struggled for the word. Family names. There used to be families. He shook off the thought. That kind of opinion could get his social credit wiped out.

Brian put his hand on Thomas' shoulder. Thomas recoiled. *Assault!* He shook his head. It was ridiculous. People used to be able to touch each other, he was sure. And there was really nothing painful about this contact. *What happened to me? What was I taught?*

"Are you okay, Thomas?" Brian sounded concerned. "Decommissioning can come as a shock. It's a huge change in your life. You won't have to worry about anything once it's done."

"It's…" Thomas swallowed. "It's a lot to take in. So many changes. Will I go back to my boxroom afterwards? What will I do when I don't go to work any more?"

Brian patted Thomas' shoulder. *Violence!*

"It's fine." Brian laughed. "You'll be perfect. Come on, we have a last day acclimatisation ritual—ah, I mean acclimatisation party for you. You'll join all the others decommissioned and I'm sure it'll be great."

"I should get to my desk. I'm still at work." Thomas wasn't sure about going to a party. He felt a little out of practice at socialising. Well, a lot. It just wasn't the done thing these days. It had been such a long time since any kind of social interaction was 'normal' that he wasn't sure he could still remember how to do it.

Brian grinned. "You can file all your work under SEP now."

"SEP?"

"Someone else's problem. Your working days end here." Laughing, Brian steered Thomas along the corridor to a door Thomas, in all his time working here, had never entered before. It had no label, so Thomas had assumed it was some kind of store cupboard. Something for the cleaners' equipment. He had ignored it for half a century. Never asked about it, never wondered. He had never seen it open during the working day.

It was open now. Brian motioned Thomas forward, but Thomas hesitated. The corridor beyond the door was painted a deep red. It didn't seem to be a very professional job: it was covered in lumps and streaks as if someone had just thrown the paint at the walls.

"Are you okay, Thomas?" Brian held the door, constantly checking behind them as if they were doing something they shouldn't. "We should get to the party. People are waiting."

"It's just…" Thomas blinked a few times. "It's just that I haven't seen what's behind this door before. It's very… colourful."

It was, indeed, a stark contrast to the uniform pale grey of the rest of the building's interior. Thomas, slightly overwhelmed, followed Brian's outstretched hand and stepped into the corridor. Brian followed and closed the door behind them. Thomas jumped at the thud of the door closing.

"No need to be nervous, Thomas. It's just a short walk." Brian led the way along the corridor. Thomas, still struggling to come to terms with what was happening, followed.

At the end of the corridor was a black door. So black, Thomas thought, that it might not even be a door at all. Just a blank space in reality – a reality he felt he was rapidly losing his grip on. Just before they reached that door, Brian turned left and opened another door. Smiling, he motioned Thomas inside.

Thomas entered. The people – too many people! – raised the glasses they held and cheered. Thomas' mind reeled. He recognised some. Ms. 47915 from accounts. Mr. 67725 from HR. Ms. 43259 from the canteen. Ms. 42986 from the front desk. So many people had their full attention on him. It was unnatural and yet it stirred a memory when this would have been something to celebrate. Thomas felt the world slipping away. He heard vague voices.

"It's too much for him."

"He's going to fall."

"Quick, get a chair."

"Sit down, Thomas. This must have been a bit of a shock for you."

"Here, drink this. It will help you relax."

Thomas accepted the cold glass pressed into his hand and raised it towards his lips. Someone stopped him. A face, a blur he could not place, looked into his eyes.

"I have to ask you one question, Thomas. Did you come here without force? Did you come of your own free will?"

Thomas managed a nod. The restraining hand on his arm removed, he lifted the glass to his mouth and drank of the soothing liquid. His mind relaxed, the tension left his body and he succumbed to the oblivion of sleep.

"Is he ready?"

"He's coming around."

"Time is short. He has to wake."

The voices filtered through Thomas' blurry consciousness.

"Mr, One will not be pleased if he's not fully awake."

Mr. One? Thomas had heard of the name but it was a legend. From hundreds of years ago. Mr. One had set up their safe place by making a deal for protection. Yet surely Mr. One had died by now. Long ago.

"Thomas. You have to wake up." Brian's voice was close, almost at his face. "It's nearly time."

Still groggy, Thomas slurred "Time for what?"

"Time for your decommissioning. You have to be conscious for it.

"Yeah, okay." Thomas tried to rise but his arms would not move. He realised they were tied to the arms of his chair. "What is this?" Suddenly fully awake, he struggled at his bonds,

"You can't fight it, Thomas." Brian's voice sounded soothing. "It's necessary. It has to happen."

"What is happening? Why?" Thomas could feel his own heartbeat in his rising panic. His panic only increased when he realised that Brian now wore a long red robe, as did the others behind him. Hoods covered most of the faces and what Thomas could see of those faces appeared to be the bottom halves of identical masks.

Only Brian's face was showing, and he held a plain white mask in his hands. Brian smiled and inclined his head.

"The 'what' in your questions will become clear shortly. I have a little time to answer the 'why', and it seems only fair to do so." Brian pulled up a chair and sat facing Thomas.

One of the others leaned over and whispered in Brian's ear. He waved them away. "It's fine. We won't be late."

Brian took a deep breath. "So, Thomas, you are no doubt familiar with the story of Mr. One, and why we have this safe haven in this city of lawlessness and chaos?"

"Of course. We are all grateful to Mr. One for the deal he made in the distant past." Thomas stared at his knees. "Even though nobody seems to know what it was. Something to do with the police still working here, I guess."

Brian chuckled. "The police are just for show. They really have nothing much to do. They are certainly nothing to do with the deal."

"But surely it's the police who keep the criminals out?" Thomas wanted to ask what the red robes and masks were for, but something told him he'd rather not know.

"No." Brian pursed his lips. "I know you've worked here a lot longer than me, and maybe you're wondering how I know things you don't know. Not everyone is suited to this part of the work." He stretched his shoulders. "Anyway. Mr. One made a deal with someone – something – far more powerful than the police. The thing is, the deal wasn't free. It has to be paid for. Every year, on this night, a night that used to be called Halloween and many other names before that. A night that has been special since the dawn of time."

"I haven't seen any unusual payments in the accounts." Deep down, Thomas had a feeling he knew what Brian meant but his mind tried desperately to find any alternative explanation.

Someone behind Brian chuckled. Brian turned and waved them to silence. He faced Thomas again, his expression serious. "You know this has nothing to do with money, don't you? I mean, I realise this has all come as a shock but deep down, you know what this is really about. Don't you?"

Thomas pressed his lips together briefly. "You're going to kill me, aren't you? I'm going to be sacrificed to some imaginary demon you all worship."

"Hm." Brian sat back in his chair. "We're not going to kill you. The 'imaginary' demon will do that. We just deliver you." He rose from his seat. "It's time. Mr. One expects payment."

"Mr. One has been dead for a hundred years!" Thomas fought his bonds as two of the robed figures moved to lift his chair. "This is insane. Why are you doing this?"

"Same reason we've done it every year, and the same reason we'll keep doing it every year." Brian opened the door and the robed figures followed Thomas' carried chair into the corridor. They chanted something in a language Thomas couldn't place while he squirmed against the ropes holding his arms.

They placed his chair directly in front of the black door. The chant reached a crescendo and abruptly stopped. Something shifted in the blackness of that door, something even darker than the darkness. The robed figures retreated. Just before he heard the door close, Thomas heard one last whisper from Brian.

"Goodbye, Thomas."

The swirling darkness fascinated and calmed Thomas' mind. It all felt so unreal. His last day at work. His anticipation of retirement. This must be a dream.

There were faces in that darkness. Twisted faces, gaping in silent screams and at their centre, one malevolent wrinkled face that stared into his soul.

The red walls with their lumpy, streaky paint came to mind. It wasn't paint. He knew that now. He saw his future, just as a spear of blackness shot from that black doorway into his heart, and his body exploded.

Gorod Prizrakov

David D Walker

I stood beside Lenin staring into the gloom of the darkening twilight as it spread across the abandoned town, the full moon not yet providing its full power to illuminate the scene in front of us.

To encourage my circulation, I stamped the blocks of ice at the end of my legs and then danced a little jig. Vladimir Ilyich Ulyanov was unmoved by my performance, keeping his paternal gaze fixed firmly front and centre. He had an advantage over me in that he had already survived forty bitter winters in the frozen north and was used to sub-zero temperatures in March. Being made of granite helped too, of course, for my silent companion was the most northerly Lenin statue in the world. He had been erected by the Soviet Union decades before the decision had been made to leave the once bustling mining town of Pyramiden on the island of Spitzbergen.

As I waited for true darkness to fall, I thought about how I'd come to be standing behind my camera and tripod in such a cold spot. Working as a photojournalist for a best-selling travel magazine had taken me to obscure places around the globe, some more salubrious than others, and Pyramiden certainly fell into the 'obscure' category. My quarterly articles, headlined 'Sam's Safaris', with my byline, Samantha Johnstone, were generally well-received, and I hoped my current assignment would add lustre to my résumé.

My assignment had been triggered by our editor sending me on a shoot to cover the opening of the Global Seed Vault the month before. He'd seen a photograph of the building's entrance and thought it looked funky, and, when tied to the vault's Doomsday insurance policy, decided that it would make an interesting story.

"And while you're up there, you might get some good shots of the Northern Lights," he'd added. "Oh, and I've heard of some abandoned Russian mining towns, nearby. They're becoming tourist spots for the brave and the bold, so take in one of those too. Very moody and atmospheric, I'm sure. Just the sort of stuff you like to shoot and ideal for our more intrepid readers looking for somewhere far from the madding crowd."

Never one to turn down a trip to somewhere I'd never been before, I'd jumped at the chance to head north of the Arctic Circle and sample the delights of Svalbard and its largest island, Spitzbergen. What those delights actually were proved elusive to my pre-trip research as the islands were not then a major tourist draw and mostly only featured as a few pages in general guidebooks to Norway, the governing state for the Svalbard archipelago. Nevertheless, I was soon on an SAS flight out of Heathrow for Tromsø, a small Norwegian fjord town already 350 kilometres north of the Arctic Circle. After an overnight stopover, I was then off to Svalbard Airport on Spitsbergen, a further 950 kilometres away as the Boeing 737 flies.

As we came into land, we flew over an iceberg-strewn sea and my Nikon D6, pressed on to the window with a rubber lens hood to cut out reflections, went into overdrive. In my mind, March was the first month of spring, but, around the airport, at 78° north, snow still lay deep on the ground in 2008. My shuttle bus took me on a snowploughed gravel road into the nearby town of Longyearbyen, past a smoke-belching power station, its emissions testament to the town's *raison d'être* — coal mining.

The power station and the evidence of one hundred years of coal extraction in the form of overhead cableways, long conveyor belts and menacing spoil tips, were a shock given the surrounding scenery, its stunning form carved by ancient glaciers. These rivers of ice had created the broad U-shaped valley that Longyearbyen nestled in. The town was circled by towering mountains, rounded in shape by eons of erosion, snow clinging to their peaks. The base of the valley was now a fjord extension of the Arctic Ocean, partly covered in sea ice near the shore, with a smattering of fragmented icebergs further out. In leads of clear water, a few fishing vessels and colliers could be seen anchored where once whalers would have been sheltering in abundance. As we drove along, we passed road signs which had a white polar bear symbol on a black background inside the usual red warning triangle. There had been a stuffed polar bear in the baggage hall at the airport too, and the animals seemed to be a local fixation.

Longyearbyen wasn't the prettiest town, nor was it like any other town I'd ever visited. It was a strange mix of dull miners' barracks, a few colourful private houses, non-descript administrative buildings for its role as capital of Svalbard, and some shiny glass and concrete newbuilds from its attempt to reinvent itself as a base of academic research into all things Arctic. The town had a church and two hotels, plus a few bars, some shops, and a couple of garages. Transport seemed to be a mix of four-by-fours, pick-ups, dog sledges and snowmobiles, with the last the dominant form. At the Radisson Hotel, when I checked in, the receptionist warned me that, although it was acceptable to go unarmed in the town centre where there were plenty of buildings to escape from any itinerant polar bears, everywhere else required me to carry a weapon as a defence against the ursine predators, unless I had an armed guide with me. When the polar bears, remoteness, pitch-black winters, midnight-sun summers, cold climate and male-dominated population were included, Longyearbyen felt unique.

I spent two days wandering around the town with my camera, trying to get good shots which juxtaposed the rusting skeletal structures of the old coal industry with the hi-tech glass buildings and satellite dishes of the new research facilities. Having largely done with its only coal reserves, leaving only one mine open, I got the feeling that Norway wanted to move forward into a brave new world funded by its vast oil and gas reserves and that Longyearbyen's conspicuous evolution was a testament to this.

The Seed Vault proved to be a giant underground library of samples from all over the world, an international insurance policy designed in the form of a genebank to protect the global diversity of crops against future disasters, natural or man-made. The vault had been sited on Svalbard due to a mix of geology and climate, but it didn't make for the most exciting visit. However, the entrance, rising out the side of a hill like a giant concrete wedge was spectacular. It was decorated by a huge illuminated artwork called 'Perpetual Repercussion', which had a stained-glass feel, and, with the hush inside the vault and its noble cause, created an almost religious aura to the whole place.

Everyone on Svalbard spoke some level of English, which made life easy for me. The population seemed to be composed largely of miners and nerdy academics, plus those engaged in supporting them, including, to my surprise, a large Thai contingency, who were part of a diaspora that I had never heard of. I'd read that in the Far North, in the four months of sunless winters, suicide rates, driven by SAD, seasonal affective disorder, were high due to the depression it induced. However, most of the population I met seemed quite happy, although whether this was due to spring, such as it was, having sprung, or the beer and aquavit being plentiful, I never worked out. To offset the alcohol, the diet was wholesome — if you liked fish and venison.

Tired of being hit upon in the few bars in town by lonely randy singletons of both sexes, I signed up for a tour to complete the second part of my assignment. The blurb promised the required combination of Northern Lights and Russian ghost town with a snowmobile tour across northwest Spitsbergen. The trip started at Ny-Ålesund, and, since there were no roads between it and Longyearbyen, a helicopter would take me and my future tour party colleagues the required hundred-odd kilometres northwest. Snowmobiles would then take our tour across to Pyramiden, the similarly-isolated former Russian settlement, before we'd head back to Longyearbyen.

A French-made red and white Puma helicopter took our mini-expedition to its start point. From the chopper's cabin, as we flew over snow-capped mountains, frozen fjords and snaking glaciers, I stared in wonderment at the passing ground below. That everything I could see had been sculpted by ice was simply mind-blowing. My schoolgirl geography flooded back to me as I recognised cirques, arêtes, moraines and other glacial features from Mrs Maddison's O-level geomorphology lessons. How I wished I could have had such a bird's-eye view back then instead of her grainy 35mm slides and dusty text books to explain the extraordinary power of frozen water. Determined to out-do my old teacher's photographs, I took plenty of shots, praying that our speed and the window's perspex wouldn't cause too many future editing problems.

Due to the stunning views, I was somewhat disappointed when our short helicopter hop ended, and we landed in a cloud of dust at the Hamnerabben gravel landing strip beside Ny-Ålesund. In some ways, our destination was a miniature Longyearbyen. Unlike the capital, its coal mining was long gone, and it was now given over to various international research organisations. Its brightly-coloured wooden buildings, in red, yellow and blue, collectively formed the most northerly permanently-inhabited settlement in the world.

The location had given the tiny village a little place in history as the departure point for Norwegian explorer Roald Amundsen's voyage on the Italian airship *Norge* to the North Pole in May 1926, with he and his crew being the first humans to visit Earth's northernmost extremity. The isolated structure of the mast that *Norge* had been tethered to before setting off on its epic voyage was pointed out to us as we drove past on the way to our accommodation in one of the huts usually used by researchers of the Norwegian Polar Institute. On the short trip, we saw evidence of the settlement's coal mining history in an abandoned siding full of coal wagons resting beside an old wooden building that looked like it was sliding into the fjord behind. Ny-Ålesund's contrast between old and new was very photogenic and my Nikon was put to work with gusto.

Over lunch, our tour group got to know each other. Our guide was Trine Riise, and I could see some looks of consternation among the male members of the party at being led by a woman across the Arctic wilderness. Their fears evaporated when Trine explained that she was an Olympic-medallist for biathlon, the sport that combines endurance cross-country skiing with accurate rifle shooting and which is a Norwegian speciality and sporting obsession. The others in the party included a pair of young Italian love birds, Georgio and Valentina, a rather formal older English couple from Surrey, Dick and Belinda, a geography PhD student from Cambridge called Parvati, a large Afro-American from Chicago named Jeff, and a blonde Russian-sounding woman called Olga.

Trine spent a long time briefing us on safety in Arctic conditions before expanding her lecture to cover snowmobile driving techniques. After getting kitted out with red thermal suits with hi-viz patches, snow boots, gauntlets, tinted goggles, ski masks and helmets, we were then let loose outside on our snowmobiles. These were large red Polaris machines, with fifty horsepower engines, a pair of short skis used for steering at the front and a caterpillar track at the rear for propulsion. The driving seat was over the engine, behind the fuel tank, with a luggage pannier further back. Steering was effected via a set of heated-handlebars behind a perspex windshield. There was a headlight at the front and a red brake light at the rear. It was a bit like riding a motorcycle, but somehow more fun. We dutifully followed Trine in convoy around Ny-Ålesund doing circuits for an hour or so until we'd all got the basics and were then led back to our accommodation.

Just as we were about to go inside, there was a bang followed by a loud screeching noise and something behind us shot into the sky, blazing a fiery trail before it disappeared into the low cloud. Although we all jumped, Jeff alone among us had fallen flat on the snow and we all looked at him as he dusted himself off and got up. He smiled sheepishly and went inside, and I could see that he was shaking slightly.

"That was a sounding rocket," Trine said, pointing to her left. "Over there is the new Andøya space centre. It's hardly Cape Canaveral, but fires small rockets high into the atmosphere to gather meteorological information and data on the Earth's magnetic field to better understand the aurora. You were lucky to see one, as the launches aren't very frequent."

During our training, Trine had kept a rifle, covered to protect it from snow, strapped to her snowmobile. After warning us about polar bears, she gave a second rifle to Jeff, as she'd learned that he was ex-US Marine Corps. While we'd been training, a special permit had been completed by local officials to allow him to carry the weapon and he was designated by Trine to be the 'tail gunner' on our future convoy. Given his reaction to the rocket, I wondered how effective he'd be in a crisis. The rest of us would ride in-between the two rifle-bearers and were given bear-scarer fireworks, activated by pulling a tab, to throw at any polar bears that got too close. Having spent several days on Spitzbergen without seeing hide nor hair of a bear, I wondered what all the fuss was about.

At dinner, possibly due to the wine and aquavit, everyone shared a little more about themselves. Our Italians were recently-married and had been keen to go somewhere different from their friends for a honeymoon. Olga was the ex-wife of a London-based oligarch and proved to be Ukrainian, not Russian. She said that she had come to visit the grave of her brother who had been killed in a mining accident in Pyramiden in the early nineties. Parvati revealed that her parents were doctors from India, but had migrated to England before her birth, and that her geography thesis was on abandoned settlements across the High Arctic. She'd already visited several such places in Greenland, Alaska and Canada. Dick proved to be a retired City head-hunter, with Belinda being his second wife and a former human resources manager. He proved to be a bit haughty for my taste, and my dislike of him was furthered when I heard him make whispered catty asides to Belinda about me being on expenses and Parvati having a jolly using tax-payers' money, while he was having to fork out thousands of pounds for the same trip. Jeff in his reveal apologised for his earlier behaviour during the rocket launch, explaining that he'd been under rocket fire during tours of Iraq and Afghanistan. He had automatically responded to the sound of what he called a *Katyusha*, a Russian word, he explained, since most of his enemy insurgents' weapons had originally been Soviet. After my own summary, I was slightly deflated that none of my peers subscribed to the travel magazine I represented, or knew my byline, but then again, competition from *National Geographic, Condé Nast* etc. was fierce in the high-end travel sector — or so I told myself.

At Trine's request, Parvati gave us a short talk on Pyramiden based on her research. She revealed that the town was named after the pyramid-shaped mountain that loomed over the settlement. We learned that the site was originally owned by the Swedes after coal was discovered there, but that the Soviet Union had purchased it from them in 1927. All this foreign activity on Norwegian territory was apparently legal under the Svalbard Treaty signed two years before that, which, while nominally granting sovereignty to Norway, allowed other countries to operate assets across the islands. Indeed, the Soviets developed several mines, and Barentsburg, was still operating, a few kilometres west of Longyearbyen. Coal mining didn't start at Pyramiden until after the Second World War, and the Soviets went on to build a small town with a population of almost two thousand people to exploit the underground deposits. All this was despite the mainland Soviet Union being rich in coal. However, its paranoid leadership was concerned that the islands could be militarised and used by NATO to snoop on the Red Banner Fleet's nuclear submarines operating out of Murmansk, to the south, and felt a presence on the islands would prevent this. The Pyramiden mine was, however, never economical, and, with the fall of the Soviet Union, after Gorbachev's reforms and Yeltsin's shock therapy economic programme, the plug was pulled on its subsidies by the newly-reconstituted Russia, and the business, along with the tied settlement, was abandoned in 1998, just ten years before our visit. Geopolitics had demanded that Barentsburg, with a population of five hundred

373

and an operating mine had been retained as the sole strategic Russian foothold. From Parvati's comments, it seemed that the Cold War had continued in the Far North, both literally and figuratively.

"What you will see, when we get there, is like a time capsule on Soviet life," Trine added, when Parvati had concluded. "I'm sure you will find it very interesting. And please remember, the town is surrounded by the Nordre Isfjorden National park, so respect the nature, keep to the track I make, watch out for bears, and then everybody will be happy. Now, we have an early start, so I suggest you all get to bed."

Before going to sleep, I went to get some water from the communal fridge in the hut's kitchen. I found Trine staring out the window into the dark, a solemn look on her face.

"Are you all right?" I asked.

She smiled a sad smile and said, "Yes, I'm fine. Just looking out for *deildegast*."

"What are they?"

"Ghosts."

A moaning noise came from outside, and I felt a shiver down my spine. "Why would there be ghosts here? It's such a small place."

"Twenty-one miners were killed here in the early sixties in an accident. There's a memorial out there. The mine was closed soon after by the Norwegian Government. It's said the miners' spirits come out of the mine at full moon to demand retribution from the owners, but, since they're long gone, the ghosts wander aimlessly, wailing at their fate."

The wind in the telephone wires is making the moaning noise, surely, I told myself, but, nevertheless, I checked outside and thankfully could see nothing moving.

Trine's talk of mining accidents reminded me of a childhood visit with my grandfather, himself an ex-miner, to the pit villages of Ayrshire in Scotland. By the time of our visit in the eighties, the tiny settlements were sparsely populated, heavily graffitied and poorly maintained. It was sad and depressing for me, so God knows how my grandfather, who'd lived in these once-bustling hamlets had felt. In Muirkirk, his home village, we had stood for a while at the miners' memorial there, its purpose similar to Ny-Ålesund's in recording the underground dead, until, after a while, my grandfather walked away, tears in his eyes. "Too many ghosts," he'd said. I'd never seen him cry before.

"Do you believe in ghosts?" Trine asked my reflection in the dark window.

"I'm not sure," I replied, slowly, wondering if I did or not. Remembering the strong emotional effect of the memorial on my grandfather, I thought perhaps that I was a believer.

"I do," said Trine. "Norwegian folklore is full of ghosts, trolls and spirits. I believe there's a reason for everything. Even folk tales are based on events from the dim and distant past, so, sometime in history, people have seen all these things."

"Well, they don't seem to be visiting tonight, Trine," I told her with an enthusiasm I didn't really feel, patting her on the back before collecting my water. As I left the kitchen, she was still staring out into the night.

When I went to my room, I found Jeff following close on my heels down the corridor. I spun round to confront him.

"The answer's, 'thanks, but no thanks'," I said, as firmly as I could.

"No thanks? What's the question?"

"I mean, I'm planning on sleeping alone."

Disconcertingly, he laughed. "Don't worry, Sam, you're not my type."

"What is your type?" I asked, now irritated by his brush off, despite me being the one giving him a warning, and wondering why I'd been rejected.

"Blonde and male. I think I'm in the room next to you. I hope you don't snore; these walls are only one plank thick. Good night."

With that, he left me standing in the corridor feeling more than a little foolish.

That night, for the first time in years, I dreamt of my grandfather and his ghosts.

The thermometer on the outside wall of our hut read -12°C when our group assembled, fully kitted in our Arctic gear, at six-thirty in the morning, just after daybreak. In March, that far north, the sun never got very high above the horizon, and, although the day was nominally eleven hours long, we couldn't expect much true daylight. Since our one hundred kilometre journey to Pyramiden involved us more or less heading east, the low sun would normally have been in our eyes for some of the journey. However, a flat grey sky overhead negated that risk, dulling visibility, and, much to my chagrin, making for poor photographic conditions. Trine told us that with the windchill effect caused by driving, it would feel a lot colder than the thermometer reading, and warned of the risk of frostbite on exposed skin. At that, we all pulled down our goggles and pulled up our masks, not wanting to lose a nose to the bitter cold. We loaded our luggage, mounted our machines and, after much revving to warm up the engines, were ready to go.

Before we set off, Trine shouted at us, "Remember to keep up. Whatever you do, don't get isolated. Svalbard is an unforgiving place!" Then we set off in convoy, lights on, high on excitement.

It took us eleven hours to get to Pyramiden. After driving south down the Brøgger peninsula, we headed east, climbing up over the Kongsvegen glacier, before dropping back down into the Holmströmbreen valley. Driving across the snowfields at the base of the massive U-shaped valleys was an amazing experience, truly breathtaking due to the sheer scale of the landscape. Our little caravan of snowmobiles seemed tiny in the vast expanse of scenery around us. Despite the poor light, I managed to get some good photographs during rest stops and when we halted for lunch at Kapp Wærn. There, we formed a corral with the snowmobiles, like settlers circling their wagons, only, for us, the danger was bears coming off the frozen sea. The lunch did not match the spectacular scenery, and we ate from pouches of hot food, warmed upon opening by some exothermic chemical they contained. Despite Trine's assurances that it was the food used by astronauts, I found it absolutely disgusting and decided that I wouldn't be volunteering for NASA anytime soon.

We survived a frightening whiteout when a snow-laden wind had funnelled down a ravine and caught us in its icy blast, but, for me, the scariest moment of the journey was the crossing of Dicksonfjorden over sea ice. I couldn't get it out of my mind that I was riding a heavy machine over ice covering several hundred metres of dark cold water underneath, and I tensed at every creak and crack lest I plunge into the depths as we forged our path across the frozen fjord. By the time we regained the shore, although it was well-below freezing, inside my thermal suit, I felt like I was in my personal sauna.

As dusk began to settle into twilight, after weaving our way through the narrow winding Mimerdalen Valley, we reached the frozen shore of Billefjorden. A short drive north then brought us to a collection of rusty shipping containers that was to be our accommodation in Pyramiden. By then, it was too gloomy to make out much of the town itself, and so we gladly embraced the interior of the makeshift hotel, tired after our long journey and driven indoors by the temperature having dropped to -18°C.

Inside the hotel, we were met by our local guide, Boris, a gangly Russian with a straggly beard, dressed in bright orange overalls, who stank of alcohol, cigarette smoke and sweat. In heavily-accented English he welcomed us to Pyramiden and offered us a tot of Armenian brandy, the best in the world, he asserted, and the same drink that Stalin had plied Churchill with, or so he claimed. No one demurred.

After our drinks, Boris showed us around the hotel, explaining that the containers had been insulated to keep out the worst of the cold, before apologising for the fact that, despite this, it wasn't exactly tropical inside. He revealed that we'd be sharing bunk rooms using down sleeping bags designed for Russian Arctic troops to take the edge of the still low interior temperatures. The lights inside the hotel were a harsh fluorescent white, and I could hear a diesel generator putt-putt-putting in the background to provide the power. All the rooms smelt of paraffin, the fuel for heating and cooking, mixed with cigarette smoke and the pervading drainy pong of chemical toilets. It was a throat-catching miasma, and I was glad we only had a two night stay.

Dinner was a grey greasy stew accompanied by watery tinned beans served up by Irina, the cook, who looked like she'd enjoyed too much of her own fare. It was washed down with ice-cold vodka and bottled water. The few other staff members of the hotel ate with us, but said little, and none looked thrilled to be in this frozen outpost of the Russian Empire.

As we ate, Boris added to Parvati's history of Pyramiden. He told us that the mine had been operated by Trust Arktikugol, a state-owned company. The town was built to be a model Soviet settlement, where people worked hard by day, but at night, could enjoy a whole range of social and sports pastimes. He made it sound like a veritable Communist workers' paradise. Men were paid well, accommodation was good, food was plentiful, the facilities were comprehensive and, for a while, he claimed Pyramiden became a sought-after place of employment. However, after financial support was cut by Yeltsin, living standards slipped, just as the coal seams became depleted. The rocks at Pyramiden were not the same geology as Longyearbyen and Barentsburg, being much older, more faulted and tougher to mine. Boris explained that without state aid in an age of widely fluctuating coal prices, it was deemed too expensive to open another seam and the decision was made to close the enterprise. Ultimately, everyone in Pyramiden lost their homes and their livelihoods. He seemed unusually sad when he told us about the town being abandoned.

Boris eventually finished and asked if we had any questions.

Jeff took a military angle and asked, "And this Soviet Utopia, you've described, since it was never economical, was it really just a coal mine? Was it not actually a KGB station used to spy on NATO?"

"No KGB here. No commissars. Purely and simply a coal mine," said Boris, but he winked, all the same.

"That's bullshit! I believe the whole operation was a sham, paid for in Ukrainian miners' lives," declared Olga, forcefully. "Twenty-three miners killed at Barentsburg in 1997 and that was after over one hundred and forty died in the air crash bringing miners here the year before. My brother died here too, in an underground accident, don't forget!"

Boris looked more serious after this verbal assault and said, "It's true that most of our miners were from Ukraine. Underground workers from the Donbas Region in the east, managers from Volyn in the west. In fact, I was born in Pyramiden, and my father was a Ukrainian miner, my mother a Russian teacher. I left in my early teens along with the rest of the population. My own family didn't survive the subsequent stress of unemployment, and my parents got divorced. I ended up in Moscow with my mother."

I thought this explained Boris's earlier melancholy when he'd described how and why Pyramiden had been abandoned. He'd obviously enjoyed happy times back then.

"Is it true you were tricked and sent back to the mainland on holiday, but never allowed to return?" asked Parvati.

"No, that's not true. That is what I believe you call in English an 'urban myth'. Families started to leave in 1994. That's when we moved out. Then, everything closed four years later when there were only a few hundred staff left. The place became a ghost town. I volunteered to come back last year to help set up tourism for the likes of yourselves. This place is still home to me, in a way."

"Why was Pyramiden abandoned and not Barentsburg?" asked Dick.

"Interesting question, given Pyramiden was the younger settlement," admitted Boris. "Firstly, there was no political will. Barentsburg was always more Russian than Soviet. For instance, it has an Orthodox church, but there's not one here. Pyramiden, on the other hand, and as you'll see on our tour, is distinctly Soviet and therefore from the past regime, with not only Ukrainians, but people from all over the Soviet Union working here, not just Russians. Secondly, Barentsburg had bigger and easier to access coal reserves than here. Better geology, basically. Thirdly, it is ice-free for exporting that coal, but here, the port is only open from June to October. We're a hundred kilometres away from open ocean, so, too far economically for an ice-breaker to plough a path and keep it clear for our meagre production. And finally, Barentsburg had the Russian consulate, so it was considered our local capital. Put in purely practical terms — particularly if you're sitting in Moscow — it made sense to close one and keep the other."

There were no more questions. Everyone looked dog-tired.

"Now, our tour of the town will begin at six-thirty, so breakfast is at six sharp," Boris declared. "However, before you bed down, there's one more thing I have to show you."

He took us to a room near the hotel entrance. On its wall was a rack of rifles over a shelf lined with pistols.

"Unless Trine or I are with you, you never leave this building without a gun," Boris told us, looking very serious. "Like everywhere else in Spitsbergen, there are polar bears around here and, for them, you're just another animal, another piece of prey, another lunch or dinner. It's never personal with a polar bear. If you want to go outside, please let me know. If I'm free, I'd prefer it if I came with you. If I'm not, then ask Trine. If you can't find either of us, then you must sign for a weapon in the log book, check it's loaded, and ensure it is with you at all times when outside. You should have a permit, but, hey, this is a Russian base, so it's okay to avoid the paperwork."

I noticed Trine shaking her head when he said this, but she didn't intervene.

"The rifles are infantrymen's Moisins, and the pistols are Nagants, as used by officers. Both were Soviet Army issue during the Great Patriotic War, so they're old, but they're still effective. You'll certainly need a gun if you meet Igor."

"Who's Igor?" Parvati asked, a nervousness in her voice.

"He's a big bastard that visits from time to time. Remember, polar bears are the world's largest land carnivores, and Igor is the biggest of the big. He must weigh about a thousand kilos and be well over two and a half metres tall on his hind legs. His size makes him very distinctive. Mostly, we see him take seals out on the frozen fjord or from the ice floes when the melt comes, but he's been seen taking down reindeer, foraging for birds eggs and rummaging through our garbage. The rumour is that he killed a lone snowmobiler last year. The man had broken down on his way to Longyearbyen. The snowmobile was found, but he wasn't. Just a trail of blood heading off into the wilderness and paw prints for a very large bear, so, Igor knows what human flesh tastes like. Also, I've seen what he can do to a reindeer carcass, and, believe me, you do not want to meet him. Remember, at all times, that although a polar bear is a sprinter and not a marathon runner, and doesn't have great hearing, it has excellent night vision and can smell prey over vast distances. So, please, be very careful out there!"

That night, I had a fitful sleep, too hot inside my Soviet Army sleeping bag, too cold outside it, my roommates' snores and flatulence interrupting dreams filled with polar bears and men with guns.

The next morning, Boris led us on a tour of Pyramiden. We went on foot, with Boris and Trine together forming our armed guard. The

380

town was strung out east-west along the Billefjorden coast. Across the fjord from us, the Nordenskjöldenbreen glacier tumbled down between two peaks to meet the frozen sea. Towering over the settlement was the promised pyramid-shaped mountain, almost a thousand metres high, with eight distinct bands of red and grey rock visible on its steep sides, too steep for snow to cling. It reminded me of a badly-iced giant layer-cake.

On the tour, I felt in danger of contracting trigger finger from repetitive strain such was the number of shots I took with my Nikon. I had taken photographs of post-industrial decay before, and always found it evocative — ugly, yet photogenic; interesting, but depressing; eerie, but highly emotive. Pyramiden, however, was off the scale in its otherworldliness, combining isolation with desolation, and certainly had the 'wow factor', worthy of an article in my employer's magazine. I felt I was an intruder in someone's imaginary Soviet townscape, almost like being on the back lot of a movie set, ready for the extras to appear *en masse* at any given moment — only, no one physically appeared.

Since we were at the shore already, we walked over to the dockside where a staithe for unloading coal in the clement summer months ran out into the ice sheet, as if still expecting colliers to call in a few weeks' time. A giant yellow crane on caterpillar tracks sat abandoned and rusting nearby in front of an enormous pile of coal which would never be shipped. A cluster of oil tanks, their paint flaking to reveal giant rust patches, had presumably in the past been full of fuel oil to replenish the bunkers of ships calling at the port so that they'd could get home with their cargoes of black gold. Nearby, a flat area with on overhead gantry crane seemed to be an outdoor warehouse of rotting mining equipment, much of it looked seized-up and crumbling under coatings of rust. In fact, the reddish-brown of rust seemed to be the pervasive colour of any metal exposed to the elements, the corrosion of the once-strong iron and steel almost a visible metaphor for the whole settlement.

To remind us of our location as we left the port area, there was a large concrete sign saying 'Pyramiden' with a red tower topped by a similarly-coloured star. We'd soon learn that Soviet symbols were ubiquitous and there was no escaping who owned the town.

Away from the coast, we headed up to the base of the mountain and a long white building that Boris described as Pyramiden's headquarters and administrative centre. Inside its dark corridors, he took us up a stairwell to an office with a panoramic view of the entire site. This, he said, had been the mine manager's office, the occupant doubling up as the local mayor. To my surprise, given he had been the villain who had cut the mine's subsidies and forced the settlement's closure, a large portrait of Boris Yeltsin hung on the office wall. A pile of yellowed *Pravda* sat on top of a gaping filing cabinet, while a copy of the last Soviet five-year plan up to 1995 was on the manager's desk, presumably never completed due to the fall of the regime four years before the end date. I felt I was in a time-warp, transported back to my childhood days when the Soviet Union was the West's bogeyman and the Cold War still threatened mutually assured destruction.

Our next tour stop was a dilapidated four-story building that had been the mine's operations centre. According to Boris, it was once the busy hub of the coal extraction from deep inside the mountain. Inconveniently, the main coal seams had been found halfway up the mountainside, and from a window Boris showed us the two narrow-gauge tram tracks, covered with wood screens and corrugated iron roofs, that ran in parallel to the mouths of the mine shafts. He told us these were the very veins and arteries of the place, carrying the life-blood of the settlement. In his analogy, one track, the artery, had been used for the miners to access their work and the other, the vein, brought coal down the mountain. Piles of spoil from the mine shafts cascaded down the mountain's steep slopes either side of the tramways, disfiguring the surface, an environmental travesty. An elevated conveyor belt at the base of the mountain had taken the coal to the port and like everything else, it now lay derelict and decayed. A large sign was set into the mountain, made of individual white letters *à la* Hollywood. It said 'Peace to the World' in Russian, according to Boris's translation. Exhortations in the same bombastic vein echoed in propaganda posters in Soviet-realism style that plastered the walls at various points, obviously designed to encourage the workforce to maximise production. Boris said that the slogan on my favourite piece of artwork proclaimed that 'Strong hands create heat and light'.

Nearby, our next stop proved to have been the miners' bathhouse, its copper plumbing now assuming a green patina and icicles hanging from the showerheads. It must have been bliss for the men to come into the bathhouse's steamy warmth after the cold ride down the mountain, and one could almost hear their banter echoing off the tiled walls as they washed the daily grime from skin made pale by the long sunless winters and their troglodyte workplace. As we stood contemplating the scene, thoughts of miners and their dirty dangerous labour made me think once more of my grandfather and his ghosts, and I shivered.

Like all of Pyramiden, the bathhouse had been supplied by electricity and heating from the power station, the next building on our tour. The large red brick building, with its two tall weathered metal chimneys and broken windows, had seen better days. Inside the spacious turbine hall, generating sets stood eerily silent, their rotors never to spin again. It was easy to imagine mechanics in overalls wandering around tinkering here and there, oilcans in hand, spanners at the ready, shouting to each other above the noise, ghosts in the machine. Boris's voice echoed of the walls and high ceiling as he reeled off impressive figures of the power station's prowess, but the one that struck me was that ten per cent of all the coal dug in Pyramiden's mines had been cannibalised just to keep the station going and the settlement alive — *hardly a recipe for economic success*, I thought. Cables and pipelines for steam snaked away from the power station under snow-covered duckboards above ground to avoid the permafrost and spread out in a tangled web across the settlement. Roads running alongside these conduits were picked out by derelict streetlamps poking out of the snow.

Moving away from the industrial zone of the settlement, we arrived at a cluster of buildings arranged around a long rectangular open space that Boris told us was the town boulevard or *prospekt*. Under the snow was a sumptuous summer lawn, grown on imported soil, we were assured. As we approached. we were dive-bombed by skuas, the aggressive seabirds screeching as they plummeted towards us. Eventually, we left their demarcated territory and Boris explained that the windowsills of the abandoned buildings nearby mimicked the cliff ledges of the birds' native habitats, and so gulls and kittiwakes, as well as the skuas, had built nests in profusion across many of the larger frontages.

Our first stop on the *prospekt* was at a large Trust Arktikugol sign which combined a polar bear, a globe and the Soviet hammer and sickle with the number '79', the site's latitude. It seemed to declare that we were on Soviet territory, so beware.

Some of the buildings around the *prospekt* were in the brutalist Soviet-style, with the corners rounded to negate the effects of the wind. Others, painted red, were more traditional wood-clad structures. The neat arrangement of all the buildings around the open space spoke of centralised planning, and I wondered if the workers and their families had been similarly regimented.

We visited 'London', the barracks used to house single men. The building — like all the others, as it turned out — was still partly furnished and had a slight mildewed musty smell. The rooms reminded me of my university halls of residence and were hardly monks' cells, their walls still decorated by busty pin-ups, while smuggled-in copies of well-thumbed *Playboy* magazines from the early 1990s sat on bedside tables, their covers stained and pages stuck together. Empty beer and vodka bottles littered the floors. Open packets of dried out Belomorkanal cigarettes lay unsmoked, their papirosa cardboard tube filters untouched by human lips. There were nicotine stains on the walls above some of the chairs and beds, testament to bored miners whiling away the hours until the next shift underground. I could almost smell the smoke. On a bedroom floor, I found some coins, one dated '1946' with the CCCP abbreviation of the Soviet Union, and a couple of others, ten and twenty kopeks, with the company logo, obviously for local use only. The evidence of sudden abandonment really hit home in all these small signs of lives lived, and together they created a spooky 'Mary Celeste' feeling for me.

More spartan than the permanent male workers' billets were a set of rooms called *gostinka*, where itinerant workers stayed, and these undecorated spaces looking more prison-like than inviting. A few rooms had mould growing up the walls where cracked windows had let in the damp and in other places the paint was flaking, all suggesting less care had been taken on the accommodation for visitors than that of permanent residents. I imagined that most of the block's clientele would have liked to get away from Pyramiden as soon as possible, job done, given the weather, the prison vibe, and the close-knit community they'd been visiting.

A smaller accommodation block named 'Paris' had been home to the settlement's single women. I found it intriguing that the accommodation blocks were named after Western cities, perhaps reflecting that life wasn't all a garden of roses under the Soviet regime and the Pyramiden residents' desire for a better life elsewhere in these fabled places when their time in the frozen north was over. I wondered what had brought young women to such a remote site to cook and clean for the miners and teach their children.

Those children had lived with their parents in a block nicknamed 'The Crazy House' which straddled the eastern end of the *prospekt's* open space. Boris explained that this name had been given to the building to reflect the madness of children running up and down the corridors, playing inside when it was too cold or dark to go outside. This building had a forlorn feel to it, the scattered evidence inside of broken furniture, the desiccated skeletons of long-dead houseplants, and even the odd photograph, forming fragmented stories of families and friends. I found the children's drawings still pinned to the walls of the family apartments particularly upsetting, thinking of their young lives, like Boris's, turned upside down when they'd been made to forcibly migrate to unknown pastures new. Strangely, one of the things I found most disconcerting was the fact that the clocks, from room to room, in the various apartments, had all stopped at different hours, as if the former occupants had been snatched at different times and spirited away.

As we emerged into the cold, after visiting the accommodation blocks, we found a herd of reindeer attempting to graze on the *prospekt*. Reindeer on Svalbard were a stunted squat short-legged version of their mainland Norway counterparts and the herd we encountered were busy pawing at the snow in an effort to expose some grass they could feed on. They ignored us completely.

Off once more, Boris took us into a blue-rendered building just south of the *prospekt*. This, he told us, was the *Stolovaya*, the communal canteen where the entire population of Pyramiden gathered to eat several times a day, there being no cooking facilities in any of the accommodation. The chairs and tables from the restaurant area had gone, revealing a beautiful herringbone parquet floor that, in my mind's eye, I saw the shades of couples gliding across in waltzes and foxtrots. A double staircase led down into the kitchen area. It was backed by a huge mosaic depicting a pastiche Arctic scene of polar bears, walruses and reindeer mixed in with trolls and other creatures. The kitchen was vast and Boris pointed out that thousands of meals has been prepared there every day. Now, it was just a museum of rusting giant mixers, walk-in fridges, hobs with burners aplenty still splattered with fat, and scales for weighing out the large quantities needed to feed an army of hungry miners and their families.

Behind the canteen, we were shown the remains of a greenhouse that, according to Boris, had been floored with soil imported from the Ukraine's rich farmland to grow fresh fruit and vegetables. Now, it looked like a vandalised glass allotment.

On our way to the next building, Boris pointed out the flat snow-covered space of the heliport with a tattered orange windsock flapping in front of a listing wooden control tower. He proudly told us that, while the Norwegians had still been going about Spitzbergen on their dog sledges, the Soviet Union had used helicopters to transport its personnel between settlements. His enthusiasm was tempered somewhat by the burnt out remains of what Jeff, as a military veteran, identified a Mil Mi-8 helicopter, and Boris had to admit to a crash twenty years earlier in which two people had died.

We then entered what I found to be the saddest building of all on the site — the schoolhouse. At its peak, the school had one hundred pupils, Boris said. We toured classrooms with blackboards, but few desks. On the teachers' tables, textbooks still lay and even though I couldn't read the titles in Cyrillic script, from the covers I worked out that history, geography, science and Russian were among the subjects taught. The rooms were gaily decorated with murals of happy children hiking in sunny landscapes with rainbows overhead that were more reminiscent of Mother Russia than the Svalbard outside the school's windows. Bizarrely, other murals depicted Disney characters and Santa Claus. *Surely not ideal images for young communists*, I thought, smiling to myself.

As I looked around at the rooms that had normally been filled with the sounds of stern teachers and chattering, laughing, singing children, my head echoed to the sound of them playing. It felt that the fire alarm had just gone off and the children had rushed out just five minutes ago, but never came back, giving the school its haunted feel.

This feeling was amplified when we came to the kindergarten where colourful building blocks, skittles and dolls lay strewn across the floor. Half a dozen little beds — for afternoon naps, I presumed — stood in a side room, tiny potties still underneath. I found the scene very poignant and thought I heard babies crying.

Back outside once more, we trooped past the tops of swings, a climbing fame and a slide poking out above the snow, more evidence of the children's presence, yet emphasising their absence, except by now, in my mind, they would always be there.

A quick visit to the abandoned hospital revealed wards of rusting bed frames and an operating theatre. As we were gathered round the operating table, we all jumped out of our skins when there was a loud banshee-like screech. It sounded as if one of the patients who had been under the knife was making a spectral comeback, but it proved to only be Jeff opening a steel cupboard whose hinges had seized. Boris showed us the maternity room and told us that this was where he'd been born. It was a nice moment and, for some reason, we all clapped. I could almost hear the cries of the newborn as I looked around and another shiver went down my spine.

Next on our itinerary, was a visit to the sports field with its small stadium of snow-covered bleachers. It was named for Yuri Gagarin, the cosmonaut who had been the first man in space. Under the snow, Boris assured us was a running track and a football pitch, with the latter the venue for the local derby against fellow Soviet citizens from Barentsburg, and international matches against the Norwegians from Longyearbyen. He said similar ice hockey matches had been played on the settlement's ice rink, down near the port.

Beside the stadium, he took us into the splendid remains of the swimming pool building. Inside, Boris made us look upwards at its beautiful roof of Karelian birch, before pointing down at the twenty-five metre pool lined with tiles, blue on its floor and white on the surround. Long side windows let in the weak sunlight, and we could see benches beside the pool for spectators to cheer on competitors in swimming galas and water polo matches. It was the noise of that excitement which filled my brain, and I wondered at how visual images were triggering such aural sensations in my mind. Even if I couldn't see them, I was beginning to hear ghosts everywhere. Changing rooms, showers and steam rooms completed the bathing complex, which, to me, was the most impressive of all the buildings we had visited so far.

However, adjacent to the pool house was what Boris claimed was Pyramiden's highlight, the Cultural Palace. The building was fronted by the statue of Lenin, who gazed sightlessly out over the *prospekt* and the fjord beyond. The centre's foyer was light and airy, with a sweeping staircase to the upper floor. Boris led us to a small theatre-come-cinema, complete with plush red seats, some motheaten and some ripped, but nevertheless conveying a sense of luxury. A memory from a television programme in my distant past came to mind, and I conjured up the Red Army Choir belting out the 'Volga Boatmen's Song' from the little stage in front of us. Behind the auditorium, we were shown the cinematography room. Beside the two big projectors were cans of film. The only Russian film I'd seen was 'Battleship Potemkin' and I wondered if any of the film cans with their Cyrillic titles held the classic. As I looked through the stack, I couldn't help but smile when I found 'Forrest Gump' and 'Jurassic Park' in English. Another room was a library of largely empty shelves, which, being a bibliophile, I found quite depressing.

As we wandered along to the corridors, more romanticised Soviet workers gazed down at us from posters, all triumphant, young, handsome and strong. These were interspersed with murals lauding the heroes of the Great Patriotic War under the omnipresent red star. I knew that millions of Soviet citizens had died in that war, but noted that the millions killed in Stalin's *pogroms* didn't get a mention in the battle to encourage Pyramiden's inhabitants to be good citizens. I supposed that their ghosts had never made it this far north.

In the sports hall, we walked on to a yellow wooden sprung floor, and it seemed that no expense had been spared to make the Cultural Palace the centre of the community. While one side of the hall had full-length windows, the other had wall bars. At each end was a basketball hoop, while five-a-side goalposts with torn netting stood ready for a game that would never happen. A disembowelled vaulting horse still awaited budding gymnasts beside beams and a set of parallel bars. A pile of rotting smelly trainers lay under a huge timetable of daily activities. Weight machines in wooden frames were in a corner beside dumbbells and a sagging medicine ball, ready for the strongmen that now wouldn't visit. No doubt the settlement's young men came here with visions of playing for Spartak Moscow or Dynamo Kiev, winning European glory, and I wondered if any of them had ever made it. In my mind, I heard their shouts and swearing at goals scored and saves made. Boris told us the sports facilities even included a firing range in the basement to ensure Pyramiden's citizens could defend themselves against not only polar bears, but, if necessary, foreign troops. Jeff nodded knowingly at this news.

On the upper floor, a series of large rooms formed a set of music and dance studios. One had a wall of mirrors with a barre for nascent ballerinas. This time, I wondered how many little girls had stood there in their leotards and tutus dreaming of joining the Bolshoi. A room carpeted in ditched sheet music held what Boris claimed to be the world's most northerly keyboard instrument, the Red October Piano. As Jeff tinkled the keys, it was clearly well out of tune. An abandoned drum kit sat nearby, its skins kicked out, and, on an adjacent chair, an accordion was fanned out, the bellows gutted. A stringless balalaika with a broken neck completed the instruments, and we all agreed that collectively they formed a sorry little collection. My mind played tricks again, as I imagined a little ghostly ensemble in the room playing some vodka-fuelled jazz, having a laugh, and encouraging each other's riffs and scales.

The last room we visited had been the meeting place of Komsomol, the Soviet communist equivalent of the Boy Scouts and Girl Guides, although, in the pictures I'd seen, and given they were driven by a political ideology, I thought of them as more Hitler Youth. Apart from some posters on the wall of striving youths with chiselled features looking into the distance and a dusty red flag, the room was empty. Boris said that it hadn't really been used since the fall of the Soviet Union, the youths encouraged to take up sports and other activities instead.

After we'd exited the Cultural Palace, Boris gave us some welcome news. "I can see you are all a little cold. Time for some lunch and a drink to warm you up."

Boris led us back down the *prospekt* to one of the most unusual bars I've ever been in. The walls were made of bottles in a striped pattern of green and clear glass with occasional brown stars. The semi-transparency let in the spring sunlight to reveal Irina standing behind a bar with glasses and bottles at the ready and trays of food heated by little burners underneath.

"There are over five thousand bottles in the walls. So, let's empty a few in case any repairs are needed in the future," said Boris, laughing. "We have a choice of vodka for you. Rossiya or Privet? And to help absorb the alcohol, Irina has prepared some delicious *tefteli* meatballs."

As I sipped my first ice-cold vodka, freezing on the tongue, burning on the throat, I looked around in amazement at the bizarre testament of human ingenuity and alcoholism, a pairing that sometimes seemed to go hand-in-hand. There must have been a lot of bored miners to be bothered to take on such a weird DIY project, I decided. Irina came over and poured more clear liquid into my shot glass, and then we all shouted "*Nostrovia!*" and downed our drinks in a oner. Somewhere, deep in my brain, a little voice told me that drinking too much alcohol was not wise in sub-zero temperatures as it thinned the blood, but peer-pressure prevailed, and I took yet another glass, before repeating the process several more times. Unlike Irina's other offerings, I found the meatballs were indeed delicious, although I worried the alcohol may have numbed my taste buds.

Under the influence of the vodka, my mind drifted again. As a child, ghost towns had meant dusty Wild West settlements of wooden buildings, the only sounds being saloon doors creaking gently and rusting tin roofs flapping in the breeze, the only movement that of coils of tumbleweed rolling aimlessly along Main Street on a trip to nowhere. Such places had usually been abandoned when the Mother Lode had run out, so, from that standpoint, they did indeed have something in common with my current location. For such 'ghost towns', the towns themselves were the ghosts, but in Pyramiden, that wasn't the case. The former inhabitants were the ghosts, in my mind, even though they had never died, and it was, for me, a 'town of ghosts', not a 'ghost town'. The whole experience was surreal.

My reverie was interrupted by Belinda coming to sit beside me.

"You saw them too, didn't you? I could see by your face," she said, her voice a low conspiratorial whisper.

"Saw who?" I asked, surprised by her question.

"The children."

"Actually, I didn't see them, I heard them," I admitted.

"Interesting how the human brain plays tricks," said Belinda, looking thoughtful. "I saw children, plain as day, but you heard them. We were both hallucinating, of course. Me, visually, you, aurally."

"What do you mean?"

"Sometimes we hallucinate due to very strong emotions or suggestive forces — that's why people see visions of God, or hear His voice. In this case, I believe we were stimulated by the pathos of the abandoned school and feeling sorrow for the children being displaced.

Women particularly hallucinate about children. Or, since the brain is a predictive machine, given everything still looked ready to be used, our brains *predicted* that we *should* see and/or hear children. In any event, we both felt their spirits were still there, like shades and spectres — ghosts, almost." Then she stopped and looked at me quizzically. "Of course, all this is assuming you're not on drugs or have mental health problems."

"No, neither. How come you know so much about this?"

"I studied psychology at university. That's why I went into HR. My degree seemed a good fit for understanding leadership and workers' problems. Instead, it was all payroll, unions and pensions."

"I thought I was deluding myself that I could hear things. And it wasn't only in the school, but elsewhere too."

"A delusion is a false belief, a hallucination is a false perception, so what we experienced was definitely the latter."

"What about Dick? Did he feel it too?"

Belinda laughed and said, "Dick has the emotional intelligence of a snowman, my dear. I'd no more admit to him that I'd been having hallucinations than I'd tell him about my fantasies concerning Jeff."

Now it was my turn to laugh. "And are you having fantasies about Jeff?"

Belinda tapped her nose and winked at me before heading off to find Irina and her bottles. I didn't have the heart to tell her of Jeff's sexual preference.

"Now, at Olga's request, we are going on a little side trip away from the main campus," Boris said, as we left the bottle bar, some of the crowd staggering a little, others giggling. The giggling stopped when Boris told us our next destination — the cemetery.

Boris led us to a building that looked like a small aircraft hangar and pulled aside its entrance doors to reveal a red Toyota pick-up truck sitting on flat tyres beside a bright yellow tracked vehicle with 'Vityaz' emblazoned across the front and rust patches all over its cabin. We were informed that this was a Russian-made snowcat.

"The cemetery is too far to walk to and it's on an island in the middle of the braided streams west of the town. We'll take this instead of your snowmobiles as the ice on the streams is too thin.

Luckily, the waters are not too deep, so this beast will get us there safely."

Thankfully, Boris seemed unaffected by the number of vodka shots he'd downed, otherwise I'd have been worried about his drunk-driving across water, snow and ice in what looked like an outdated and ill-maintained Soviet-era castoff.

We started our journey on a snow-covered road of sorts and headed towards a large low yellow building with '1972' in big letters on one gable. We stopped, but didn't get out, and Boris explained that we were looking at the settlement's collective farm. He added that chickens, pigs and dairy cattle had been kept to provide fresh meat to supplement locally-caught fish and the vegetables grown in the greenhouse we'd seen earlier. These all contributed to the spirit of self-sufficiency that the local management wanted to engender, despite the far-flung location.

Further into our trip, we careered off the road. The off-piste snowcat ride from then on was more roller-coaster than Rolls-Royce as we bumped and skidded our way to a small plot outlined by the points of a picket-fence sticking out of the snow. Inside the plot, a number of narrow concrete pylons emerged from the white like periscopes, each with a red star on top. It seemed there was no room for crosses, not even of the Russian Orthodox variety, in a Soviet graveyard.

After we all got off the snowcat, Boris pulled out a plan of the cemetery and showed us that there had been over forty funerals during Pyramiden's existence, including five children and three women. The others, he said, had all been male miners in their twenties and thirties, mostly killed in accidents. Under our feet, he told us, were concrete tombs, as the bodies would otherwise have been pushed out of their graves by swelling permafrost. The concrete also protected the dead from passing carnivores. After consulting his plan, Boris led Olga to her brother's grave, wading through the snow to her sibling's plot. The rest of us stayed at a respectful distance. Our silence was interrupted by a shout of "Over here!" from Parvati.

She was standing beside a pylon under which the snow had been disturbed, exposing a cracked concrete slab. Underneath, a broken coffin lay empty.

"Probably some damned Arctic fox or polar bear got in after the concrete cracked due to the cold weather. The bloody foxes are always digging up my roses at home if I put a bit of bonemeal or dried blood around them," said Dick, staring down at the messy site.

Trine had gone very pale under her weather-beaten tan. "Maybe it's a *gjenganger*," she whispered.

"A what?" asked Jeff.

Trine frowned and then said, "I think the English word is 'revenant'."

"Someone who comes back from the grave, you mean?" asked Parvati. "Like a zombie or a vampire?"

"Or a *fantasma*, a ghost." Valentina whispered, before shivering.

"Stuff and nonsense!" exclaimed Dick. "There's no such thing as ghosts," he added, before muttering, "They're so excitable these Italians. Honestly!"

No ghosts? I thought. *Your wife and I have been seeing and hearing them all day.*

When Boris came over to our group after leaving Olga to pay her respects, he seemed quite spooked by the open grave, crossed himself, and ushered us back on to the snowcat. As soon as a weeping Olga climbed on board, we were off, and I was sure that we were all glad to be heading back to the relative warmth of the hotel and a coffee followed by a hot shower.

As darkness began to fall, I decided I'd go out to complete my assignment by trying for some photographs of the Aurora Borealis, the Northern Lights. Although we'd enjoyed daylight earlier, I'd learned that Svalbard endured a long grey twilight before it got properly dark, so I waited until after dinner to venture out, knowing that the best time for the aurora to appear was after nine, and that closer to midnight was best. In Longyearbyen, there had been too much light pollution in the safe areas, and in Ny Ålesund the sky had been too cloudy. However, during our tour earlier that day, the sky had been clear, and it looked like this had persisted into the night, so I had high hopes that the conditions would allow long-exposure shots should the aurora appear. I knew that photographing the phenomenon under a full moon would be tricky, but I'd read that if solar activity was high, I was likely to get some extraordinary shots since the foreground would be lit and the background sky would be a darker blue or black.

Given I was carrying a tripod in addition to my trusty Nikon, plus a bag of lenses, I decided to take a pistol instead of a rifle with me, to ease my burden. I wasn't sure I could hit a barn door with a firearm, but I hoped the noise would frighten off any prowling polar bears. There was nobody about as I left the hotel, so I put a scribbled note beside the gun register stating my intentions. I added a head-torch to my insulated ensemble and set off for the *prospekt* and the platform beside Lenin's statue. I hoped that the platform's height above the town would give me enough elevation to see moonlight reflecting off the glacier on the opposite side of the fjord, adding drama to my shots. As I trudged up the hill, my way was lit by the moon over my shoulder and my torch. The reindeer had gone to wherever reindeer go at night. There was near silence across the town and the only sound was from my feet crunching on the snow, an ice crust having formed under the clear night sky when the temperature had plummeted.

I felt confident to be out on my own, despite all the dire warnings about polar bears. I had, after all, survived encounters with over-friendly greyback gorillas in Uganda, ravenous hyena packs in Kenya, and a bloat of hippos on a river in Botswana, so a bear was, to me, just one more predator to add to that list. Truth be told, I was almost hoping to meet one and get some wildlife photographs to supplement the rusting ironwork and snowy landscapes that currently dominated my portfolio from the trip.

As I walked, I sang an old Scottish folk song my grandfather had taught me at his knee.

The Northern Lights o' Auld Aberdeen,
Mean home sweet home tae me,
The Northern Lights o' Aberdeen,
Are all I long tae see.

After setting up beside Lenin, and doing my little jig, I was still frozen despite my multiple layers. Since the magnetosphere hadn't started its light show, I decided to go for a prowl inside the Cultural Palace behind me, thinking I'd to get some moody interior shots lit by moonbeams streaming through the windows. I unlatched my camera from the tripod and tried to get in through the main door, but it was locked. I remembered then that Boris had locked each building on our tour after we'd exited. He'd said it was to keep out vandals coming over from Longyearbyen on their snowmobiles, or his compatriots from Barentsburg sailing over to purloin souvenirs since Soviet-made stuff was more durable than modern Russian trash. Looking along the building, my head-torch caught the glint of a window half-open, and I managed to climb in through it.

I wandered along a corridor into the gym, expecting its tall windows would do the trick of providing enough light to shoot by. As I looked around for a suitable composition, I heard strange screeching noises and saw an upturned wooden box start to move across the floor towards me. My heart skipped a beat, I could feel the hairs on my arms and the back of my neck rising, and I almost wet myself. My mind, filled with daytime ghosts and empty graves, jumped to one conclusion — a poltergeist! Neither the fight or flight instinct seemed to kick in, and I was transfixed, my head-torch illuminating the box like a wartime searchlight. The box got closer and closer, seeming to hover over the wooden floor, the weird noises emanating from it increasing in volume. As it skittered towards me, it hit one leg of the vaulting horse and the box turned over. From inside it, two Arctic fox cubs took one look at me along the torch beam before they skedaddled out the gym still screeching as they went. I breathed a huge sigh of relief. Then I heard a shot fired.

My confidence about handling prowling carnivores evaporated on hearing the shot. Scared to be out on my own with a polar bear on the loose, I clambered out of the window and headed down the *prospekt*, back in the direction of the hotel as fast as I could manage in my thermal suit and snow-boots, leaving my tripod and lens bag behind. As I passed the school, in the bright moonlight, I noticed a figure lying in the snow. I went over and found Dick, rifle in hand, his pale face contorted like Munch's 'Scream'. He was dead. A bloody trail revealed what had happened to Belinda, obviously dragged off by their attacker. I hoped that the poor woman's end had been swift. I gathered my breath and then headed on towards the hotel.

As I half-ran, half-walked, out of the corner of my eye, I thought I saw movement in the gap between the canteen and one of barrack blocks. I knew it couldn't be the bear, for it would be busy devouring poor Belinda. I paused. An indistinct shape floated back across the gap, making no sound whatsoever. I reversed course, not wanting to meet whatever it was. I caught another glimpse of movement and ran over to the schoolhouse. I tried to get in, but the door was locked, and I cursed Boris and the souvenir-hunters that had caused him to secure it. In my panic, I ran off down the side of the school, and then realised I was heading away from the main settlement. I turned and caught hints of something silently following me like a menacing shadow. It was too big to be an Arctic fox, the wrong shape for a reindeer, and if it wasn't the feasting bear, I couldn't think of an animal that fitted the bill. In my terror-filled mind, the only thing I could think of was a ghost.

I tried to run faster, but, despite an adrenaline rush, I was hampered by my bulky outfit and oversized footwear. I saw a low building in front of me, illuminated by the moonlight. The farm! The roller door at its end was open and I went inside. I desperately pulled on the chain beside the opening, but it hadn't been oiled for years and rust had taken its toll. The door stubbornly refused to budge. I told myself that it didn't matter anyway, as ghosts could float through man-made barriers. I moved further into the building to avoid my approaching nemesis, unsure of its spectral powers to detect my shaking whimpering frame.

Plunging deeper into the farm's interior, my head-torch light bouncing off the walls, I ran past stalls still caked with manure and hay and stumbled over half-empty feeding troughs filled with mouldy God-knows-what. One decade on since their removal, the whole place still stank of animals and their shit. By now, I could hear the ghoul that was chasing me crashing about inside the building, obviously angry and looking for someone to vent on. I turned into a side room, my heartbeat pounding in my ears, and I knew I was in danger of hyperventilating. My head-torch showed the space was fully lined, floor to ceiling, in blue tiles, with stainless steel tables in the middle of the room, and little channels cut into the concrete floor. On the walls were racks of choppers and big knives. Butcher hooks hung from a rail above me. Now I understood what the channels were for – blood! I was in the slaughterhouse. Gruesome images from 'Texas Chainsaw Massacre' flashed through my brain, and I knew I had to get out.

In desperation, I looked around for an exit away from where I could hear the phantom approaching, but I couldn't see one. There was deathly quiet for a few moments and I backed against the wall furthest from the doorway. Then my torch lit up the opening. It was filled with the most enormous white figure. This was no hallucination, this was real. It took me a few seconds to process that I wasn't looking at a ghost after all, but a giant polar bear — Igor!

I now truly understood the word petrified, for I felt turned to stone, unable to move, incapable of even crying out. I also knew what was meant by visceral fear, my mind filled with deep, instinctive terror. I could have turned off my torch in an effort to hide, but Boris had warned us of the bear's good night vision and enhanced sense of smell, so there didn't seem much point. The only sound in the room was the echo of Igor's grunts from the tiled walls as he stood swaying, sizing me up. He dropped down on to all-fours and looked like he was gathering himself for an attack. I pulled the pistol from my pocket, but found my gloved finger was too thick to fit through the trigger guard. By now, Igor's head was moving from side to side, his ears went back, and he growled, showing an alarming array of teeth. I tore off my glove and managed to find the trigger. I pulled with all my might, a shot went off, the bullet ricocheted around the room but went nowhere near the bear. The noise and flash had no effect on Igor whatsoever and he started to move slowly towards me. I was trapped and I was going to die.

When Igor was about five metres away, I felt a jolt go through my body, like an electric shock. My hair stood on end and a shiver ran down my back. Beside me, a man had appeared. He was dressed in a miner's overall, his face black with coal dust, a helmet on his head, and in his hands, he held a pickaxe. Without fear, he charged at the bear, swinging the pickaxe. Igor almost bowed down in front of the man, let out a squeal, and turned tail, fleeing the slaughterhouse. I had never felt so relieved in all my life, and collapsed against the wall.

I looked up at my saviour standing over me, smiling. "Thank you, thank you, thank you," I said, then realised he must be one of the Russian hotel staff, and I dragged out, "*Spasibo, spasibo*," from my memory. He didn't say anything, just stood there, smiling at me.

I got up, dropped the pistol, lest he thought I was going to shoot him and held up my camera instead. I tried my broken Russian once more. "May I take your picture, *pazhalusta*, please?"

He smiled some more, so I flipped up the flash and let off a few shots. He winced at the flash, then smiled again and waved to me before turning and walking off after the bear. "*Do svidaniya*, goodbye," I whispered.

I followed him out of the slaughterhouse, questions about him cascading through my brain and I decided to catch him up. Then my head-torch battery gave out. I felt my way past the smelly animal stalls until I saw the main door. I froze. A tall broad silhouette was framed in green light, filling the open space. The menacing figure glided silently towards me like a dark wraith. The revenant! I screamed, and then everything went black.

I knew I was dead. I was floating on my back over snow. Above me, shape-shifting curtains and pulsating spirals of green light danced in the heavens against an indigo sky, the spirits of angels come to take me with them.

"Shit!" said a voice, interrupting my divine vision. "Almost dropped you."

I found I could turn my head, so I did. I was being carried by Jeff.

"I'm not dead," I said, and then began laughing.

"Nope, but you're damned lucky. Two bears were spotted earlier prowling around. One of them cornered Dick and Belinda. Dick must have been trying to protect her and managed to get off a shot, but then he died of a heart-attack. The bear took her. We found her body. It wasn't a pretty sight."

"Why did you come after me?"

"We heard the first shot in the hotel, and Boris, Trine and I came out, all armed. We saw your note and knew you were out someplace, along with the two old folks. We found them first, then spread out to try and find you. I saw footprints heading in the direction of the farm, so I came over this way. I heard a second shot, so I ran over lickety-split. The aurora and snow means you can see a ways and I wasn't far off when I saw a big ol' bear come haring out the farm. You must have really scared him. He was in a hell of a hurry, that's for sure."

"I think it was Igor. It wasn't me that frightened him. It was the miner."

"Miner? What miner?"

"Didn't you see him?"

"I didn't see nobody. Only the bear. Here we are at the hotel. Let's get you inside. You're a bit delirious."

Inside the hotel, we passed the foyer where Dick and Belinda lay side-by-side covered with a tarpaulin. Jeff carried me into the lounge and put me down on a settee. Boris, Trine and the remnants of our party came in, all with worried looks on their faces that turned to relief when they saw me.

I recounted what had happened, my flight, my being cornered in the slaughterhouse, and my saviour turning up in the nick of time to attack Igor with his pickaxe.

"He must have been one of your staff, Boris," I suggested. "Can you get them to come here, I'd like to thank him properly."

"My staff? But none of my staff were out. We checked before coming to investigate the shots."

"You must be wrong. Maybe you'll recognise him," I said and reached for my camera. I flipped on the monitor at the back and flicked through my last set of photographs. Much to my consternation, all that I had recorded were a series of images from inside the slaughterhouse showing the butcher hooks and knives, along with a bright blob where the flash had bounced off the tiled walls.

I was confused. "That's funny. I took his picture, I'm certain, but there's nobody in the photographs. There was a miner, I swear. I don't understand."

Boris looked at the screen and then at me. He smiled. "Did you forget, Samantha? I told you at the beginning, Pyramiden is a *gorod prizrakov* — a ghost town!"

Afterword

Roo B. Doo

Well well, Dear Reader. Now that you've consumed this enormous anthology, I hope you've left a little room for the Afterword. I promise you, it's wafer thin.

With all the madness going on in the world, I've turned to Jesus for help. Seriously, have a prayer...

Our Starmer
Now Labour's in power
Shallow be his game
The time has now come
The UK's undone
What on Earth! He brings depression
We can just about afford our daily bread
As he takes away our bus passes
And gives them to those who trespass in small boats
And lead us not in prosperity
But deliver us from energy
For now it's his kingdom
Power hungry for glory
It's the same old story
Sausages

About the Authors

Jane Nightshade

Jane Nightshade is a former corporate writer turned horror, sci-fi, and crime fiction writer. Her non-fiction writing about horror and crime film and television has appeared online at Horrornews.net, Horrified Magazine, and Ghouls Magazine.

Her fiction has appeared or will appear in twenty-five+ anthologies, magazines and podcasts, including FlameTree for print and NoSleep for podcasts.

She is the author of A Scream Full of Ghosts, a single-author story collection from Dark Ink Books, and The Drowning Game, A Novella of the Supernatural, available in digital form on Amazon. She is also editor of and contributor to the anthology Jane Nightshade's Serial Encounters, from Hellbound Books. Her second collection of single-author short stories, Ghosts Never Leave, will be published in 2025.

Stephen Johnson

Stephen Johnson is a retired Naval Officer, husband, father, and Chihuahua dad serving 22 years on four different ships over his career. His first novel, **The Fizz Prophecy**, is available in paperback and hardcover on Amazon. He has also published **Terror Tales from the Bluff City** trilogy. The series is based on short science fiction horror stories from his hometown of Memphis and can also be found on Amazon based on the witch doctor Madame Marguerite focused on Beale Street and the Peabody hotel.

His short stories appear in anthologies from Scare Street's **Night Terrors** Volume 8 and 17, No Bad Books' **Released**, Breaking Rules Europe's **Death Ship**, and Ink'd Publishing's **Hidden Villains**. His Drabbles have appeared in publications from Macabre Ladies, Black Hare Press, Brilliant Flash Fiction, Raven and Drake, Crow's Feet Journal, Ghost Orchid Press, Black Ink Fiction, and Iron Faerie Publishing.

Ian Caswell

Ian is a nondescript, near pensioner, who lives with his wife in Bangor, Co. Down. In his past he has had more jobs than anyone could reasonably shake a stick at, from motorcycle couriering during the Northern Irish troubles, an apprenticeship as a trainee auctioneer, melon farming in the Negev desert, and a year or so spent making leather goods. He has also written for motorcycle magazines based both in the UK and the US. Following a period when he eventually wised up and knuckled down, Ian now works in IT.

L.N. Hunter

L.N. Hunter's comic fantasy novel, *The Feather and the Lamp* (Three Ravens Publishing), sits alongside works in anthologies such as *Best of British Science Fiction 2022* and *Ghostly*, as well as several issues of Short Édition's *Short Circuit* and the *Horrifying Tales of Wonder* podcast. There have also been papers in the IEEE *Transactions on Neural Networks*, which are probably somewhat less relevant and definitely less entertaining. When not writing, L.N. occasionally masquerades as a software developer or can be found unwinding in a disorganised home in Carlisle, UK, along with two cats and a soulmate.

https://linktr.ee/l.n.hunter
https://www.facebook.com/L.N.Hunter.writer

Jim Mountfield

Jim Mountfield was born in Northern Ireland, brought up there and in Scotland, and has lived and worked in many other places since then. He currently resides in Singapore. He is the author of over 100 short stories published, sometimes pseudonymously, in various magazines, newspapers, webzines and anthologies and he blogs regularly at www.bloodandporridge.co.uk/wp/.

Nicola Lombardi / Joe Weintraub

Nicola Lombardi has published in Italy the novels *The Gypsy Spiders, Black Mother, Night Calls, The Red Bed, The Tank,* and *i*, as well as seven collections of stories since 1989. In addition, he has published novelizations from the films of Dario Argento (*Profondo Rosso* and *Suspiria*) and translated works by Jack Ketchum, Seabury Quinn, Charlee Jacob, F.B.Long and many others for the Italian market. In 2021 UK's Tartarus Press published his collection *The Gypsy Spiders and Other Tales of Italian Horror*. Full bibliography at www.nicolalombardi.com.

J. Weintraub's work includes fiction, essays, translations, poetry along with over 50 dramatic works produced in the USA, Australia, India, and New Zealand. His translation of Eugène Briffault's classic gastronomic text *Paris à table: 1846* was published by Oxford University Press. More at: https://jweintraub.weebly.com/

Mark Ellott

Mark Ellott is a part time motorcycle instructor, delivering training for students who require compulsory basic training and direct access courses. He has semi-retired from his main job as a freelance trainer and assessor working primarily in the rail industry, delivering track safety training and assessment as well as providing consultancy services in competence management.

He writes fiction in his spare time. Mostly, his fiction consists of short stories crossing a range of genres, and has stories in all but one of the previous Underdog Anthologies – and now in this one.

His first five novels, 'Ransom', 'Rebellion', 'Resolution' 'Reiver' and 'Renegade' are now available in print and eBook formats. Hardback copies are in the works too.

He has also published two volumes of his own short stories, entitled 'Blackjack' and 'A Moment in Time' as well as a collection of Morning Cloud Western stories entitled 'Sinistré, The Morning Cloud Chronicles'.

https://legironbooks.co.uk/about-the-authors/mark-ellott/

Bill Diamond

Bill Diamond is a curious traveler. He lives in Colorado where the Rocky Mountains are both an inspiration and a distraction. He writes to try and figure it all out.

Lee Bidgood

Lee Bidgood currently resides in the south-east of England. He used to work in the UK civil service but was given the opportunity to lose his job and save the country some money. Now free, however, he is expected to make a full recovery.

Lee's work has appeared in 'Treeskull Stories', 'The Good, the Bad and Santa', the third and fourth Underdog Anthologies and again in Underdog Anthology 18, 'The Hole in the Veil'.

https://legironbooks.co.uk/about-the-authors/anthology-authors/lee-bidgood/

Gary Thomson

The author lives and writes in Ontario. He has spooked readers – and himself – with short fiction in *Horla Horror, Pulp Modern Flash, AgnesandTrue*, among others. He seeks calm by riffing Beatles and blues on his Hohner harmonica.

Daniel Royer

Daniel Royer is a writer of short fiction. He is a California State University, Bakersfield graduate with an English Degree he's not using. Royer works as a full-time welder to support his true passion, which is tomahawk-throwing. His stories have been printed by Ponahakeola Press, SFReader.com, The Sirens Call Publications, Drunken Pen Writing, and some other outlets you've never heard of. He used to have cats.

https://legironbooks.co.uk/about-the-authors/anthology-authors/daniel-royer/

Greg Patrick

A dual citizen of Ireland and the states, Greg is an Irish/Armenian traveler poet and the son of a Navy man. Also, a son of the Traveling People, he is a former Humanitarian aid worker who worked with great horses for years. He loves the wilds of Connemara and Galway in the rain where he has written many stories. Greg spent his youth in the South Pacific and Europe and currently resides in Galway, Krakow, and sometimes the states. He now writes and travels.

Jason Battle

Jason Battle knows that monsters do exist. They are much worse than any imagined by Stephen King, Mary Shelley, or any contained within these pages. Jason writes non-fiction by day and fiction by night outside Chicago where he resides with his beautiful and patient wife and imaginative son. Jason has been published in multiple non-fiction scientific and medical journals, short story anthologies and online fiction publications.

Fay Jekyll

Fay is a psychological thriller author, currently working on her debut novel.

She enjoys nothing more than a humorous or sinister twist in a good tale.

Outside of creating short stories, Fay enjoys winding up her pet cat, visiting art galleries and writing in third person.

Austin Muratori

Austin is a writer, photographer and filmmaker from a small town in Michigan. When he isn't telling stories or creating, he can be found enjoying a Coca-Cola and spending time with his 4 year old son.

Facebook:
https://www.facebook.com/austin.muratori?mibextid=ZbWKwL
Instagram:
https://www.instagram.com/am_news_dude?igsh=MWh1c2plbXY2b2lnZw==

Bernardo Villela

Bernardo Villela has short fiction included in periodicals such as *LatineLit* and in anthologies such as *There's More of Us Than You Know*. He's had original poetry published by *Exist Otherwise* among others and translations published by *AzonaL and Red Fern Review*. You can find some of his other works here: https://linktr.ee/bernardovillela.

Bill Freas

Studying under esteemed writers Sonny Sykes and Charles McClelland, Bill Freas continued his education at West Chester University before he was hired in 2002 as the head writer of a TBS sketch-comedy pilot that ultimately did not make it to series. Subsequently, he optioned or sold over two dozen scripts, which included shorts, features, and pilots. As an author, he has written more than twenty published short stories, including three full collections. His produced credits as a writer span multiple genres and mediums. Currently, Bill also heads up Oceaniacom Films' development department, where he oversees the development of US and international film and TV projects for the Australian company. Along with script, development, and production consultation, Bill is also a staff writer for Vancouver production company Foresight Entertainment, with which he has had an active partnership for over fifteen years.

Chris Blinn

Christopher Blinn lives in Marshfield Massachusetts with his wife and three sons where he has worked for the Massachusetts Bay Transportation Authority for the past twenty-six years. He is the author of several short stories, the most recent being One Night in Roswell in Knight Writing Press, 'What Really Happened' and 'Rodent Independence Day' in Three Cousins Publishing 'The Trouble with Time'.

Ginger Strivelli

I have written for Marion Zimmer Bradley's Fantasy Magazine, Autism Parenting Magazine, Flash Fiction Magazine, Third Flatiron, Silver Blade, Greenprints, Solarpunk Magazine, several other magazines, and several anthology books.

Katherine Kerestman

Katherine Kerestman (B.A. English and History, John Carroll University; M. A. English, Case Western Reserve University) is the author of *Lethal* (Psychotoxin Press, 2023), *Creepy Cat's Macabre Travels: Prowling around Haunted Towers, Crumbling Castles, and Ghoulish Graveyards* (WordCrafts Press, 2020), and *Haunted House and Other Strange Tales* (Hippocampus Press, 2024), as well as the co-editor (with S. T. Joshi) of *The Weird Cat* (WordCrafts Press, 2023) and *Shunned Houses: An Anthology of Weird Stories, Unspeakable Poems, and Impious Essays* (WordCrafts Press, 2024). More than 60 of her Lovecraftian and gothic poems, essays, and short stories have been featured in *Black Wings VII*, *Penumbra*, *Journ-E*, *Spectral Realms*, *Illumen*, *Retro-Fan*, *Dissections*, *Off-Course*, *Lovecraftiana* and other discerning publications. Katherine thinks *Dracula* and *Wuthering Heights* are the greatest books ever written, and is wild about *Dark Shadows* and *Twin Peaks*. Her name is etched among the inscrutable glyphs of the Esoteric Order of Dagon and the Dracula Society. Interested parties may stalk her at www.creepycatlair.com

Mark Dozier

I earned a Master's Degree in Creative Writing at the University of Florida and have had a short story published in the *Mississippi Review*. I was the associate editor of *Multi Images*, a photography magazine and served as the Teachers Workshop Coordinator at the National Geographic Society's headquarters in Washington, D. C. In addition, I taught in the United States, as well as in the Singapore American School and in Sierra Leone.

K.T. Booker

K. T. Booker (they/them) lives and works in Northern California and writes strange stories and poems when they have free time. They have published or are forthcoming in Tales from the Crosstimbers, Witch House, and Whetstone Magazine, among others. You can reach them on X at @KTBookerWriter.

Paul Northgraves

Born and raised in Kingston Upon Hull. Started writing stories this year at the age of 38.

Spends his spare time writing stories and reading horror books.

Love sports. Season pass holder at Hull City AFC and rugby league team Hull FC and plays baseball for the Hull Scorpions.

Lives with Marie, my partner of ten years.

Kelly Piner

Kelly Piner is a Clinical Psychologist who in her free time, tends to feral cats and searches for Bigfoot in nearby forests. Her writing is inspired by Rod Serling's *Twilight Zone. Most recently,* Ms. Piner's story, "Euthanasia," was chosen as *The Best of 2023* by *After Dinner Conversation.* Her short stories have appeared in *Litro Magazine, Scarlet Leaf Review, Dragon Soul Press, The Last Girl's Club/Wicked News, Rebellion Lit Review, The Chamber Magazine, Drunken Pen Writing, Lit Shark Magazine, The Literary Hatchet, Weirdbook, Written Tales and others.* Her stories have also appeared in multiple anthologies.

Robert Bagnall

Robert Bagnall was born in Bedford, England, in 1970, and stood for parliament for the Green Party in 2024. He has written for the BBC, national newspapers, and government ministers. Five of his stories have been selected for the annual 'Best of British Science Fiction' anthologies. He is the author of sci-fi thriller '2084 - The Meschera Bandwidth' and two anthologies, each of which collects 24 of his ninety-odd published stories. He can be contacted via his blog at meschera.blogspot.com.

Tanya Delanor

Tanya Delanor is a huge fan of graphic novels, cheese and tomato pizza, and Dr. Strangelove. But not necessarily together! Her work has appeared in Independent Persons Press, Poem Hunter, January Ember Press, Tigershark, and Pure Slush. Tanya writes stories of dreamworlds with an eye on reality. She is currently working on a story about two dragons pulling Earth as a chariot towards the stars. But that is another story for another day.

S.W. Duffy

I am a retired Professor of Cancer Screening, spending much of my free time writing fiction. In the past, I mainly wrote short stories. These have mainly had supernatural themes and have often had the setting of the great and mysterious city of London, where I lived for some years and worked for many more. Leg Iron Books has published many of these stories, for which I will be eternally grateful. When not writing, I do a lot of running, martial arts training, boozing and crossword puzzles. With the recent expansion of my free time, I have moved into writing full length novels. We'll see how that goes. Once again, my deepest thanks to Leg Iron Books for providing an outlet for my stories over the years.

https://legironbooks.co.uk/about-the-authors/anthology-authors/stephen-w-duffy/

Yvonne Lang

Yvonne's work has featured in a range of publications, from Your Cat Magazine to Siren's Call, as well as ranking highly in competitions. Her flash has featured on Trembling with Fear, 101 words and Fairfield Scribes. Her work has been published in anthologies by Café Lit, Knight Writing, Three Cousins, Black Hare Press and Schlock with her debut horror novelette featuring as part of Demain's Short Sharp Shock Series. She resides in Yorkshire with her husband where she writes down her weird thoughts despite appearing more or less normal on the outside.

website: (I am not on social media) www.yvonnelang.co.uk

Max Jason Peterson

Max Jason Peterson (maxjasonpeterson.wordpress.com) is a professional member of Sisters in Crime and the Horror Writers Association. With horror and mystery creations in *Mystery Magazine*, *Coastal Crimes*, *Mystery Tribune*, *JOURN-E,* and the *Virginia Is for Mysteries* anthology series, this Halloween night owl can often be found reading comics with cats or shooting b&w film in the noir nightscape.

Kevin Ground

Kevin Ground is a third age neuro-divergent author who creates Gothic Victorian Ghost and Horror stories. That sit side by side with contemporary works, re-imagining the horror of modern day life and situations. Find out more by visiting www.kevinground.com. Disturbing for the Discerning.

Annie Knox

Annie Knox is an award-winning actress and author. She is also the founder of Snake Bite Books, an indie horror publishing company preparing to release its first anthology. Her recent published work includes *Mister Reaper*, featured in the *Elemental Forces* anthology by Flame Tree Press, and *Incorporeal Tax*, featured in *The Perfectly Fine Neighbourhood.* In her spare time she is a keen boxer/kickboxer.

Liam Hogan

Liam Hogan is an award-winning short story writer, with stories in Best of British Science Fiction and in Best of British Fantasy (NewCon Press). He volunteers at the creative writing charities Ministry of Stories, and Spark Young Writers. Host of the live literary event Liars' League for twelve years, he's now escaped London, but remains a Liar. More details at:
http://happyendingnotguaranteed.blogspot.co.uk

Paul Lonardo

Paul Lonardo is a freelance writer and author with numerous titles, both fiction and nonfiction books. Paul has placed short fiction and nonfiction articles in various genre magazines and ezines. He is a contributing writer for Tales from the Moonlit Path and an active HWA member. Follow the author on X: @PaulLonardo / Instagram: PaulLonardo13 / Author website: www.TheGoblinPitcher.com

Adam D. Stones

Adam is a Mechanical Engineer, working in the aerospace industry. When not tinkering with precision machinery at work, he tries to find time to write amid all the myriad responsibilities and demands of life. He has a passion for science-fiction and spaceships in general.

His earlier stories have all been published in every Underdog Anthology, starting at Underdog Anthology XV. More are on the way.

For the occasional musing on life, beer and the weather: Twitter/X: @adamdstones

https://legironbooks.co.uk/about-the-authors/anthology-authors/adam-stones/

David D. Walker

David D Walker is a retired executive who turned to writing late in life. Born in Hamilton, Scotland, he now lives in Guildford, England, after a long and varied career in the international energy industry. His novels include the whodunnit, *Torres del Paine*, set in the Chilean National Park, and *Blackmail,* a World War One thriller set in France, both published by Matador. He has also contributed to other LegIron Books' short story anthologies.

https://legironbooks.co.uk/about-the-authors/anthology-authors/david-d-walker/

Roo B. Doo

'Buffering' is the twelfth story in the Ronageddon series of stories and follows on from 'Fright Club', which appeared in *Underdog Anthology XXIII: Spring Broke*.

Want more Roob? A collection of 18 of her short stories are available in *Just Call Me Roob*, or she can be found on the internet, ably assisted by Clicky, who may or may not be a) an alien dolphin and/or b) from another dimension, lolling about her Library of Libraries, writing synchromystic shambles at:

www.roobeedoo2.wordpress.com

https://legironbooks.co.uk/about-the-authors/ruth-bonner-roo-b-doo/

H.K. Hillman

H. K. Hillman is the creator, or perhaps creation, of Romulus Crowe, Dr. Phineas Dume, Legiron the Underdog and a growing cast of bizarre and hopefully fictional characters. Now pretty much retired from science, he hides out in an ancient farmhouse in Scotland with a Viking who calls herself CynaraeStMary. The house includes a deer skull in a holly tree, a gallows stone in the wall and holy water comes out of all the taps.

Here he spends a lot of time thinking up horrible stories, and running the tiny publishing house called Leg Iron Books, helped by Roo B. Doo, who he's never met.

No, he doesn't understand how any of this happened either.

https://legironbooks.co.uk/about-the-authors/h-k-hillman/

LEG IRON BOOKS

Also available from Leg Iron Books:

Underdog Anthologies
'The Underdog Anthology, volume 1'
'Tales the Hollow Bunnies Tell' (anthology II)
'Treeskull Stories' (anthology III)
'The Good, the Bad and Santa' (anthology IV)
'Six in Five in Four' (anthology V)
'The Gallows stone' (anthology VI)
'Christmas Lights… and Darks' (anthology VII)
'Transgenre Dreams' (anthology VIII)
'Well Haunted' (anthology IX)
'The Silence of the Elves' (anthology X)
'Tales from Loch Doon' (anthology XI)
'Mask-Querade' (anthology XII)
'Coronamas' (anthology XIII)
'The Dark Ides of March' (Anthology XIV)
'The Darkness at the End of October' (Anthology XV)
'Slay Bells in the Snow' (Anthology XVI)
'The Wrong Kind of Leaves' (Anthology XVII)
'The Hole in the Veil' (Anthology XVIII)
'Have Yourself a Very Little Christmas' (Anthology XIX)
'A Dark Spring' (Anthology XX)
'A Day Off for Angels' (Anthology XXI)
'The Shadows under the Tree' (anthology XXII)
'Spring Broke' (Anthology XXIII)
    All edited by H.K. Hillman and Roo B. Doo.

Fiction

'The Goddess of Protruding Ears' by Justin Sanebridge
'De Godin van de Flaporen' by Justin Sanebridge (in Dutch)
'Feelgood Original Christmas Stories' by Justin Sanebridge

'Ransom', by Mark Ellott
'Rebellion' by Mark Ellott
'Resolution' by Mark Ellott
'Reiver' by Mark Ellott
'Renegade' by Mark Ellott
'Blackjack' a collection of short stories by Mark Ellott
'A Moment in Time' short stories by Mark Ellott
'Sinistré (The Morning Cloud Chronicles)' by Mark Ellott
'The Mark' by Margo Jackson
'Feesten onder de Drinkboom' by Dirk Vleugels (in Dutch)
'Es-Tu là, Allah?' by Dirk Vleugels (in French)
'Jessica's Trap' by H.K. Hillman
'Samuel's Girl' by H.K. Hillman
'Norman's House' by H. K. Hillman
'The Articles of Dume' by H.K. Hillman
'Fears of the Old and the New' short stories by H.K. Hillman
'Dark Thoughts and Demons' short stories by H.K. Hillman
'You Can Choose Your Sin… but You Cannot Choose the Consequences' by Marsha Webb
'My Favourite Place and other stories' short stories by Marsha Webb
'Musings of a Wanderer' short stories by Wandra Nomad
'Just Call Me Roob' short stories by Roo B. Doo

Non-fiction:

'Ghosthunting for the Sensible Investigator' first and second editions, by Romulus Crowe

Biography:

'Han Snel' by Dirk Vleugels (in Dutch)

Printed in Great Britain
by Amazon

50811525R00235